Kingdom Come

I was going to say something profound, but the time for that has not come yet. Instead, I say "wait for it" to those that rooted for me, and I say "did it anyway" to those that didn't.

One

"*Take me to the repair shop; fix me up, a broken toy. Forget about me now and then; perhaps I'll be another's joy.*" I hummed through the steam of the warm water.

The water rolled off my back as I climbed out from within the tiled walls. Nearly slipping on the floor as I struggled into my jeans, which were a little tighter than I remembered, I continued to sing, "*Play with me when you want, until I fall for another boy.*"

My reflection caught my attention as I muttered my song, "*You'll never get to play again…*" I shook out my short hair like a dog and gave my most crooked grin, noting the ever-present two white stripes below my right eye.

"*I'll become another's toy.*" I walked into my room and pulled on a sweater, then clipped a dog collar around my neck. My telltale costume, so to speak.

"*You'll never get to play again, because I'll belong to a different boy.*"

I swung open my bedroom door and was immediately (and unfortunately) welcomed by a friend, who was standing there waiting for me.

Okay … I'm using *friend* loosely here. Dan "Dragon" Stanton wasn't anyone's friend; he was a rival, an enemy, a piss-baby strategist, and a cheat. Sure, some people, like Randy and Ronin, liked him, but they weren't exactly sociable people either. Sadly for me, Lilithia Heights was a small place, and I was pretty well known around the arena and around town. I guess Stanton decided to come bug me before any of the others — Dan hadn't been getting much action lately.

Mind out of the gutter, my friend. By action, I of course meant battle time. We were warriors, Lilithia's main attraction. All the towns had warriors, and all the warriors were preparing for the big tournament coming up later in the year. Each town had a different way of running its arenas and gearing up for the big events. Some cities set it up like an elite club, allowing only the most privileged warriors to compete. Others staged brawls in the basements of seedy taverns on the weekends. Others were more open, making us a public spectacle. Lilithia had nearly every waking second of our lives filmed. In Lilithia, it was a reality show, but instead of shrieking at each other while getting our nails done, we fight. If personal drama is slow, then our supervisor, Vince Viktor, sets us up in rotation battles in the arena. There's a set three per day, and the rest are up to us. Some can get pretty brutal, but it's never anything personal. Usually.

"Hey Dan-o," I said as I brushed past the tall, blond man. "What can I do for you?"

I headed towards the cafeteria, attempting to get far enough away from him that I didn't have to look at him or smell his playboy cologne. He had to jog to keep up.

"It happened again, Benji. I was checking in on you. I thought you got hurt."

"Me? Please, everyone knows I sleep with a knife under my pillow."

One more thing: we were kind of being hunted. This had been going on for a while, and no, it wasn't part of the show.

"A knife under your pillow isn't... Benji, you sleep heavier than Jeremy does when he's on Crane's meds!" Dan scowled and crossed his arms. Well, he wasn't wrong.

"So what happened? System failure again? Tech crew's slacking," I muttered as I shoved open the large white doors leading to the cafeteria. The smell of baked goods and sausages hit me — I really was hungry. A few warriors turned to wave. The rest rolled their eyes. I ignored them and raided the toast and muffin department.

"You are a danger to yourself and others," Dan continued.

I continued to hum my song while Dan painstakingly explained all the ways I could have fallen victim. I silently mocked his thick Boston accent and made my way down the hall to where my actual friend, Frankie, was lounging, eyes closed. That boy had a habit of falling asleep anywhere. It was a talent I envied.

"Benji, you need to listen to me. This is serious!"

"Danny, do you have anything interesting to tell me? Or are we going to keep playing 'Damsel in Distress'? As any damsel will tell you, I can handle it myself!" I snapped. I'd been a warrior for over twelve years. I could handle an ambush.

Dan tugged at his scruffy chin, and I hid my annoyance by fixating on a stain under my boot, on the yellowing white tile.

At that moment, as if to prove Dan's point, the lights went out and an alarm sounded.

Frankie woke, leaping to his feet with a snort, and in the red glow of the emergency flood lights, we all shared a look, worried who the next victim would be.

"Is anyone in the Pit right now?" I asked. My voice betrayed me, coming out like a squeak.

"I think Dolly was in there kicking it up with a Vu. something," Dan said, looking at Frankie for confirmation.

"Don't you ever look at the boards, Dragon? She's going in with the Mummy," Frankie answered. "But not for a few hours. I'm not even sure if anyone is training yet." He scratched at his faux hawk anxiously.

"Then what the hell is going on now?" I bounced on my toes, ready to sprint at the first sign of trouble. Wasn't about to stand around and get hit myself.

I might've played it a bit casual with Dan earlier. The threat was real. Not one of us had any idea who was behind the attacks, but around six warriors had already been seriously hurt, maimed, or taken out of commission. And every attack had been accompanied by technical glitches — dropped lights, system shutdowns, alarms, the works. Some of the victims couldn't even compete anymore, maybe wouldn't ever again, not in Lilithia at least. I sure as shit didn't want that to be me.

After a few tense seconds, Matt, our little tech-nerd, came over the loud speaker, "False alarm! That's on me. My fault. Sorry, everyone." I could hear someone start to argue just as he flipped his mic off again. The three of us simultaneously let out a breath and stared at each other, laughing nervously. Things had been tense for a while.

We were all standing there trying to figure out what to say when Chrissy came around the corner, arm in arm with my roommate, Angel. Chrissy had been my closest friend for almost a decade; she was one of the few warriors I knew without a massively overinflated ego, plus she was an ace with the crossbow. When she saw us, she rushed forward, dragging Angel along behind her.

"Oh, Ben, you're alright! Thank god it was a mistake," she muttered as our eyes met.

Dan leaned against the wall, pretending (poorly) to be composed. "They really have to start getting their act together!" He rubbed at his arm.

I watched Chrissy release her death grip on Angel's arm and sit down beside Frankie, "I just can't stop thinking about what happened last week." She shook her head, blond curls bouncing. "Limbs shouldn't bend like that!"

None of us were there, but we all heard about what had happened to Static. Charlie "Static" Stinson had been lying in the centre of the empty arena, unconscious but mangled nonetheless. He wasn't even set for battle; no one knows how he got there.

I shuddered at the thought.

"Don't worry, it won't happen to you." Angel said. Her eyes twinkled with mischief when she spoke. "Not big-time enough. Who would care?"

"Want to say that to my face?!" I swung my fist in her direction, but Frankie pulled me back before I could make contact. She was a grudging friend. We tended to go head-to-head over the dumbest stuff, but I couldn't stop myself from getting angry at some of the things she said. Angel "Beauty" Lannister knew exactly how to set me off.

"No fighting!" Frankie said, gripping my shoulders. "We can't afford to fight each other right now. We don't have any clue who's doing this, but Viktor tried to tell us he's investigating. And he's been trying to hide it from the civilians, so it's obviously not supposed to be happening. I — I'm afraid we're going to have to deal with this person ourselves…"

Managing to cool down just a little bit, I brushed his hands away and crossed my arms.

"Relax, she's right," Chrissy said. "You'll be fine."

"You hear who got taken out yesterday?" Frankie said. All eyes shot to his direction.

"What?! No, who?" Chrissy whimpered.

"Roberts. The poor kid didn't have a chance."

Dan laughed harshly. Frankie was young and not very bright, but he was observant. Frankie somehow knew every news story half an hour before the media did.

"Yeah, in the locker room after practice." Frankie shook his head. "They seem to be targeting the Valiants mostly, though some Volatiles have gone down too."

Valiants, Volatiles, and Vultures — that was how Lilithia classed its warriors. It relied heavily on how we did battle, our strategy and all that. I was a Volatile if you couldn't tell.

"Viktor doesn't like us talking about this," I said.

"Hey, since when are you one to follow the rules?" Dan asked.

"Since I don't want to be next!" I growled back. Dan and I had been partnered up for a while, but we didn't get along. Neither of us were methodical. My emotions got the better of me more often than I would like to admit, and Dan was just plain reckless, sometimes stupid.

Chrissy's blue eyes were wide with worry, and her hands shook a little bit. Leaning over with her curly hair in her eyes, she sighed. I didn't know what to do — clearly, none of us did. Even Angel bit her perfectly manicured nails and closed her trap. All I *could* do was sit myself beside my friend and put my hand on her shoulder.

"Everything's going to be alright."

It wasn't. Little did we know, that was only the beginning.

About a month after Matt's little mix-up, Chrissy was attacked. She wasn't injured too badly, not compared to everyone else, but she was left with a concussion. She had to leave the dorms for a while to stay with her sister. It was hard to focus on my own training, knowing that my small list of friends was dwindling. At least this time, it wasn't my fault. That's what I was telling myself anyway.

I needed a distraction, so the day Chrissy left, I asked the boss for a match. He set me up against Frankie and Ronin. Oh, sorry, make that Scene Fest and Wolf Man. (As boss man Viktor always said, "Stage names on stage, kids!" The arrogant blowhard.) I was looking forward to it.

I went to the locker room early to unwind, trying to prep my mind for the battle ahead. The place was brightly lit for the most part. The dull blue lockers that held all our weapons and gear formed three long aisles, which meant I couldn't quite see the whole place, but at least the drone cams wouldn't be in here so early. Who could complain?

Call me paranoid, but the girl who stood alone in the room, feeling like she was being watched, could.

Instinctively, I grabbed my short dagger from my locker and peeked around the corner, checking the other two aisles. There wasn't anyone there. I wearily went back to changing and stuffed my clothes into the little blue locker. My armour, like most of the other warriors', consisted of two metal-plated shoulder pads and the fancy sheaths for my old-fashioned duel swords.

My armour was pretty skimpy, but then a lot of warriors preferred not to wear any at all. Dan had steel gauntlets that ran to his elbows —

real fashion forward, that one — and knee pads, but that was it. Armour restricts movement, and a lot of us see it as a cop-out. Warriors that wear too much armour are seen as weaker, unable to take a hit. The knights died out hundreds of years ago, but there's still a law put in place by the higher-ups — or the council that organizes our tournaments — that we must wear armour for the sake of "preservation." Not a thing I cared a lot about, personally. Maybe they required it for the same reason they prefer us to have stage names: for show.

My paranoia eventually got the best of me, so I hopped on top of a bench and looked up into the vent, but the grate was stuck tight and it was too dark for me to see inside. Instead, I jimmied Frankie's locker open and pulled out a heavy flashlight. I knew he had one in there; only god knew why. With my knife resting between my teeth, I hopped on top of the bench, then climbed on top of a locker and ripped the grate free. I shone the light through the dark space, but there was nothing there.

"What's going on?" A gruff voice came from below.

I jumped, hit my head on the aluminum duct above me, and slipped back to the ground. I had to sit for a minute as I came back to my senses.

"I thought someone was watching me … can't be too careful around here," I offered.

People questioned things I said or did a lot. When people spoke of me, my sanity was more often than not the topic of conversation, so I guess I was just used to explaining myself.

The guy standing on the opposite side of the aisle had his back to me, but he was very large and he had a baseball hat pulled down low over his face. I didn't recognize him, but then again, I don't tend to notice the new recruits until they're punching me in the nose.

The man let out a small chuckle, then quietly closed the locker, turned, and walked out, humming a song — the same song that had been stuck in my head for the previous three months. *"Take me to the repair shop…"*

"Wait!" I called after him. "How do you know…?"

But the guy was gone.

I sat in a daze for a few minutes until footsteps pulled me out of my trance enough that I could mumble a "hey" to whoever had just entered. It was Dan. Of course, I'd been paired with Dragon again. I suppose the fact we didn't get along just made us all the more entertaining — Viktor did like to set up for maximum drama.

He offered a snort but ignored me and changed into his gear.

"Do you have any idea where my jacket is? It isn't in my locker," he said.

I shrugged my shoulders and pushed myself off the bench. "No clue, man."

This battle was pretty much the same as every other against Scene Fest and Wolf Man, except Frankie managed to stay upright a little longer than usual. Me and Dragon met outside the gate of the Pit — Lilithia's own grand arena — as our opponents showed off for the cameras, one waving his arms and grinning while the other rolled his shoulders and his eyes. We walked in with ready weapons; granted, they were dulled since we weren't actually supposed to kill each other. Or so they say.

Across the dirt, on the other side of the arena, Frankie grinned and juggled his daggers.

"Give up, K9!" he teased. "Run now! With your tail between your legs!"

"In your dreams, Scene Fest!" I growled, baring my crooked teeth.

Dan and I had argued over how we should take them down, but eventually we both rushed them. Frankie sidestepped me but fell into a puddle of blood from the previous matchup. He wasn't too pleased and ended up squealing and hollering so loud I couldn't keep myself from laughing manically at his misfortune.

He continued to cry out. I doubled over, still laughing, until Dan yanked me back up.

"Hell! K9, focus!" he snapped.

I shrugged gleefully and slashed at Frankie viciously. He rolled out of the way, as I expected he would. Then he came toward me quick and swiped at me with his daggers, but I easily swatted him away with my sword. I was just about to take a run at him again when the lights cut out. I stepped away from our opponents, tripping over myself in a panic; everyone knows bad things happen around here when the lights go out.

I heard Viktor's voice over the speaker, *"Matt! What in Apollo's name is going on?"*

"I ... I don't know, sir!"

"Well, fix it!"

I looked through the dark as best I could. Exit stage left. I tried to make my way to the gate when I felt someone in front of me. A second later, my nose started stinging. Someone had punched me square in the face, leaving me dizzy and concussed. I fell back a bit but managed to stay upright thanks to strong hands on the buckles of my shoulder pads.

"Matt, get the lights on!" Josh hollered over the loudspeaker.

The security alarm cut out, but the connectivity warning was still sounding, meaning there was still someone else in the system. I could see Matt's computer from where I stood. A symbol of a skull was playing across the screen. The thing looked deformed and thoroughly unsettling, but maybe that was my eyes playing tricks on me. I had just gotten whacked in the face, after all.

Viktor wailed so loud the feedback nearly shattered our eardrums. *"Take it back!"*

"I can't!" Matt cried.

"What do you mean 'you can't'?" Josh asked.

"There's someone else in the system. They booted me out!"

"Take it back by any means!" Viktor shrieked once again, his voice booming through the arena.

"All attempts at escape will fail, and all attempts at recovering your systems are futile!" The person holding me up growled out into the stadium.

I choked on my blood as it dripped down my nose and onto the man's hand. I shakily brought my hand up and tugged his wrist, smearing even more blood around as my face went numb.

The backup generator cut off. The guy must have done it from a remote device. He turned his head to face me.

The last thing I heard was the familiar sound of Matt and Josh bickering.

"Josh, I'm back in. I'm writing a new firewall but files are missing..."

"The boss is going to kill us, Matt."

Shortly after that, I passed out.

Two

"Mystery, mystery, what can I say? Why … *why*!? Stupid, stupid, stupid … *stupid bird…*"

I rolled my head as my nose throbbed, and groaned as dried blood around my lip cracked, pulling at my skin. I sat resting my back on a hard surface, struggling to open my eyes. It was a feeling I knew all too well, and I knew what the medic, Louis "Ichabod" Crane, would say. I could just picture him standing over me, looking down at me with disdain over that beak nose of his, scratching the hideous scar on his neck. The man disliked me — thought I was too reckless. He wasn't wrong.

"No, no … I want to fight. I don't need to go to medical," I murmured.

"Good!" a voice answered. It wasn't Louis.

I leaned forward quickly and desperately tried to clear my head as fast as I could. I held my hand up in defence as I opened my eyes. The room was dark and full of shadows that seemed to move. There was a single overhead light, but that didn't really make it any easier to see the rest of the room.

"K9's not going anywhere anyway."

I flinched. Though smoother this time, the voice still sounded ghostly. Hollow and forgotten by time. I peered through the darkness, past a steel table, hoping to see who was talking. Leaning in until something tugged against my left wrist. Lucky me, a handcuff. The other end was secured to a tall steel pipe.

I scowled and placed my hand on my head as it started to pound, realizing that I might be in serious trouble... But I guess it was nothing compared to what I'd dealt with before.

"Caw, caw says the crow. Down, down you will fall..." He went back to muttering. "Deep, deep in the darkness, out of hell you will crawl."

I stood slowly, clearing my vision and tasting blood. I couldn't see the man's face, but I could see the outline of his body: broad shoulders, about six feet tall, and the longest, messiest hair I'd ever seen. From what I could tell, it was a tangled black nest.

"Who are you?" I asked quickly.

He lifted his head but didn't turn to face me. "The crow, the plague, and the end for you."

"What's your name?"

"N-no more questions!"

I stumbled slightly. This was not someone I could negotiate with, and this was not a situation I could fight my way out of. Not right now anyway. I put my head down and tried to regroup. There was some way. There had to be. I could still play him. Everyone has a weakness. It's usually the first thing they show you.

The man slowly walked around the table and put his hands up. "D-didn't mean it..."

I looked back up, and he was miserably fidgeting with his sleeve. "Crow, bird, death, monster, freak," he said, then continued with his poem.

"Nameless and faceless
A monster at the core
Useless and careless
Here forevermore."

"I know that poem," I muttered to myself. He turned his back to me and started to speak again, ignoring me.

"Every night I burn
My feathers turned to ash
Like that of a baby crow
Rooting through the trash."

"A Ravin is a raven, but a crow is more ... more, more, more...!" He shifted papers around and reorganized them before he shouted in what sounded like pain or fear and threw everything off the side of his desk. He slammed his hands down and grunted out another verse.

> *"I do my best to please them*
> *And keep the voices down*
> *But sometimes when I hear him*
> *I feel I start to drown!"*

This wasn't right. He was clearly angry and in some form of emotional torment, but hearing the boom of his voice, I couldn't help but take a step back, accidentally slamming my shoulders into the steel. As the handcuffs rattled against a pipe, I realized I'd made a mistake.

I cringed as the man turned around, shouting once again. "Never should have done it! Thing of evil!"

He started reciting again.

> *"He took my beauty*
> *And burned my beautiful wings*
> *And now I'm left to hear him*
> *As others start to sing."*

He clenched his fists and shook his head.

> *"I am still a being of light*
> *Suffering in darkness*
> *One thousand degrees of anger*
> *Leave me sitting in distress."*

He threw his back against the wall as he cried out. He cradled his head in his hands and took in a ragged breath, calming himself down as he slid to the floor. I tugged at my restraint silently — listening to it grind against the pipe — until he looked at me again and slowly parted his lips as he spoke. "Why the crow? Why...?"

"I-I don't — "

"Don't know? How could you ... just a K9...? No monster here, only the bird.

> *"Your eyes are half-asleep,*
> *and your heart is soft to the core.*
> *All the things they say,*
> *made my mind and body sore.*
> *But you smiled and shook,*
> *and now I miss you more."*

His voice was instantly deeper, angrier — almost sinister — as he sneered at me.

I decided to risk a question, maybe indulge this psychosis if I had to. "Do you like poetry?"

He tilted his head and took a step closer. He was almost out of the shadows. I could see that he had ink splattered across his shirt and skin. His hair was even darker than I initially thought, too; it had a tint of blue to it. I took that moment to say my own poem.

> *"They told her to be violent*
> *And now they fall silent*
> *For fear of insanity..."*

His head tilted downward and a menacing grin took over what I could see of his features.

> *"She asks questions in her mind*
> *But nothing she will find*
> *For fear of final clarity."*

He stared for a moment, pleased. He tried to hide his face by biting his lip and haphazardly rubbing his head, causing his hair to stick out farther than it already did. Now that he seemed to have calmed down, I did too.

"Please tell me why I'm here," I asked softly.

His face fell, and he walked back to the other side of the room, covering his entire body in shadows again. "Don't know that one."

I sighed. "Please ... at least tell me I'm not in danger."

"Can't do that! No more questions, please! *Leave my loneliness unbroken!*" He hollered at me in anguish. His body jolted suddenly, and I dodged to the left as a speaker hit the wall beside me. I hesitantly turned to where it hit the wall. There had been enough force behind the throw that it dented the metal of the wall slightly. I straightened up again, and the man turned around, completely refusing to meet my eyes or even look at me.

"W-wants to know, wants to know ... *dirty little secrets!*"

He slammed his hands down on the desk, and the room lit up with the light of about ten computer monitors mounted to the wall. The man cackled as the light cast his shadow across the room, making him look bigger than he probably was. Some screens were running code; others had security videos playing. The most disturbing were the pictures of the other warriors, the ones who had recently been injured or quit, with large black Xs stamped across their faces. Chrissy was one of them. The colour in her face drained when she told me what happened, but in the picture, her cheeks were just as rosy as they always had been. I know I needed answers, but my anger just kept burning. I wasn't sure how long I could hold myself back if this is what I would have to keep looking at.

But then he pulled *my* picture up and typed *Eliminated*.

I struggled to free myself, but as I looked up, I saw that the man was staring at me, so I asked what should have been my first thought when I woke up. "Did you do this to everyone?"

He looked down. "A crow, a murderer."

He looked away, and my attention was caught by something else. There was a picture taped to the wall beside him with the eyes scratched out. It looked like it had taken many darts and knives over a short period of time. This picture was of a friend. A close, rude, and potentially dangerous friend ... Dan.

"K9, K9, K9."

He repeated my name over and over again. His breathing was

shaky, and he looked like he was having a hard time keeping his composure. He pressed his hands to his face with a sigh. "Broke my heart, and they broke my body."

"Who did? Maybe I can help?"

"The bird was supposed to get rid of you! B-but can't... Crow's going to be in trouble..." I watched him carefully. "So much trouble, so much pain."

He started choking on his sobs and then slid into his seat and bit his knuckles.

"Who are you going to be in trouble with?"

"People."

"What people?"

"People who can hurt the bird!" He snapped, only momentarily pulling his hand away and — I'd imagine — shooting a glare at me.

I tilted my head and grimaced. "I can help you — "

"Never again! No more pain, no more lies ... no more *help*."

"Tell me who you are." I didn't like begging for answers. I didn't like the feeling it gave me. He stood and walked out of the shadows, showing me his face for the first time. He had sad, green eyes and a jagged scar that ran down his chin and turned into a cross on his neck. Ink stained his cheek, and he looked at the ground, those green eyes shifting only slightly. They didn't sparkle, they didn't shine — in fact, they just looked dead. Their colour was vibrant and startling, but they also looked weary and a little bit emotionless, with no hope or happiness inside them at all.

I had never seen him before.

"The madness keeps me safe."

He walked forward, and I raised my hand in defence, maybe to stop him from getting too close or maybe to show him I wasn't an enemy. He carefully let his fingertips touch mine. I inadvertently flinched. Startled, he pulled his hand away and drew it to his chest, looking cautious, eyes wide and shoulders hunched.

"It's okay..." I said.

He did it again, and I tried not to pull away this time.

His hand shaking slightly, he slipped his fingers between mine and watched our movements as I let the tips of my fingers touch his knuckles.

My hand was shaking; this had to be the single weirdest way of escaping certain death. He watched as he lightly held my hand in place, downturned green eyes following every movement. He let himself smile sadly as he closed his eyes. After a moment, I slowly pulled my hand away, and his smile faded as he dropped his head. He grimaced and stepped back. His lip quivered as he opened his eyes again and tilted his head at me.

"What's going on?" I asked softly.

Blinking, he shook his head, "Don't want to hurt anymore… Stabbed the bird in the back … revenge…"

His eyes glazed over, and he listlessly let his head roll to one side. My voice caught slightly as I attempted to lean over so he could see me properly. "Please take the handcuffs off?"

Snapping back, he started to rub his neck and pace back and forth. "O-okay…"

He looked nervous, so I offered a sympathetic smile. "I'm not going anywhere."

He stared at me, then let my hand free and took a moment before stepping back. I rubbed my wrist and looked up at him. He was watching every movement I made, and his pupils were dilated, eliminating most of the green. Stuttering, he took a step back.

"Did you … do all that?" I asked.

He glanced at the monitors. "Crows are very resourceful."

"Impressive."

I looked over the monitors until I found a live feed of the training room. Dan was punching his punching bag and yelling at Josh and Matt. I turned around to look at the man, and he stammered like he had been staring. He raised his hand and opened his mouth to say something, then thought better of it and closed it again, his shoulders hunched the entire time.

"You took them out, didn't you?" I asked. He fidgeted and then finally nodded.

"Didn't want to." His voice was much different, quieter. "He would hurt the crow if the crow said no, and … and — and then he said he wanted K9 and the crow couldn't, he just couldn't — too tragic, too … too — "

"Wait, you mean me? I'm the 'K9' you're talking about?"

He tilted his head, pupils filling out again. "Y-you…?"

"K9 is just a stage name, so to speak. My real name is Benji Keanin."

"No! Yes…? K9, the target … couldn't… She's just a little dog … pretty little dog," he said in broken English as he lifted a slim, shaking finger to point at me. This man was clearly struggling to speak, maybe even to think clearly. There was something about him, though.

"Why wouldn't you just take me out like everyone else?"

He looked at the ground again. "Too tragic."

"What's tragic?"

I watched him bite his lip at the question. He wrung his hands, not giving me an answer. Though he was standing closer with a curious look.

His head was tilted, and he looked from my eyes to my lips. If this were anyone else, my combat training would have kicked in, but even though it was clear this man could hurt me badly, he didn't feel like a threat. Not like most other people. The air he carried was too familiar.

"Who's next?"

He jumped back, startled.

I asked again, "Who are we taking out next?"

"H-help the bird?"

I nodded. "You shouldn't be alone, especially if you're going to be in trouble."

He glanced at the monitors, then back at me. A wicked grin took his face, and he pointed at the picture of Dan up on the wall. Slowly, he let his expression drop, though, and he shook his head, "Not again … always get hurt; can't do it again. Dog is going to get hurt…" He ran his hands up over his eyes, then into his hair.

"I can at least look out for you even if you don't want me in the arena," I offered. It wasn't much, and I wasn't sure I was doing the right thing, but I had to do something. I needed to know why … maybe I could stop it.

Three

He didn't speak much, and I didn't want to bother him, so I stayed quiet. At some point during the evening, I had gathered the courage to ask him a mildly important question. "Y-you never told me your name…"

"Crow."

"Just Crow?"

"Just Crow."

Late in the night, Crow left to "research" Dan. I kept an eye on the monitors to make sure he didn't get caught. He made his way back through the halls and tunnels of the building, careful to stay out of sight. I figured that, while given the chance, I should try to research him myself. Honestly, I had no idea where to start; I didn't even have a proper name. I started going through files on the hard drive, until I got into his email — which was luckily not password-protected — and opened one from an anonymous sender.

> *Get the job done or you're finished. Your next hit is Benjamina Keanin AKA Benji "K9" Keanin.*
> *She is the biggest threat to us. Take her out, kill her if you have to, just make sure she won't get in the way.*
> *Your payment will come through once it's done.*
> *Don't let us down.*

I read it over and over. I could be a threat to whom? To what? I searched through other messages from this person and came across one that was likely the first sent.

Soul,
Your new alias will be Crow, in reference to your surname of course.
We expect you to do a thorough and clean job. Never let anyone see or notice you unless necessary or otherwise stated.
If you fail to do your job we will eliminate you.
Good luck and good hunting,
Doctor Frankenstein

Okay, so his name is Soul, a.k.a. Crow.

The clunk of boots on tile startled me from my search. I started to panic as the door opened, rattling as it did, and I struggled to clear the email from the monitor. I was a bit too late, and the door slammed shut. I tried to stand up quickly to cover what I was doing, but my chair toppled back, leaving me crashing to the floor and cracking my wrist. I hollered in pain and felt a large hand grip my belt. He hauled me to my feet and gripped my shoulder.

I opened my hazel eyes to see green staring back — very angrily, might I add.

"I'm sorry," I blurted. "I didn't mean to snoop."

He readjusted his grip and exhaled shakily.

"The bird's nest is his own," he growled.

I held my breath and nodded, but curiosity got the better of me.

"Who … who is Doctor Frankenstein?"

Crow sneered and shook his head.

"You created me
As long as you live, you'll never be free
But I'm a busy man
So dead you'll have to be."

I still had no idea what he meant, but I doubted it was a good idea to ask.

"Your name is Soul?" I asked. He whipped around and squeezed his eyes shut.

"D-don't…! Crow — don't…" He looked as if he were trying to work something out in his head. I decided to take a chance.

"Yes, your name is Soul and your alias is Crow; mine is K9 — "

"No! B-Benji … K9?"

I put my hand on his neck. "Soul, just breathe — "

"They'll hurt the bird! They'll *kill* you!"

He still had one hand firmly on my shoulder, but his head was hanging low.

"Soul, I am not going to let them get away with anything. I don't know much, but I know that you don't *want* to do any of this." I wanted to help this man. Something about him was just so … *lonely*. It radiated from him.

He let me go and looked at my wrist as he spoke softly, his hand swinging at his side. "Please … don't hurt the bird. He has nothing left…"

I watched him shake his head and quickly glance around. "I'd never lie to someone who doesn't deserve it."

He looked back up and examined my face, looking slightly relieved, though still wary. Despite his broken English and messy exterior, he appeared to be a very calculating and intelligent man. He would have to be to work most of the programming on that system of his.

He lifted my hand up and pinched my wrist, earning a small growl from yours truly. I half expected him to flinch again but he didn't; he only let my hand go and went digging under his desk. He pulled out a case and opened it. Inside were various medical supplies, goopy plaster spilled across each plastic package. Watching him, I grimaced as he pulled out a couple bandages after a glance back at my hand. I was a little hesitant. Does he even have any training? Has the plaster compromised the integrity of the bandages?

He held his hand out and motioned for me to walk forward, but I shook my head.

"I'm fine."

"The crow can't let the dog be hurting." He gently grabbed my hand and put the other on my waist, leading me to the table and making me sit in his overly large desk chair. He lightly poked at my wrist and held it to the light. Wrapping the bandage tightly over my wrist, he caused me to scream a little louder than I'd meant to. I kicked my legs and bit my lip, but he wouldn't meet my eyes as he wiped away some plaster.

"Have you done this before?"

"Yes."

I tried to get another good look at him, but wild hair covered his eyes. He absentmindedly brushed it back, getting plaster stuck in it and getting his long fingers tangled in the black — and now white — mess. His chin was slim and framed with a short goatee; his cheeks were rather hollow and outlined by thin black sideburns that turned into the aforementioned goatee. He also had high cheekbones, one of which was cut and still a little bloody.

He paused in his actions, then he dumped most of the contents of his medical case into the trash and stepped back, ready to run his fingers through his hair again. I grabbed his wrist with my good hand, and he froze like a deer caught in the headlights. He started to look defensive but didn't move; instead, he opened his mouth to speak as I pushed his fringe off his face. There was still plaster mixed in, so my hand stuck a bit as I tugged.

He whined softly and pulled away, nearly tripping over the table. Turning his back and muttering, he repeated my name over and over, as if to get used to saying it.

"K9 helped the bird. The K9 helped … the K9 — trust … trust, trust, trust. The bird can trust the dog…"

He nodded to himself as though he had made up his mind. He straightened, sat in front of his computer, and started typing. I leaned over his shoulder and watched as he hacked his way into Lilithia's media systems and programming. Every screen in every home on every street of this city was under his control.

He leaned in toward the computer's microphone and spoke.

"Tonight at eight o'clock, another 'hero' will be taken out. You cannot save him. This is his warning … the bird will catch the worm."

He let out a joyful laugh and turned to face me. He clenched his teeth excitedly and waved his hands about. I responded with a shrug, and he motioned to my wrist and wrung his hands. I got what he was going for — mass fearmongering.

"What did I ever do to you? Let me go already!"

He grinned as he let out another cackle, sounding very much like a crow or bird of some kind, and then cut the connection to the media servers. The screens went dark. He was still staring at me, eyes locked, with that half-mad expression on his face. I'll admit that I was a bit unnerved by it. He probably saw it in my face; he didn't bother to hide his amusement.

He stood and started putting on his armour — a long trench coat-style jacket with a metal shoulder pad jutting out on the left side, and feathers from that of a raven or crow fixed to it. He quickly tied his boots, then looked at me, standing to his full — and intimidating — height for the first time. "Will the K9 help the crow?"

He held out his hand. Dropping my aching wrist to my side and reaching out with the other, I took it.

Getting progressively more excited, he managed to keep a straight face as he dragged me through the halls, keeping to the shadows and back halls that not many people use anymore. They were close to collapsing, and we were all pretty sure they were haunted.

"What about my gear?" I asked.

He stopped and thought, then shook his head. "The bird wants to play ... out of his mind punishing, whispering demons rise and the bird will have a prize — Crow wants to have his fun, the K9 needs her rest, the worm needs to feel helpless and fearful."

I was confused, but I followed him anyway.

He stopped outside the gate and quickly turned to me, not meeting my eyes. "Do you love him?"

I was rather startled by this sudden question. "Who? Why?"

Soul wrung his hands and stared at his boots with bitter eyes. "The worm, Daniel Stanton. Do you love him?"

I looked down and shook my head. "I can't deny there was a point I found him attractive, but I've never loved him. There's something about him that just … isn't right."

Soul's exterior stiffened again and he nodded curtly. "Good. Tonight the crow has his fun."

"W-wait…"

"He won't die."

He opened the gate and shoved me into the light. My legs got tangled together, and as I slid through the dirt, I cast a small displeased glance back at him. The arena was full of fans, and sunlight was peeking through the glass panels in the roof.

Dan was standing opposite me, his weapon raised to Randy's. He was a bit to my left. Randy "Mummy" Curio always had bandages around his head. Today they were practically flowing off of him, unwinding. Dan called out my name and ran forward. I pushed myself to my feet and met his eyes just as the lights cut out and Soul came over the loud speaker.

"Did you miss your girlfriend?" he taunted in a gruff voice.

The lights came back on, and Randy was lying on the ground, out cold. Dan looked around him, confused, and then looked back at me. I tilted my head at him, and the lights went out for the final time. He shrieked in pain. A moment later, I felt an arm around my abdomen dragging me back out of the arena. When everything came back on, Dan was lying face down in a pool of his own blood, his knuckles white as he gripped his head. A bloody pipe lay beside him. "Remember me, *Danny*?"

Soul stood in the dark entrance to the Pit, a spot that hid him from the cameras and the crowd. Dan's eyes widened when he caught a glimpse of the pipe, but he hadn't noticed the deranged-looking man. Seconds later, Soul was gone.

Soul initiated a fail-safe that momentarily crashed all cameras and security feeds, letting us get out of the main halls without being seen or tracked.

It seemed that Soul was used to being invisible, and he appeared to be very good at it.

Soul really only seemed able to speak smoothly when taunting: I guess he needed time to give it thought and preparation.

I followed him to the barracks, where he pulled me behind him and held his breath. An alarm shot out, and the cameras came back on. Well timed.

"Now what do we do? They'll be looking for us."

He searched his pockets, then slammed his hands back against the wall. He ran a hand through his hair and tugged at it, squeezing his eyes shut. I rested back against the wall and flinched as he started mumbling. Suddenly standing up, he threw me over his shoulder.

"Scream."

"What?"

"Do it or trouble." He was threatening.

I weighed my options, and he was right. I screamed like I was in pain, and I could sense his relief. He stopped halfway down a hall and looked at the camera. I kicked my legs and he started laughing, his shoulder jabbing my ribs slightly. I tried hitting his back, but it barely affected him. He continued quickly down the hall and kicked open a door. After looking up, I saw it was mine. The door clicked closed again, and he put his hand on my back as he slid me off his shoulder and onto my bed.

As I grunted, my wrist shifted. Soul paused his movements to make sure I wasn't too hurt; I could still feel his hands around my back as he watched me carefully. His eyes were fixed on mine for a single moment before I sat up. He stumbled back, wringing his jacket in his hands as what little colour he had drained from his face.

"Crow?" I said. He turned to me but kept his head down. "Crow, come here."

His head shot up but he did, and sat down beside me. He was still strangling his clothing and glaring at the floor with wide eyes.

"Soul, when was the last time you got any rest?"

He continued to play with his jacket but stood up, tilting his head back and forth. "N-need to go back. The bird will get caught if he doesn't — "

"Soul." He sat back down and swallowed hard, staying silent as I scolded him. "When was the last time you slept?"

He started fidgeting and sweating, but then his breath became more ragged, falling into a pattern of sobs. He seemed extremely agitated and looked like he was about to yell, like he did before. I wondered if he did this whenever he had a hard time dealing with whatever emotion he was feeling.

I quickly placed my left hand on his cheek and he leaned into it, whimpering. A tear rolled down his face and he pulled away, shaking his head. Softly, I grabbed him again and made him look at me, both hands on his cheeks. His lip stuck out as he watched me with awe.

"Go get some rest," I instructed. He nodded, but didn't take his eyes off mine. "And please … trust me."

He nodded again and closed his eyes, taking a deep breath. I dragged my thumb over his soft skin and let my hand fall as he opened his eyes, startled.

"I need one last thing," I asked carefully.

He leaned forward eagerly. "A-anything…"

I gave him a soft smile and tilted my head to the side. "I need you to knock me out."

He suddenly jerked back and stood up. "N-no, the bird can't do that!"

"Trust me, Soul. That way, when they find me, they won't know I'm helping you." He scratched his head and nodded hesitantly. Closing my eyes, I felt him touch my hair before he backhanded me across the side of the face and I hit the bed.

When I woke up, Matt was standing beside me, Dan was yelling at Frankie again, and my head was pounding. That last one was becoming a bit of a habit. Josh was sitting in the corner, still in his security guard uniform, carefully taking notes in a large journal. Or maybe just doodling.

"She's up!" Matt called.

Dan spun on his heel and bounded over, brushing his shaggy blond hair to the side of his face. The welt on his forehead was clearly visible and still crusted over with blood, but it didn't look nearly as bad as I thought it would, considering. Dan didn't even seem to notice it, thick headed as ever. "I want to know who the hell did this," he said.

"I-I don't know..." My vision was still blurry, but I could see Matt was holding out a few painkillers and water. "I was drugged, or at least I think I was."

Dan stomped his feet as he walked, shaking the room. "We'll get a nurse down here to do a rape kit — "

"What?! No! No, I'm fine. Well, at least that ... part of me is. My wrist could use a — oh, never mind." I held my right hand up, a cast already in place.

"Louis was already prepared," Matt offered. "He patched it up while you were out. Grumbled about it a bit, but you know him."

I nodded, then ran both hands over my face as pain radiated through my nose, temples, and brow. Dan looked like he hadn't slept, which he probably hadn't considering my clock said 3 a.m.

"Viktor put me in charge of finding this son of a bitch," Dan said. "And Frankie wanted to help."

I asked Dan quickly, "How the hell did you know that guy, anyway? He asked if you remembered him, and your face went white as a sheet."

"Long and personal story, Ben. And I don't know him. He just ... reminded me of someone I used to know."

"Well, I'm involved now too, and I want to know."

"I'll tell you tomorrow. You need to sleep — "

"I'll sleep when I'm dead. Tell me."

"At this rate, you *will* be dead pretty soon. I'll tell you tomorrow! I'm going to need your help with the investigation anyway." Dan's grey eyes went from drilling a hole in mine to shooting glares at Matt, Josh, and Frankie as he left the room.

"Rest up. We'll get a statement from you in the morning," Josh said, eyeing me.

Matt stepped in. "Maybe in the afternoon. You look beat."

I scowled at them both. It was part of Matt's job as producer to be concerned about me — I was one of his stars — but Matt was a friend too. I knew his concern was genuine. Still, I didn't want to be questioned about all this.

Matt tipped his blue cap, and he and Josh walked past the resident pink-haired punk rocker and out the door.

Frankie sat rubbing his arms. "I know we've had our differences, but I hate fighting you — mainly because I always get hurt or embarrassed or both — and I really don't want to be next. I'm not, am I?"

For a moment, he looked nothing like a warrior. The only thing he'd be a threat to is the contents of the refrigerator. I shook my head, "I wouldn't know, Frankie, but I sincerely doubt it."

"Okay, I'm here if you need anything. Just give me a holler." He turned his back and his bright hair grazed his shoulders.

"One more thing" — his eyes were sincerely full of worry — "you weren't lying about the sexual assault, were you?" His voice shook a little, and I remembered his sister was killed because she reported a case a few years back.

"Wouldn't lie about something like that," I replied softly.

She had been a wonderful girl, and she hadn't deserved to die over a man's lack of restraint. Frankie had hunted the guy for weeks before he found him, and it's no secret around the base that he killed the culprit, but they never had enough evidence against him.

"I'll be fine once the psychological trauma wears off."

He nodded and gave a weak smile before closing my door. I rested my head back on the pillow and looked at the ceiling. This was the only part of the building that looked like a regular home, aside from the small kitchen on this side of the base. The rest of the place was all white panels and tile floors, very clean. Except one area where Jekyll and Hyde seemed to hang out; it looked abandoned and dirty all the time. But we didn't ever go near there. I happened to value my life.

For some reason, Vince Viktor, the man upstairs, loved Jekyll and Hyde. They were warriors too, tacticians with a mean streak. Most of us hated them; their sadism had cost people their careers. My hand drifted across my chest when I thought of them. We had a history.

I stood and walked into my little bathroom, shaking off the residual dizziness. The bathroom was connected to another room, Angel Lannister's, but she was always with her boyfriend, Ronin, so I never actually had to share it. We had a grudging friendship.

I looked in the mirror and rolled my eyes at the blood stuck to my nose and eyebrow. I was a mess. A shower could fix that, though. After heating the water, I peeled off my top, which was coated in sweat and blood, and dropped it onto the floor. I tried to keep my right hand out of the water as I soaped up.

I got out and threw on some pajamas that the guys would never let me live down. Pink sheep-skeleton PJs aren't exactly something the world-renowned K9 should be caught in.

I looked at the dripping black-and-white mop on my head and shrugged before strolling back into my room and falling onto my bed. I hoped Soul remembered to get some rest too.

I pushed that thought away as the world left me again.

Four

My eyes hurt as I sat up in bed. Though the world was a blur, I still took a confused look around, only to find a piece of paper lying on my desk. I cleared my throat and ran a hand through my hair to clear my mind before I read it. It was messy penmanship to say the least, although it was nothing compared to Matt's.

> *K9*
> *I'm not stupid. Confused. I don't know anymore.*
> *Can't put words together well, start to panic and lose control. Please give me time.*
> *Sorry.*
> *Crow*

I read it over a second time. The first statement looked hesitant. He probably wasn't used to writing, but he had explained himself. He didn't speak in the first person because he couldn't. It was not his fault, not that I ever thought it was. I couldn't believe he honestly thought I didn't understand that he couldn't control it. Sure, he didn't deal well with stress, but he had a system of calming himself down. I could understand that.

I tucked the note under my pillow and threw on some jeans and an old T-shirt, grabbing a jacket and putting on my dog collar on my way out to meet Dan. He'd emailed early in the morning and insisted we get together so I could help him with his investigation into the attacks. As much as I didn't want a damn thing to do with it, and as little as I wanted to hang around with old Dan-o, I knew I had to stay on top of what he was finding.

"So, princess," Dan started, as we made our way through the crowded mid-morning streets of Lilithia. We had met at, and promptly left, the cafeteria to go walk through town. "Are you sure you didn't get a look at this guy? I mean you were stuck with him for, like, a day and a half."

I shook my head. "I was drugged, remember?"

He stayed quiet and kept walking.

"And don't call me *princess*."

He nudged my shoulder and gave me a sideways smile, something that suddenly made me very uncomfortable. Dan had always been a charmer, a flirt, but this time it felt different, like something was wrong. It felt like he was trying to lull me into a false sense of security.

I kept my eyes down and followed him out into the street. People turned to stare (they always did — we were the stars of the town, after all), but I kept my head down.

"So where are we going?"

Dan pointed to a tall red brick house down the street. "What, you don't recognize your own best friend's childhood home?" He grinned at me.

We walked up and knocked on the door. I was greeted with a smiling face.

"Benji! What are you doing here?"

"Hey, Chrissy, how are you feeling?" I tilted my head and crossed my arms.

She shrugged. "I've been better, but at least the drugs are out of my system. What happened to you? Don't tell me this guy got to you too?"

I looked down. My strawberry blond friend shook her head. "Are you alright? Why does something tell me that it was your own fault."

I nodded and let out a laugh. "Yeah … you're probably right. I'll just walk it off."

"That's why we're here actually," Dan cut in. "We both got it the other day. Warriors are being attacked almost every day. Do you remember anything about when you were hit?"

She rubbed her arm and shook her head. "I felt a pin prick in my neck and arms holding me back. I … I was in my room. It shouldn't have happened. I thought I was safe…"

She shook her head and wiped her face in order to keep composed. I put my hand on her shoulder and she looked back at me.

"I know the door was locked and no one else had a key. I heard something metal clang, like the air vent or something though," she said.

She still seemed a little shaken. She was a long-range combatant and had rarely had to deal with any kind of direct enemy contact.

"Once we find this guy — and I promise you we will — I'll let you know, and you can come back to work. Josh is putting new security measures in place and he's changing the locks."

"Okay. Thank you, Benji."

For a few seconds, she looked relieved. Dan let out an impatient sigh and tapped his foot, so naturally, I had to draw out the conversation. "How's your big sis? Still trying to convince you to leave this behind?"

Chrissy instantly rolled her eyes and snatched my shoulder. "You have no idea! All of this has just made it worse. I even tried to convince her I'd be safe in another city, but she just wouldn't go for it."

"What? You can't leave Lilithia!"

Chrissy was the first partner I ever had in this place. Back then she was kind of stuck up and I was a little brat. No one wanted to work with me and no one wanted to train me; she had a proper fit when Viktor assigned us. She'd take my shots before I could reach my opponents, and we ended up fighting with each other more than anyone else.

I always figured she was just there for the fame until the day we were up against Dan, who had just joined, and a guy that resembled someone from my childhood. I couldn't even hit him. It was pathetic, but halfway through the match, Dan got close enough to Chrissy to toss her into me. I had been about to call her a few names when I noticed the tears in her eyes. I helped her up and we ran, and she told me about her sister wanting to pull her out of the competition if she didn't win at least once.

She wanted to be like her mother. She wanted to make her proud. So I've made sure she's never had a losing streak since. We've been an unlikely pair, but we've made it work.

Chrissy sighed and let her hand fall from my arm, holding my hand tightly in hers. "I'd never go anywhere without you. And besides, I'm a grown-ass woman! Annie can't tell me what to do!"

"I'm sure she thinks otherwise…" I dropped my gaze but nodded nonetheless.

"Benji Keanin, I'm not leaving you alone to fend for yourself with all of this going on. I'm just … taking a break."

"Because you know I can't do it without you?"

Pearly white teeth shone under her pink lips, and she tossed her perfect hair over her shoulder. "Exactly!"

Giving a laugh, I shook her hand and started walking away with Dan.

"Oh, by the way, a bunch of us are getting together next week. Angel wanted me to ask you to come," she said.

"Of course, just email me the day before." I sheepishly grinned. I have a hard time remembering stuff like this.

She waved as we walked down the path and back to the street. She was staying with family until this was over, but she had guts for wanting to come back. I had to give her that.

"Now where, boss?" I asked.

Dan scratched his head and shrugged. "I honestly don't know. Some people we couldn't get locations for, and the rest left town. Two of them are comatose at the base."

I nodded and did up the zipper on my coat. "So much for your 'investigation,'" I mocked.

"You know what? What is your deal lately?" He stopped walking and turned to face me. "You've been acting weird all day. Would you even care if this guy gets off scot-free?"

I shook my head and looked down; the rage in his face would have been intimidating if so many people hadn't stopped and stared.

"This guy did who knows what to you and countless of our co-workers *and* friends, and you're questioning the logic behind asking people what they remember?" Dan raised his hand to his head, touching the gash he got in the arena. "Come to think of it, *Ben*, how exactly did you end up in the Pit when I got attacked? You say you were drugged, but I saw you before everything went to shit, and you looked pretty damn lucid to me."

I bit my lip and spun around to face him. "With all due respect, *Danny*, you have no idea what you're doing. This guy will stop at nothing, and I don't think some pathetic, half-assed investigation is going to save anyone's life. Why don't you grow up and stop playing detective?"

I was inches away from him. My faced burned with irritation. He looked like he was about to snap too, but I didn't back down.

"You're either with *us*" — he spat at me — "or *him*."

I was 100 percent okay with siding with *him*, but I took a step back. "Fine."

"Then let's go."

Dan stormed off down the street. It was crowded and people parted for us, partially out of respect and partially out of fear of an angry Dan.

We trudged along silently as the streets got darker; the crowd thinned but disappeared abruptly. The days are pretty short here. I'd followed Dan to the oldest part of the town, all the way to the north. One of the outer walls that surrounded the city partially stood in ruins to separate the market from the wasteland. All the cities have walls like this, and people may travel as they please, but they can only pass through the gates at certain parts of the borders.

This area, the old town, was now mostly a burned-out ruin, abandoned after a civil war. It was eerie how quickly it went from being populated to a ghost town. But the buildings were still structurally sound for the most part, and it was on a small hill, so we could see the angled-down buildings that made up most of the city — a beautiful sight when the sun sets. We'd often use this part of town for open battles. Graffiti and overgrown plant life aside, it was rather nice.

That's our city for you for you — nice view, war-worn buildings, and gory TV. Lilithia Heights! A pretty pretentious name for such a hole. I wouldn't give it up for the world.

Every city has a base like ours, and warriors too, but none of them measure up to us. We got to prove that in the tournaments. Though I doubt the warriors in other cities were being slaughtered like us.

Once every year, a tournament is held featuring warriors from all the cities. The high council gathers to discuss possible war threats and the details of the Tournament of Survivors. They're kind of the peacekeepers who mediate everything. Since the Tournament of Survivors was created, there has been less fighting. Our business was set up to prevent war.

One day someone figured out that if the gladiators and their old-fashioned style of sorting things out was brought back worldwide, then people would get their fill of violence from us and crime rates would go down. It worked for the most part. It was a method brought about when society was nearly in ruin from having to adapt to how the world was changing — or falling apart, really. Apparently, world leaders at the time hadn't believed what was happening until it was too late, but we all know how people feel when change happens. The government was nearly abolished. No matter where you go, it's the same set-up, and every ten years, they send warriors chosen from the tournaments to be thrown into an even bigger battlefield. Beyond that, the cities keep to themselves.

Not many cities are like ours, though. We only have a very basic way of broadcasting with almost ancient tech, and the fact that we straight out battle… Other cities are more organized, civilized, and methodical. But we were the first to bring back the gladiators, and we stayed true to the most basic, brutal aspects of battle. Makes for really good TV anyway.

The Tournament of Survivors is a little more Lilithia's speed. Two combatants from each city are sent in — one male, one female — and fifteen cities compete. We don't kill each other (if we can help it). The fatally wounded are booted out of the competition. There's a monitor that relays our vitals, and if they drop to a certain point, we're pulled. Of course, accidents do happen.

Whatever city is left wins. There's no reward other than the pride of being the city's champion, but it's every warrior's dream.

When I looked up again, we were outside of a cracked old building.

"Why are we here?" I asked.

"Are you going to freak on me again, princess?" Dan asked with a sigh.

I shook my head at him. "I told you to stop calling me that. My name is Benji. My code name is K9. And no, I'm fine. Now, why are we here? I'm exhausted."

"I have one last idea, then you can go home and rest," Dan said. "If my gut is right, we'll find something here. I knew this kid a couple years back. He, uh… Something happened. I doubt he has anything to do with it, but it's still worth a shot. The building should be around the corner — dammit!"

There were four buildings that looked exactly the same. This must have been the source of his sudden discouragement.

"I'll take these two," I suggested. I gave him a pat on the back out of pity then took off toward them, trudging through the trash in the courtyard.

The stairs were rickety and dangerous, but I did my best to stay upright, ignoring the minor splinters I got when I tried to hold onto the railings. Most of the doors were open and most apartments only had two or three rooms, so it was quick work to check them out and move on.

I was in the bedroom of a particularly messy unit — the poor people who had to leave it behind probably missed their family photos — when I heard Dan's muffled shouting.

I opened the window closest and shouted back, "What was that?"

"Check the eleventh floor. I'm not sure what room."

"On it."

I turned back to the room and sprinted out. The hall was in the same disordered state, but I made my way up the staircase to the eleventh floor.

The flora-infested building was a dark brown colour, with peeling paint and rolling carpets. All the doors were open, so it didn't take me long to conclude that I wasn't going to find anything in this building. With a sigh, I exited and crossed the courtyard to the next building. Also not much to tell other than that I hit my wrist while falling down a flight and a half of stairs that caved in and left me on my back in the lobby, dazed and confused.

I shook it off and stood up, nearly falling over in the process.

I was going to wait another moment, but I heard Dan shouting, telling someone to stop running and to get out of the shadows, so I bolted out into the fading sunlight and into the last building. I assumed that Dan was on someone's trail by the way he was shouting, and once I met him on the ninth floor, he stopped his shouting and looked up at me.

"You're bleeding again…" he said.

"Thanks, captain obvious; a fall from two storeys can do that. Who are we chasing?"

He scowled and shook his head. "I don't know. I thought I saw someone come in here… Dear *god*, I need to start running more…"

I left him there and hauled myself to the eleventh floor.

The doors were all open once again, so I stuck my head in each until the last door. The window was open to the fire escape, and there were papers scattered across the floor, covered in what looked like fresh ink. I slowly pushed the door wider and walked inside. There was a certain feeling to the room. It felt older than the others somehow, like it had been abandoned long before the war ravaged this side of town.

I knelt down to look at one of the sheets of paper on the floor and dragged my hand through the ink. Sure enough, it was still wet.

I picked up a paper that looked like it had been dropped moments before. A creak in the floor caught my attention, and I spun on my heels, ready to fight. Dan was at the door, wheezing.

"What did you find?" he asked with a cough.

"I don't know. It just looks like some drawings. Hold on…" I walked into another room and found a wall covered in them. The older ones were blue in colour, while the new ones looked black, and familiar; they were drawings of people that had been attacked recently. Chrissy, Ronin, Roberts, and Juno and Beanie — friends of mine, a sibling team who'd been attacked in the street a month earlier — were all up there, rendered beautifully in black ink. Dan's profile was warped and splattered rather than sharp like the others. There was also a second one of Dan, in blue ink. I was sure it was him, but he looked much younger. His hair was really long, and his usual smirk was replaced with a goofy grin. There was another drawing next to it of a boy, maybe a few years younger, laughing. He had short hair sticking up in a mohawk and a space between his teeth. If I had to guess, I'd say the two of them were in high school.

The newer ones were slightly messier but still very skilled. Dan hobbled in next to me and pulled the picture of the boy off the wall. "This is Absolom Ravin. He used to be a friend of mine; the three of us actually went to school together. I doubt you remember that though."

"I never talked to you. I don't recognize him," I told him quietly.

"He was such an innocent kid. He was kind of everyone's punching bag, but he … he knew he'd be a champion one day. He was one of those guys who would ask out the head cheerleader and then be run up the flag pole by the football team, and *still* have a crush on her."

I thought a moment. "Did that actually happen?"

He ignored me. Dan hadn't taken his eyes off the paper. His hand shook. "He was always on his own. He was so ... *good*. I just really don't... It can't be him."

I tilted my head towards him. "What happened to him?"

Dan shrugged like he didn't want to answer me. "The worst thing you can do is jump to conclusions. Let's investigate more before we start speculating."

He nodded to himself and walked out of the room.

So he had changed his name from Absolom to Soul; as someone whose name was "Benjamina" I could understand the impulse. Especially when everyone wants to call you "Mina."

I turned around, finally, and noticed the closet. Well ... I noticed who was leaning against the closet. I jumped back and hit the wall with a thud. Soul held up his hands to show he wasn't going to do anything. He didn't say anything. He just leaned on the door frame and watched me with those sleepy eyes.

"This is going to get personal, isn't it?" I asked, already knowing the answer.

He looked at the floor, then slowly brought his eyes up to meet mine.

"That's what I thought."

He stepped back into the closet, and I gave him a soft smile. What had changed between now and when he knew Dan, and why did he hate him so much? I needed to get Dan to talk.

"Are you coming, princess?" Dan called to me.

"Get lost, Dan," I called back. "I'll get back on my own."

"Fine!" he snapped. I waited, listening as he stomped down the stairs and stormed out of the building.

"Soul, I have to talk to you," I stated as I turned to the window. I climbed onto the fire escape and up to the roof. That little room was making me claustrophobic. Soul quietly followed.

I looked up at the sky, probably only minutes before sunset. Soul stood by the fire escape and waited patiently.

"The bird didn't do anything wrong," he mumbled nervously, making me turn around to face him.

"No, not at all." I shook my head and sat down at the edge. "I just want to know how you got mixed up in this mess."

He wrung his hands as he sat down beside me.

"Painting … fighting … *underground* fighting. The bird was hunting the worm…

> *Scared and hunting*
> *Midnight black wings*
> *Hunting the worm*
> *And what he brings*
> *The devil's night*
> *And demons sing.*"

"He hunted…" Soul struggled to continue as his voice cracked.

"You mean Dan?" I asked as I tried to get a look at his face.

He nodded and then looked up. "And the demons. Demons … demons; the gemini did this … the gemini… The bird never found them. A note found its way to the bird. I-it told him…" He paused and took a breath, wringing his shirt in his hands. "… me… where to find the worm. *A time, a place, a name, a face* … that's how the bird found the nest. A home."

He seemed to be struggling more than usual.

"Soul, you don't need to force yourself when you speak to me. So, they told you to go to the base, and they gave you the office?" He swallowed hard and nodded. "And that's when you got an email about getting rid of various warriors?"

He squeezed his eyes shut and nodded, with a slight whimper. "The bird refused. It would be wrong! But the monsters found the bird and … and…" He started hyperventilating and grasping at his shirt with shaking hands.

"Soul, relax! It's just me, K9."

He shook his head violently and gasped for air again. I placed my hands on his cheeks and he started to calm down, keeping his eyes shut. "Who were the monsters?" I asked. "What did they look like?"

"Didn't see … too dark. They burned the crow … said he was dirty, a no-good animal. A monster like them." He let go of his shirt and jabbed at the air in front of him with shaking movements and slim fingers as he tilted his head to the side, slightly.

"They burned you? Where?" I could feel my heart speeding up, my stomach knotting with every word he said. Whether the burn itself was bad or not, it must have been a terrifying experience. He pulled the collar of his shirt down to reveal a really bad burn in the shape of what looked like a skull, right smack on the left side of his chest. I put a hand over my mouth and felt a chill run down my back. "It doesn't still hurt, does it?"

Soul still didn't meet my eyes, but he tilted his head back and forth before giving a small nod.

"Crow, I promise that we will find Dr. Frankenstein and his monsters — "

"The crow *is* a monster," he said quietly, shoving his hands into his lap. I placed one hand on his cheek again, smearing ink over him and myself.

"No. You aren't a monster. You do the dirty work because you *have* to, not because you want to. But you are a *crow*: you are brave and strong, and you're just protecting yourself. You are far more beautiful than a simple animal, far more important. *Animals* have no morals … just like monsters. And that's not you."

His eyes were wide with wonder and his cheeks went pink. I ran my thumb over a small cut and then dropped my hand to my side. He didn't take his eyes off me as I stood and stretched. It was night now, and I knew I should probably get back if I wanted to grab dinner at the cafeteria instead of preparing a meal for myself. Which would be nice, considering I can't cook.

"Did you get some rest yet?" I asked. Soul got to his feet and nodded, keeping his shoulders hunched. "Good, we have a lot of work to do." I gave a soft smile and he nodded. It would be nice to see him smile; I wondered what that would look like.

We climbed down the fire escape and left the building. My life was a mess. But I found it fun. Or I would if Soul wasn't being hurt because of this. I lightly patted his arm as I walked past him and back out toward the market. Hopefully, I could make it home without any further incidents.

Five

As I walked through the market, I got hit in the head with a bouncy ball. Considering how many kids play here, it wasn't a huge surprise. Rubbing my head, I bent down and I picked it up. I saw a few boys run over, along with one girl. Probably the culprits.

"We're so sorry, Miss K9!" one shouted.

"Hey, I used to do the same thing not that long ago. Don't apologize for living your little lives while you can." I smiled at them. The little girl looked completely dumbstruck, and the boys were just giddy.

"What happened to your hand? I watch all your fights, and it didn't happen there!" the girl said.

I glanced at my wrist. "I'll let you in on a secret…"

I bent down to their height so we could see each other evenly. "You've heard that people are getting hurt and leaving, right?"

They all nodded.

"Well, the same thing happened to me. The only problem is, I don't think the person who's attacking everyone is completely sure of what they're doing. I don't think they want to be doing it."

"Do you know who it is?" the girl asked, as I rolled my shoulders.

"Maybe." I smiled at her. "What's your name?"

"Rosie," the girl said. "But my warrior name is Razer!"

"Well, Razer, it's all going to come out soon, and I don't want any of you to jump to conclusions. Find all the facts, the who *and* the why, got it?"

"Are you going to get in trouble?" one boy asked.

"Aw, come on, you said you knew all about me! Of course I am … just trust me."

The kids looked at each other and then back at me. "Why are you telling us this?"

I shrugged and smiled. "I guess that's so the most important people, the kids like you, will believe in more than just yourselves. Even K9 needs a team sometimes."

"Nothing's black and white anymore," Rosie stated. Smiling, I patted her head, tousling her flame-red hair. My attention was drawn away suddenly as I stood in the cool air.

A shout from a booming and hoarse voice that I only recently came to know forced me to turn my head. "*K9!*"

I straightened up and saw Soul at the end of the street, a look of fear and anger on his face.

"You kids need to go." My nerves tightened in my gut once again.

They nodded. "Is that him?" the shortest boy asked.

I looked back at them and grinned before sliding to the ground and swinging my leg out behind me. Sure enough, someone fell to the ground with a thud. The kids scattered, shocked, and people ran as I stood again and looked towards the person who had attempted to attack me. There was a knife next to his hand and, even though he was wearing a hood, I could tell he was disoriented.

"Let me guess…" I sighed. "You're one of the *monsters*?"

"That's one way to put it, Vixen."

Vixen. That voice rang through my head, that thick Irish accent. It was one I'd never forget.

"Hyde," I growled. My voice shook, but I was still strong enough to stand my ground.

The figure recovered to his full height and flicked his hood back.

He smirked and stalked towards me, his shoulders hunched. A crooked, gnarly grin distorted his face. "Someone has to stop your little game. Tsk tsk, little doggy. Attacking fellow warriors? Really?

Someone has to stand up for justice."

I stepped back, and a wave of anger came over me. Nothing about Hyde or his twin could ever be called "just."

"What do *you* know, Vulture."

I felt a hand on my shoulder and spun to defend myself with a punch. A second figure staggered back as I struck him in the nose. He looked up at me in a rage. Jekyll, Hyde's ugly twin. He rushed forward like a bull. He was a huge man. Scars covered his face and his hair hung just above his ears. He radiated ferocity. Laughing was all I could do to keep from panicking.

I stepped to the side and tried to hold in a light giggle. "You're wasting your time here."

A thick arm wrapped itself around my neck from behind — Hyde made another move. I dropped all intent of making fun of them and kicked backwards, hitting his knee and causing him to drop me, though Jekyll was now standing upright, ready to strangle me.

"Hey, bozo!" A small voice called out from behind them.

Jekyll took a step forward as a piece of wood splintered across the back of his neck. He took a sharp breath as he slowly twisted his body around to see the young girl Rosie, who was with her friends, holding a shattered piece of wood.

"Rosie, run!" I shouted at the girl, startling her. She backed up and grabbed the boys before she could get caught by Jekyll, swinging his long arm out behind him.

I took that opportunity to kick him in the face and then turn back to Hyde and jump on his back. Once I compared our sizes, I realized this may not have been the best decision. The two are unnaturally large men. He grabbed at me but I squirmed away from his grasp, so he threw himself back against one of the market food stands, with me still holding on tightly.

With a shout of pain, I let go and hit the ground, cracking my wrist for about the fourth time today. Jekyll threw his own knife up and caught it, then leaned over me, threatening me with it. I promised I'd never be a victim again, as scared as I was ... I wouldn't. I gave one last-ditch effort and kicked my legs up, nailing both of them in the chest and knocking them backwards a couple steps.

Sitting in the dirt, I watched the twins grunt and wheeze. By the time Hyde's rage returned, Soul had made his way over and tackled him before he could make another move. They grappled a moment before the larger of the two (so ... not Soul) had the other pinned down. Hyde's hooting and hollering was deafening as his brother tossed him the knife he had been waving. He was ready to slash Soul's throat.

Soul pushed his hand against his attacker's face.

"What's wrong, dirty little bird?" Hyde taunted, laughing and holding onto Soul's cheek, his knuckles white. "Not as skilled as you thought?"

"Who's this now?" Jekyll asked. His laughed mimicked his brother's but it was rougher, deeper. "That man — dirty black hair, scarred face — looks an awful lot like Danny-boy's supposed attacker. How do you know him, Vixen?" Jekyll spoke loudly, like some kind of circus ringmaster, making sure the entire marketplace, and the newly arrived drone cams, could hear him.

Desperately making sure his face was hidden from the cams, my friend gave one last push, then spat in Hyde's face. Reeling back, the attacker gagged as he wiped it clean, leaving Soul an opening to roll him over and punch him a few times in the face. Hyde's knife hit the ground and bounced away.

"Monster..." Soul said. He started to recite:

> *"I've learned to fight the monsters in my head*
> *But how do you fight*
> *The monsters under your bed*
> *When they start to scratch and bite?"*

Can't hurt the bird! Not anymore."

I coughed and held my stomach with my sore hand as I crawled towards the knife. I grabbed it and began to shout loudly at the first attacker, trying to distract him and stop him from terrorizing the kids who had hit him.

"Get away from them and you'll walk out of here alive," I warned.

"You really think you can beat me, Vixen? You can't even stand!"

He lunged forward, trying to grab me. He didn't see the knife until it was too late. I slashed at him as he came toward me and caught him in the arm, carving a large gash into his bicep. He grasped at his arm, letting out an agonizing howl. Hyde growled, tossed Soul to the ground, and ran to his brother, grabbing him and holding him up.

Jekyll's face was pale, and the amount of blood draining from his arm was enough to make him stagger. Hyde roared in frustration then turned and hauled his twin off down the street. A trail of blood followed them as they ran off.

I let my head fall to the ground and sighed in relief, even laughed. Soul did the same, before he pulled himself over to me on his stomach and sat on his knees expectantly.

"I'm fine," I said, trying to suppress a cough. "Maybe a broken rib or two." I hauled myself to my feet and yelled out in surprise as pain shot through my middle. "You're not hurt?" I looked at Soul, who had settled enough to stop shivering.

He shook his head and looked around. "Too many people…"

"I know. You should go, and make sure you get your arm bandaged —"

"Excuse me…" I looked up to see the little girl standing in front of us. "You dropped this."

She held out a piece of paper and he gently took it from her hand, unfolded it, and stared at the ink drawing with a smile. "Thank you," he mumbled quietly.

I was holding myself up by his shoulder as he looked back at the paper, then at me. He smiled, folded it back up, and handed the paper back to Rosie.

"Soul, you need to go. Too many people have already seen us together."

"The dog is hurt — "

"Just go! I've been through worse than this!"

I gave him a small shove and he nodded, a sly smile creeping onto his lips as he pushed his way through the crowd and, hopefully, to safety. I shook my head and started laughing. Rosie unfolded the paper and looked at the blue ink drawing. "What is it?"

She held it up. It was an ink-splattered crow with the outline of a girl dancing, and underneath it were the words "someday you'll be a hero." I smiled and watched which direction he ran in.

"Was that him? Was that the man you told us about?"

I looked back at the little girl and grinned. "Yes, it was. You helped us a lot today. Thank you. Someday you *will* be a hero, for more than just us."

"You really think I could be like you someday?"

A wave of gentle pride swept over me, and I nodded my head. "I do. Just try not to get yourself into as much trouble as I do, for both our sakes."

She giggled and started to walk back to her friends, before turning around and calling to me, "Tell your friend that he's my hero, too!"

I smiled at her. She and her friends ran off home. I decided to do the same.

I stumbled into the kitchen, but no one was there.

Trudging through the tiled walkways to the lecture hall, I was about 100 feet away when I heard shouting. Rolling my eyes, I kicked the door open, ready to make my big entrance.

"I need all of you to listen to me!" I called out, interrupting their argument. "There is more than one person in on this!"

Viktor, Dan, and Louis stood in a circle in the middle of the hall. They jumped and turned toward me as I huffed in the doorway. Viktor looked annoyed at my intrusion.

"And how exactly would you know that, Miss Keanin?"

I looked at the front of the room as I held my side. "Mr. Viktor, I was just attacked by Jekyll and Hyde — in the middle of the market no less!"

He stood and gave me a cold, questioning look. "What?"

"Those goons jumped me! They tried to kill me!" It might be for the best if I leave out the fact that Soul had a hand in my survival. "Dan, did you manage to find anything else about the guys going after us? Those brothers are in on this. I can *feel* it."

He ran a hand through his hair as a light flickered above him. "Not a damn thing."

I nodded. *Good.*

"Are you alright?" Louis asked, putting out a cigarette. He walked towards me.

"I will be … I'm a bit hungry, but I'm good. It's cool." I took a step back. The last thing I needed right now was Louis "Ichabod" Crane in my business. Guy gave me the creeps. I shook my head.

Viktor chose that moment to speak again. "K9, enough wild accusations. Warriors have a go at one another sometimes. That's how it works. You should understand that better than anyone."

"Look at me! They clobbered me. Who just attacks another warrior in the street? We can't rule them out!" I looked at Dan. It hurt to breathe, but my bones were burning with anger.

Viktor turned to Dan and Louis, completely ignoring my comment. "Crane, take a look at K9. Dragon, I want this guy's head on a *spike*. The real culprit."

I wasn't going to let him have that. "I know you like to keep your lapdogs close, but there comes a point when they need to be muzzled! That point is endangering civilians."

"Mind your position, Keanin!" Viktor's arms fell to the side of his fancy vest as he hissed my name. "*You* work for *me*. I'm sure you don't need to be reminded of how quickly that can change."

His white hair, tied perfectly at the base of his neck, swayed as he stalked towards me with his head high. No one knew how old he actually was, but he still had strong hands and a posture that suggested a history in battle. One of those hands lightly pet my hair as he tilted his head and pouted, "You have a bump on your head. No wonder you're being so rash; you've a concussion!"

"I am fine! I know what happened. It's on camera!"

"Yes, well. I'm afraid we *did* see the footage, but by the time it came in, it was horribly distorted. Couldn't tell a damn thing. No need to worry, my dear. I assure you I'll be looking into your claims regardless." His half-lidded eyes creased in the corners as he waved for Louis to cart me away.

Damn old man used to be one of us. There used to be a code of honour here. I'd known him for so long, but I'm just not sure if he lied or not. It kind of made me mad.

I fumed at Viktor and cringed at the thought of Louis examining me. But I followed Crane to his medical facility. He made me lie down while he poked at my abdomen.

"You've been busy." He poked hard above the bruises and I flinched.

"You did that on purpose," I growled at him.

He snorted and looked down at me over his crooked nose. "I know what I'm doing, K9. I'm actually very good at my job."

"No broken ribs?"

He shook his head. "Not this time, but if you keep getting into fights between your fights, you're going to start suffering from exhaustion. Honestly, what were you thinking?" He shook his head.

I sat up on my elbows and winked at the exhausted medic. "You know I'm only doing it to make your life more difficult, Crane."

He slowly leaned forward, his arms bent out at an unnatural angle and his back arched like a cat. His top lip curled a little bit. "I. Hate. You."

Leaning back again, his face suddenly turned serious. He met my hazel eyes with his cold, icy blue ones.

"Do you really think that Jekyll and Hyde are involved in all this?" he asked.

I took a moment to think about the question. I had been purposely over the top with my accusations, maybe as a way of deflecting some of the attention from Soul and myself. I didn't know if the twins were really involved. But the attack was strange nonetheless. They kept to themselves; they weren't even part of the usual rotation. They've never interacted with me on any level since the day they joined the league. I was almost starting to hope they forgot who I was. Who am I kidding? I could never be that lucky.

I looked up at Louis skeptically. Maybe he was trying to bait me into revealing something; I wouldn't put it past him. They called him the Headless Horseman, but that was just a stage name. It didn't stop him from trying to keep a leg up on everyone, though. I mean, he did kind of creep everyone out, but he wasn't the kind of guy to get in league with Soul's "monsters." Was he?

"Yeah. I really do," I stated finally, studying his face.

His thick brows knit together, making him look cross-eyed but contemplative. If he really was involved, he was a pretty incredible actor.

He looked back up at me suddenly, face frozen in a scowl. "Hmm, alright then. Go on. Get out of here."

"Gladly!" I hopped off the table and jogged toward the door.

"And eat something, would you?"

"I *was* on my way to the cafeteria!" I cried out behind me as I shoved open the door. I squeezed my eyes shut and hoped someone saved me some food.

I saw Josh leaning against the wall as I walked back to my room. He was still in uniform but clearly off duty, so I convinced him to bring me a sandwich. Even after I settled down, it was hard to calm the jitters in my body. It was a long day, and it didn't look like it was about to end anytime soon.

"Holler if you need anything else." Josh said, already on his way back out the door.

"Thanks, Josh," I called after him, with a mouth full of spicy-grilled-chicken sandwich.

I sat on my bed and ran over what happened. I'd have to tell Soul he made that kid really happy. Somehow, after a while, I managed to fall asleep with a smile on my face and a half-eaten sandwich in my hand, despite the day I had.

Six

After spending the morning training, I walked down to security and knocked on the door. "Josh, open up. It's Ben!" I heard a crash. The door swung open and a dishevelled Dan appeared, glaring down at me. I entered the office and took a seat with a slight laugh. There were wires everywhere, as well as half-empty plates and cans of soda. "This man needs a maid," he stated humourlessly. "I've been here since breakfast. Frankie's bringing me lunch, then he's going out. I only have one hall left. Would you mind taking a look at those three cameras?"

Nodding, I started the playback. The video was from the day Dan was attacked, showing a view of the second-floor training room. I saw nothing, so I sped it up. The only people in the video were Ronin, who was lifting weights, and Jekyll and Hyde, roughhousing on a couple of mats. I'd give my left arm if I never had to see them again. I hit fast-forward again.

My back hurt from the plastic chair. We'd been sitting there for an hour and had found nothing. My mind was starting to wander.

"Hey, Dan?"

"What?"

"What are we going to do when we find this guy?"

He scratched his scruffy chin. "I don't know … run him out of town … hang him … put him in a fight against, like, twenty guys? Whatever we want, I guess."

I didn't want to do any of that.

"Got it." I felt a little sick. Should Dan find out, he'd kill Soul. Judge, jury, executioner. I don't even know what Dan would do if he found out I was helping Soul. I couldn't let that happen, but if I said anything, Dan might start to catch on. Instead, I diverted the conversation.

"Are you going out with the crew tonight?"

"Yeah, why not? I need a break from this hunting. It's taking up my every waking minute."

Dan and I took our time on the last two security tapes, which took another hour and a half. He made sure he watched every file, but based on the time stamps, there were clearly some missing. My temperamental companion shouted profanities as he slammed his hands down, noticing the same thing.

"He got to them first! Now how am I supposed to figure out how to find him?"

I took a breath and mentally cracked my knuckles: time to put my powers to work. "Forget it, Danny. This guy knows what he's doing, and he doesn't want to be found. We'll get him on something else. Now, I'm hungry. Let's just go meet everyone."

He scowled and side-eyed me. "Maybe..."

I dragged my finger across his collar and pressed my cheek against his as I massaged his shoulders. "Please come? We can talk later."

Dan got to his feet and grabbed my hands, swaying back and forth for a moment before nodding. He wrapped an arm over my shoulder and grinned like the sleazy dog he was. I resisted the urge to lean over a trash can. But at least he had dropped his focus on finding Soul and was following me like a puppy. I probably would have high-fived myself if given the chance.

Sam's Choice was the best restaurant in town. It was packed, so finding our friends was a task in itself. Most of us had dinner here at least twice a week, but they weren't set up at our usual table. The lights were dim, and I was a little bit distracted by the smell of bread sticks, but I spotted a flash of blond through the crowd and waved to Chrissy. She sat at a table with Angel. Dan followed, making flirtatious eye contact with various waitresses before walking smack into the table and receiving a barrage of mockery.

"Did you guys manage to find anything?" Angel asked. She was the first to speak up, which was unusual — Angel rarely cared about anything that didn't involve, well, herself. Lovely woman, I swear. She must have been worried that she'd be next.

"No, but there are some files missing. We're going to have Josh and Matt try and trace them tomorrow," I said.

Angel looked at Chrissy, then Dan, then back at me. She seemed suspicious, almost as though she thought one of us had something to do with it, which, of course, was true. But she didn't have to know that.

"Maybe it's Dan," she said. "He's been spending all his time on this investigation and getting nowhere."

Dan made a sarcastic face and crossed his arms, waiting for one of the staff to recognize him and send over a round of his usual beer. "Yes, brilliant. I hit myself over the head with a steel bar. All for what, exactly? Attention?"

Chrissy shrugged. "Wouldn't put it past you."

I could barely hear over all the restaurant noise, but I still made an effort to seem half-responsive.

"Oh! Look who it is, the lovely couple!" Chrissy hollered gleefully, probably completely hammered already. I turned my head to see Eloise and Frankie walking toward us, holding hands. She gave a shy smile while his cheeks turned pinker than his hair. As they sat down beside me, he quickly mouthed a thank-you to me, and I silently nodded.

They were the target of conversation for most of the evening. After an hour or so, I started to notice Angel getting agitated and looking around the restaurant.

"What's wrong?" I asked.

"Ronin said he'd be here."

Ronin was her current boyfriend, one of a long line of them, but she seemed to be really into it this time.

I looked around and shook my head. "He probably forgot, or he's avoiding us. You know how he feels about crowds."

She nodded sadly and ate her meal, as slowly as humanly possible.

When our small group got back, Matt stopped us at the gate. He was holding a camera in his right hand.

"What is this?" Frankie looked at him curiously.

"The cameras were knocked out, the live feed is down, and the power's been cut, but the boss still wants us to broadcast. Josh, Jeffery, and Louis are helping," Matt answered.

Everyone exchanged nervous glances, so I spoke up. "You know what? We should round everyone up, send them to the lecture hall. Only one person gets hit at a time, right? If more of us are in one place, the better our chances of stopping him, or better yet, catching him."

Nodding, Matt radioed his counterparts and told them to do exactly that. It took a couple minutes and it was all chaos because of panic and infighting, but we did it.

"Shut up!" I shouted. Everyone turned to me and gawked. "Are we missing anyone?"

Our warriors looked around and shook their heads, until Angel stood. "I still can't find Ronin!"

Looking at her, I grimaced. "Everyone stay here. Randy, Frankie, you're going to help me look for him."

Frankie nodded. "You got it, boss."

"Why us?!!" Randy snapped grouchily at me. "Because you know him better than anyone else, and Frankie can easily go unnoticed in the dark."

"I'm going with you!" Angel followed me to the door. From the look on her face, I knew I couldn't stop her even if I wanted to.

We grabbed our weapons then took off toward Ronin's room; Randy and Frankie headed towards the training room. The backup generator had kicked in, but the lights in the long, white corridors were so dim we could hardly see where we were going, never mind search properly. Angel held her nunchucks to her chest nervously as we ran through the halls as fast as we could.

The door to Ronin's room was ajar.

"Wait here," I said, and bit my lip as I slowly opened the door. I could hear someone rummaging through Ronin's things. Sadly, Angel could too. She shoved me aside and pushed her way through.

I looked around her to see Soul with his back to the door.

"What did you do to my boyfriend?" Angel's words were sharp, her voice dangerous.

Soul held Ronin's "log" in his hand (really, it was a diary). He tossed it onto the table and shook his head.

"Not good for you." His voice was raspier than I'd ever heard before. There was something in his hand and Angel seemed ready to attack; I needed to stop this.

"Drop the weapon," I warned.

He started to turn around but only shook his head and chuckled. "Did you a favour, you'll see."

He dropped what was in his hand — a bright, smoking flare — and ran past Angel, who thrust her leg toward him, trying to trip him on his way out. I stepped to the side as he tripped, stumbled past me out the door, and hit the wall in the corridor with a thud.

Soul looked back at Angel, then shook his head, touching a cut on his lip and standing to his full height. I watched him straighten, then calmly walk down the hall.

"Benji, where are you?" Frankie's voice came through the radio.

I grabbed the radio from my belt and spoke into it. "Get to Ronin's room!"

I quickly put my sword back in its sheath and ran to the side table, grabbing the logbook and slipping it into my jacket. Angel set to frantically searching the room, obviously hoping to find some clue about what happened to Ronin. She was desperately trying to keep herself from crying out of frustration as she looked around the trashed room.

I stepped into the bathroom, wanting to clear it of anything that could be linked to Soul. Instead, I found Ronin face down in the tub, which was full of ice cubes.

"Angel! Get in here!" I yelled. "Grab a blanket or towels!"

My arms strained as I pulled Ronin out of the tub and laid him on the floor. He was still breathing, but his lips were blue and his limbs were bound.

Angel ran in holding the huge, blue comforter that had been on the bed, but dropped it upon seeing her boyfriend on the floor.

Frankie ran in a second later and helped me untie him, then wrap him in the blankets. The three of us lifted him and took off toward the medical facility. Both head medics were in when we burst through the door of the med centre. They told us to set Ronin down on a gurney and started rushing about. Angel stayed behind to keep him company as Frankie took off to brief Dan and the boss.

I let Louis know what had happened, then went back to my room. I read Ronin's logbook and was surprised about the things it said, referring to Angel. It looked like he actually did care about her. But the other pages... He took too much pleasure in hurting people. Angel wasn't like that. She hated people like that, but Ronin always acted so upset when he hurt others, so you would never know. I shook my head and flipped to the last page. It only got worse. I had to put the book down and close my eyes, trying to think about something that wouldn't make me feel sick.

I must have fallen asleep thinking about everything because — once again — I woke up in a cold sweat with a sinking feeling in my gut, probably due to the fact I was going to have to deal with the aftermath of what happened to Ronin. I couldn't tell Angel about his log though ... I just couldn't. It would kill her. I decided that I was going to have to talk to Ronin before anyone else did. I needed to find out what he knew about Soul. After cleaning myself up, I walked down to the medical office.

"Hey, Jeff?"

A bespectacled man with messy brown hair stuck his head out from under a desk and smiled. I was glad Jeff, the head medic, was in. I wasn't in the mood to deal with Louis.

"Benji, what can I do for you?" He said.

"Is Ronin awake yet?"

He nodded and pointed toward the bed he was in. I nodded thanks at Jeff and walked past him and over to the bed. "K9? What do you want?"

I held up his logbook and he stiffened. His lips were still blue and he clearly had a chill, but he still grabbed for it. I pulled it back half an inch and sneered, "I read it, you know. I particularly like the part about how much you *love* to play the innocent hero. You enjoy not having any competition?"

"I didn't mean that..."

"Prove it to me and I won't out you to the *public*."

"That's got to be extortion — blackmail!"

I shrugged and leaned closer to him with an angry grimace. "I have a feeling I'm going to do a lot worse very soon. Now, are you going to do better?"

He didn't say a word; he only glared at me. There were footsteps entering the room, so I stepped back and hid the journal again. Dan hardly acknowledged me, and Angel raced to Ronin's side. After smearing her red lipstick all over his face, she sat herself beside him and pushed his hair away from his eyes.

Angel looked up, apparently surprised to see me. "Benji, what are you doing here?"

"Just wanted to see how our patient is doing."

Angel eyed me for a minute, apparently suspicious.

"Any details on the guy who attacked you?" Dan asked.

"He hit me from behind and we grappled. I think I got a decent look, though. He looked sleep-deprived and just overall sad. He told me to just leave the base, and when I refused, he attacked me again and knocked me out. I woke up here."

Angel shook her head, running to her boyfriend's side and holding him gently.

"Brutal," Dan muttered. "Anything else?"

Ronin looked at me and then back at Dan. "I think he had a scar down his face. On the ... left, near his chin."

I swallowed hard and looked at a determined Dan. "I'm going to find this guy if it kills me," he said.

Well, if it had to be one of us...

Angel sat down with her boyfriend, and Dan and I left.

"We need to look for common factors between the victims, things that might link them together," Dan said as we walked.

"Got it. I have a fight later, though. It's against Carmel — "

"Say no more."

I walked back to my room. Inside, it was too dark to see but I knew the layout by heart, so I walked towards my bed.

I must have miscalculated the angle because I walked right into what felt like a brick wall. I fell backwards and landed on my behind. I groaned. My head, wrist, and mind hurt so much I decided to stay there. I rested my head on the floor and ran my uncasted hand through my hair.

"I'm going to die today..." I shook my head and heard the light click on. Blood rushed to my head as I bolted up and looked around.

Soul slowly tilted his head and gave me a worried look.

"You scared me. That was you I ran into?"

He stared a moment, then quickly returned to his senses and

nodded. "Be wary of the candy, poison bite, and twisted heights..." he said. I pulled myself to my feet and dusted off my clothes, trying to understand what he meant.

"Are you talking about Carmel?"

Soul cocked his head to the side, thinking.

"Carmela McCarthy," I continued. "One of the downtown crew. I'm fighting her today."

He nodded slowly.

The last part about "poison bite and twisted heights" had to be about her weapons. As gladiators, we were given access to new toys, to test them. Everyone knew she'd been experimenting with hallucinogens. For this fight, I planned to coat my swords with a tranquilizer, a high enough dose to cause paralysis but only momentarily (or at least that's what Jeffery, the head medic, claimed).

"The doctor wants to know..." He held out a piece of paper, a printed-off email.

> "Why is K9 back? We told you to get rid of Keanin. If she knows anything about you, she'll hunt you down and then come after us! I'd tell you to fix this but your incompetence has already lowered our expectations. Do not fail us again."

My crow-like companion had a sly smile that completely defied how he should be reacting to that email.

"The dog and the bird were such a good herd..." He motioned for me to turn the page over but kept his eyes on the floor. There was a list of names scrawled messily in blue ink.

"People that they want you to go after?"

Soul nodded.

"Well in that case, I'll take Matt. I'd really prefer if he didn't get hurt. The guy can't even take a friendly punch." I looked back up at him and ran a hand through my hair. I could procrastinate, right? All I'd have to do is scare him...

"The weapon is fear
It will shed thousand a tear
In an astronomical year
And bring shame
To many a domineer."

I focused again. Soul was getting agitated and had started pulling his hair and biting his lip.

"H-he's a friend? Hmm-mm … don't…" He tried to steady his breathing but stuttered and tugged his hair harder.

"No! Soul, it's okay, I'll tell him to go. He'll understand, no problem," I said, trying to reassure him. His breathing steadied and he nodded, still not meeting my eyes.

"I'm telling the truth…" I stepped forward and twisted my body so he could see my face, even with his own angled toward the floor. "I'm not going to walk away, no matter what."

His eyes were wide but he swallowed, then nodded, not looking away.

"Th-thank you…" he murmured after a moment. His voice cracked but he didn't seem to notice. He walked to the door then turned to say something, stuttered a moment, and then shook his head and headed out the door. That jacket of his swung around the door frame, and I was left staring after him. He was definitely in need of a friend. Your mind goes to a dangerous place when you're alone too long; it either runs a mile a minute or there's nothing, just blank.

I put it out of my mind as I shoved the paper under my pillow and left for the change room.

Carmela "Carmel" McCarthy was ready to murder me.

"Weren't you in charge of finding this guy, anyway? What is up with that?" I dodged her dagger and rolled straight into a wall. The arena was packed, and fans in T-shirts were cheering our names —

though I was getting booed more than I usually do. Carmel and I had walked in immediately following another fight, so we had to dodge not only each other but the old blood that hadn't soaked into the dirt yet. It was making me a little nauseated. "And how the hell did you not get hurt when you went missing?"

I snorted, holding up my wrist.

"Look, I'm sorry your boy toy got hit, but I had nothing to do with it … and screaming at me isn't going to get Jeremy out of the medical ward!" Contrary to his personality and outward appearance, Jeremy was a Volatile, like me. He'd followed Carmel around like a lost puppy until Soul got to him a month before we met. As I thought about his recovery, I hit the release button and my sword extended into a chain — a one-time deal that Viktor let me test out on the dip-dyed ditz. She shrieked — and I mean *shrieked* — in pain and stumbled back. I moved my arm in a full circle and she jumped away, whipping her head from side to side.

"Feeling the effects of Jeff's cocktail?" I asked smugly. She wailed like a banshee and ran forward, staff ready to hit me upside the head.

"Don't you dare bring me into this!" Jeff shouted from behind the gate. Jeff was the head of medical, Louis Crane's boss. Louis was there too, probably to support Carmela. The medic on the other side of the facility smirked and flicked his cigarette through the grate. The Headless Horseman was the perfect name for him; the old scar across his neck gave him the illusion of being decapitated. He scared me, to say the least, and I'm someone that interacts with him on a regular basis.

He was a part of the "downtown" side of the base, where people like Carmela, Jeremy "Dracula" Vamp, and Jekyll and Hyde were the head honchos. They were questionable — probably killed people, were drug dealers, addicts, thieves … stuff like that. That was not to say that other people were not, but it was far more dangerous with them. There were also nice, normal people living on that side of the base, but they often only slept in their rooms and then spent the rest of their time with us.

Dan, Frankie, Chrissy, Beanie and Juno, and I were the big names over here, but we mostly ignored the drama around us. We didn't beat people up if they hadn't done anything to deserve it — that didn't mean we didn't scuffle with each other, though.

I was pulled out of my thoughts when Carmela jabbed me in the stomach, and I fell back. She stood over me and smirked. "Some star fighter you are. You look more like a skinny, little rat to me."

I swept her legs and got to my feet, retracting my blade and holding it to her neck. "Yeah? Well, you look more like the one caught in the trap to me." I dug the edge of the sword into the ground beside her head, and she held her hands up in defeat.

Josh called the winner, and I took a bow to the crowd. "And that was with one hand, ladies and gentlemen!"

I walked out with all the swagger I had left in me, then went back to my room, fell into the shower, and rinsed the blood from my head. The bruises were already starting to form, but I reminded myself they were battle wounds that I should be proud of. Even if they hurt.

Seven

It was almost midnight. I had procrastinated more than I should have, but my bed was so warm and soft. There wasn't much I could do from there, though…

I threw a bag over my shoulder and went to the storage room. More than enough things that could be useful were there. If it were anyone else, I would have just woken them up and told them to walk with me, but Matt isn't someone you can just wake up. There were two pipes sitting in the corner of the room, so I grabbed those, then found my friend asleep in his office. I prepared myself for the clang and pounded the pipes against each other.

"What..?" Matt squeezed his eyes and groaned.

"It's Benji. Get up."

"Five more minutes…"

I hit the pipes together again and he sat up, scowling behind sleepy eyes.

"What's going on?"

"I need you to come with me, fast." I went to his closet and threw clothes into the bag for him as he put his pants on and rubbed his face.

"What's this all about?" he yawned.

"Just come with me. If you have a wallet, grab it." Matt seemed to perk up. He grabbed his keys and wallet, then followed me through the halls.

Once outside I pulled him closer and he leaned in with wide eyes. "You were on the list. Of people getting hit."

"What!" Matt reared back and took a step away from me. "Like … to be attacked?! H-how do you know that?"

Shoving my hands into my pockets, I gave a sigh.

"Benji, tell me you didn't have anything to do with what's been going on…"

"I'd love to Matt, but I can't."

Suddenly, I felt as though someone was watching us. I turned to look around, but I couldn't see anyone so continued. "I was supposed to be gone too, but he couldn't — he wouldn't. So I tried to get myself out, but it's bigger than just a personal vendetta … though there is one of those too…"

Matt stared at me like I had three heads. I sighed and rolled my eyes. "His name is Soul. His code name is Crow. Someone hired him to eliminate us one by one, and if he doesn't, they'll hurt him. I have to help find out who did this, for all our sakes, without him getting hurt again."

"Yeah, and who does he have a vendetta against?"

"Hmm? Oh, just Dan." Everyone hates Dan for one reason or another.

Matt nodded. "Why can't we just tell Mr. Viktor?"

"Because he's been covering it all up so the fans don't freak. Plus, I can handle it myself!"

"Then why did you tell me?"

"Because I didn't want our best IT geek to bite it."

He shook his head. "You can't do this yourself. I'm going to help too … I think I'll stay away from the base for the time being though, at least until you go public with this information."

My hair blew off my face and I nodded. "Thank you."

"One more thing." He pulled me close by the shoulder. "I think we were followed."

I nodded and stepped back. Instead of walking him to his sisters' apartment, we walked into the woods. There were a few cottages, but all we wanted to do was deter whoever was stalking us. "Maybe it's your friend?"

"No, Crow would have let us know he was here. This ... doesn't feel right..."

From the corner of my eye, I saw a dark shape moving through the trees. Matt saw it too. He flinched and picked up the pace, obviously nervous.

"Hey, Matt?"

"Yeah?" he whimpered.

"Remember when we were in school, and you wanted to be a director?" I rolled my shoulders and stretched my neck, getting ready for a fight.

He looked incredulous. "What the ever-living hell does that have to do with this?"

"You used to carry a camera around everywhere. You wouldn't happen to have one on you right now, would you? If we die here, I want proof that Crow didn't do it!"

Shakily, Matt pulled out the camera and aimed it into the woods. He filmed our very quick walk back to the dorms — and the terrible sounds of heavy breathing and crunching leaves all around us.

I threw open the door to my room and dragged the disoriented blond boy in with me.

"Why the hell are they following us? They're trying to k-kill us! I'm going to be sick..."

I dropped my head and pointed to the bathroom. Matt quickly ran in and did just as he said he would. When he came back, holding his stomach, he pulled my desk chair over and I sat on my couch, set in between two bookshelves.

Matt shook his head and his voice cracked. "Are we just going to hide here for the rest of our inevitably short lives?"

I gave a quick laugh. "I'll talk to Dan tomorrow and we'll sort it out." Pulling out his little camera, Matt sat himself on the cushion beside me. He kept one eye on the door but pressed the tiny buttons until the video started playing on the screen.

"I can't see a damn thing," I stated.

"I see shadows. In the trees. Oh, my god, how did we make it out of there. There's so many of them!"

"Matt, you're panicking. Did we make it back in one piece?" He gave a sheepish nod. "Then whatever is on that video didn't get us. And if it didn't get us out there, do you think it will get us in here?"

"There's a good chance!" He cried.

I rolled my eyes and shoved him off the couch. "Matt, we need to rest. Let's look at it tomorrow!"

His hands balled up as he set the camera on my desk. His voice cracked when he spoke, and tears started to make his eyes shine. "What if it's *them*? What if it's Jekyll and Hyde?"

Though my heart stopped for a split second, I sat up and leaned forward. I pointed my finger towards his nose and gritted my teeth, "Don't you dare. You can't throw that back at me."

"They could *kill us*, Benji! They hate you, and they won't think twice about crushing some little pipsqueak like me!"

My legs moved before I could even think, but I stood and grabbed his jacket. He was a kid, easily the youngest here, but I wasn't going to think twice about slugging him. He was a little bit smaller than me. As I leaned over him, we both realized this for the first time. He bit his lip.

"Don't be a coward." I jolted him towards me for emphasis. "If you ever use them against me again, I will end you. I never should have told you."

His eyes suddenly changed. He was still on the edge of tears, but he grabbed my hands and shook his head. "I'm not using them. I want you to realize how deep you are! If it is them — for the sake of argument — they will stop at nothing to get what they want! Benji, you know what they're capable of. I'm just trying to —"

"Trying to what?" I snorted, letting him go and sitting back down. "Whether it's them or not, K9 doesn't run. Never has, never will. Whoever it really is, let them come. I'm not afraid." I leaned back on the pillow as Matt climbed onto the bed and shot me a glare. I pretended to ignore it as I drifted off, though from the racket he was making, I doubt Matt was having as easy a time as I.

"K9? Ben, open up! Are you alright?"

A furious pounding on the door matched that of the pounding in my head. It had to be Dan yelling. Matt shivered, curled up in the middle of the bed. He was still dead asleep. I looked back at the door and saw it was barricaded with my desk and a few drawers. I punched Matt, abruptly waking him up.

"Matt, do you know how much the twins can bench?"

"Yeah, I know everyone's stats. It's my job."

"Then do you really think *that* would stop them?"

I didn't let him answer as I shoved everything to the side and opened the door.

"Benji, what happened with Jekyll and Hyde? They're all up in arms about you being the one trying to take everyone out! Apparently, you and some guy attacked them in the market?"

"*What?!*"

A shower would have to wait until after I'd worked up a sweat.

"Who the hell is this guy, Ben?"

"Where are they? I'll kill them!"

Dan silently pointed toward the cafeteria and I grabbed my swords… Well, I grabbed *one*. It's hard to hold a weapon when you have a cast on your hand. I'm not even sure it needs to be there anymore.

Biotech has progressed so much we heal faster than the human race used to be able to, all for the purpose of preserving the warriors. And that would come in handy when I tore Jekyll, Hyde, and anything else in my way apart in a few short moments.

I busted through the door to the cafeteria. The two buffoons were parading around like heroes for "revealing" who the hunter was. Granted, no one believed them.

"You two!" I yelled.

They spun and grinned like a pair of hyenas.

"You *stalked* us yesterday. Don't deny it. You think I'm going to let you walk away from that? Walk away and then pin this whole debacle on me?" I drew my sword from its sheath and gave it a quick practice swing as I leapt forward and pressed it to Jekyll's neck. True to their story, despite being twins, the two were different. Jekyll was an average-looking man, scraggly sideburns and sharp cheekbones under slick hair. He'd always looked like that. Face scarred from acne too. Hyde had always had the potential to be an attractive man, but there was something in his eyes. He had neatly cut hair but he lacked his brother's brains, which he more than made up for with his bloodlust.

"Calm down, little doggy… You might end up in the *crosswire* again," Hyde singsonged from beside his brother. I cringed and shrunk a little bit on the spot.

"Don't you mean 'crossfire'?" Jekyll smirked. His voice, unlike his brother's charming fluidity, was stronger, more intelligent.

My breathing increased and my voice caught. "Don't play dumb. You both know exactly what he said."

Dan stepped up and began speaking for those in the room who had no idea what was happening. "Can *someone* tell me what the *hell* is going on?"

Hyde snatched my shoulders and pulled me off of his brother. "I'll tell you! She's the one hunting us! She and this monstrous pet of hers attacked my brother and me in the marketplace! The guy she was with has been attacking warriors all along!"

"That's a lie!" I shouted, and lunged at them, getting right in their faces.

They faced each other, then caught me as I came at them and tossed me at Dan and Matt. The three of us crashed to the ground in a groaning heap as the brutes towered over us, ready to fight. I rolled off the boys and Dan stood up, roundhouse-kicking them both in the jaw.

I leapt at them and swung my weapon, barely catching them in the stomach, not hard enough to do real damage. The warriors around us had started either recording on their personal handhelds or leaving, as the fight was getting ugly and showed no signs of letting up.

Dan was shoved back by Jekyll, who reached for the knife he kept in his belt. Meanwhile I had somehow managed to get stuck with the larger, angrier of the two. Hyde swung his pipe at me, and I hopped back as he came towards me before falling over and crawling as far back as I could.

"You should have known you weren't going to survive after encountering us — "

"Can it, Hyde. I like a good fight, but I don't get off on slaughtering innocent people!" I said.

"You know damn well that plague-infested *freak* isn't innocent…" Hyde hissed. Like the snake he was, the statement dripped with venom, and it hurt.

"I know *damn well* Crow does what he has to, to survive!" I kicked at him, but he easily dodged my feeble attempt and raised his pipe again. I was ready to take a hit, simply out of spite, when the door was quite literally broken down. Everyone froze, including our assailants. We watched as the interloper pulled the axe embedded in the door free and dragged it across the ground behind him. If I hadn't known who the heaving, black-clad man was, I would have stayed frozen like everyone else in the room. Instead I shoved my blade forward, catching Hyde's leg as I leapt up and jumped from the floor to a table.

"You shouldn't be here — "

"Shouldn't — shouldn't be *alive* … not after *them*." Soul held his axe up and pointed towards the twins. "Hunters become the hunted!" A grim chuckle turned into a sick laugh, then into an all-out cackle. A sinister grin contorted his features as he rushed towards Hyde.

"Sh-she's with him!" Hyde hollered. "She'll… Ah!"

Soul didn't give him a chance to finish; he took a great big swing at his face. Hyde dodged it and glared at us both as he booked it across the cafeteria to the kitchen. Jekyll took the distraction as an opportunity and jabbed at Soul with a knife, which he quickly regretted when Soul dodged the blow and tossed the brute over his shoulder and onto the floor. Jekyll's knife clattered to the ground. Soul closed his eyes, trying to steady his breathing as he bit his lip and hunched his shoulders, swaying slightly.

"Murderers…" he mumbled. "You should have buried me then, should have thrown the crow into a grave! Murderers! *Murderers!*" He slammed both hands onto the table I was standing on. I lost my balance, falling onto my back. A result of exhaustion — or, you know, a few lingering concussions.

Soul was shaking his head, violently mouthing the words.

"It's okay, Crow, it's okay now." I was still lying sideways on the table as I tried to comfort him.

"K9…" he said.

I touched his shoulder, and he quickly looked from my hand to my eyes.

"It's okay," I repeated.

He suddenly jolted up and with his axe, deflected another attack of Jekyll's knives. I rolled off the table and onto the floor as Soul twisted his body so his attacker wouldn't reach him. A second later, Hyde was back. He headed straight for Dan, who was staring at Soul. I had to haul him out of the way as he stuttered, "B-but I thought …?"

"Snap out of it, Dragon," I said, shaking him. "You look like you've seen a ghost!"

He was completely blank as he watched the two men grapple. Then Hyde snarled and jabbed at me with his knife. I jumped to the left to avoid him, but he cut pretty deep into Dan's leg. Dan fell to the ground, whining. I grabbed my blade and tried to retaliate, but I couldn't counter such brute force and was quickly overpowered. I had fallen to one knee and nearly given up when the pressure against my blade was suddenly gone. I looked up to see Hyde hunched over and staring at his shoulder, where a common kitchen knife was embedded. He ripped it out with a shriek louder than Dan's caterwauling. I scrambled to my feet to get away from the bloody gash and looked up to see a horrified Jekyll and an almost deliriously angry Soul. He quickly grabbed his axe and started backing towards the door with a mad grin. In one terrifying second, our eyes met and then he spun on his heels and ran.

Josh, Jeff, and Louis ran in, ready to do their respective jobs. A horrified look was shared between Jeff and Louis. Jeff went right to work on Dan's leg. He turned to me and growled, "You better have a damn good explanation for this!"

"What in god's name?!"

Everyone in the room looked up to see Vince Viktor saunter through the splintered doors, and over the debris.

"Jekyll, Hyde! Dragon! ... K9?" He stopped and stared at me. I had never been a problem for him. Until now.

"Sir! We were warning everyone here that we were attacked when she just ran in and hit us!"

"Bullshit!" Dan hollered back. "Everyone here can verify that a guy ran in and defended everyone from *them*!"

"And did anyone recognize *the guy*?" our boss asked. Everyone cautiously shook their heads, and then he turned to the onlookers, who mumbled between themselves, then agreed on a solid "no." "Dan, Benjamina, I want this handled. And you boys" — he turned to look at Hyde and Jekyll — "get to my office."

After he left, everyone breathed a sigh of relief and grimaced. Everyone saw me say something to Soul. Why did none of them say anything? That was when I saw the giant TV screen in the dining hall. Matt had already put the video on replay. The headline talked about how this hit man could be doing this for fun, like Jekyll and Hyde, but also mentioned that it was rumoured he was forced to do it against his will, for one reason or another. I looked at Matt and mouthed a thank-you before I started helping Jeffery drag a nearly unconscious Dan to his infirmary. You would think a man who had lost as much blood as he had would be a little bit easier to carry.

Jeffery laid him out and grabbed his equipment.

I stood awkwardly at Dan's side, then Jeff dismissed me with a wave.

Back in my room, I dragged myself to the bathroom. I climbed into the shower as pathetically as anything, warm water burning my cuts and soothing the aches that come with too much strain being put on your body. Pants didn't even seem worth it. They never really do, but today especially. Granted, they were required for a social gathering, and I really hated skirts. I sighed and gave in to a pair of torn jeans. Chrissy wanted everyone together tonight. It didn't seem like the best idea, but it would be relaxing, more or less. Until then, a nap was in order.

The door to my room easily swung open, and I stepped onto the grey shag carpet, not expecting to see a bloody Soul leaning against the door. I jumped back and he touched his jaw carefully with a disappointed look. "Mistakes follow that which calls itself a murder."

The crack in his voice sent a pin into my chest and what he said was even worse.

"You were just — "

"No!" He held up his hand and started pacing. "No, the worm belongs to the crow. Hmm — mm, kill … kill … kill the worm. No — no! M-me … me, Crow, gets to kill the worm; no monsters, only … monsters…"

His face went whiter than I thought possible, considering how pale he already was, and his eyes seemed to water. He looked like his heart had just broken.

"The bird … *is* a monster…"

I wanted to say something, but there wasn't anything he would let me say, and nothing seemed to be as *consoling* as I wanted it to be. He dropped his jacket to the floor and ran his ink-smudged and shaking hands over his face, smearing blood over his cheeks and nose. His breathing was ragged, and he was completely horrified by his realization. He slid his back down the closet door until he was sitting on the floor.

"J-just as bad as them…" he whispered, hands still covering his mouth.

"No." I carefully knelt in front of him and took his hands. "You can't destroy a demon without becoming one. There are no guardians — no angels in this world, and just because someone does bad things doesn't mean they are a bad person. So many of those people are survivors. None of us can ever be angels." I put my head down and squeezed his hands. "And maybe we shouldn't try to be."

My voice was shaking more than I wished it would. He shook his head, giving me a puzzled look. "But … the dog *is* a saviour, an angel…"

I gave a breath of laughter and looked up at him. "There's no such thing as angels, Soul. You either die in pain, or you become a bigger monster than the ones you're fighting. We need to create our own happy endings, as monsters and demons if it comes to that, so are we going to get our justice? Or are we going to fool ourselves into believing the world is fair?"

Soul looked up at me, a very sad look still painted under all that blood.

"Come on," I said, "let's clean you up."

He looked away, pulled himself to his feet with a grunt, and walked towards the sink in the next room. His shirt, stained with ink, was all bloodied and torn and no longer nice.

"Thank you," he whispered, so quietly that I almost didn't hear him. Red rolled off his hands and into the drain.

"Out damn spot — out, I say."

He seemed to go about the motions mindlessly, while mumbling something every few seconds that I couldn't quite catch. He pulled his shirt off like a child would, getting his head stuck in the neck hole, and stared at his reflection in the mirror. Blood was running down his torso from small slashes and cuts, and from what had soaked his shirt. There was a lot of blood, but it wasn't all his. His eyes glowed through the blood that was on his face. He closed them and inhaled. Something went horribly wrong today, something that made him think he was going to end up as just another nightmare.

I took a rag from the sink and wiped his face, water dripping from his chin. He grunted when I touched his lip by accident, and cried out as I continued to soak up the blood from it.

After he was cleaned up, he sat silently while I walked to Angel's room, feeling conflicted about whether or not I hoped she would be there. She was.

"Benji, I saw what happened with those thugs. Are you and Dan okay?"

"He'll be fine, and don't worry about me. I was wondering if you had any of Ronin's shirts here."

"Of course. Why do you need one?"

"No reason."

She eyed me suspiciously but didn't ask any other questions. I waited as she put her book down and walked to a shelf. She pulled out a black T-shirt and held it up for me to see.

"That's good."

"Are you still going to Chrissy's tonight?"

I gave a sigh. "I guess I should. It would be good to take a break."

"And to see your best friend? Don't forget Chrissy was attacked. You need to support her too."

I smiled and nodded, then walked back into my room, locking the door behind me. Soul's lip was bleeding again, but he didn't seem to care. He didn't look at me when I sat down beside him. I could almost physically feel his sadness.

"I wish ... I wish so bad that you didn't have to go through this, Soul."

He shrugged. "Everyone gets what they deserve."

"Jekyll and Hyde will if I ever get my hands on them."

He shook his head, trying to shake away a hint of a smile.

"Here." I handed the shirt to him. He put it on slowly.

"We should get out of here before Dan tracks me down." I stood and he followed me to the door. Before I opened it, I turned to him again. He had produced a baseball cap from his back pocket. He slipped it on over his hair, which didn't do much to keep it from going all over the place. I should really buy him a brush. Come to think of it, the cap looked a little bit familiar, but I brushed it off.

He silently followed me down the halls and to the exit.

Eight

Once we were outside, Soul took his hat off and shook his hair out. He seemed to be having an issue with his shirt. It looked slightly too tight — not that I'm complaining. He tugged at it to loosen it, but that didn't seem to help.

Suddenly he stopped walking and stuck his arm out in front of me. I too had seen the bouncy ball and attempted to catch it, but I only ended up flailing my arms out before I noticed that Soul already had it in his hand. He stared at me and slowly started to smile. We started giggling like school kids as a group of children ran over. I recognized them as the ones from a few days ago.

The girl, Rosie, shrieked. "It's K9!"

I waved to them and Soul tossed the ball to the boy closest.

"I watched the cafeteria video this morning! It was so cool how you just broke down the door to jump in!" one boy said to Soul.

Soul shrugged and rubbed his neck, blushing at the attention.

"And you're so amazing, like fast and … big!" The kid puffed out his chest and flexed his tiny arms. A smile started to break on Soul's usually serious face as the kids chattered on about this morning's fight.

"How did you see it? The main cameras were still down until twenty minutes ago."

They shrugged.

"It aired and then cut right after Mr. Viktor came in. I checked and they said it was a technical glitch," Rosie said. She was still staring starry eyed at Soul.

I looked at my friend and he shrugged his shoulders. "Not a snitch, just a glitch?" he said.

"H-how did you meet K9?" Rosie softly interrupted.

Soul bent down to her height and rested his nose on his knees. "She saved me," he mumbled quietly.

"How?"

He smiled. "She trusted me."

"You saved her too, right? The other day in the market, and today and this morning," she eagerly stated.

"He did," I said.

Soul glanced up at me wide-eyed as I crossed my arms. I wondered what went through his head at times like this.

"I hope you do well in the tournament next month," Rosie said before she turned to go. Her blue dress danced in the wind as she ran off with her friends.

Soul stood again and I smiled. "See, they like you too. The little girl seems to *really* like you."

His cheeks turned pink, and he faintly grinned as he picked up his boots again.

"Where are you off to?" I asked.

He shrugged and stuffed his hands into his pockets. "Home."

I nodded as I watched him walk away, but then stopped him before he could get too far. "Please stay safe."

"For K9?"

"Who else?"

He smiled again and walked off, leaving me with my thoughts and a sinking feeling in my stomach. But that may have been because I was hungry...

"Chrissy! Open the door, it's Benji," I had been knocking for a few minutes before my stout friend reached the door with an empty bottle of wine in her hand.

"Tell me you didn't drink all of that by yourself…"

She grinned like a five-year-old and hiccupped. Who was I kidding? She could empty an entire cabinet. I walked inside and dropped onto the couch. Everyone was already there — Angel, Eloise, Juno — and everyone had a glass of wine in their hand. Chrissy poured a new one and tried to hand it to me, but I stopped her.

"I can't stomach that crap and you know it."

Rolling her eyes, Chrissy tossed a can of beer at me instead, which I gladly caught and gulped down.

"So … who was that you were talking to earlier?" Angel asked slyly.

"Ooh, does someone have a boyfriend we don't know about?" Chrissy added.

"I want to know! Tell me… Is he cute? Or hot? Or that kind of attractive in-between that makes you want to smash your face off a wall?" Juno's brain often went into hyperdrive as she spoke. It tended to get annoying.

"Breathe," I ordered. How one's mind could run so fast astounded me. "I don't know what you're talking about —"

"Yes, you do! I saw you talking to someone during the Jekyll and Hyde incident," Chrissy called from the other room.

"Was it him you were talking to? He was definitely hot," Angel added.

"Guys, it's not — I don't… You really want to know, don't you?" I already knew the answer to that.

"*Yes!*"

The word simultaneously rang out, so I heaved a sigh and shook my head. "Angel, yes, that's who I was talking to. Chrissy, yes, it's the same guy that ran in and saved Dragon and I. Juno, you'd be surprised; he's actually very sweet."

"Really? I saw the video." She exhaled, puffing her lips up and shaking her head. "I swear he was pretty hot… Are you sure he's not both?"

"Yes."

"Benji! You *never* just jump into relationships!"

I threw my hands up, nearly spilling my beer over my face. "Whoa! Who said anything about being in a relationship? You all *know* I don't do those!"

"So who is he then? What is he to you?" Eloise softly threw in her question.

"A friend —"

"With benefits?" Chrissy asked, giggling.

I spit out my drink and coughed as Chrissy high-fived Angel.

"God, no!" I didn't want to think about him that way. At all.

"How did you meet him?" Eloise asked.

The cat was out of the bag.

"When he tried to kill me," I said.

Everyone went silent until Angel spoke again. "And we thought Eloise had a strange taste in men." Though her words were playful, her voice was dark.

"I — is that the guy who's been attacking everyone?" asked Eloise.

Juno gasped. "It does look like him!"

"Ben, what are you doing?" Chrissy said, concern in her voice. "Why would you be hanging around that guy?"

"Listen, none of that is his fault." I could hear the desperation in my words. But I needed them to believe me. "He doesn't *want* to hurt anyone."

"Bullshit," Angel cut in. "Ronin has scars from what that guy did to him. What's wrong with you?"

"Well, a lot is probably wrong with me … but in this particular case, I'm on your side!" I went on. "He's being forced to do it against his will. I promised I would help him track down the people that 'hired' him. The same people that *branded* him."

"Do you know who those people are yet?" Chrissy asked as she gave me a disapproving once-over.

"No, but I think those bastards — Jekyll and his nutcase brother — have something to do with it."

"Do you think it's a good idea to go after them, with your history?" Chrissy asked.

"Not at all. Can we talk about something happier?"

Angel was in the middle of taking a drink, but she raised her hand and waved it around until she finished swallowing. Then she blurted, "Ronin proposed to me! He said he finally realized that he had taken me for granted before and that now he wants to marry me!"

I nearly fell out of my seat. "And you waited until now to tell us?"

"Yeah, I told him I would. He didn't have a ring or anything but it was so sweet, and I really don't want to lose him." We all congratulated her and then moved on to Eloise.

"My life has been kind of boring lately."

"Come on, there has to be something," I said encouragingly.

"Well, you said you didn't want to talk about it, Ben, but your 'friend' from this morning told me to leave the base. He said I would know when it's safe to come back."

"Don't worry about it. Something tells me you can stay." I was slightly aggravated that he talked to her without letting me take care of it.

"What do you mean?"

"Once I get back tonight, Dan is probably going to call him out. Or kill me. Either way, things are going to go public soon."

"Okay … let's go back to talking about happy stuff. What's new with you, Juno?" Eloise asked.

After stuffing a handful of chips into her face, Juno shrugged. "Not much. Beanie and I are waiting for that new video game; it has dinosaurs in it."

Everyone rolled their eyes. Whenever something involved dinosaurs of any kind, Juno and Beanie were first in line.

I had taken off once the party started winding down. I couldn't shake the feeling of being watched again. The rest of the girls were staying at

Chrissy's. Chrissy was planning to return to the base the next day, and she, Angel, Eloise, and Juno were going to go together. For the time being, I was pretty much on my own.

I really wished I wasn't because, let's face it, the world was against me, and I remembered that once I saw Dan storming towards me on a crutch the second I got back into the barracks. I considered making a run for it, but he got to me before I had a chance, snatching me by the hair. Honestly, I can't blame him for being angry. I would be too, but really? The hair? Cheap.

"Ow! Danny, let me go and I'll explain."

"Oh, you're going to explain alright." He dragged me into his room and sat me down in a chair as he glared at me.

"How do you know him?" His voice was far calmer than I'd expect from looking at his face.

"What are you talking — "

"Don't even start. How do you know Absolom?"

I glared back and crossed my arms. "It's Soul now."

Dan ran a hand through his hair, looking like he was about to wring my neck. "He's not right in the head, Ben, he — "

"Shut up! What happened between you two? Why does he hate you so much?"

"That's not your problem!"

I stood up and walked to the door. "It is now. It became my problem when he risked his life against Jekyll and Hyde."

Dan slammed his hand over the door and leaned closer, almost too close. "I'm just trying to protect my girl…"

"I'm not your girl. I never was, and I never will be."

He somehow got it into his thick head that this was the perfect moment for him to make his move. I was way out of my comfort zone when he kissed me, and if I could live it again, I would have hit him with his own crutch. Many times. Instead, I shoved him backwards and he landed on the ground with a yelp. Spitting in his direction, I walked out.

I went to my room and slammed the door shut. My gut was in knots, and I thought I was going to throw up, but no one was around. The only person not still at the party that I could trust was Matt, and I didn't want to drag him into this any more than I already had.

I shouldn't have been able to fall asleep, but after brushing my teeth for an hour straight and then climbing into bed with a knife in one hand and a pager in the other, I managed.

Nine

The next day, I returned to the scene of the attack in the market, hoping to find something left behind by Jekyll and Hyde or someone who witnessed the whole thing.

Dan had obviously had the same idea.

"Benji, are you here to help me investigate? This was where you were jumped, right?"

I was momentarily floored. He had the *audacity* to speak to me?

"Are you kidding me? Don't act like nothing happened! Dan, I will *smite* you if I have to."

"Calm down, princess," he started. I didn't give him time to finish as I walked right up to him and slammed my knuckles into his nose.

"*Dammit!*" I hollered as I shook my hand. Dan screamed profanities at me and held his face in one hand as he steadied himself with the other. I looked up in time to step to the side as Dan was shoved forward by a boot to the back courtesy of my friend Crow.

Dan rolled over on the ground and looked up to see a very angry man standing over him, axe raised.

"Soul! No!" I called to him, and he looked up with worried eyes. Dan shouted for backup and I started to tug at Soul's sleeve. "We need to go."

He stepped away from Dan and gave me a look that said, "Aw, but I just got here!" Sure enough, a moment later, Randy, Ronin, and Jeremy showed up, ready to hit Soul with every weapon in their arsenal. He quickly hooked the blade back over his shoulder and started running. I did the same, struggling to keep up.

"My fault... Should have waited!" Soul said, aggressively shaking his head.

"Don't beat yourself up about it ... I think *they* got that covered."

He nodded, grabbed my arm, and pulled me into an alley, a shortcut to the base. We both dodged people as we ran and knocked over garbage cans and small stands in order to slow down our pursuers.

We burst past security and down the first few halls. My lungs were on fire; I am not made for running. Soul, on the other hand, simply wiped two drops of sweat from his forehead and looked at me with remorse.

"Stop doing that. How were you supposed to know it was a trap?"

"Here, pretty puppy," called Ronin mockingly.

"And her pet bird... That guy creeps me out, Ronin," Randy said.

We silently made our way down another hall only to find Jeremy waiting for us, surrounded by a group of warrior wannabes. Sharing a look, we rushed past them, throwing a few to the side while dodging others. We turned a corner as they gathered themselves again, and I shoved Soul down one hall and waited for the grunts to find me. Once they saw me, I raised my eyebrows and bolted down a different hall. I was very close to collapsing, but I pushed as far as I could.

This was the most running I'd ever done at one time. Halfway across town and a wild goose chase through the base? Would not do that again.

I led them through any hall I knew wasn't a dead end until I got back to the main corridor. Having made it to the entrance of the arena, I leaned against the gate for a moment to catch my breath before I realized Randy and Ronin had joined the larger group on our tails. I cursed my terrible luck and even more terrible decisions, then ran forward.

Soul had reached the other gate. He was holding my swords.

Fighting our way out seemed the best possible action at that point. We nodded at one another, silently agreeing to meet halfway.

The sunlight in the arena was mocking me. The dull glow of the dirt was almost blinding as I ran out into the centre of the Pit, which was crammed full of people. The crowd started to shout in surprise, disappointment, and even delight the second they realized that this wasn't the fight they were here to see. I pushed my boots into the dirt as hard as I could, but I still couldn't move fast enough.

I had my hand on the hilt of my broadsword when a gunshot rang out. I felt my abdomen burn. Soul and I fell into each other a second later. I placed my hand over my stomach, my breathing becoming increasingly painful. I cried out again and rested my forehead against his shoulder, biting my lip to hold back any more screams. His breathing was just as ragged. I felt him slide his arms over my body, only pulling his hand away for a moment to stare at the blood.

On one hand, I could still feel my legs; on the other, I was starting to shiver so aggressively it felt like I was going to throw up. I was terrified.

Soul squeezed his arms over my shoulders again. I winced.

"K9?"

"Soul, you need to go—"

"N-no! ... If the bird leaves..." He started trying to calm his breaths, reverting to whispering. "I don't want the dog to die..."

I breathed against his shirt. I desperately wanted to let go of my stomach and hug him back. "They will kill you, Soul. I can't ... I wouldn't be able to stop them ..."

"No ... no, it's not fair..." he whispered. I could feel him start to shake. "K9..."

"Please..."

I could feel his body slowly start to stop shaking as he inhaled sharply. He practically radiated with the pain of it. "For K9?"

"Who else?"

He nodded to himself and whimpered one last time as he started to sit back. I touched his face and quickly kissed his cheek, much lazier and sloppier than I intended, but it was getting so hard to use any fine motor functions, I was happy I could even do that much.

He gently put me down and I sat on my hands and knees. He stood up and fearfully started to turn his back and run, only to realize Dan was on one side and Josh was on the other, perched above the gate, holding a gun.

"*Take the shot*! Take it, kill, do it!" Soul shouted, his lip shaking as he held out his arms.

Dizziness hit me as I fell onto my stomach, feeling blood drip from my mouth into a pool that was forming next to my cheek. I inhaled a bit of dirt as I started to cough, bracing myself for the gunshot … but nothing happened. He gave me one last terrified look, then unclipped his axe from his back and got ready to start swinging.

"That's my Crow," I solemnly muttered before closing my eyes.

> *"The flames that singed my torso*
> *Now burning back again*
> *Not for me this time*
> *But for a former friend.*

"If the K9 dies, then so will you…"

I opened my eyes slightly to see him standing protectively with his weapon raised and the most anger I have ever seen in a pair of eyes. A sudden and merciless surge of pain ripped through me again. I let out a scream before I blacked out.

Ten

"*I'm so sorry…*"

A raven is a raven, but a crow is more.

My friend didn't believe it, but he was far more like a crow than a raven. They are pretty much the same bird, but ravens are prideful, bitter towards the world, and pampered. Very proud birds.

Crows, on the other hand, seem to exist to do their jobs, whatever those may be. They are like people: they become what the world wants them to be, despite being such beautiful and intelligent creatures. They do their jobs and they do them well because they are strong and know that, one way or another, they have to keep surviving.

Crows and ravens are not the same bird; the crow is okay with what they have become … and I knew that, someday, my friend would be too.

Eleven

Light pierced through my eyelids as I woke up.

I held my right hand against my face. I immediately noticed that something was off, but my mind was too scattered to think of what it was. All I could focus on was the quick pain that shot from my back to my front. I opened my eyes fully, gasping, and noticed that I was lying in a hospital bed. I sat up and lifted my shirt slightly; blood-splattered bandages covered my entire middle.

The window to the right of the bed reflected the small room. To my left, Soul was asleep in a chair with his arms crossed. He couldn't have been comfortable. After a few seconds of painful silence, Louis walked around the curtain, his bony face twisted into shock when he saw me.

"I-I thought you were in a coma… How do you feel?"

"What in god's name happened?"

Louis quickly managed to compose himself. He gave a sly smile and tilted his head. "You don't remember?"

"I remember running and then…" I scowled and smacked the bed. "Some ass-clown shot me!"

Louis jumped back and started to chuckle. He cast a look over at Soul as we both settled again. He pointed his chin at Soul.

"He's been here every night, you know. I keep trying to send him back to wherever it is that he came from, for proper sleep, but he keeps telling me he needs to be here in case you wake up. Sometimes he'll say 'one more minute,' then lose track of time and fall asleep. He did that tonight." Louis's hoarse voice was calm for once, a little more nasal than usual.

Watching Soul, I smiled softly. This was the most peaceful I'd ever seen him.

"Is it true you can hear someone talking to you when you're in a coma?" Louis asked. He always had been morbidly curious — some of us joked that he was secretly a mad scientist, experimenting on poor saps in the basement. I gave it a thought. "I do remember hearing something, but it might have been a dream."

Louis nodded. "It *is* possible. You never know what the body's capable of." He raised an eyebrow. "By the way, the boss has decided to let your friend join the league. Dan and his men have been all up in arms about it, trying to turn the public against him. Frankie, Chrissy, and Matt have headed up the retaliation, though. They aren't having an easy time with it, but they're trying to have your back. You might want to keep them around. Do you want me to call them down?"

"No, that's okay. I'll talk to them tomorrow. Thanks."

Louis nodded and went to his desk. I wondered if he ever slept; he always seemed to be busy with paperwork.

I swung my legs off the side of the bed and whispered to the sleepy bird, "Soul, wake up…"

He stared to shift his weight, then slowly rubbed his eye with his knuckle, pouting like a small child.

"Wake up, oh protector of mine…"

Slowly, he opened his eyes, then, startled, he jumped up and bit his lip. He looked relieved and remorseful at the same time, but mainly surprised. Before I knew what was happening, his arms were around me and I had a face full of his matted hair. Chuckling, I slowly slid my hands around his muscular shoulders and he nuzzled into my arm. I felt safe.

Ordinarily, I would put on a tough face and tell you I didn't need it, that I let him hold me for his benefit and not mine, but that wasn't true. This time it was nice to know someone was there, that maybe I wasn't on my own for the first time in a long time.

His breathing started to slow and he slipped to an arm's length away, keeping his hands on my shoulders.

In truth, I wasn't done with that hug.

"How long was I out for?"

He looked at the ground, then kicked the toe of his boot against the floor. "Eight days." His voice was raspy like he had been yelling, and his eyes were red.

"How are you?" I asked genuinely.

He shrugged his large shoulders. "Better now … but tired. No … worse; worried, scared…" He put his head down and I wrapped my arms around his neck. He rubbed his face against my hair, and I stroked his own blue-black mess.

"All my fault…"

He shook his head back and forth, looking distressed, but all I could do was laugh. Stepping back, he stared at me.

"Soul, none of this is your fault. It was just a wrong-time, wrong-place kind of thing. All of it."

Tilting his head, he sniffled.

"It's not your fault," I insisted, straightening. "And we're going to win this. We're already winning!" I twisted a piece of his hair around my finger, and he gave a sheepish smile and a nod.

"What next?"

I thought a moment. I really didn't know but I was kind of hungry. I looked at the clock and saw it was 5 p.m. I slid off the bed, grabbing the clothes, changing—maybe getting a little motion sickness — and then going in search of my boots. I looked at the side of my bed, then the end of it. I even checked under it. And where on earth were my shoes? I swear, if Jeff tossed them to get me "upgrades" again…

I stood up and crossed my arms. "Shoes. Now."

"Looking for these?" Louis was holding them up, smirking. "No arch support at all." The medic clicked his tongue. "You really should think more about your lower back."

"Ya, ya." I jumped up and snatched them from his hand. "Thank you," I said, scowling.

I couldn't lie. I wondered again if he had anything to do with Frankenstein and those demonic brothers.

"Why are you here helping us anyway?" I asked, narrowing my eyes. "I thought you hated this side of the base."

He shrugged, then looked up, his eyes searching every corner of the room. He was looking for drone cams, I realized, but there were none.

Louis sneered back at me and spread his arms, letting his dark hair fall in his eyes and speaking much more urgently than his ordinarily bored tone would allow. "This is all a show. The name, the attitude. Why do you think I proudly display this instead of hiding it?" He ran his thumb along the grotesque star that tore across his throat. "Look, I know I take too much joy in the violence. I'm the Headless Horseman! But I'm not one of them. I'm not like Jekyll and Hyde."

"We'll see," I said coldly. I didn't want to, but I believed him.

"I'm with you," he said, adopting his usual neutral expression. "I'll process your release, but I suggest that you take the rest of the week to rest." He paused a minute before opening the door, as if he wanted to say one more thing, but instead he slid out of the room.

I hopped into my shoes and strapped my two broadswords to my waist, fastening them with buckles on either side. I stomped to the medic's door and threw it open, hurrying out into the hall. Someone had hell to pay. But first, I needed one or five of whatever kind of baked goods I could smell coming from the cafeteria. Soul trailed a few steps behind me as we walked, seeming very quiet.

"What's been going on around here while I was out?"

"The dino wanted to fight with the bird ... all in good spirits. Stay out of sight when not in a fight; they don't like the bird."

"Beanie did? How did you figure?" I asked.

"Quiet avoidance ... threats, silence." He shrugged his shoulders and put his hands in the pockets of his worn jeans. "Birds don't do well alone, but the dog knows... The dog can help."

I smiled as I cast a look back at him. "I thought Chrissy and Matt were helping?"

"Bobcat doesn't trust the bird… Blames him for what happened to the dog. H-he needs to do better. Needs to prove he is good to K9's friends… Will the dog help?"

I stopped walking and turned. Then I gave him a soft smile and nodded. "For Crow?"

"Who else?" He grinned. We started walking again, and I pushed open the door to the cafeteria. People stopped and turned to look. I guessed Soul didn't really hang around here more than he had to, but he stood tall anyway. I appreciated that. I spotted Chrissy, Angel, and Frankie at the back of the room and tugged Soul along with me as I made my way to them.

"I heard you were on our team?" I slid into a seat across from Chrissy.

"Benji! Are you even supposed to be up right now? How are you feeling — "

"Because you look like crap," Angel said, giving me a playful smirk.

"Anyway…" Chrissy elbowed our friend. "Are you okay?"

I snatched her muffin. "You know … I'm just *so* hungry."

She shot me a disgruntled look, then turned to Soul. "I'm Chrissy, or Bobcat. Whatever you want to call me."

Soul nodded sheepishly.

"F-Frankie…" The pink-haired guy gave a small, nervous wave. "I think Eloise is still cleaning up from her and Angel's last fight against Carmel and Sugar. She got a bit beat up. Those two are mean."

I nodded to Frankie's words and then felt myself get shoved into Soul's side by someone to my right. Soul calmly raised his eyebrows as he pulled his arm out of my way and watched me elbow the girl beside me. When I looked up, Juno was grinning like a cat, and her brother was doing the same on the other side of Soul.

"Jun, Bean, how nice to see you…" I shoved her off me and rested my head against the table, clutching my stomach and trying not to be sick. I glared at her, and she grinned again and ran to the other side of her brother, mouthing an "oops."

"Those two are Juno and Beanie, or the Dinos," I explained to Soul.

"So, why don't you introduce the guy you're willing to risk not only your life but your job for?" Juno asked teasingly.

"Everybody, this is Soul Ravin, otherwise known as Crow."

He quickly put his head down and avoided eye contact.

"I really don't care who he is. I just want to know what the hell is going on," Angel said.

Soul looked at me, then unbuttoned his shirt a little bit to show her the burn. "Need to find them, and Dr. Frankenstein."

"Two men did that to him when he refused to go after someone," I said seriously. "Someone with the alias 'Dr. Frankenstein' was the one who sent those goons. The one who forced Soul to work for him. We need to find out who that is."

Soul cut me off with a sharp tone. "And the worm... He needs to know what he did."

"I don't know what Dan did, but I can promise you I'll let you have your fun sometime soon — that is ... if I don't get my hands on him first," I reassured him.

"K9 *can* help..." His face twisted into a sinister grin. I tried my best not to let anyone know how much I loved that.

Speak of the devil, Dan chose that exact moment to make an appearance. No longer on crutches, he moved far faster than I, and barely gave Angel, Soul, and me time to stand. He easily brushed past me, shoving me back down, and faced Soul. Dan was slightly taller than him because of the way Soul hunches forward, so he tried to intimidate Soul by standing over him. But my Crow had his own strengths.

"You're supposed to be dead," the slimmer man hissed.

Soul angrily grabbed his collar and switched their positions, slamming him into the wall. "J-just ... shut up! Shut up, *shut up!*"

Soul dropped his head as he almost choked on his own breath; a small whimper escaped him and then he began to holler. I stood again, walked up to Dan, and socked him in the nose for the second time that month.

"He isn't, unluckily for you."

Soul raised his head. His face was red and he was shaking slightly. "You don't deserve what you have…"

Dan smirked, then kneed Soul in the stomach. As Soul lurched forward, Dan kicked him back, sending Soul grasping at the table, holding his ribs.

Furious, I swung my leg up, catching Dan's jaw. I instantly regretted it; the pain that ripped through my middle was nearly enough to make me pass out. I fell to my knees on the ground beside Soul, clutching my now-bleeding abdomen.

"What is happening?!" The entire room froze when we heard the echo of the voice of our employer. Viktor stepped into the room, tidy and composed as always, his face a mask of cool contempt. "What are you three doing? If you must fight, please take it up in the arena. I would appreciate it if you would stop getting my facility all bloody."

"Let's do it, Danny. Neither of us are going quietly," I hissed.

"I'll see *you* in the Pit," Dan said, taking a step toward Soul. He spat in Soul's face.

Soul wiped his face with both hands and slammed his fist down on the table. I pathetically crawled into my seat and ran both my hands through my hair, tugging at the ends and growling at the thought of Dan.

"Stay with the boy and the cat," Soul pleaded. I refused to do that, of course, and so did the others, so we followed him as he stormed off.

When I caught up to him, he shot me a look of annoyance. "I'll let you go but this is my fight too."

He opened his mouth to refute that statement and stuttered. Then he just rolled his eyes, knowing he wouldn't win.

I rushed to the change room, tailed by Chrissy, who had apparently followed me in so she could start throwing complaints at me.

"No, no, *no*!" She said, stomping up to me. "You're going to die! Dan will kill you and then Soul will kill him."

I barely heard her as I tossed my T-shirt off and motioned for her to help me slide my black vest on. She obliged with an irritated sigh.

"God, you are so stupid,"

I tightened my boots, then strapped my armour over my shoulders. It was silver, and it had tattered fur sticking out of the edges.

I really need to upgrade. The thing was badly scratched and uncomfortable.

I made sure my swords were secured properly, then ran out to fight, despite Chrissy's protests. Soul had obviously already clashed with Dan. He was standing to the side, bleeding and gathering his thoughts. I strode over and pulled out one weapon. Dan kicked Soul in the side, and I swung my weapon down on his shoulder. His own armour rattled my sword and caused me to step back.

"Why the hell are you helping him try to dismember me?" He stepped up to me and flicked my stomach.

"Don't touch the dog!"

Soul tackled him, and the two fell to the ground with a thud. Soul punched Dan in the face a few times before he started to calm down and back off. "Y-you left... You abandoned the crow! He n-nearly died!"

Sitting back, Soul ran a hand over his cheek.

"Dan, what did you do to him?"

"Oh, don't tell me you've fallen for *him* now! Or are you forgetting what happened last week? Matt!" Matt's little screen flickered to life and part of a video started playing. I knew exactly what it was before it started. It was a video of when Dan tried to... Okay, we're going to say "seduce" me, but clearly it was a weak effort. Soul glanced at me, then put his head down. He shook his head, embarrassment and misery playing on his features. I started to walk over to him but Dan flicked me again, only harder, and I dropped to my knees, groaning and clutching my middle.

"Stanton, you've made a big mistake here. We both know how that happened!"

He raised an eyebrow.

"Soul, you have to believe me! Matt should have the rest of the tape somewhere!"

He called from his little office. "I'll check, but it was already edited when Dan gave it to me." My eyes darted back to Soul from my seat on the ground. I silently pleaded for him to believe me.

"It's all right there on the video," Dan said smugly. "K9 isn't exactly known for her honest and reliable nature."

"You can't make me look like a cheater. I don't do that!" I hauled myself to my feet, all the anxiousness and stress transforming into pure rage. "I am so *sick* of being made to look like the bad guy! I am so sick of people trying to walk all over me and tear me down and use me!" I spat, practically foaming at the mouth. "I am sick and tired of everyone thinking *I've* done something wrong. The truth ain't clear but trust me! I am not the villain here!"

"I got it!" Matt yelled.

I was seething as I turned to the screen again. Matt played the whole video, from me trying to storm out to Dan forcing himself on me, to me shoving him. It was all there.

"It became my problem when he risked his life against Jekyll and Hyde," I heard video-me say.

Soul stormed toward Dan with a fire blazing in his eyes. Dan smirked, but he held up his hands and took a step back. "I can't read people perfectly. Usually she's totally into that!"

I stepped closer and Dan took another step back, almost tripping over himself.

"Okay! I get it. You're mad. But I'm sorry!"

"S-sorry," Soul said, gritting his teeth and clenching his fists. He squeezed his eyes shut and stammered out a few sounds before his voice boomed through the arena.

"You left me to die!"

It was a shock to hear him speak properly, especially now.

"The gemini… It was them! They did this; they killed Absolom and awoke the crow…" He tried to clear his head as his voice cracked. "See this!" He pointed to the scar on his chin that dragged down around his neck. "A pipe and razor wire! D-Da ... *worm* walked away! ... Absolom hollered ... He screamed and he shouted for his *friend*, but Danny just walked away! Danny watched the gemini beat and bloody his *brother*, but Danny only cared about himself, not his scared, hurting friend!"

He screamed.

"Th-they took a pipe ... and they didn't stop... Still feel the blade." He scratched at his throat and chest. "Can't breathe..."

"I didn't — " Dan started.

"Shut up! Danny knew; he mouthed a sorry." Soul quickly chuckled. "Didn't mean it. They beat, and they beat, and they beat ... until Absolom was gone and there was nothing left to choke, or cut, or beat. Absolom died. H-he bled, then he died."

Soul shook his head and slammed his boot against Dan's chest. "Can't think straight... Too much damage, all because Absolom's childhood *hero* turned into the worm, pitifully squirming away ... afraid of the bird. Does he ever wonder what became of Absolom? Did he ever care that his only friend died at the hands of the gemini? The ... the razor still burns ... and the pipe still pounds..."

Soul placed his axe against a terrified Dan's neck. "Absolom's last wish was to see Danny again, on his knees grovelling for his life." Soul's eyes were red and his entire body shook, but a terrifying and sadistic grin spread across his cheeks. "So, grovel."

Dan sent a look at me and waved his hands around. "Aren't you going to stop him?!"

I shrugged. "Why should I?"

Soul pressed his axe down harder.

"Who are the gemini, anyway?" I asked.

"I-it's Jekyll and Hyde," Dan said, his voice breaking. "Benji, please! Call him off."

Soul raised his weapon above his head, and Dan squealed like a pig. Then I placed my hand on Soul's shoulder.

"But…!"

"I know. But you should be going after Jekyll and Hyde, not Dan. You two were young. He got scared." I lowered my voice and leaned closer, feeling the heat from his face. "He wasn't as brave as Absolom was."

"K9 doesn't know what that was like! The … *sting*! The burn. The agony. The constant pounding, oh … hmm-mm…"

He dropped his weapon and held his head in his hands. I stood there for a moment, taking in the damage the twins and Dan caused; then I unhooked my armour and wriggled out of my top as fast as I could.

Dan muttered a "What the hell?" as I looked down at myself, disgusted. I dropped the black vest to the ground. I could feel the weight of their eyes on me. Dan, Soul, and hundreds, probably thousands, more. The X-shaped scar running over my shoulders, crossing at my sternum, and running down below my ribs was a bit of a distraction.

"It does burn," I said simply. "That razor wire, the boot pressed into your back? They used to make it hard to sleep at night. Then I find out the same guys who did it were joining our league." I shook my head. "I was glad they were joining. That I'd get the chance to hurt them. I'm not afraid of them. Never was. What I was afraid of was that eagerness. I was afraid of what I would do to them, afraid that I would enjoy destroying them as much as they enjoyed destroying me. Afraid of what I'd become if I did."

I looked from Soul to Dan and back. "Well, I'm not afraid anymore. Everyone deserves what they get. Right, Soul? They are going to get hell."

"*Hell hath no fury like a woman scorned,*" he stated as he raised his head and glared at Dan. He exhaled, glanced at me, a look of determination set in his gentle features, and then turned his back on Dan.

Dan looked from me to Soul, like we were insane. He slowly placed his hand on Soul's shoulder. Soul stood there but didn't face him.

"I was afraid, but I *never* should have left you, Absolom," Dan said. He looked genuinely miserable.

"*He* is dead," Soul stated bitterly as Dan stepped back. "I am Soul. I am the crow, the plague. I am death ... and won't forgive the worm."

Twelve

Followed by my bird-like companion, I kicked open the door and went to my locker. Frankie stood slack-jawed in the middle of the room for a moment before he ran out so Soul and I could talk. I struggled to open my lock as Soul watched my movements. "What?"

"Didn't know … *how* bad…"

"No one did."

I smacked the locker with the palm of my hand. "Look, if you still feel angry towards Dan, you can kick his ass after we find out who hired you, and *after* we get rid of Jekyll and Hyde."

"Okay. W-wasn't going to kill him yet. K9 was going to stop the bird; he knew it. Only needed to scare him… Lost control…"

I slowly looked towards him, meeting his dark green eyes. "You could have fooled me."

"The bird will still have his fight." Soul started unbuckling his armour and put his jacket in his locker. When he turned back to me, I smiled softly. I so desperately wanted to feel like this was going to end well, but deep down we both knew something would go wrong. Neither of us trusted Dan anymore, but at least he wouldn't be running around trying to kill either of us at every turn.

"Something wrong?"

I looked back up to see that Soul was only a few steps from me.

"I don't think I thanked you for staying with me every night while I was in the hospital. That was comforting to hear."

"C-couldn't leave the dog, too many enemies. Too ... scared to leave her." He walked closer and tilted his head with a soft smile.

"You're starting to handle stress better. You're able to calm yourself easier."

"Because of K9." He scratched his neck. "Maybe. Don't know."

"I think it's because you're interacting more. Learning how to be around people again," I suggested.

He simply nodded. "Crow's used to talking like this... Not going to change."

"I wouldn't ask you to. I'm just saying that it's good." I tried to open my locker again. "No one should be that isolated."

I tugged at the lock again with most of my strength, the rest of which was being used to keep myself from passing out. Soul put his hand on my shoulder, and I took the hint to step back. I sat on the bench and lifted the gauze on my stomach; my wound wasn't torn open, just a bit bloodied. It hurt like hell, though.

When I was done inspecting the damage, Soul handed me my shirt and I struggled my way into it, unable to lift my arms too high. I felt like a child, sitting there with my head stuck in the sleeve. That was until Soul tugged the bottom of it and helped me find my freedom again. I felt the beads on my hair pop up past my ears and bounce against my neck again.

I looked up at him, seeing a trace of a smile on his face. His hand was suddenly beside my face. I flinched slightly, surprised, but he only picked up a beaded strand of my hair, inspecting it carefully.

Soul's eyes sparkled with curiosity, but before he could get any words out, Jeff ran in looking like he was going to beat someone. In fact, he did. He started swatting Soul with his clipboard. "If I had known you were going to get her into something like this I wouldn't have had Louis let her go!"

Soul held up his arm in defence until Jeff stepped back and composed himself, first straightening his glasses, then moving to his jacket.

"Relax, I just checked. Nothing's torn open, and there almost no blood — "

"You unwrapped the bandages?!" He held his hand over his forehead in exasperated grief. "I hope you feel a very intense pain."

"Oh, believe me, I do!" I crossed my arms and Soul sheepishly twiddled his thumbs, mumbling an apology and inching closer to my side.

"*Can every warrior, all medics, and all on-duty security personnel please make their way to the lecture hall. That's the ward one lecture hall. Thank you.*"

The announcement tore out of the speaker directly over our heads, causing Soul to jump back. He turned abruptly and walked out of the locker room. I jumped up and went to catch up with him, one hand on my middle and the other in my pocket.

"The bird won't let it happen again. K9 needs her strength … just in case," Soul absentmindedly stated as he looked back to the floor. I smiled to myself and followed him down the corridor and into the lecture hall. Chrissy beckoned us towards her. We pushed our way through the crowd of noisy warriors and took two seats next to her. When I sat down, she handed me a package of sweets.

"Thanks, Chris."

"You doubted I would feed you?" She whispered. "Honestly, how did you survive here without me?"

I shrugged, brushing her off. I tore into the package and popped two into my mouth.

"Ladies, gentlemen, here and at home." Viktor spread his arms as he walked to the front of the room, followed closely by hovering drone cams. "As we all know, something very tragic happened to our favourite little warrior dog last week. K9 was shot and injured very badly. She spent several days in a coma, but has now, thankfully, made a full recovery."

Viktor smiled as the crowd present politely applauded. Several warriors turned to smile or to sneer at me.

"But after a tireless investigation," he stated, shuddering and shooting a subtle look at Soul, "very little has come to light. We've all heard the accusations against her and her interesting new friend. But do we believe them?"

I lurched forward in my seat, held back from jumping out of it completely — and probably tearing out my stitches while I was at it — by Chrissy on one side and Soul on the other. Viktor was using it for show. The attacks, Jekyll and Hyde, my injury, all of it. He was twisting it to get ratings. Well … I guess I couldn't blame him for doing his job, but he hand-picked me for the league! He could have had a little sympathy.

"We all understand the circumstances, the danger we're all in," Viktor continued, his voice as regal as ever, "but I have tried to make the best out of this horrible misadventure. I know some of you still have some … *strong* … feelings on the matter of K9's innocence and on the mysterious Mr. Ravin. I'd like to announce that Mr. Ravin has agreed to take any battle that is asked of him in order to repent for what he has done. From here forward, Soul Ravin will be fighting in Lilithia Heights as the warrior known as Crow."

I stopped midchew and looked at Soul as he slowly stood, at Viktor's insistence. Why, on god's green earth, did he agree to that? He fidgeted, refusing to meet my eyes.

"Now, speaking of battles, Lilithia's qualifying battle for the Tournament of Survivors is one week away. The grounds used will be on the abandoned side of town instead of the forest. This year, we will have six women and six men. I trust most of you know the rules, but just in case…" He paused for a moment. He sighed and rubbed his temples. "All arrows and weapons will be replaced with dull edges. Please don't kill each other until the Tournament, and even then restrain yourselves, *please!*"

Everyone gave a collective chuckle, though we all knew it was entirely possible.

"We are announcing contenders this evening at the city square. Be prepared to attend all interviews — cocktails and other various drinks will be served," Jeremy added quickly, leaping from his seat in the front row. He's always been the boss's favourite lapdog, and he oversaw a lot of public events on Viktor's behalf.

"Thank the lord...," our boss muttered under his breath. "And can everyone dress appropriately this year?" Viktor stretched his neck, gripping his podium with white knuckles. "That means you, Franklin. No tuxedo T-shirt this time! Ladies in dresses, gentlemen in suits, jackets, the works." The boss glared at Frankie, who no doubt would wear the printed shirt — underneath his suit jacket if nothing else.

I dumped the last of the candy into my mouth and felt a nudge from Chrissy. "Do you even own a dress?" she asked.

I thought about it for moment. I might. I hadn't seen the back of my closet in a long time. For all I knew, there was literally a skeleton in there. It wouldn't surprise me. I gave a shrug. "I think I have one. If not, do you mind if I steal one of yours?"

"No, but I doubt any would fit you." She eyed my skinny frame and I scowled at her. She had far more curves than I did and she never failed to remind me. I shot her a flat look. Around us, everyone was standing up and filing out of the room.

"I guess I'll check out the closet then," I said, shrugging.

"Why is it," I muttered to myself as I sprinted across the base, trying to make it to the gala on time, "that everything decides to happen the exact day I wake up from a coma?"

I tripped, of course, laying myself out face first on the dusty ground. The fall wouldn't have been so bad, except the pain from the bullet wound shot through me, causing me fall into a hysterical sort of laughter that turned quickly into sobs. Pressing my hands down, I sat up, making sure I hadn't bled through the black fabric. I pushed myself off the ground, dusted myself off as much as I could, and continued on my way as if nothing had happened. I turned the corner and saw Soul and Chrissy. Chrissy turned toward me, raising her eyebrows.

"Shut up," I said as I made my way to the drink table. Chrissy and Soul both followed quietly.

"What the hell?" She asked.

"I fell," I said, glancing down at my dusty outfit. I had quickly thrown on the very short high-neck dress that I'd found in the back of my closet.

"It's not just that. How old is that thing? And, those?" She pointed at my feet, holding in a laugh.

"What?"

"Combat boots? Really? Viktor said to dress *appropriately*," she said, not even trying to suppress her giggles now.

I rolled my eyes at Chrissy and crossed my arms again. I looked at Soul, who also seemed to be holding in a laugh. I scowled at both of them and downed the whole drink, pouring the bitter pink liquid down my throat. Whatever it was burned my throat.

"Alright, ladies and gentlemen, please give us your attention," a familiar voice said. I saw Jeremy standing on the stage, looking as tired as ever, and started following my companions to our seats.

"I guess I should be impressed," Chrissy whispered as we pushed our way through the crowd. "I didn't know you even owned a dress, Ben."

"Neither did I." I shrugged. The three of us began to weave our way through the crowd toward the stage.

Chrissy started to giggle.

Soul rolled his eyes. "Looks nice," he muttered, more to himself than to me, "ripped or not."

I froze and looked down. "*Ripped*?!"

Looking down at my dress, I noticed a massive tear that ran up the side and stopped at my hip. You could clearly see my faded blue boxers. I felt my face go red and I tugged the tear closed. After a quick look around for something to keep it from flying up, I pulled two bobby pins from Chrissy's hair. I pinned it in place as best I could and held my hand over the rip... Hopefully, no one would notice.

"Lilithia Heights." Victor's booming voice echoed through the microphone. "It is a city of warriors, both recognized and not. This year, a change. We will add two players to the qualifying round of the Tournament of Survivors, for a total of six women and six men. Our warriors risk their lives every time they go out and fight, every time they set foot in that arena. No matter what they encounter, they always get back out there. These twelve warriors have shown Lilithia that they have what it takes, and I would be proud to see any one of them represent us this year in Rhys-Mordred. Our first contender embodies these qualities wholly and fervently. I'm pleased to announce that our first selected warrior is" — Viktor paused, and we all sat mentally screaming for him to hurry up — "Benji 'K9' Keanin!"

Chrissy started clapping loudly, along with a whole host of Lilithia residents. *I* sat dumbstruck as Viktor nodded to me, then announced the next two to take part in the tournament. "Chosen for their resilience and impressive skill set, Jekyll and Hyde!"

My face went white as a sheet. I didn't need to see the video on the big screen to know that. The twins grinned at each other and shook hands as they celebrated, feigning surprise. Chrissy grabbed my hand and gave an anxious look.

"Contender four, chosen for her speed and agility ... Carmela 'Carmel' McCarthy!"

My pulse quickened; all these people hated me.

"Contenders five and six, for their outstanding ... outstandingness ... Jeremy 'Dracula' Vamp and Frankie 'Scene Fest' Gent." Viktor searched for them and threw his hands up in frustration when he saw Frankie on the screen with a printed T-shirt under his fancy jacket, proudly puffing out his chest.

"Contenders seven and eight ... Angel 'Beauty' Lannister and Christina 'Bobkat' Bokitski!" I squeezed Chrissy's hand. She practically shook where she stood. "Contenders nine, ten, and eleven are Cindy 'Sugar' Candice, Randy 'the Mummy' Curio, and Eloise 'Dolly' Bentley!"

I dreaded this. Vamp was on Dan's side; so was the Mummy. Sugar and Carmel have always had a vendetta against me, and Angel was selfish — she wouldn't hesitate to take me out either. None of that really mattered though, since Jekyll and Hyde would make it their first priority to eliminate *me*. There was only one spot left. I doubted I was going to be happy to hear the name called, but I had to hope it wasn't going to be someone else that wanted me dead.

"Our final spot, which is being awarded partially out of punishment and partially out of compensation, will go to our new recruit, Soul 'Crow' Ravin!"

I spun to the side at a breakneck speed but Soul didn't seem to be surprised. He didn't seem to be fazed in the slightest, but I knew better. I grabbed his slightly shaking hand.

"Just a reminder… From here on in, all fights will be preapproved. No one is allowed to get hurt before then. Is that clear?"

Viktor gave me a level look, then flashed his well-known, charming smile at the crowd and strode off the stage.

Chrissy stood in horror. "We … are going to die…"

I was still holding both Soul's and Chrissy's hands when everyone started to move away from the stage.

"I hear music," I said. "Should we celebrate or something?"

"No! I have to go write my will!" Chrissy said dramatically.

"Oh, come on," I said, rolling my eyes at her. "You're overreacting. It's not all that bad. Frankie and Eloise are in too."

"Easy for you to say! You brought this down on us in the first place," she snapped. I jumped back, surprised at the heat in her eyes.

"I have to go," she said, looking miserable. She dropped my hand and headed to the bar without another word.

I looked back at Soul. What little colour he had had drained from his face.

"B-big mistake… Shouldn't have … shouldn't have in-involved the dog…" He started to scratch his head and bite his lip, hard. His voice shook as though he was feeling nauseous.

"One way or another, I was going to get involved, whether you'd let me or not. I'm not one to let things go so easily." He whimpered and shook his head violently in protest. "Okay, you need to listen to me, my crow-like friend. Have a little faith in me and stop blaming yourself. I've taken care of myself for years. I can handle most of these guys, and I would have taken on the twins at some point anyway."

"Yes, but — "

"No! This is my war too, and nothing's going to change the fact that we're both knee deep in this!"

"K9's fight too…" He nodded. "K9's stronger than the crow, fearless." He perked up a bit and smirked at me. His smile faded into a nervous and uncertain grin as he put his other hand over mine. Slipping my hand behind his head and rubbing the back of his matted hair, I leaned forward and pressed my forehead to his.

"Going to win," he stated, smiling broadly.

I grinned back and nodded. "We're going to win."

Soul began nodding his head in time with the music; his grin stayed in place. I swayed my shoulders as he grabbed my hands and pulled me toward the dance floor under the fairy lights, his grin getting wider and wider as we walked. I recognized the song; it was popular a few years back. It was one of those really high-energy hits; you know, the kind that made you want to bounce around and just dance like crazy… But that might have been the booze. I stopped counting after four.

Soul spun me around and I leaned back against his chest. I could feel him chuckling happily — it almost sounded childlike. I turned to face him again. We both froze on the spot when we saw Frankie throwing his arms up and shaking his hips like it was payday. What made this even better was a very pink-faced Eloise and a very angry Viktor, who stormed across the dance floor, snagged Frankie's collar, and dragged him off to the side to scold him.

Soul took my hand again, and I put the other on his shoulder. I sang a little and bounced around, and he held me tighter. I couldn't complain; he was warm and gentle.

The song faded to another just as upbeat as the last, and I noticed Eloise standing awkwardly at the side of the dance floor. I waved to her, and she very elegantly made her way over. Frankie, who had managed to escape Viktor's fury, proudly followed.

"Was it worth it?" I asked him, waving a hand at his ridiculous T-shirt.

"Every smack!" His pink fluorescent hair was all over the place, though it was previously combed back. Eloise fell into his arms and they danced together, twisting and turning, her long green dress billowing around her as if she were a living fairy tale. I felt Soul wrap his arms across my shoulders and rest his chin down.

"Looks like a princess," he muttered.

I nodded. She was more beautiful than I could ever hope to be. She was a young warrior, and relatively unmarred. As for me, I was full of imperfections, my life written all over my body in a web of scars.

When I pulled away from Soul, he was still grinning from ear to ear.

"What's wrong?" he asked gently, searching my face.

I raised my eyebrows. "Nothing. I'm sorry, did it seem like there was?"

He smirked and rested his forehead against mine. "Jealous?" he taunted.

I stepped back and he was grinning mischievously. "Chrissy, how many drinks has he had?"

"Only one, I think." She went back to her obnoxious dance battle against Juno. I turned back to the crow and eyed him warily. Suddenly, he took my hand and pulled me away from the crowd.

"Watching, waiting, snatching, hating..."

"Who is?" I asked, nervous.

"Worm ... waiting for the dog to be alone. Try to..." he stopped himself and swallowed painfully. "Trying to *use* K9 ... again..."

I looked back and, sure enough, Dan was standing and staring at us.

"He wouldn't dare," I reassured Soul.

Soul straightened up and played with one sleeve of his blue shirt. "Warning."

I smiled knowingly. "Thank you." He nodded, his bottom lip pouting even though he looked pleased with himself.

"Stupid shirt… I swear, one day I'm going to burn the contents of his closet…" Viktor shook his head, his greying ponytail swinging as he moved.

"Frankie's a little odd, but he isn't bad at what he does," I told him.

"I agree wholeheartedly," Viktor said, grinning. I got the sense that he wasn't actually that bothered by Frankie's outfit. Maybe he just didn't like Frankie because he's a better warrior than you'd expect. "What about your friend," Viktor continued. "How has he adjusted to the base?"

I turned to look at Soul, giving him the opportunity to answer for himself.

"O-okay, sir…" Soul dropped his head and played with a button on his shirt, pressing his lips firmly shut as his eyes went wide.

"Respectful, I like that. A lot of other cities have already gotten wind of the situation, and they aren't as understanding as Lilithia, so if either of you win the tournament, watch your backs. I've tried to put a good word in but they just don't get it." He took a swig of whatever was in his glass — probably some fancy Scotch that wasn't available to the likes of us — and sighed. "I don't know many details, K9, but I'm leaving everything up to you and Dragon."

"Thank you, and don't worry. Dan and Soul won't be going at it until after we find out who wanted everyone gone."

"Very good. Best of luck in the tournament, you two." He dismissed us.

"Shall we head out?" I asked, pointing my chin toward the road just outside of the town square. Soul nodded and followed me out, looking around anxiously.

"Nervous…"

I turned my head and looked at my companion. "Why?"

"Bad things happen in the dark…"

I looked up at the night sky. "It's not dark … not here. The stars shine far too bright here for it to get really dark. And we can still see the light from the party."

I smiled. I really liked being out at night, but most days I was too exhausted to stay out late. Our breath was visible. I had to grab my shoulders as I shuddered. It would be snowing in a few weeks, and despite my complete hatred of hot weather, winter wasn't exactly my favourite either.

"We have to win," Soul spoke quietly.

"Heaven help us…" I replied. The world was against us, and it seemed that no matter what we did, we were born to lose. "We will. We have to, if we want to live."

I followed Soul past the iron gate at the front of the building — a feature that made it look more like an asylum than a … whatever it was before the warrior's league swept in and took over.

"Training tomorrow?" he asked. I nodded and started to walk away, only to be stopped after three steps when he grabbed my hand.

"Please … p-please stay out of the spotlight…"

"What do you mean?" I asked, looking up at him.

He grimaced, clearly trying find a way of wording what he wanted to say. "N-no one's explained… They don't understand why K9's helping the bird, a-and they don't want us to win. At all. The boss … he said the crow didn't do anything he didn't have to, to survive … b-but there was better ways to handle it…"

"And no one except maybe Chrissy and Matt are willing to believe us?"

He nodded nervously and looked at me for an answer.

"They don't need to right now. We'll show them once we know the whole story; we'll make them confess and then let Mr. Viktor choose their fate, okay?"

He shrugged his shoulders. "Okay." He paused for a moment, searching my face. "K9?"

"Yes?"

"The bird's not bad … is he? F-for all … all he's done … you…" — he slowly put his head down — "do you … *care* about h-him?"

I couldn't take my eyes off of him. Of course, I cared about him. Of course, I cared about what would happen to him. I nodded. He bit his lip and hunched his shoulders so much he looked as small and scared as he did when we met.

"I care about my Crow, and I always will. That's another thing you should never worry about. I've got your back."

I squeezed his arm, then started walking away.

I smiled as I heard him mumble to himself, "*My* K9…"

Thirteen

By the time I got to the dining hall, I had discovered that I was among those few who didn't party too hard the night before. Chrissy, on the other hand, had decided to wake me around 8 a.m. with three slow knocks on the bathroom door, asking for some painkillers. Turned out she'd kept the party going on her own once she'd gotten back to her room. She'd been staying in Angel's room since she got back, and Angel moved in with Ronin.

I grabbed a cheese-filled breakfast sandwich from under a heat lamp and sat down on the cafeteria bench in between Chrissy and Angel.

"How's your head, Chris?" I asked, a little louder than I needed to. Chrissy groaned and shot me a menacing look.

"Lightweights!" Frankie shouted from behind me, walking up to the table with his own breakfast. He plopped down across from us, apparently no worse for wear even after a night of hard partying.

"Frankie ... please..." Eloise said. She had been following him. She sat down beside Frankie, holding her head. "This is worse than your twenty-fifth birthday, Benji."

To my amusement, most of the room seemed to be hungover. For once, I wasn't the one suffering the effects of too many shots of tequila. It felt good.

"Where's that little birdy that usually sits on your shoulder?" Angel asked through gritted teeth.

I rolled my eyes. "He isn't a pet."

I slapped Chrissy's back. "You intend on training anytime soon?"

"Not with you, I don't." Her angry glare stung a bit, but I shrugged it off. Chrissy could be pretty emotional at times, and I could tell she was nervous about the qualifier.

Soul stepped over a few moments later, hair still dripping wet and soaking his button-up shirt around his neck, distracting me from my conversation.

I looked at him for the first time in a while; he had the same broad shoulders, the same tired eyes and pouting mouth. He constantly looked curious about something but also like he was about to fall asleep. There was still ink smeared over his arm and cheek that didn't seem to want to fade, and his hands were very different from the rest of his body. His strong build and height gave him a pretty intimidating look, but his hands were smooth. His fingers always seemed to be typing or tapping, barely noticeable most of the time.

He'd started to stand taller. He looked bigger and he didn't hide his face by looking at the floor. Granted, he was still pretty easily taken off guard.

He caught me staring and his cheeks went pink, but he didn't look away. Turning away slowly, I rested my chin on the tops of my hands as I went back to listening to Chrissy argue with Angel.

A moment later, a jolt of fire ran through my body. My arms and legs spasmed uncontrollably for what felt like an hour, and I fell to the ground, a groan of pain escaping my throat. The second it was over, I jumped up and snatched the steak knife off Chrissy's tray. I spun to see Carmela and Cindy — Carmel and Sugar — smirking back at me. Carmel was holding an electric something or other, which sat in her perfectly manicured hand spitting blue fire.

I lunged at them, ready to slit their throats, but Chrissy grabbed my wrist before I got the chance.

"What do you two want?" she hissed.

The two looked at one another and burst into laughter.

"We just wanted to see the travelling freak show!" Carmel said.

"Yeah, we heard the clowns were back in town," Sugar added.

I crossed my arms. "Is there a point?"

They looked at each other again before smirking, "We just wanted to let you know that it's going to be four versus two in this little battle next week."

I gave Carmel a confused look before Sugar jumped in. "Yeah, our boyfriends and us versus you and" — she waved in Soul's general direction — "*that*."

"Wait, your *boyfriends*? Who would be desperate enough to date you two?"

And then it hit me. "Jekyll and Hyde."

"Of course! They're *so* hot…"

"Yeah" — Carmel jumped in again — "I dumped Jeremy after he woke up. Jekyll is just so much more … *dangerous*," she finished, licking her lips. I couldn't help but cringe.

"Dangerous? Listen, Candy-corn, those guys are monsters. Psychopaths, sociopaths, complete abominations of the human race!"

"Oh, like you're any better," Sugar spat.

I pulled my hand out of Chrissy's grip and pressed my knife against Sugar's face. She tensed, standing perfectly still.

I moved my face close to hers. "You wanna say that again?"

I stepped back again. She exhaled and rubbed her cheek, then stepped slowly around the table to where Carmel stood.

"Don't bother with her, Sugar. The real monster is right here." She motioned at Soul with her stun gun, or cattle prod, or whatever it was. "Don't they call a group of crows a 'murder'?"

Sugar let out a sharp laugh, then smacked the side of Soul's head with her open palm. He didn't react. Carmel sniffed and jabbed her prod into his ribs. He tossed his head back and screamed, his shout ringing through the hall.

I tried to lunge angrily after them, smiling wickedly at the thought of what I would do to them, but was again caught and held, this time by two people — Chrissy, who held my waist, and Angel, who had got a hold of my shoulders.

"Cool down. Calm — calm down!" Chrissy said, struggling to hold me back.

I was so angry I didn't notice the pressure from her arms around my stomach until a moment later, when pain flared up through my wound. I felt like I was shot a second time. Reluctantly, I dropped the knife onto the table and held my arms up in surrender.

Chrissy and Angel let me go. I scowled back at them as I took a seat beside Soul, who was clutching his stomach and struggling to breathe. He had rested his head on the table as he choked and gasped for breath. I slid my glass of water toward him as he started to breathe properly again. His eyes were red and watery as he looked up at me, still holding his side.

I motioned for him to take a sip of his drink, and as he did, I lifted his shirt to see how bad it was. They had increased the voltage. From the pain I felt, there's no way I could have a burn as bad as Soul did. But that wasn't the worst part. I was certain I had seen this same burn before.

"Take off your shirt," I said quickly.

He looked over at me, his cheeks reddening.

I scoffed. "Just do it."

He complied, unbuttoning the shirt and pulling it off his shoulders slowly.

I studied the shape of the raw wound on his ribs, then moved my eyes up his chest to a much older scar, just below his collarbone. It was nearly identical to the new one in size and shape: a skull, strangely distorted, with its cruel mouth hanging wide open. My chest tightened.

"What?" His voice was once again shaking. He licked his lips.

"It's the same," I said shakily, waving my hand between the two marks on his body. "The two marks, they're…"

He touched the old scar with his fingertips. "But this… They weren't the monsters?"

I jumped up from the table and, without saying a word, ran off in the direction that Sugar and Carmel had gone.

I had followed them back to their locker room with no weapons and no knowledge of whether or not friends of theirs would be lurking. I had to be extra careful while breaking into their lockers, so I took a screwdriver from the toolbox by the door and jimmied the latch on Sugar's little blue locker. I found nothing in it except the clothes she was wearing earlier. I moved to Carmel's locker and found exactly what I was looking for. The cattle prod sat on the ledge, just waiting for me to take it.

Before I got a chance to examine it properly, I heard the door open. I spun on my heels, jumped behind the lockers, and held my breath.

"You got the smart one, but I got the pretty one," a strong Irish accent said.

"Yeah, but she's the forgetful one too." Jekyll chuckled cruelly, the way he would when he was getting ready to attack. "And Carmela's not as good in a fight."

I peeked around the corner to see Jekyll and Hyde pulling off their workout gear.

"Hey, did you take a look at that last message from the doctor?" Jekyll said.

"Pfft, yeah. But I didn't answer him or nothing. I swear he thinks we're his servants."

I bit my lip and silently walked behind the lockers, making sure they weren't looking, then bolted out the door. I ran through the halls until I was back at the cafeteria, wheezing and holding one hand over my middle.

"I-it was them! Jekyll and Hyde." My brain was running a mile a minute as I tried to explain to everyone through my gasps for air. They all looked at me blankly. "Listen. They were talking about Frankenstein, right there in the open locker room. I think they were, anyway. They're involved! They must be."

I smacked my hands together and looked at everybody, pleased with myself.

Angel rested her head on her hand. "And what exactly would be their motivation?"

I shrugged my shoulders, "I don't know — any excuse to hurt people, probably!"

I looked at the zapper I had just stolen from Carmel. It was a weird contraption, a mix between a cattle prod and an electric branding iron. It had to be a custom build; it was clearly designed to dole out as much pain as possible, and to leave its mark.

I made sure the thing was turned off, then examined the end, looking for the pattern that matched Soul's scars. There was no pattern, no skull, only zigzagging lines. I tossed it on the ground and pushed my hair back, feeling defeated. I sat beside Soul and dropped my head to my hands.

"I was so close … and it's the one room that doesn't have any cameras!" I shook my head and sighed. Soul kicked his legs over the bench and knelt by the broken pieces of metal.

"Possible … they s-switched the branding plates."

I leaned forward and he held up two separate pieces, both with threads on the ends.

"Interchangeable," he stated.

"Just have to find the plate she used!" I pumped my arm in the air, hope returning again.

"Benji, do you have any idea how hard that will be to do? Think of all the places it could be hidden." Chrissy rubbed her head and looked indignant.

"They wouldn't have hidden them though; think about who we're talking about here! Their egos are too big to ever even think of getting caught." I ran my hand through my hair, thinking. "I'll get Josh to unlock their rooms when they're not around — "

"Josh won't do it. He can't know. We'll cover for you *if* you don't leave any evidence," Angel said.

"N-no…" Soul spit out.

I patted Chrissy's back with a grin as I bounced off before he had a chance to argue.

"K9! Bad idea… Don't do it!"

I heard him trip over the table as he tried to follow. I turned to see him muttering as he straightened himself out and ran after me.

I pulled the knife from my boot and jammed it through the framework, pushing the lock back and hip-checking Sugar's door open. Soul wrung his hands as he recited a poem, trying to keep his nerves at bay while I started rummaging through a drawer. I quickly made my way around the room, trashing what I felt was necessary before making my way through the bathroom to Carmel's room.

"The dog has focus, the bird is nervous."

I took a quick glimpse at him.

"Hocus pocus, such a disservice."

I shook my head as he pushed his hair back and started looking through trinkets on the shelf.

"This?" I turned again to see him holding a small piece of metal in the shape of a skull. I jumped over the bed and looked; it matched his burn perfectly. We both grinned. Suddenly, the lock started to rattle. Soul pulled me towards the bathroom door, putting his finger to his lips. I cringed for no more than a second before Soul shoved me back into Sugar's room and to the door. He made sure there was no one around before he dragged me out into the hall, back to safe territory. Luckily, everyone was training so we were okay.

That is, we were until we ran into Dan.

"What's going on?" he said, grabbing my shoulders. "Why are you so out of breath, princess?"

Soul stepped forward and stood tall, giving Dan a menacing look.

"I told you to stop calling me that." I pushed Dan off and walked past them both, the metal plate still tight in my hand.

"What is *wrong*? Why are you acting like all the time we've spent together is nothing?" Dan growled at me. "I can understand him being mad, but you?"

"All the time we've spent together? You mean fighting on the same side while you made passes at not only me, but every other half-decent girl you saw?" I looked him over. "Learn some loyalty, then we'll talk."

Soul smirked and followed me until Dan spoke up again, stopping us both on the spot. "I loved you, Ben."

I didn't bother looking at my scruffy co-worker. "That's nice." And also not true by any means.

Soul stood clenching his fists. I turned to look at him, silently begging for him to ignore Dan. He grumbled and sneered but he obeyed and followed me down the hall.

"You have to learn to ignore him. He's just trying to work you up," I explained to Soul.

He was currently working on the punching bag pretty well. He sent a few more punches, then looked up at me. "Sorry…"

I looked back at him and slowly gave him a smile. "Don't worry about it."

He shrugged, then moved on to defence training, taking up his axe, and I grabbed my swords. I swung one sideways and then the other downwards. This caused me to have to twist my arms as he started to retaliate. We both absentmindedly swung, then deflected.

"I've never seen you really go at it," I said as he brought his weapon down, causing me to fall to one knee. "How about we go out to the arena in a few days, get some *real* practice?"

He thought a moment, then nodded. "The K9 will lose, though."

I laughed louder than I ever had in my life. "Is that a challenge?"

He grinned as he pushed his blade down harder, a mistake I had to remind him not to make again. I kicked his legs out from under him.

"You may have strength, but I have speed." I lunged forward and dug the blade into the handle of his axe. He could effortlessly hold me back, so he gave me a shove and then held his weapon over me, indicating that I should stay down. Dropping it to his side, he pulled me up with one hand. "K9 is reckless."

After we'd gone at it for a few more rounds, Matt ran in and sat down with his lunch.

"What's happening, Kreature?" I asked.

Matt shrugged and took a bite of his sandwich. "Not much, but I can tell you one thing…" He paused to swallow, and I raised my eyebrows. "The crowd loves you two. And I mean *loves*!"

He took a few more bites as Soul and I switched weapons — not the best idea I'd ever had, considering I could barely lift his.

"Any other news, Matt?" I asked.

He nodded excitedly, choking down his food, making his eyes water. "Yeah, Sugar and Carmel found out what you did. They announced that they're leaving you two until last and that they're going to kill you, no mercy. I've been asking around, and no one is even going to try and get in their way, so you guys are pretty much on your own. Sorry."

I shrugged. "Anyone drop out yet?"

"Nope, they all figure they should eliminate each other and then let you and the twins battle it out. Take on whoever's left standing, since you'll be broken and out of breath."

"Smart." I leapt back, barely avoiding being hit with my own swords. I planted the sharp end of the axe on the ground and swung myself around, kicking Soul in the side, which caused him to drop one weapon. I hauled the axe over my shoulder and fell onto my behind in the process, but considering it caused him to fall back and drop the other sword, I was okay with it.

I pressed my boot into his chest, and he laid flat on the mat with his hands in the air.

"What do you think will happen if you win? I mean, I know the other cities have an idea of what's happened, but they aren't as forgiving as Lilithia, I guess. You'll be targets," Matt said.

"We are going to win, and we are going to out the person

responsible, prevent it from happening again, and then blah, blah, blah … happily ever after." I faced him, striking a little pose for the cameras, and waved my hand around as I spoke, not realizing that Soul had gotten back up and grabbed his axe, placing it directly in the centre of my shoulder blades.

I held my hands up and sighed as my hair fell in front of my eyes. "Cheap."

Fourteen

Two days until the tournament, and training was excruciating. Jekyll, Hyde, Cindy, Carmela, Jeremy, and Randy had all made it very clear to the public that they were going to kill the traitor. *Traitors*.

Matt, who's in charge of all promotion as well as overseeing the media, had suggested we make a retaliating statement. I *thought* we already did that but evidently not.

I was on my way to give my statement when Soul joined me, lip bloody and more ink smeared across his face.

"What is it exactly that you do when I'm not around?"

He gave a shrug and wiped his lip. "Unimportant."

I grimaced and eyed him as we walked into one of Matt's many studios/offices. He greeted us with a smile. "All set up… You just have to say your piece."

I followed to where he was pointing and rolled my neck; this might get ugly. He flicked the camera on and I leaned forward with Soul wringing his hands behind me. "You know Jekyll, Hyde, and their little followers? They tried to say we were the villains, and that's just not true!" I glanced back at Soul, who smirked and looked at me with mischief in his eyes. "Sure, most of you know I'm not one to play hero. I always do what I have to for the greater good. But a hero? No way. Heroes don't tend to commit homicide."

Soul shook his head. "The dog is no liar, either. Not this time."

"So trust me when I say I am not going to be playing the hero this weekend. I am not going to be playing nice. I've sharpened my toys, I've been training, and I have an ally this time … and he's stronger than anyone you've dealt with before."

I heard Soul crack his knuckles behind me. I grinned.

"If it's a war you want, it's Armageddon you're going to get."

"Suffocating, walls closing in on me." Soul examined an ink stain on his arm. "Dying, crawling free, is it worth trying to see?"

A crease formed between his eyes as he started to try and rub the ink off. I turned back to Matt's camera. "Are you willing to risk being locked in an abandoned area of town with a revenge-crazed lunatic and her bird? Or would you rather not feel what it would be like to live in hell just yet?"

I swallowed the lump in my throat and stared at the floor, rubbing my hands together. "You're going to get what you deserve. It's just a matter of time. This is your warning. Drop out now and live a little longer."

Matt switched the camera off. "Perfect. That's going to play great with the public. It'll have the Jekyll and Hyde fans seething."

He moved around to his desk with the handheld and connected it to his small computer. He switched the thing on, and blue light lit up his face. He looked confused.

"What the hell?" Matt said.

"What?" I asked, moving around the desk to stand behind Matt. "What's wrong?"

"It's been wiped. The whole thing. All my videos…" Matt held his head and groaned.

I kicked a chair across the room and Matt jumped, but didn't look up. "Goddammit Matt, I swear we'll get to the bottom of this."

I strolled out into the open arena, feeling like a million bucks.

I'd been given new armour for the coming events, courtesy of Josh. He'd always been enthusiastic about what we do. It was slightly more revealing than I would have liked, but I couldn't complain. There was a simple band that would go around my top, taped down with the same thick tape I use on my wrists, and silver shoulder pads. Brindled grey fur stuck out from the bottom of the plates, as it did on my old armour, though this was much shinier and unscratched.

Let's be honest. Half of what we do is a popularity contest, and the best way to get attention is to look good, or at least unique. It showed off my scars, not by accident, I was sure. They would get peoples' attention. Other warriors' armour was just ridiculous sometimes. You wouldn't believe it.

It *was* a reality show, after all.

When Josh waved me over, there was a mix of cheering and booing in the crowd. Some were just curiously chattering. I raised my swords in an X, and they gave up all mixed feelings and applauded out of respect.

Matt waved Soul in, and it took every ounce of self-control I had not to start jumping up and down. He looked amazing and intimidating in his armour. The crowd shut their mouths and waited. They had no idea I was going to be battling Soul today, and half of them doubted that I should even be fighting at all. I wasn't too worried. Two weeks was enough time to heal from a bullet wound, right?

Soul dragged his axe across the ground as he walked. I didn't know whether he was trying to look intimidating or whether he was just tired, but either way, I was slightly more than nervous. We met at the centre of the arena and he looked down. I followed his eyes and saw a crimson stain on the ground. Inhaling sharply, I tried to clear my head. That was my blood. This was where I got shot. I wearily turned my head, just in case the sniper was there, just in case he wanted to eat steel.

I snapped back to focus and turned back to my partner, who was now holding out his hand with a mischievous smile. It was a smile I would have liked no part of, so despite showing him the respect due, I stepped back, waving my finger.

"I know that look. I invented that look," I said.

He grinned and dropped his hand, taking a few steps back as well.

The dirt slabs placed around the arena were great for hiding behind if you were playing at long-range combat. Neither of us were though, except for some smoke pellets and flash-bangs.

Sadly, the flash-bangs were not part of *my* arsenal.

We circled for a moment before he started to lift his axe. I felt behind me for one of the slabs. I grabbed it and managed to jump back, pulling my knees close to my chest in order to make it over.

His blade came down and became embedded in the dirt. He tried to tug it free but I was too quick for that — cat-like reflexes, they say. I pounced on him, and we rolled over on the ground until we were crouching face to face. I held my blade out to block him from his weapon. I wasn't expecting his next move though. He grabbed my arms and threw me over his shoulder.

I landed on a rock right in the centre of my back. As I whined and tried to shake off the uncomfortable feeling, Soul scrambled on his hands and knees back to his weapon. I rolled back onto my front as he kicked at the dirt and pried the handle upward. I refused to lose, friend or not, so I leapt up again and ran over to him.

Once again, I didn't expect his move, a sidestep to the right. If I hadn't thrown my hands out, I would have done a face plant right into the clay, and I think Soul knew that because he started to snicker. I quickly climbed on top of the stone and faced him again; he was ready for an attack but I had better plans. A smoke pellet. As I let it fall to the ground, he stepped back, making an effort to see through the smoke.

I jumped behind a different stone and called to him. "Oh, my Crow, such a horrible mistake." He started creeping up behind the stone I'd been behind a minute ago and looked over the top, becoming confused when he didn't see me there. "You thought this fight would be fake."

He ducked behind the rock, and I lost sight of him. I was about to risk a look over the top of the stone I was behind, but an axe four inches above my face was enough to change my mind. Hollering, I stood up and blocked an attack with one sword while I used the other to swing at his middle. He hopped back and snatched my wrist while still blocking the other. His strong grip caused me to drop the sword in my right hand while my left arm started to give out, and I was forced to drop to my knees to hold him off. The blades sparked against each other, grinding against each other, getting closer to our skin before he nearly sliced his own arm open. Lunging away from him, I reached for my second weapon, but he kicked it out of the way, leaving me with one sword and very slim chances of winning.

As I've mentioned before, Soul is a rather large man — extremely fit and slightly taller than myself. You wouldn't expect him to be able to move as fast as he does. I was practically running backwards as I deflected every swing. I backed right into a barrier and fell over, landing on my shoulders and neck as Soul stood over me, tilting his head.

I grunted as I rolled over, grasping my chest as I tried to take a moment. Soul wasn't one to show mercy… This is good for us, just not right now. I clawed myself to my feet and pressed my blade as hard as I could towards his chest, easily held back by his axe.

I was breathing heavily and feeling slightly beat up. My opponent didn't care. He hooked the edge of his weapon around mine and pulled it from my hands.

"Quit?" he asked loudly, with a gleeful smile. Cheeky bird.

I sighed. At this point, it would be a good idea, but a few young, familiar voices in the crowd stopped me.

"Go K9!"

"You can beat him! You can beat anyone!"

I don't know why Rosie and her friends liked me so much, but I couldn't disappoint them. I turned to their direction and saluted as Soul ran towards me. I ducked and grabbed his leg, lifting him off the ground and shoving him over my shoulders. He cried out as he hit the ground and dropped his battle axe, giving me a chance to slide it away — since I can't quite toss it yet.

Within a moment he was up again, eyeing the various weapons that had piled up behind me. We both knew I wouldn't let him near them, but he took a chance and ran forward anyway. He ran straight into my knee and tensed his muscles as he stepped back far enough for me to lean over, swinging my leg up and catching his jaw.

We both stood ready to defend ourselves, me being in worse shape than him. He took shot after shot, which I managed to dodge before landing a few to his stomach. He was off balance enough that a single kick to the chest sent him to the ground. I ran for my sword, but he caught my ankle and pulled me back before he did the same. I went after him and stepped on the handle before he could get it off the ground. I grabbed a handful of his hair, and he shouted as he tilted his head back. I laughed, then shoved him away. We grappled again, getting caught in a game of mercy.

I bit my lip as he pushed my hands back. I cried out when he finally held them at my sides, still holding them very tightly. Turning me around, he gave one good shove and I was back on the hard, dusty ground, holding my wrists and praying he was as finished with this battle as I was. Smelling blood and sweat, I could feel him behind me again, so I sat up and grimaced as he used his axe to pull me towards him.

You will move according to anyone's will if there are sharp enough objects involved.

He was holding the axe way too close to me, and only with one hand. For those of you that don't know, that means it was close enough for me to wrap my arm around the handle and pull it from his grip, and that's exactly what I did.

Or what I *tried* to do... Once again, he was very strong.

He yanked it back while my arm was still over it, looking at me intensely. I squeaked as he slowly pulled me towards him and the edge of his weapon jabbed my shoulder blade.

"Y-you're good..." I stuttered, trying to catch my breath. I cursed myself for not including any speed or sprint exercises in my daily strength training.

He smiled happily and I decided to make my exit. I scrambled away as fast as I could while avoiding having my flesh torn open, only to feel a hand snatch my hood. I indignantly slumped my shoulders as he stood and lifted me off my feet. I pouted as Matt zoomed his stupid camera in. I continued to pout until Soul spun me around, now holding the buckle of my shoulder-plated armour. My fake pout fell and I stared at him, a pleasant smile still plastered across his face. He wasn't smug about it, and while I seemed to be in a bit of pain, having taken a few bumps and bruises, he seemed pleased that I put in decent effort against him. He tilted his head, silently asking me if I gave up. I didn't want to, but there was no way I could keep fighting, so I held out my hand and gave a sheepish smile. His face softened, and he grabbed my hand as he set me on the ground.

"That was the biggest challenge I've had in a long time. Thank you, Crow."

"P-pleasure, K9," he stuttered, pretending to be out of breath too.

We both knew he was fine. We gathered our weapons and I held Soul's arm in the air, the way a traditional boxing or wrestling match would have ended. He looked down at me nervously. Slowly, people started to cheer, delayed probably out of shock more than anything else. I spotted the kids in the front row throwing their arms up and pointed them out to Soul. Rosie waved at him, her cheeks almost as red as her hair. He returned the wave, along with a proud smile.

She screamed and shook her friend by the shoulders. Yeah... She's going to end up *just* like me.

After taking in the applause for five minutes, Soul and I went our separate ways. I headed straight for the showers, eager to rinse all the dirt and sweat off of me. As soon as I left the locker room, I was met by a man who shoved a microphone in my face.

"Hey, K9! My name is Robert Harold, interviewer for *The Invisible Man*." I cautiously shook his hand. "I'm the new reporter. Mr. Viktor is sending me to Tournament of Survivors and wants me to interview all possible candidates."

I nodded, a cautious look still apparent on my face. *The Invisible Man*? Really? Who gave this guy his name? Dr. Frankenstein?

"So," he said, his wide mouth stretched out farther into a smug smile. "How do you feel after that battle against Crow?"

I shrugged, glancing at his cameraman. "A little beaten up. I'm probably going to be feeling it tomorrow, but overall, it was great. I'm really confident in our chances."

"So, there's no hard feelings then? There's no competition between the two of you?" He held out his microphone again and I scrutinized him.

"No, this was all training. No one's ever seen him fight; I wanted to be the first. There's no reason for there to be competition between us."

"*Friendly* competition, then? Very good. You both have my best for this tournament. I hope to catch up with you again."

Never had I ever heard such a fake "good luck" from someone in my life. I shrugged him off and left for dinner.

Fifteen

Today was the final day of freedom and of not fearing for my life. Tomorrow was the battle royal, which could last minutes or days; there was no telling. Everyone's nerves were high, and to an extent, they'd formed teams: for example, Randy and Jeremy, Jekyll and Hyde, and the "lollipop guild," and then Chrissy, Angel, Frankie, and Eloise.

And yet Soul and I were on our own. I couldn't let anyone else fight for me; I couldn't let them get hurt too. We had to win, though, and I had a plan to do that, assuming Sugar and Carmel got knocked out before the brothers went after us. I'd run over the plan in my head a million times and it was only lunch. I pressed my fingers to my temples and gritted my teeth.

"Ben?"

"Gah! What?" I looked up to see Chrissy staring at me.

"So you didn't even bother getting dressed today? Or are pink boxers your new look?" I glanced down to see I was in my sleeps and felt my nose and cheeks burn. Standing up slowly, I silently walked out of the cafeteria. I was cursing myself for being distracted and putting on the wrong pants; my face was still red when I ran into Soul. He looked like he was in the middle of a serious thought or a mental breakdown. His hair was sticking out more than usual, and he had his hand across his cheek. He curiously glanced at my outfit, then shook his head and went back to his thought.

"What's wrong?" I stepped in front of him, and he evaded me by turning his back. I stepped around him and leaned forward so he could see me from under his hair. This only seemed to stress him more.

I slid my hand over his and he closed his eyes tightly.

"K9 said it was them… K9 said it was the gemini. She said they were working f-for…" His voice cracked and he bit his lip. He started to press his hand against his cheek harder, and I reminded him my hand was there by running my fingers over his knuckles. "Hmm-mm, c-came … back… Hurt — hurt the bird! Not the knife! Not the knife! *Should have killed you, dirty crow, should have killed you then*!" He pressed both hands against his face as he screamed. "*Murderers! Murderers! Murderers!*" He sobbed and slid down the wall.

I bent down beside him. I felt I needed to speak softly to him otherwise I would be the one taking the hit. "What happened, Soul?"

His lip shook as he dropped one hand, uncovering most of his face, which was contorted into a blank, disturbing look. "Soul isn't here right now…" —his eyes were going in and out of focus — "but if you'd like to leave a message…"

That thoroughly creeped me out. Usually, he would go into a fit and then need to recite poems or riddles to calm down; this time he completely bypassed that and went straight to lunacy. He rested his head back against the wall and started to get a sheen of sweat over his pale skin. I'd never seen this before, and it scared the hell out of me. I placed my hand over his again and he slowly opened his eyes.

"K9?"

"Hey, what was that about?" I carefully asked.

He looked confused a moment, then shook his head. "Wh-what?"

I met his terrified eyes, and he started to move his right hand away from his cheek, revealing a small, deep cut. It looked like his skin had come into contact with some form of toxic chemical. Blood started flowing the second he took his hand away. I think I stopped breathing for a moment before I screamed for both Jeff and Louis. Soul rested his head back and I grabbed his cheeks gently.

"Soul, you have to stay awake… This was Jekyll and Hyde, wasn't it?"

He wearily nodded and wiped his face. "M-my office ... the knife..."

"They got into your office?"

He nodded again and rolled his head to the side. "Was there something on the knife?"

"Burned ... didn't cut."

His eyes closed, and I wasn't able to wake him up again. If Jekyll and Hyde were trying to get him out of the competition, it seemed like they had succeeded. After I shrieked for the medics again, Louis finally showed up with his bag and shoved me out of the way.

"So what happened to him?"

Jeff was trying to work things out. His glasses were tilted to one side, and he was still shaken up.

"I don't know. I ran into him in the hall, and he told me that Jekyll and Hyde busted into his office. He said they didn't use the knife to cut him though — "

"No, they probably just held it against his skin. There was enough of the chemical to literally burn through his flesh, which resulted in his nasty wound."

"Do you even know what kind of drug it was?" Josh asked, walking into the medical ward while still buttoning his uniform.

"No, but he should be fine now ... no permanent damage." He faintly smiled and let me go wait for Soul to wake up while he talked to our security guard.

I looked at my sleeping friend. He was clearly having a nightmare. He kept clenching his fists and grimacing, then relaxing again. Pressing my hands against my eyes, I drifted into my thoughts ... no sleep last night, likely none tonight, and Soul was out like a light. I desperately hoped he would wake up soon. I glanced back up and sighed. This shouldn't have happened to him. I needed to find Dr. Frankenstein before he actually killed any of us.

"So," Josh said, leaning against the wall behind me, "what was he doing before this?"

"I don't know."

"Where was he going?"

"No clue."

He grunted and pulled his cap from his head. His knuckles were bloody and his fingers were a little cut up. He was always bruised; he trains with us but he doesn't have the speed or stamina. He's said he's happy with his job though, just happy to be here.

"You can't keep giving me attitude. I'm trying to help."

I felt my hands ball up, and the next thing I knew, I was standing in front of him. "I know it was you that shot me! I saw you before I passed out. I … I don't blame you. I know you were just doing what Dan said. But how do you think I feel right now? Jekyll and Hyde are gunning for us, and the one guy that's supposed to be looking out for me put me in the hospital!"

He didn't answer me. His face went white and he looked down.

"I'm sorry, Josh; I have to take care of this."

I turned back to Soul, told him to find me when he woke up, and squeezed his hand. Then I ran out of the room and straight for my locker. Josh followed me without a word, just wringing his hat between his hands while he jogged to keep up.

After grabbing my weapons, I knew exactly where I was going. I assumed that Jekyll and Hyde would be in the dining hall, as they usually were around noon, so I kicked the door open and stormed in, one sword already raised. I embedded it in the table beside Hyde and glared at them and their girlfriends.

"Care to explain why you tried a sneak attack when you know very well that I wouldn't stand for it?"

"Yeah, about that… It wasn't anything personal, but our boss wanted us to test his new drugs, and let's face it, everyone hates your friend," Hyde said.

I whacked the jewelled end of my sword over the back of Hyde's head. "Who do you work for, boys?"

They looked at each other, then laughed.

"Dr. Frankenstein, of course," Hyde answered. "But you already knew that, didn't you?"

Hyde shoved me back and Jekyll jumped to his feet. He punched me in the stomach with enough force to nearly reopen my almost-healed stitches. I fell to the floor, hollering in pain and grasping my stomach. I bit my lip so hard it bled as I kicked my legs and pressed my forehead into the floor.

"You're going to wish you hadn't done that!" I wheezed.

I recklessly swung my sword up and slashed Hyde's cheek wide open. I barely got to my feet before Jekyll reached for me. Ordinarily, I would clean the blood off my weapons before attacking again, but this time the blood was a warning that we were done playing nice.

"That's enough!" Suddenly, Josh dropped his hat and stepped between me and my opponents. "You want to fight, you can fight in the arena! You will not be trashing the place again!"

I had to hunch my back as I rested my prized steel blade over my shoulder. "You're just a little killjoy, aren't you?"

"Okay, fine, you're mad at me! I'm sorry, but let me do my job."

The twins stood opposite us, snickering and high-fiving each other. They looked quite proud of themselves until Josh turned on them. He stomped over to Sugar and grabbed her wrist, nearly lifting her out of her seat. Had to admit; Josh was strong for someone with little training.

"Where did you get this?" He pulled a silver-and-black device from her hand and examined it closer. I peeked over his shoulder and looked from the trigger to the skull-shaped brand on the end of it. I ripped it from the security guard's hands and flipped it around a few times.

"I trashed this! I tossed it on the floor. How'd you fix it?"

Josh held up his hand to stop me. "I have my own questions. Where did you get it?"

The four quickly looked amongst themselves, then grabbed their lunches and bolted. Josh had an unsettled look, and he motioned for me to follow him as he left the cafeteria. He scratched his chin as he stomped through the painfully bright white halls to his office, shushing my questions as we went. It was near the front entrance, a few corners away from the locker rooms, and the door was slightly open. As it usually was.

He was a quiet man. He kept to himself and Matt mostly, but he wasn't intense. Josh was always the one to bail us out of trouble. I think I forgot that at times.

His hand was on the doorknob as Soul came around the corner and staggered towards us. He had a bandage below his eye and a frustrated scowl. And bed-head.

"Good, I was going to have to tell you too."

"If you made me wait, I'll make you wait." I snapped at him, then embraced Soul. "Feeling any better?" I wasn't really upset with Josh, just frustrated.

Stepping away, Soul nodded slowly and looked at Josh. I guess I did have to deal with him at some point, and giving him the cold shoulder really wasn't helping. "So why did you pull me out of there? What was with that look on your face when you saw that device?"

He sighed and rubbed his arm, his fluffy brown hair falling over his left eye. "Because I built it. Come into my office and I'll explain. I don't need the cameras hearing."

We had to push through trash and fast-food containers to fit the three of us inside his dark little office, and I'm pretty sure something ran across my boot, but once we were inside, Josh immediately started rooting through his desk. He swore a few times and then looked through the closet, throwing memory cards and handheld cameras out of the way. His arms fell to his sides, and he turned to look at us with embarrassment.

"It was mine! I don't know how they got it. No one knew about it!"

"I'm begging you to start making sense," I said. I crossed my arms, bored and confused.

Josh cracked his knuckles and sat himself down on the edge of his desk. "I built a custom-designed branding staff for Mr. Viktor. Pretty unique little thing, a cross between a taser and a branding iron. My prototype was a lot bigger, but it looks like the same technology. I wouldn't be so worried, but there are so many similarities I had to check for myself, and ... I'm not seeing my prototype anywhere around here."

I had to put so much effort into not commenting on the state of his office I thought I was going to explode. Instead, Soul and I checked the bench by the door and under the desk again. Nothing.

"Why on earth would he ask you for that thing?"

"A branding staff? I don't know. It's not my place to ask questions."

My body froze and I stood up. I searched my jacket pockets for Ronin's log. I never did give it back to him, and I guessed that was a good thing because, as I flipped through the pages, something caught my eye.

I trailed my finger across the page as I read, trying to remember what I had seen a few nights after I stole it. I got a paper cut, but that was the least of our problems. "I knew it."

The tapping of the keyboard was distracting me, and when I looked up at the screen, well, I didn't need to read any more. The two of us crowded around Josh in his desk chair and the monitor, and watched Angel slip into the office. She came back out a few minutes later, carrying a long grey staff. She looked both ways, then ran down the hall. It was time-stamped over two months ago.

Josh dropped his face into his hands and gave a defeated sigh. He shivered like he was going to be sick, sinking further into his seat.

Rolling him out of the way, Soul flexed his hands and started typing. He found all the footage she had been in that day and followed her from the office through the building to an empty dorm room. She pushed her long hair out of her eyes and took a deep breath. I did the same and grabbed Soul and Josh's shoulders.

I wasn't happy to hear the voice coming from the speakers. I felt like I got punched in the gut again.

"Is this it?" Angel asked sheepishly.

"This is exactly it, my dear."

Vince Viktor took long, swift strides until he was in the frame. He held out his hand without a word, a sly smile on his face and his suit as neatly pressed as always.

"Oh Maat," Josh sputtered, "I did this…"

Maat, his goddess of choice. She wouldn't have mercy; none of this felt very just.

"No, it's not you." My voice cracked, and I looked away from the screen. I wished it wasn't real. Of course, I always thought Mr. Viktor was an arrogant bastard but … I didn't want to believe this. Back on the video, Angel handed over the branding rod and she smiled proudly.

"You did perfect, Beauty. Can I count on you again when I need you?" He laid his hand on her hair and then gently lifted her chin with the tip of his finger. His voice was so smooth, all three of us knew he wasn't asking.

Soul stood and crossed his arms. He pressed his lips together and his brows creased, but Josh sat shaking his head. The two of us looked up to Viktor for a long time… Did he really do that to us? His monsters were the only ones that weren't hit, so it would make sense. But why Angel? Why did she do this to me? We were friends!

I choked back the fear building inside me and stumbled out of the office and down the hall. I called Angel's name as loud as I could as I went, until I ran into Eloise.

"What's wrong?" she asked, with as much urgency as her soft voice could possibly muster.

"None of your concern. Just tell me where Angel is."

"I'm right here; *what* is your problem?" She stepped out of the lounge and gave me a funny look. Her old T-shirt sat unevenly over her shoulders when she crossed her arms. It took her a minute to realize that I had grabbed her by the shoulders and threw her up against the wall, one hand holding her back and my sword in the other.

I choked up a bit, drooling on myself, and shouted, "How could you do that?!"

"Do what? Benji, are you alright?" She was acting genuinely

confused. I hated her even more.

"Don't give me that. I saw what you did! I saw you give him the prototype!" I cried. My grip was slipping on my blade and I couldn't look at her, but I felt her body tense below mine.

"You're goddamn right I did," she hissed. "But you don't have any proof. You can't prove his identity."

Her voice was only loud enough for me to hear. Eloise stood quietly, waiting to jump into action if she had to.

"Why? Wh-why would you do that?" I asked, a little heartbroken.

She scoffed and grabbed my upper arms. "Because Viktor's going to keep me safe!"

"From who?! Angel, from who?"

"From people like you and your *friend*!" She spat at me and I dropped my weapon, shoving her back again. I'm pretty good with a sword but I wanted to use my fists. "You better be careful with this, K9. You might get rabies."

I shouted and planted my fist in the wall beside her head. She hadn't flinched. "Are you trying to scare me? Huh? Because I'm not leaving the qualifier, and neither is Soul or Chrissy! How could you turn on us like that? How could you abandon us when we need you? Don't you understand what's going on?"

"Believe it or not, you aren't the most terrifying thing out there!"

She pulled herself from my grip and strutted off down the hall, clinging to Ronin's arm. Her heels clicked, getting farther away, but I didn't turn away from the wall. My knuckles throbbed something fierce, but I couldn't move. I just tried to call to her one last time. I trusted her; she was my friend. She'd tried to hurt us. Hurt Chrissy, and Soul. And Frankie and Eloise and Charlie! All my friends… She was one of them…

"You've got to be delusional, Angel. He's not protecting us, and he never was. You're on the wrong side."

Soul was oddly easy to be around. I had been standing quietly in the hall for a while, and I wanted nothing to do with anyone until Soul gently coerced me back to my room to rest.

We sat beside each other, and I lifted my hand and grazed his fingertips, causing him to flinch and then wrap his fingers around my hand. His eyes followed the movements and he tilted his head to the side. His hands were really soft, probably because of the ink and how hard he'd had to scrub them to get it off. I could hear him sigh slightly as he looked back up at my face, sad green eyes looking worried. His cheeks turned pink around his scar as I smiled softly. Reaching out, I tugged his goatee.

He whined slightly as he leaned forward. "D-don't like that…"

I let him go and ran my thumb over his chin, his pupils filling out again. A light laugh escaped my mouth as he gently pushed my hand down, not looking away. I put my head down and closed my eyes, my bottom lip started feeling like it was going to bleed again, not anything out of the ordinary for me.

I knew Soul was still watching me; he seemed to be trying to get a good look at my face.

"I'm glad I met you."

Suddenly, Soul sat back and raised his dark eyebrows, "C-crow? Really?"

I nodded and sighed. "Yeah, I needed a crow in my life. You're a good person to have around."

"*They* don't think so," he said. I nodded quietly and felt my shaggy hair tickle my cheek, "They don't have to. I just think you should have more faith in yourself…"

I drifted off and slipped backwards, waking myself up by hitting the fluffy mattress. It smelled like my shampoo and a little bit like cotton candy. It was a soothing scent, but I had no idea where it came from. Tired, I exhaled out of aggravation and held my hand over my eyes, blocking out the light. It'd been a rough couple of days. I felt Soul's weight leave the bed and the light clicked off. Instantly, I was out again.

Sixteen

My muscles tensed and I bolted up. It was the day of the qualifier.

I was still half-asleep when I realized I wouldn't have time to shower. I had to leave right away if I wanted to at least have a chance of showing up at the city square on time for the tournament opening. That was what happened when you didn't get proper sleep every night; you ended up being late for life-changing events.

I tied my boots and slammed my locker shut, running out of the locker room like my life depended on it. I slid my arms through the buckles of my armour, then bit down on the strap to keep it in place as I secured my swords to my hips, over a belt of potential fire power.

I saw Chrissy up ahead of me, her metal-pleated skirt rattling as she walked.

"Chris, you feeling okay?"

She turned and gave me a terrified smile.

"Okay? *Okay*? I'm going to die out there because they know I'm with you, and you ask if I'm *okay*!"

I held my hands up in self-defence. "We'll take care of ourselves. Just keep yourself safe."

She nodded and let her anxiety drift away as much as possible. Speaking of drifting, Soul wandered over, struggling to buckle his shoulder pad. He kept reaching behind him for the strap, but it kept swinging away. I finished buckling my own armour before I reached around his chest, pulled the strap to the front, and fiddled with the buckle. When I tried to step back, the mesh under his coat got caught in the steel over my left shoulder. Putting my hand on his chest, I tried to pull free. Tearing Soul's jacket, I freed myself, slamming into the wall behind me.

"Yeah ... you two are going to do *great*." Chrissy rolled her eyes.

"Nervous?" I asked my tall partner.

He smirked and shook his head slowly. I patted his arm, then walked out of the gate. The air was cold. I was probably going to regret not bringing a jacket. Soul had jumped into step with me, and I noticed him shiver slightly. At least I had a hood that would block the wind a little bit; he didn't even have sleeves. We were standing in front of the abandoned side of Lilithia, our battleground.

"No sweater?" I eyed him with slight disapproval, and he returned that with a sheepish look. We soon joined the others taking part in the tournament at the edge of the abandoned road, and I gave a terrified Eloise a hesitant thumbs-up.

"This is all your fault," Frankie whispered to me, also scared and angry.

"Hey!" I snapped. "Just watch out for yourself, otherwise I'm taking you out first."

"*I'm* going to be a target?! It's because of your soft spot for the clinically insane that we all have prices on our heads. *You* aren't my problem, mutt!"

"I'm going to be if you keep talking! Now I know how you got your code name — "

"Yeah? How?"

"Since you're always causing a scene!"

Poor Eloise got caught in the middle as we both reached around to strangle each other like children.

"Count us out of your little anti-hero justice club!" Frankie sneered.

I spat at him and he stumbled back, ready to swing at me again.

"Scene Fest, K9, why on earth is it that every time there's trouble afoot, one of you is involved?" the boss scolded as he walked past us to the microphone. I reacted by stepping to Soul's other side, putting a bit more distance between Frankie and me. Eloise nervously held her hands in front of her but looked up at Soul.

"Sorry we can't help you anymore. We just… We can't have Jekyll and Hyde after us."

"It's not your fault, Eloise." I sighed. Soul nodded slightly. "Like I said, we'll do better on our own anyway."

"One plus one, a little bit of fun; two plus two, we may lose a few…" Soul sheepishly wrung his hands and shrugged. We couldn't have anyone else to worry about. We had to win, if only to get out of this city so we weren't run out by an angry mob…

The drone cams circled like vultures, ready to follow us into the grounds.

"Ladies and gentlemen, warriors and soldiers … this is the qualification tournament. You all know that if you are one of the last two standing, you will go on to the Tournament of Survivors, which will be held at the Isle this year."

Soul started to get agitated and rubbed his arm roughly, silently trying to keep his nerves down. I grabbed his hand and squeezed. He slowly took a breath, then calmed down again.

"Each entrant will be given a five-minute start, and you may begin your battle once the bell is rung." He was about to start calling names. I knew I would be first again, and Soul would be last.

"*Devil's night, and demons sing…*" I kept my head straight and spoke softly, hoping no one else would hear me. Soul squeezed my hand back tighter than before to let me know he understood.

"K9, you may proceed."

I exhaled and stepped forward. Soul was still holding my hand, and he slowly let it slip from his grasp. I cast a smirk at the rest of the warriors and tugged my hood over my ears. I was in no rush, walking past the barrier like I owned this place.

Mr. Viktor announced the next person to enter. I started walking faster.

Five contestants later, I was standing outside of the same building where Dan and I went, where I'd found Soul. I started to climb the stairs and quickly made it to the eleventh floor. Making my way through the trashed room, I climbed onto the fire escape and up to the roof. The flight of stairs had collapsed long ago, and this was the only other way up. It was a good spot to be; I could see the entire area and everyone in it. All the streets were dusty and empty except for some kicked-over trash cans and stray plant life. Vines climbed the outside of crumbling buildings, but none of the brush was thick enough to hide in. Viktor didn't want us to hide anyway; it wouldn't make good TV. The bell was rung and I started looking for potential threats. Too many of the others were waiting to catch Soul or me. I paced up and down the roof as I searched for my partner. I couldn't see him but I heard shouting ... something about a bird.

Jekyll and Hyde were arguing with each other. Their voices carried through the streets. They paced up and down through the centre of town; you would be forced to run into one of them no matter where you were going. The crossroads in that area were pretty much unavoidable.

Stress and maybe some hunger bit at my stomach. I couldn't see Crow, but that didn't mean Jekyll or Hyde couldn't.

"Die, bird!" The voice had come from behind me.

I swung my head around and saw Jeremy Vamp on the roof a few buildings over, swinging his double-sided daggers at Soul, who was facing him. For the first time in a while, Jeremy's muffled voice wasn't obscured by sleepiness. Jekyll and Hyde had heard him too, and both bolted towards them as Soul gave Dracula one good shove, causing him to yelp as he grabbed at the fire escape to keep himself from falling six storeys.

"So much for the devil's night and demons sing." I said, sighing and unsheathing my weapons. I walked backwards, preparing for a running leap to the roof of the next building.

"Don't do it."

I stopped dead and turned to see Randy at the top of the fire escape. "You can't make that jump. Maybe you should thank me by dropping out."

"I very well *can* make that jump." I sneered back at him. "The only way you'll get me out of this competition is by defeating me fair and square."

"So be it." Randy sighed and tugged his whip from his belt. I swung my swords, then stepped forward, knowing that I can't leave Soul for very long with Jekyll and Hyde on the way. He was terrified of them. And rightly so.

Randy and I circled each other until he was where I was just standing. He lashed his whip, wrapping it around my arm and leaving a little red welt on my cheek where the leather hit. I slipped it down to the hilt of my blade, and then I ran. The wind pushed my hood back, and I kicked off as far from the edge of the brick as I could, not only making it to the next building but also dragging my bandaged foe after me and leaving him hanging over the side of the brick wall, gripping his whip, which was still wound around my sword. This building was far shorter than Soul's, but Randy was still terrified to fall. He'd probably break at least a few bones.

"K9, come on. Let me up! Fight me face to face!" He spoke tough, but his voice shook.

I smiled sweetly and waved as I angled my sword downwards and let the whip slide free. He screamed as he fell, hitting the ground roughly and crying out.

"I'm going to kill you, K9! You're dead!"

I nodded as I walked away. "Okay! Let me know when all your bones fuse back together first, though."

"*Randy 'the Mummy' Curio has been eliminated! Eleven warriors left!*" I heard the smooth voice of Robert Harold call out over a speaker as I grabbed the ladder of the fire escape and slid to the ground. In seconds, I was running out of breath and still some distance away from where Soul had been.

Our more rugged enemy's voice boomed through town in deceiving echoes. "Find the damn boy!"

His accent made me cringe. It's not that I don't like Irish accents; it's just that I don't like theirs.

"If it comes down to us and the girls, you best believe I'm taking you down," his gruesome twin snarled. I don't know how close to them I was, but it made me nervous to pass open streets or alleyways. I slowed my steps and tried to breathe as quietly as I possibly could. Hearing heavy boots stomping the ground towards me, I tried to slide into the darkness of an alleyway.

A soft hand suddenly slid over my mouth and the other around my stomach, pulling me farther into the shadows. I struggled and tried to swing my sword back, but my grip was loose and the arm over my stomach was also holding my hands to my sides. Panic struck me as I kicked my legs up and tried once again to break free, but then it hit me. If this were a threat, I would probably be dead. Letting my boots rest on the ground once again, I settled enough that the person holding me back rested his head beside mine and whimpered softly. I could identify that whimper anywhere.

Soul let his hand fall from my mouth and sighed. When I turned around in his grip, he had his eyes closed tightly. Leaning against him, I ran a hand through his dirty hair

"We should go."

He nodded, then stepped away. I started to panic as I faintly smelled the scent of blood. I checked my arms and then grabbed Soul. He had a long gash down his chest, but it wasn't very deep and shouldn't be a problem. That being said, I was still worried about it.

"*Here, birdy, birdy, birdy…*" Hyde sang mockingly.

I started to push him farther down the alley and into a back street, which was a little too open for my taste. After a shared look of frustration and anxiety, we took off towards the wooded area near the entrance.

When we hit the treeline, I fell to my knees, gasping for air and holding my stomach. I wasn't completely healed yet, and each breath pulled at my skin. I tried desperately to steady myself, but I was hardly given a chance since, a second later, Sugar and Carmel jumped out of the darkness.

Standing and stretching out my back, I threw my arms up. "Are you kidding me?!"

I got my sword ready with one hand and held my wound with the other. Sugar and Carmel shared a look and started laughing.

"Aw, is the doggy hurting?" Sugar mocked.

"Just think about how *happy* Jekyll and Hyde will be when we knock you two out of this competition for them."

Happy? They'd be *ecstatic*.

I half-heartedly swung and knocked the grenade out of Carmel's hand; then I turned to Sugar. She was a bigger threat. She had skill with her metal staff, but she lost all the colour in her face when she heard Soul unhook his axe from his back and clamp his left hand firmly on the handle.

She shook. Her shaking hand took Carmel's and the two whispered to each other. Sugar kept looking at Soul with his axe in his hands, then looking at me and flinching.

"You can't leave! We have to do this," Carmel declared. I looked at Soul and he shrugged his shoulders, just as confused. Suddenly, Sugar tossed her friend away and struck her with her staff. "I don't want to fight someone else's battle! I *will not* fight Crow. Think about what they must be going through, think about how sacred you were yesterday! I can't do it, Carmela. I don't want to get hurt for *them*."

"B-but..."

"I quit! I'm out. I'm leaving. This is a sick game!" She turned to us and tossed her weapon down. She stormed off with Carmel, who was reluctant but seemed pretty grateful to go. A few short moments later, I heard Robert announce that they had left the competition as well.

"Wait here," I told Soul as I started to climb into a tree in order to get a better idea of where the other contestants were. There were only nine people left, with seven to be eliminated, and I didn't want to be one of them.

"Hey, birdbrain, you want to take another shot at me? Here I am. Go ahead!" a familiar voice shouted.

Scowling, I dropped to the ground. "Dracula," I said, greeting Jeremy, who was limping towards us from the forest path.

"Maybe I'll even get to impress your girlfriend when I stick my blades into your heart," he taunted.

"Nothing about you is impressive, Dracula," I said flatly.

Soul stepped towards him. I knew I didn't have to worry about him being on his own; he was very good and very intimidating.

"Eloise 'Dolly' Bentley, and Frankie 'Scene Fest' Gent have both been eliminated! Seven warriors remaining!" I smirked and stepped back as Soul swung at Dracula. They exchanged blows for a few moments before I heard someone else heading towards us. I prayed it wasn't Jekyll or Hyde, but I noticed the rattle of a metal-plated, pleated skirt. At least that eased my mind.

I held my weapon tight but allowed her to walk through the trees and stand by my side.

"Who are you rooting for?" Chrissy asked jokingly.

I scowled at her. "Who do you think?"

She smiled as she watched the two now-aggravated men try to kill each other. "I've always liked crows more than bats anyway," she said, scratching her head.

Jeremy missed his one last swing and was whacked on the head by the blunt end of Soul's axe. He dropped to the ground like a wet rag, out cold. Soul had won.

I sighed and looked at Chrissy. "I guess this means it's our turn?"

"It's seems so. Just try to stay away from the face." Chrissy was already looking tired, but she lifted her arms into a defensive position.

"Where's your crossbow?"

"Jekyll caught Angel and I in a lock-up, so I had to ditch it. Choked Frankie out with my bare hands though."

I raised an eyebrow; that was *one* way to win, I suppose. I left my sword in its sheath and sent a punch towards her. She dodged it and fell straight onto my knee. I started to fall back, but instead I leapt onto a low-hanging tree branch. I scampered up the tree and swung into an open window beside it.

"K-K9?"

"It's okay, Soul, I'll only be a minute!"

I knew Chrissy wouldn't be able to make the jump from the tree to the window. That was the disadvantage of her curves and her short stature; she was strong but her centre of gravity was lower. She couldn't throw herself around as easily as I could. I finally found the upside of having shoulders wider than my bony hips.

I watched her land on the ground on her back. She struggled for a minute, unable to breathe. Eventually, she let out a sigh.

"You win. I quit," she said shakily. "I'm going home to sleep. You need this more anyway."

I let out a laugh. "Thanks for helping us out!"

She waved her hand in the air before pressing both palms against her temples and walking off. I jumped back out the window and hit the ground again, biting my lip to keep from crying out. I gritted my teeth as I stood and looked at Soul, ready to start moving again. He was staring up into the trees, so I stepped over and followed his line of sight. There was a crow sitting just above him, watching us. It cawed, then dropped onto his shoulder. Soul looked nervous for a moment but quickly relaxed and held out his hand. The bird jumped onto it and cawed again.

I hesitantly petted the feathers on its neck, and the bird stretched out, tilting its beak and blinking. It walked up Soul's arm and settled on his shoulder again, making itself comfortable.

"A crow … imagine that." I smiled at Soul. He still looked nervous, trying to shoo the bird away.

"Go … not safe."

The crow decided to emit its protest by shrieking right in Soul's ear. Turning his head, he grunted as the bird settled again.

"They can recognize faces. Maybe he's seen you before," I suggested.

My friend looked like he was hit with a sudden realization. "Y-yes … but really? Y-years ago — bird was caught in a net…"

"You pulled him out?"

Soul nodded.

"Their memory is better than a human's," I said.

The bird got my attention again and I looked at its eyes … a soft brown, like most crows', but it was different somehow. Kinder maybe. Pretty small too, maybe it's a juvenile. Soul tried to shake it off again, but the bird just latched onto his jacket. Sighing, he accepted our new companion.

"We should track down the others now — "

"*Angel 'Beauty' Lannister, Chrissy 'Bobkat' Bokitski, and Jeremy 'Dracula' Vamp have been eliminated! Four warriors left!*"

I think my heart stopped for a few seconds. I had been looking forward to procrastinating on fighting Jekyll and Hyde, but it looked like that was out of the question. I could feel my face drain of colour. I scowled.

"We should finish this, now. C'mon, my birdies."

Seventeen

We managed to make it back to an old warehouse without being caught by our foes, though we could hear them nearby. I rattled the padlock that held the two large wooden doors closed, but it was securely fastened. I turned and ran a hand through my hair. Soul was staring at the ground and a shadow covered his eyes.

"I know that look," I started. "This place was used by underground fighting rings. This was where it happened, wasn't it?"

He turned his head slightly and inhaled slowly. His little bird left his shoulder and started picking at the lock. I could sense how angry Soul had suddenly become. He ripped his weapon off his back and cried out as he brought it down on the lock. The crow cawed loudly in surprise as it fluttered backwards.

Soul's large form was seething as he pulled his axe out of the metal. I glanced at the bird as it jumped on my shoulder.

"S-Soul? We don't need to — "

"No. Need to see where it happened, where it was all taken f-from him," he stuttered, seemingly preoccupied with pulling off the lock. After he did, he shoved open the heavy doors.

Our crow seemed to share a look with me before I stepped forward and followed Soul inside. There were still bloodstains and barriers up, but the most disturbing thing was the pipe and wire still lying in the middle of the floor. There were scratches in the dirt near them, like someone had tried to drag themselves out of a fight. I had to look away.

The incident with Soul must have been the very last thing to happen here … and nobody had bothered to clean it up.

I was dragged into my memories, a place I was not fond of. I felt pathetic and angry for letting it get to me, but I could still feel the razor wire wrapped around my arms and across my chest, gradually getting tighter. I grunted as I bit my lip and tried to bury the thought again. All I wanted was to get rid of the men who did it so they could never do it to anyone else, but more than that, I wanted to make them feel the same pain. I wanted to make them *suffer* for what they did, make them live the nightmare that plagued me for years, and then end it. Once and for all.

The crow cawed in my ear and brought me back to reality. Soul was staring at the bloodstain, the grip gradually getting tighter around his axe. Inhaling, I decided it was high time we shoved back: play dirty and cheat. But first, I had to bring Soul back to his senses.

Almost silently, I strode over to him, then reached around, placing my hand on his forearm. He quickly brushed it away.

"Get out."

"What?"

"Get out, leave. Hide. They're going to die today. K9 doesn't need to get caught in the middle."

I scoffed and crossed my arms, speechless for a moment. After finding my words again, I roughly spun him around to face me. "I want to kill them. I want them dead. I want to go to battle with them. I will cheat and I will *slaughter* anyone who gets in my way. You aren't going to get in my way … are you, Soul?"

He stood over me and snarled, "K9 needs to go. *Crow's* fight today. Going to kill, going to bleed, it's all for naught if the K9 can't lead —"

"Stop it."

He froze and tilted his head, looking slightly angry and slightly confused at the same time.

"Wh — "

"Don't. Don't play your little poems with me; we're both fighting them. Whether it's as friends or enemies is up to you, but don't tell me this doesn't concern me. They're my doing anyway."

I tugged the band around my chest slightly lower and showed more of the scar on my chest. He looked at the ground, then back at me, frustration shining in his eyes.

"N-no! Need to go… Can't let K9 do it!" he shouted.

"Why! Tell me why!"

I didn't need to look down to know he was clenching his fists as he mouthed something to himself. He pulled his hair back hard and took a deep breath, trying and failing to calm his nerves.

"The crow is already a monster! Y-you shouldn't be one too!"

"Too late, *birdy*! It's been a long time since *I* was the one to step back from a fight!"

"C-can't!" His voice cracked as he gave a high-pitched shout, pacing back then stepping up again. He roughly grabbed my shoulders and stuck his pointed nose against mine. He gently let go with one hand and pressed it against the side of his head, looking like he was dealing with some internal turmoil. Sighing, he dropped his hands to his sides.

"Th-think … I … l-love you!"

He stared at me intensely, trying to fight the regret seeping across his gentle face. After an agonizingly short moment, he dropped his head and started to grind his teeth and pull his hair, obviously trying to keep himself from sobbing. He let out a whimper as he tugged at his black mane. His chest rose and fell quickly; he appeared to be having a hard time breathing. He was whining and whimpering every few breaths.

It felt like he was playing a cruel joke on me, but I tried to work through how it could ever be possible as I picked my jaw off the floor. Soul — he couldn't … right? Out of everyone we knew … *me?* It's not true. It's only because I was the first real contact he's probably had in years. Right?

My breathing was shallow, and I was feeling light headed — probably out of hunger more than anything. I pushed my hair back and tried to swallow the lump in my throat.

"Y-you don't mean that…" I stammered.

"I do! I meant it! D-don't want to lose my K9!"

He still had his back to me, but I knew his hands were covering his face, fingers buried deep in his matted hair. I kept staring blankly at the ground in front of me. I started to tug at the tape on my top and bit my lip. I'm not good with my feelings — anyone could tell you that — but maybe… I don't know. Maybe…

I internally groaned. *What* am I feeling? I've never felt like this before. I don't think I like it. It's confusing — and stressful. Soul seemed to strike my nerves the first day we met, and since then, maybe I'd developed *something*, some kind of feelings for him too? And just maybe … I was okay with that?

I wrung my hands and looked back at my friend, who was wobbling back and forth now, biting his knuckles on his left hand. Quietly stepping over to him, I pulled his hand away from his face. He resisted at first but then let me, keeping his eyes fixed on the ground and his bottom lip tucked under his teeth. He looked like he was traumatized by what he said. Gently, I kissed his knuckles, tightly holding his fingers between mine.

"I don't want to lose my crow, either."

He let out a huge breath, almost as if he'd been holding it since he'd said … what he'd said. Biting back a smile, he managed to regulate his breathing again. It was the only sound I could hear aside from my own, but it was almost rhythmic. My cheeks were hot, and I didn't want to meet his eyes, but I smiled to myself anyway.

"I'm not letting you do this alone." I grabbed his chin and perked up again. "Soul. Okay?"

He smiled brightly as he threw his head back, pulling his face from my grip and then rubbing his forehead against mine. "*My* K9."

I gave a light chuckle as we stood together quietly, hoping for just a few more seconds with each other. But all good things come to an end.

Our companion let out a loud caw. And we turned to see the door slowly swing open. The air got denser and we both drew our weapons, preparing for the worst. We both knew it was the worst we were about to face. Two silhouettes stepped through the open door.

"Now wasn't that sweet," said Jekyll, showing us every tooth in his ugly mouth.

I smirked, then cracked my neck.

"Yeah, we should thank you for arguing, otherwise we wouldn't have thought to look here," Hyde added. Keeping with the theme of buying time, I spun on my heel and tossed a smoke pellet at them, giving me enough time to grab Soul and hop behind one of the barriers. A desperate attempt to say the least.

"Oh, Vixen ... such a shame you fell for such a worthless creature," Jekyll said.

Soul sneered and looked at me for instruction. I was at a loss until I saw a half-broken bottle nearby, and cut my hand open when I leaned forward to grab it. It radiated pain, but I ignored it as I started to fill the bottle with the smoke pellets from my belt, and glass, keeping my back to the brothers. I could hear their footsteps on the dry sand floor, coming closer and closer. The warehouse was dark; it was hard to see very far and it smelled like must and mould. It was the perfect place to fight them.

"We know that was you that burned your mark into Soul's chest. Everyone else is afraid of you but we're not. We're just going to get rid of you, and then we're going to find out who Dr. Frankenstein is ... unless you want to save yourself the pain and just tell us?" I spoke while working frantically on the bottle, making sure nothing went off.

A hearty laugh rang out. "You hear that, Hyde? They think we'll tell them."

"It would be easier to kill them. It just so happens that I have my wire with me now. Shall we get it over and done with?"

"We shall."

I stood and let out a shout as I threw the makeshift grenade directly at them. I ducked back down as smoke exploded into the area and shrapnel flew out. Those little bombs are just filled with chemicals but they pack a surprising punch. I heard one man cry out in pain, then a thud. I risked a glance from my hiding spot and saw Hyde unconscious on the ground with Jekyll standing over him, shaking him in an attempt to wake up him up. He pulled his hand back and anxiously stared at the blood dripping from it.

Soul and I stood up, pulling our chosen weapons free as the crow started to … almost *laugh* at Jekyll's misfortune. He was outnumbered and likely outskilled with the two of us combined. But he wasn't without his talents, and he had a large hammer, which he was prepared to swing at us should we come any closer.

The beads and crystals on the string hanging from the hilt of my sword hit the blade, creating the only sound in the little warehouse aside from heavy breathing. My steps matched the clangs and I smirked, the wolf gradually getting closer to its prey. Soul's voice stopped me, though, and I turned to see him seething as he glared daggers at the brothers.

> "One, two, skip a few;
> three, four, a demon's roar;
> five, six, look at this mix;
> seven, eight, it's too late;
> nine, ten, I'm about to sin…"

Soul started to walk, then sprint, then run at Jekyll. He raised his axe and leapt up; then he threw it downwards with all his might, trying to break either the weapon or the resolve of his opponent. Soul was in a rage and I wasn't about to stop him. Jekyll was able to block Soul's axe with his hammer, but he grunted under the weight of the two medieval weapons *and* Soul's strength and dropped to one knee. I looked for an opening, and Soul jammed his boot into Jekyll's ribs, causing him to fall back and start gasping for air.

Soul bitterly let him get some of his breath back before narrowly missing a swing and having the hammer smash into his stomach. I watched him fall back and elected to join the battle, swinging my swords at random toward him, from above and the side. Jekyll did his best to dodge and block my moves, but he was nearly backed into a corner.

Pure aggression ran through me as I remembered the day my world ended. I brought both blades down on him, but he blocked, shoving me backwards. I landed on my back in the dirt, gasping for air. I stared death in the eyes with a smug look on my face. Yes, his hammer was directly above my nose, but I had faith in a tiny friend.

The crow swooped in and flapped his little wings as quickly as he could while he pecked at Jekyll, distracting him enough for me to roll out of the way. He cursed at the bird. Soul stormed towards him, dragging his axe with one hand and holding *something* in his other. I stayed on my stomach, prepared to leap up again, but Soul dropped the axe and hit Jekyll with a pipe, swinging as hard as he could once, twice, three times before moving behind him and forcing Jekyll to look in my direction.

"Pity the man who has none ... *fear* the man who has but one," he growled into Jekyll's ear.

Jekyll shrieked as Soul wrapped the razor wire around his neck and yanked. There was no mercy in his eyes. No mercy for the man who caused us and countless others terror and pain. In this moment, I was more afraid of Soul than the day we met — and also proud.

Jekyll moved to avoid being cut but it didn't happen. The wire didn't go too deep. He would be fine, but he was starting to fall unconscious.

"Cross the crow again and see what happens..." Soul tossed the much-larger man to the ground. He flopped down, out cold. Soul kicked him hard in the ribs. "Not done with the gemini yet. They will be *humiliated*. Fester and then you will see, K9 and Crow are capable of so much more..." Soul stepped over him, the bottom of his coat dragging through the blood and dirt. "Later," he said. "Later you will hurt."

I sat in shock at what he just did, not only how composed he managed to stay, but also the brutality. He didn't kill either of them. That was a huge surprise to me. Though I suppose if he had, then we would have been pulled from the tournament. He was clearly struggling to not finish both brothers off, though; his hands were shaking a great deal and his breathing seemed ragged.

I sat up and he held out his hand. I looked from it to his face and he shook it, urging me to stand up. I nodded and let him help haul me up. Pulling my hair back, I took a deep breath. They were out cold. Soul was staring at the ground.

"How many left?" he asked.

My mouth feeling dry and still struggling to breathe, I shook my head. "There isn't anyone left… We won! Soul, we beat them all!"

He looked up and grinned. "We did it!"

I threw my arms around his neck, and he gladly returned it by clinging to me and smiling into my hair. I stepped back and held him at arm's length. "We won!"

I laughed and shouted as I grabbed his hands and leaned back. I'd wanted to do this for a small lifetime, ever since I was a kid. He smiled brightly and stood taller. Then he grabbed my hand and started to drag me out of the warehouse, running as fast as he could. I heard the call of our little friend and stopped long enough for him to soar over and rest on Soul's shoulder.

"Lock."

"Lock?" I asked.

Soul pointed to the broken metal on the ground by the door. I smiled and grabbed his hand again, jumping and dancing as we walked. My cuts and bruises were at the back of my mind as I hopped and dashed to keep up with Soul. I did this a few times before I saw the boundary getting rather close. Soul saw it too and smirked.

"Race!" he cried.

"What? No!" I exclaimed.

He started to jog. I quickened my step in an effort to keep up, then tripped, slipping and landing on the ground. I scowled jokingly and pushed myself back to my feet, following him as quickly as I could. Soul reached the gate before I did, barely breaking a sweat. *I* was extremely out of breath, and feeling like I was about to pass out. Silently, he watched until I caught up, and then held his hands in front of him.

"Y-you're going to find Jekyll and Hyde in the abandoned warehouse," I said to Josh, who waited just outside the concrete barrier that sectioned off the area. He and the medical team were on hand, ready to jump in and pull out the injured contestants. "Just follow this path. And make sure you have a lot of bandages."

"Yeah, we know," Josh replied. I furrowed my brow as I watched him and Louis climb into a little cart and drive off. A few moments later, they radioed back and Robert stepped to the microphone.

"Jekyll and Hyde have been eliminated! Your champions and this year's entrants in the Tournament of Survivors are Benji 'K9' Keanin and Soul 'Crow' Ravin!"

Chrissy and Matt pushed us onto the stage beside Robert, and he raised our arms into the air. Other fighters either cheered or scowled but the rest of the locals were going crazy. I had forgotten about the security feeds relaying to the main screen and broadcasting to the main station. And the drone cams had been hovering around the area the whole time. I wondered how much they'd seen. I smiled brightly despite my embarrassment, and celebrated with everyone.

"They will be taken to Rhys-Mordred Isle in three days, enough time to speak with friends and family, gather their things, and — ah!"

Lock, who was previously sitting atop Soul's shoulder, jumped onto Robert's head, then onto my own armour, distracting the announcer.

"Wh-what was I saying?" He shook his head and put his hand on my back. "Good luck in the tournament."

He walked off and I threw my hands up. Chrissy stood and started shouting our names. I blew her a kiss, which she answered with a true fangirl squeal. I looked out over everyone until I spotted the person I was looking for. A gangly, dark-haired man was clapping proudly, a massive grin spread across his youthful cheeks. I grinned and waved. He waved back, slowly showing the same grin. Soul caught the exchange but avoided me when I looked back at him. He was clearly jealous and making very little effort to hide it.

Eighteen

After the crowd had cleared and we had walked back to the base, we met up with Chrissy, who had bandaged her head tightly, and sat down for a very late dinner.

"So how does it feel to finally come out on top after weeks of being screwed over?" she asked.

"I can't tell you how excited I am right now! I could scream!" I was bouncing in my seat, barely able to eat — and that's saying something.

"I need you to win for me, at least knock someone else out of the game for me … please?"

"Chrissy, we're going to knock them *all* out."

She bumped my fist and started to eat as fast as she could. I sat back and looked across the table at Soul. His worried green eyes looked nervously back at me.

"Hey, at least you guys'll be free of the twins for a while — "

"What did we ever do to them?" Juno and Beanie hopped over, making Soul jump and grind his teeth in annoyance. They sat on either side of him and rested their heads in their hands.

"What's up, lover boy?"

"Leave them alone, Bean. They forgot the cameras were on them," Chrissy said, her mouth full of food.

Juno burst into laughter. "If they forgot the cameras were on them I think we would have seen a lot more than that! Or didn't you see the way he was looking at her?"

The twins hooted and hollered as Soul's eyes went wide.

"Uh..." he stammered. His cheeks went pink. He slowly got up from his seat and started to walk to the fridge in the back. I sighed at the twins and turned back to Chrissy.

"They didn't mean anything by it. Aren't you going to go bring him back?" she asked.

"He's fine, just went to get a drink." I watched him as he bumped into Frankie. I doubt they would be too pleased with each other.

"Uh oh..." Bean whispered, making me turn around again. I prepared myself to run over and stop an argument, but Soul stepped back and put his head down. Frankie stayed silent a moment, then held out his hand to a surprised Crow. Soul cautiously shook his hand, and Frankie quietly congratulated him before walking back to Eloise and Jeremy. I kept an eye on him as I started to pay attention to the twins and Chris again. "So ... I have to ask," Juno started. "Was that a publicity stunt? Like, to get the crowd to sympathize with you?"

"Not that I'm aware of?" I scoffed at her, but she seemed honestly intrigued, along with Beanie. After a few moments, I shook my head and rubbed my eyes. "I'm just so confused."

"So that was real?! He wasn't faking?"

"Are you kidding me, Beanie? I don't think he's even capable of something that cruel," Chrissy snapped.

"I don't know ... I ... What if he was? I hate this, something about it feels wrong," I said weakly.

"Don't be scared that you have feelings for him. You *are* human," Chrissy said, trying to reassure me. I shook my head and looked down, jumping slightly as Soul sat down beside me. He radiated anxiety.

"M-mad ... at the bird?"

Glancing back up at my Crow, I shook my head. "Why would I be mad?"

"Did something ... wrong?"

I leaned against his shoulder and looked up to his eyes. "Never."

He smiled happily and held his hands in his lap.

"So … *why*, then?" Beanie flicked a grape at Soul, continuing to question us. Soul thought a moment, lightly touching his index finger against his lip before shrugging.

"Can someone give me a hand? Maybe a pellet gun!" a voice suddenly called from behind us.

We all turned to see Matt run in, shouting and waving a net around. The next thing I saw was feathers. Lots and lots of black feathers. I jumped back and grunted as the bird landed on Soul's shoulder, hitting me with his tail feathers and surprising us all.

I looked up at Matt, trying and failing to hold in a laugh. "What the heck…?"

"Don't even *ask*," Matt said.

"Can't be here," Soul told the bird. He cawed and tilted his little head back and forth. Soul shook his head and lifted him off, setting him on Matt's shoulder. "Go home, Lock."

The bird screeched in protest but allowed Matt to take him back outside.

"H-how did he even get in here?" I asked, struggling to breathe properly as I cackled at Matt's misfortune. Upon seeing his humourless scowl, the twins joined me. I pressed my hands over my face and shook my head. I was exhausted.

"Benji, you feeling okay?"

"I'm so tired, Chris." I was still laughing slightly and she shook her head.

"I'll walk you back to our rooms."

We got up and headed out of the cafeteria and back toward the dorms. She was quiet until we were out of earshot of everyone else.

"So…?" She nudged my arm and grinned ear to ear.

"What?"

"Tell me, what's going on with you and him?"

My eyes rolled back in my head and a groan escaped me. "Not much."

I side-eyed her and she gave a wild smile. "Have you kissed him?"

I turned my head fully and scowled. "Really?"

"I was just wondering… Have you ever even kissed *anyone*?" She pursed her lips and shoved her hands into her pockets.

With a tired sigh of exasperation, I tossed my arms to my sides. "Yes, Chrissy. I have done a *lot* more than that."

My scowl decided to remain in place long after a yawn that interrupted my friend's rambling.

"Okay, but has *he*?" she asked.

I had to think for a moment. I doubted it, but it was possible. Soul really didn't seem like he would have recently, but he might have had someone before this whole ordeal.

"I'm not sure," I responded.

"Maybe you'll be the first."

"I don't see how that would matter. Now please stop telling me things that will keep me up; I really need sleep right now. Good night."

I pushed my door open and closed it before she could say another word and make things worse.

I didn't need that.

I did not sleep at all that night, and it was clear I wasn't going to sleep for the next couple weeks. The day kept playing out again and again in my head. I couldn't get the image of that room where Soul had been attacked out of my mind. I had to get up in the middle of the night and go researching, out of curiosity. I trusted Soul to tell me whatever he could, but I also knew what Jekyll and Hyde were capable of, and I wanted to know exactly what happened. All I knew was that they had attacked him with a pipe and razor wire…

I had gotten out of bed around 3 a.m. and sat down at my dusty old desktop. Pulling up the search engine, I started typing in the names of everyone involved with what had happened: Jekyll, Hyde, Dan, and Soul — at the time, Absolom.

I watched old fights of theirs, some of which were brutal. Soul, or Absolom, was a little monster. He was only about twenty-two. He still looked like a kid. He was fast and stealthy, able to go unnoticed until he swung his baseball bat or whatever he could get his grubby hands on. In every video I found, he would make a plan with Dan; then they would go after their opponents. At the end, he would gloat a little bit but still look for Dan's approval.

It almost made me sad to know how much he would end up hating Dan.

My eyes were starting to water from staring at the screen for so long, but I wasn't ready to quit. The last video I pulled up was them against Jekyll and Hyde. Dan still had long, greasy, blond hair and barely any scars. Soul had a short mohawk and a terrified look, in contrast to his usual smirk. Dan ruffled his hair and they called for the battle to start.

They were doing so well! I kept thinking there was no way that this was when it happened … and then Soul was knocked to the ground and Jekyll hit him with the pipe. After a blow to the head, Hyde joined his brother, whipping Soul with the razor wire. There was blood everywhere, and Soul desperately tried to claw his way to safety, pinning himself against a barrier. In the corner of the screen Dan was scrambling towards the exit… I knew how it was going to happen but still.

Soul was screaming in agony and fear. He called for Dan as blood ran down his face and neck, staining his shirt and the ground. Kicking at Hyde, he was trying to keep him at a distance. He cried out again as Hyde dragged him away from his hiding spot and into the centre of the warehouse.

Soul's eyes met Dan's and he mouthed an apology as he ran out. Soul screamed his name and kicked out, but Jekyll kept beating and Hyde kept whipping him.

Dan didn't come back.

None of the people watching wanted to get involved. I couldn't blame them but someone, anyone, should have stopped them. The back of Soul's head was bleeding badly; the blood didn't stop. The gashes on his arms and chest were wide open. I recognized some of those scars. He was unconscious as Hyde rolled him over with his boot and dropped the wire across his face, stepping on it and forming the most noticeable scar on his body, the scar running down his cheek and across his neck.

I felt sick to my stomach and delirious with sleep deprivation. I wish I had never seen that. Curiosity didn't kill the cat but it sure did break the dog's heart. Sighing, I rested my head on the desk. Some people think heartbreak is only metaphorical, but from the pain — no, the *hollowness* in my chest — I had to disagree.

Nineteen

I lost all hope of fighting my way out as I looked up into dark grey eyes. He was easily about a foot taller than me. I was just a kid… Why did I think I could do this? A whimper escaped me as I dropped my little knife and started backing up. I was facing two very large men and I was on my own.

I can fight … I'm pretty good for not having any formal training! But I don't think I can fight them.

"I q-quit! You win!"

A loud laugh rang out from the one with slicked hair. I could feel the panic building in my stomach and started to turn the other way. Pain seared into my head and I hit the ground… Tears burned my eyes. I'm only a kid! I'm so stupid and I'm going to die here!

"P-please! I just want to go home!" *I sobbed as I heard one of the men walk over. I pressed my hands over my head and pulled my legs to my chest. I screamed as my long hair was yanked back and I had to stand.* "Hyde? Do what you want with her."

I fearfully turned my head to see one pull a camera out of a man's hand and start filming as the razor wire was draped across my chest and around my arms.

"I said I quit! P-please leave me alone! Why are you doing this?"

I heard a laugh from the one behind me. "Relax, Vixen … it will hurt less if you relax."

It felt like my heart stopped as he viciously tugged the wire back, slicing through my arms and chest. He continued to pull harder and harder as I screamed and shrieked and bled and cried. I struggled as hard as I could, tears falling from my eyes as my muscles tensed, and my voice started to feel like it was on fire. I was trying as hard as I could to break free but I couldn't. The feeling in my stomach was indescribable; I felt like it was tensing and like I was going to drop dead at any moment. I could feel the burn of every razor across my chest and over my ribs. I was being torn apart like a pig in a slaughterhouse.

I lost feeling in my hands as the blood poured over me and the ground.

"Henry! Johnny!"

My voice cracked and I was suddenly out of breath. Every inch of me was shaking from one feeling or another. Oh god, oh god, oh god ... I'm going to die!

I cried out again, pathetically, more like a whimper than anything. I'm dying at nineteen... I'm a kid; I never even got to fall in love!

I could feel a boot pressing into my back, making the wire cut into my bones. The blood covered me, my hair, and was probably spraying out onto the demon behind me. My head hung, but I looked up long enough to see the crowd gasping and muttering.

"Let her go!" *I heard Henry shout. I silently pleaded for him not to get involved.*

"Not today, boy-o."

I heard a loud shot, then a thump. "Henry!" *My brother called out.* "No! No no no. H-He's dead, you freaks!"

I cried out again and started shaking uncontrollably. Is ... is this what having your heart broken feels like?

I hit the ground and lay still as I sobbed. I feel broken ... and words couldn't describe the feeling sitting in my stomach. Suddenly, Johnny hollered in pain and I shut my eyes, biting my lip. This is not defeat ... this is death.

"Let's go, Hyde."

"We're done here, Jekyll." Two Irish accents conversed happily.

Dirt and dust hit my face and I wept openly. My best friend is dead ... and my brother wasn't moving either.

"Johnny! I'm sorry! Henry ... I'm so, so sorry!"

Twenty

Someone was shaking my shoulder roughly. I sat up, groaning and holding my stomach in both arms. I started to feel tears roll down my cheek and I squeezed my eyes shut tightly.

"I'm so sorry," I whispered again. I felt my throat catch, my shoulders heaved a few times, and I slowly, shakily wiped my hands over my cheeks.

"K-K9?" Soul looked down at me with wide eyes.

My heart dropped and I was sent into a panic. What if it happens to *him*? What if I had to relive that moment when I lost one of the people who meant the most to me? I didn't let myself feel like that anymore. I fought harder — dirtier. I never let myself love anyone after that. My first reaction was to spin around in my chair and drag Soul into my arms. I shook my head as I tangled my fingers in his hair and pressed my face into his neck. I couldn't let it happen again.

My dishevelled friend hesitantly let out a breath and slid his arms around my waist. I kept both hands wrapped around his neck as I pulled my elbows closer to me and tried to keep my lip from shaking.

I was *afraid*.

For the first time in a long time, I was afraid. Not something I'd truly felt since that day. I was afraid of losing a friend, someone I care about, but no one had to know.

I finally managed to calm my breathing again and leaned away from Soul. His hair was still flat and messy from sleeping on it, and there was far more worry in his expression than I had ever seen before. His top lip stuck out as he patiently waited for an explanation.

"Promise me ... promise me that you'll be okay. That no matter what, you're not going to let me ... that you won't let me down?" I could feel my voice crack and swallowed down a lump in my throat. I looked into his eyes. His expression changed from concern to sympathy.

"Promise."

Exhaling, I looked down and ran a hand through my damp hair. I closed my eyes again and tried to shake the image of Henry getting shot, only to have it replaced with an image of Johnny lying in the hospital.

I whimpered again; I would never be able to get those out of my head…

My cheek tingled as Soul's soft hand grazed my skin. I looked forward and he tilted his head. Taking a deep breath, I shook my head. He tilted his head the other way, giving me a small smile.

"Who…?" Soul started.

I smiled softly to myself. "Henry was my partner. He died because of me. W-we were kids and I — I can't let it happen again. I grew up and lost everything all in one day … night. But I'm not the same person I was. I'm not a stupid, innocent kid anymore! I couldn't kill them, Soul. I froze up, and it's not fair! I have to pay them back for what they took from me."

I grimaced sadly and wiped my face again. "Johnny… Well, I hoped you would meet him."

I looked up at him once again and his beautiful, sad green eyes stared back curiously. He suddenly nodded, but his mouth stayed fixed in that little pout of his, slowly turning into a gentle smile as he ran his hand over my hair.

"Can we see him today?" I felt like a child asking permission to go to the park. It's silly, I know, but I didn't want to force him. He nodded vigorously and smiled brightly. My mood was lifted and I sent him off to clean up, then got in the shower myself.

I didn't want to even try eating today, but I sat down with Soul nonetheless. The cafeteria was almost empty. My mood was still low but I didn't want to drag anyone down. It's not their problem and no one should have to know, so I put up a smile and leaned on my hand as I watched Soul happily munch on his toast.

"Don't fake … don't like fake," he mumbled with his mouth full.

"I'm not." I reassured him as a true smile tugged my mouth up my cheeks. "I feel better now."

I was telling myself more than him but he still gave a disapproving look, making me quiet down a little bit and look downwards.

"Thank you," I whispered.

His tilted his head and gave me a confused look, which was really kind of adorable and hard to take seriously with his cheeks puffing out like a chipmunk.

"For waking me up earlier," I explained. "That was… I don't want to live it again."

He swallowed what was in his mouth and shook his head. "D-don't thank! The bird was … worried."

He stopped for a moment, obviously thinking. "Bird's been alone for so long … *so long*."

"You aren't alone anymore, Soul." I smiled softly at him.

"F-forgot what it was like…" He started to shake his head and mumble to himself.

"I've been meaning to ask you," I said.

He threw his head up to look at me.

"Do you have any family? *Someone* had to be worried about you."

He slowly shook his head, heaving a sigh. "Left. Warn — warned him. Said, 'Don't fight, Absolom, you'll get hurt. If you fight you'll never see us again'… and he didn't. H-he said he'd be fine but they left… He was lonely. Still go home, *want* to go home… No home anymore. The bird is not welcome … and they were right." He bit his lip and his brow creased as he gave a worried look, staying far away from my eyes.

"That's why you go to the little apartment on the abandoned side of town? You grew up there?" I asked.

"*He* did."

"It's been a long time. Maybe they've changed their minds. No matter how long it's been, you're family. They're probably worried sick. Up until last week, they probably thought you were dead. They'll feel bad about telling Absolom he couldn't come home if he fought, trust me." I grabbed his hand and he nodded. We just sat there for a while; the room was quiet.

"He has a sister."

I spun to see Dan standing behind me.

"She was five when he left," he continued.

Standing, I gritted my teeth. "Who asked you?"

"Hey, do you think *he* would have told you?" Dan growled back.

Soul had his gaze fixed on the floor below him. I knew the emptiness he must have felt in his chest, the numbness in his hands… We've all felt it at some point. I almost couldn't blame him, given how I'd been treating my only family lately.

"Thanks, Dan! That was really helpful!" Dan shouted mockingly, doing a terrible impression of my voice as he walked away. I could feel my cheek twitch slightly as I watched him go.

"Tina…" Soul muttered as I turned back to him. He hadn't moved. "His sister's name was Tina. *Tiny Tina* … always smaller than the other kids. Absolom had to protect her, he … he worried so much…" He started to tear up and buried his hands in his hair.

"She misses her brother. You might not be Absolom anymore, but you're still her family." I thought of my own brother as I grabbed his hands. "Little girls will always worry about their brothers. No matter what."

He nodded but refused to look at me.

"You should see her. Tell her you miss her and that you're okay."

He nodded and opened his mouth to say something, waiting until his lip stopped shaking to speak. "B-but…"

He had to pause and breathe so I finished his thought. "Your parents?"

"Mother."

"I'll do the talking if you want. I just don't want you to leave without seeing her."

Soul nodded and faintly brightened as I pulled him to his feet. We grabbed our jackets.

The air was crisp. Snow might fall any day now. Soul didn't seem bothered by it, but I tightly hugged my chest and shivered.

"Where to?" he suddenly asked.

I shrugged to myself, then looked around. Johnny was probably done with his physical therapy by now so we could head there, but Soul probably wanted to get his visit over with.

"Where ever you want — "

"To meet Johnny?"

Giving a hoot of joy, I nodded and started walking. "Okay, he lives this way."

I got to the door of a relatively nice house, but before I even had a chance to knock, it opened, revealing the smiling face of my brother. I hardly had a chance to say hello before he dragged me into a bone-crushing hug.

"Ugh! Can't … breathe…"

"Sorry!" He muttered as he let me go and grinned. "I can't believe my little sister got into the tournament!"

I turned to look at Soul. He seemed surprised and a bit relieved, probably recognizing Johnny as the lanky man I waved to as we were celebrating yesterday. He chuckled as he let his head fall back.

"Brother," he muttered as he started to smile.

"What? Were you jealous?" Johnny asked.

Soul dodged the question by shaking his head and holding out his hand.

"Johnny, this is Soul — "

"Yeah, I got that much. I want to know the story behind this. Get in here. It's freezing!"

I pulled Soul into the doorway by his jacket, following my brother down the hall. His limp was still very prominent — he'd never fight again — but it was nice to see him walking at all. He did still have to use crutches sometimes, though. They were currently lying on the floor in the living room. He had a habit of tripping over them, even though he had been using them for almost ten years.

"I know you, Benjamina. Your moral compass may not always point north but you are not a bad person."

I grimaced. What was he talking about?

"So please tell me, for the love of everything that is good — including pie — that you didn't fall into that whole reality TV game. Tell me you weren't faking a story with him, and please tell me that you weren't acting out there at that warehouse."

I sighed and plopped onto a couch that was covered in stuffed animals, preparing to tell him our story.

About an hour later, my thin brother was sitting in shock and his chocolatey brown eyes were wide.

"This is bad. Everyone thinks that *you* were the ones who were in the wrong. Do you need any help with anything?"

I thought a moment and shrugged. "I don't know — "

"Yes."

I glanced at Soul. The crow-like man had a determined look on his face and jitters in his hands.

"Media... K9 can't do it *and* fight in the tournament."

I scowled but my brother nodded. "Ordinarily I would tell you not to underestimate her but I think you're right. You need someone on your side to tell the world what actually happened and to dispute what they say happened. I'll do a press release tomorrow if I can get permission."

"Thank you, Johnny." I stopped and thought about when Jekyll broke his spine. "For everything."

"You're my sister. I've looked after you since you were three. Even if we've been distant, it's always going to be my job." He cast a sad smile towards me as he sat back in his chair, petting a stuffed dog.

"No, I mean for *everything*. It's my fault but I'm never going to let it happen again, to anyone."

He smiled and shook his head. "You've changed so much ... but you're still my little girl."

My heart sank, but I smiled anyway. I've disappointed him by becoming a fighter, ignored his calls out of guilt, but still he's so supportive, so happy that I'm getting to compete. I'm not going to disappoint him again. I'm going to finish it.

"You know, until I met Soul, I was so carefree. I was able to go about my day without any problems. But now I remember that I can't forget my emotions. That I'll need them for when the time comes." I pinched his leg and he yelped. "I'm going to fix everything."

Johnny rested his chin across his fingers and tilted his head. "Yeah, I like this ... whatever *this* is. Keep her safe, Soul. I like you. I don't want to have to get rid of you."

"And there's the brotherly love," I joked.

We laughed together for a moment. I only realized now how similar we sound.

"Where's Skipper?" I asked.

"He's out with Rory, doing his rounds. I'm sure you'll see him around at some point," Johnny assured me. Skipper is our dog. He does therapy with Johnny, and he's become a good companion for him since the incident. Johnny rarely goes out anymore.

"We should go now — " I paused and reached behind me, something poking into my back. I pulled out a small stuffed bird. "Hey! I remember you!"

Johnny chuckled quietly. "I kept meaning to give that to you. Corbin's been sitting on my couch for years, just collecting dust. Maybe you can put him to good use."

I nodded. "I think I can. I'll see you later, Johnny."

"I love you, Ben. Be good, Soul…" Johnny pointed to him and squinted as we left the room.

Closing the door behind us, we started walking to the end of the little lane. "Where to?"

Soul gave a frustrated sigh and grabbed my hand as he led me to his sister's house. I looked down at the stuffed animal. Corbin was a little crow. I used to fall asleep with him sitting at the end of my bed. I always liked to think that he and Bernie, a little stuffed dog I used to have, were best friends. I still had Bernie.

I stumbled a bit and looked at the ground; a good deal of snow had fallen while we were with Johnny. Groaning and scowling, I had to pull my legs up higher, snow still sticking to the fur on the top of my boots.

"Cold?"

I shook my head. "Annoyed more than anything."

He tugged on my hand and I stumbled closer to him. I noticed him smile contently but he still looked nervous. The fur of the stuffed animal tickled my fingers, and I gave it one last look before I held it up for Soul to take.

"Give it to your sister. I don't need it anymore."

He hesitantly took it with shaking fingers and stopped walking long enough to hold it with both hands and smile. "A crow."

"So she can still be close to her brother — "

I was cut off by the call of that exact bird. I looked up to see Lock circling above us. He dropped down to the ground quickly and started rolling around in the snow before getting up to look at us. He cawed and hopped up to Soul's shoulder, blinking, then tilting his little head.

I petted his neck and he stuck his black beak out. "We won't be here much longer, little bird."

Soul nodded and scratched the bird's head. Lock leaned into Soul's cheek and then crowed again and flew off to the northwest.

"You don't think he knows…" I hesitantly asked.

"Not possible…" Soul tried to tell himself.

I know these birds are smart, but I don't think he *knows* where a place is by name. Maybe humans aren't the only ones that've evolved…

Twenty-One

Soul held the stuffed animal tightly. He sighed and looked at me, seemingly for reassurance. I touched his cheek with a frozen hand and he closed his eyes, nodding as if he knew what I was thinking. Smiling softly, I rubbed his cheek and then shoved my hand into my pocket and followed him to a door. He muttered to himself as he kneaded the toy, then finally built up the courage to knock. After a few moments, he violently shook his head and whipped around, trying to rush past me. I quickly stepped in front of him and crossed my arms, raising an eyebrow.

"S-scared…"

I could feel my expression soften and I sighed. "I know, but this is important."

The door opened and he slowly turned around, hunching over slightly, like a wounded puppy. The bird was still held tightly in both hands as he looked curiously at the woman who opened the door. His lip shook and I put my hand on his shoulder, making him jump slightly. The woman looked tired, but when she examined Soul's features, her hand shot to her mouth and she gasped, having to grab the door frame for support.

"A-Absolom…?"

He bit his lip and offered a nervous smile. "Y-you were … right…" he told her quietly.

"We thought you were dead. I'm sorry, I'm so sorry! It's my fault! I should have never said that you couldn't come home — it's been seven years, boy!"

I nearly had to laugh at the range of emotions running over the woman's face, but I stopped myself as she roughly pulled him into a hug and held him there with a hand on the back of his neck.

"We saw you in the tournament... Tina didn't seem to register that it was you. They didn't call you by your first name either."

He debated something in his head and then stuttered, "N-not Absolom... K9?"

I stepped forward as she released him. He put his head down, looking a little bit sick.

"Absolom? Are you okay? Talk to me..." she begged.

He looked sad and tried to swallow his nerves as he struggled to speak. His voice cracked and he looked like he was ready to have a breakdown again. "C-can't — don't s-speak ... *K9!*" He cried out my name and rubbed the side of his head as he closed his eyes and bit his lip, breaths coming in heaves.

"Soul ... it's okay, just breathe."

He nodded and tried to steady himself, still whimpering.

"Mrs. Ravin, my name is Benji..."

"Yes, I know, my daughter is a fan — why won't he talk to me?"

I looked down, thinking about how to explain it. He started to wring his hands.

"Trying!" his voice cracked again.

"When he was twenty-two, he was in a battle against — "

"Those two men, what were they called? Jekyll and Hyde?"

I nodded. "That ... *bloodbath* left him with brain damage. He has a hard time pronouncing what he means to say sometimes."

"I thought he died that day..."

Soul held the stuffed animal to his face and nodded. His mother, who was a thin and fragile woman, gently touched his face. He squeezed his eyes shut, his tears gently spilling over her skin.

"We missed you, Absolom..."

He shook his head. "Not Absolom…"

"He's changed his name," I told her. "He has too much history associated with that name. He prefers Soul."

She looked nervous for a moment, but her aged face softened and she even laughed. "Tina used to call him that; she couldn't say his full name. Come inside, would you? It's freezing."

As we hesitantly followed her, his mother closed the door behind us and then held him at arm's length.

"My little boy…" She started to cry as she shakily touched his cheek, moving his hair back to see the scar down his face. Her voice caught as she sobbed, but he wouldn't meet her eyes. He just kept staring at the floor and kneading his bird.

"A — Soul … I never should have said what I did."

He shook his head. "B-but he was wrong… The boy was wrong and you were right. Never should have fought because he lost the fight." He looked back up at his mother and she pursed her lips as tears fell.

"I love you so much. We thought … we thought you were dead."

Soul shook his head.

"Why didn't you come home? Why didn't you come see your sister, to let her know you were okay? She watched all of your battles. We both did."

Soul looked at me with sad eyes, sadder now more than ever.

"T-told him … told him he couldn't come home! Told him he wasn't… 'Not my son, not my boy. You leave, you never come back. You can't ever see her again.' Told him you didn't love him! Told him he was nothing to love!" Soul cried out and quickly bit his lip to stop himself from falling apart.

It didn't work and I had to try as hard as I could not to jump in. And I didn't, not until he brushed past and tried to open the door. I roughly grabbed his jacket and hauled him back, causing him to stumble. He looked at me as though I had just refused his dying wish. His expression changed a second later and he started to tug at his hair. Both he and his mother were falling apart at the seams, faces stained with tears and hair sticking to their foreheads.

His shoulders shook and he started to zone out.

"Soul, Soul! Hey, it's okay... You're okay now."

"B-but ... not — not welcome here ... not anymore." He grabbed my wrists, placing my hands on his cheeks.

"Yes, you are. I was awful to you, and if you left again it would be my kingdom come," his mother said.

After meeting his mother, I had a feeling that *letting* him leave again would be *my* kingdom come.

He turned to look at her and she gently touched his hair again.

"My little boy isn't little anymore."

Soul nodded and inhaled, calming down a bit.

"I really wish you had come home... Where did you go?"

He shrugged. "Home."

She looked at me.

"An abandoned apartment building," I explained.

"We lived there before he left. You weren't alone, right? Tell me you had someone ... anyone?" She looked at me again and I slowly shook my head.

"M-met K9 a month ago..." he stated quietly.

"That's nearly seven years of being alone, boy!" she interrupted, smacking him on the shoulder.

He jumped away and grabbed my hand. I struggled to hide my laughter, and he scowled at me. She sighed and hugged him again. He closed his eyes and smiled back softly.

"S-seen the battle?" he asked her.

She wiped her face and nodded proudly.

"Every second." She winked at me and I immediately looked away, pretending not to have seen. My cheeks burned but I tried to ignore it. Unfortunately, she wouldn't let me fade away into the background as she now directed her full attention to me.

"You are a far better warrior than I knew." Her features seemed to soften. "I've seen you before; his little sister, Tina, is a huge fan. She knows all about you. You're very good. Keep him in line, won't you?"

"I'll try, but lately it's been the other way around," I admitted.

She tilted her head, looking very much like an older and more feminine version of Soul. "That's odd," she said, looking at Soul. "He was always an unruly child. Danny needed to look after him. How is he? Do you still talk?"

I grimaced as Soul tried not to twitch his cheek.

"Well ... they don't... " I sighed and thought a moment.

"Traitor ... his fault," Soul grunted.

I nodded, as did his mother.

"I always knew that boy was going to be bad news."

I watched the woman shake her head as she motioned for us to follow her into the backyard. Soul had to duck under decorations and ribbons hanging from the ceiling as we followed his mother back into the cold.

"Tina, I'm making hot chocolate. Come inside, we have company."

A small voice shouted back, "Okay, mama!"

I looked around the small yard. There were snow angels and snowmen all over the place. You could tell a child played there. I had to admire her dedication; the snow had only been on the ground for an hour or so.

"T-Tina?" Soul's soft voice asked as a tiny girl jumped out from behind a snowman.

She stopped and stared at him and he offered a nervous smile. The next thing I knew, snow was flying into my face and he was lying on the ground with his little sister sitting on top of his chest and hugging him tightly.

"I knew you would come back! I knew it! I missed you so much, Soul!"

He laughed as he sat up and pushed her back enough to look at her. If she was only five when he left, she had to be about eleven or twelve now ... but she was so small! She was so small for her age, "Tiny Tina" seemed like almost a cruel nickname. Soul happily patted her head and stood up, keeping her in his arms. She leaned into his shoulder and started to play with his hair.

"E-everyone said you were dead. I was scared that it was true … but I saw you on TV! I saw you save Benji from those mean guys! And — and at the battle… I don't like them but you beat them!"

She was so happy to see her brother, until she spoke again. "Soul? Why were you gone for so long? I waited for you to come home every day."

He looked down and I watched the smile slip from his face. His sister put a tiny hand on either side of his face and pouted.

"You have a new scar."

He nodded sadly and she traced it down his neck.

"You look different," she concluded.

Grimacing, he slid the back door open, stepping back into the warmth. The temperature change was enough to shoot a pain through my ears and cheeks as I closed it behind me and followed him over to the kitchen table.

"I don't really recognize you," she told him again. "Why won't you talk to me? It's been so long!"

He closed his eyes and a small smile took over his face. "Sometimes," he started softly, "people change."

His mother was watching from the counter, looking star-struck. I walked over to her and stood quietly beside her.

"He was her hero," she told me. "He would always have to look out for her because she was so small. Her sight has always been impaired and she stumbles a lot, so he would carry her around on his shoulders."

"He doesn't really talk about her, though. I understand that he didn't think he would ever see her again," I replied.

"Thank you for forcing him to come back … if not for me, then at least for Tina."

"Don't thank me. He needs her; she seems very loving and he needs that."

"How long have you been looking after him?"

I thought for a moment. "It's been a little over a month."

She chuckled and handed me a cup of tea. "A lot must have happened then. He really does care for you, you know. He was never one to throw his affection around willy-nilly."

I brushed away her comment with a light laugh, then followed her to the table. The four of us sat down. Tina made herself comfortable on Soul's lap.

"You look different. You were shorter and … spikier before." Tina put her hands in Soul's hair and gave her best attempt at untangling it.

"I've tried that, kiddo. We're going to need a brush and two bottles of conditioner in order to straighten *that* out," I said.

She looked at me, startled. Her black hair framed her perfectly white skin — even paler than Soul's — and her eyes widened. "Y-you…!"

I smiled and took a sip of tea.

Once she stopped staring, she looked back at Soul, slapping both his cheeks and pressing her forehead to his. "Why didn't you tell me she was with you?!"

He stared back in shock and a grin tugged at my cheeks.

"You are amazing! I've seen all of your work!"

She said it as though I was some sort of artist, which was laughable at best.

"I've been working with your brother lately —"

"Oh, I know! I saw the tournament!"

She struggled to control her emotions but eventually calmed down and looked back to Soul, braiding a piece of the front of his hair. "Do you really…?" She looked at us expectantly, nudging her head in my direction.

He tilted his head and looked at me, both of our cheeks turning pink. He looked down for a moment and I could feel my heart beat in my throat. Then a smile pulled at his cheeks and he nodded. I calmed down again and looked at my tea as I grinned.

"That is so cute," she whispered, drawing out the "cute" for far longer than she needed to. Her eyes were practically bulging out of her head as she bit her lip, grinning. After a moment she calmed down again and stared at her brother. "Why do you look so different? And why won't you talk to me? Mama doesn't tell me stories like you did. She doesn't know the warriors and she won't do voices…"

There was a look of pain on his face. He wouldn't be able to tell stories anymore. He took a minute to put words together, mouthing a few, then shaking his head.

"Hair got longer, joined too many fights, legs got longer, and seen all new sights." He mumbled as he tilted his head and petted her hair again. "C-can't … speak well anymore. Scars … don't go away, barely fade. Don't … don't know how to look or dress. I'm no princess." He smiled and poked her nose.

My friend had very pointed features, but his sister looked much more delicate with her very round nose and small bones. Like a life-size china doll.

"G-got hurt… Can't talk." He looked at me, then debated something again. "Trying… It's hard. D-don't know what to — how to… Don't know." He sighed and shrugged. "Best I can. Remember the stories … only … can't tell them… Little Tina, C-Crow is sorry. So, *so* sorry…"

My brow was set in a worried fashion and I watched him bite his lip. Of all the people this could happen to, it happens to someone who truly doesn't deserve it.

"You're my brother. You were gone for a really long time. I missed you so much." She hugged him again, little arms barely reaching fully around his neck. "Don't say sorry."

He laughed despite the tears in his eyes and hugged her back. His smile was still so innocent, and the world hadn't seen it enough. I shook my head and looked back at my tea, swirling the mug in my hand and sighing.

"K-K9 got this…" He handed the stuffed bird to her and she held it out in front of her, examining it.

I chose that moment to speak up again. "His name is Corbin. I got him when I was your age. There's a legend that says crows were the advisors to the gods and to native tribes. Look for him if you get worried or lonely."

She hopped off his lap, walked around the table, and threw her arms around me.

"Secretly, I think it kind of looks like him," she whispered to me.

I grinned and nodded. "I've got to agree with you on that one!"

She stared at her new friend as she walked back over to Soul. His bright green eyes followed her and I turned to their mother. "I have to ask, where do the green eyes come from?"

"I've wondered that for years; his father had brown eyes like me."

I talked with his mother for a while as Tina told Soul all about her life. It was nice until my pager started to go off. Getting to my feet, I clicked the button to answer the message. It wasn't exactly a pager as much as a walkie-talkie I could turn off, which was nice because the alarm sounded like a siren.

I left the room quickly and picked it up.

"*Ben, we got a problem!*"

"Dan? What's going on? Why are you so out of breath?"

"*Someone went through your room! Soul's office was trashed and his tech was torched. We're trying to put it out, but we have no idea what's going on!*"

"I'm on my way back."

I clicked the button and burst back into the other room. "Soul, I don't want to drag you away, but the base is out of control. We've got to go."

I grabbed my jacket off the chair and ran out the door. I wasn't going to wait for Soul. He needed time to say a proper goodbye. A moment later, however, he was at my side, dodging people and buildings.

Once we got to the gate, I cursed under my breath and pushed past security upon seeing the smoke still hanging in the air. Soul moved as fast as he could, pushing me to the side in order to get to his office. There were people standing around talking about the damage. It was chaos. It seemed that Jekyll and Hyde had been in the arena all day, but I knew that Dr. Frankenstein — Viktor — was still behind it. I wondered who he manipulated into doing his dirty work this time.

Groaning, I clutched my stomach as I stood in the doorway. I really did have to start hitting the treadmill. Soul was desperately attempting to recover some of his tech, but the entire room was scorched. After regaining some of my breath, I stood up and walked into the room.

"No! L-lost ... *everything!*" Soul hollered as he picked up a speaker.

I sidestepped to the left just seconds before it hit the wall beside me, just like when we met, only this time the speaker smashed into about five pieces. Grunting slightly as a piece hit my arm, I brushed away some dirt, then looked back up at a very angry warrior.

"No more proof... Can't — can't prove it was the gemini!"

"The correspondence between you and Frankenstein is lost, but we have solid evidence that they didn't get! Besides, after the tournament, we're going to out them for good and they'll confess; they've already admitted to working for Frankenstein!" I reassured him.

"Frankenstein ... Viktor ... the letters! N-now ... gone!" He continued to shout, even punching the wall a few times, twisting his wrist in the process. I was going to try to tell him again that we had more evidence, but the anger in his face startled me. I wouldn't want to get in his way right now. He pushed past me and snatched a camera. I shrugged and followed my partner down the hall.

"*Hell to pay!*" he shouted and cursed as he darted through the locker room, grabbing his axe, and then bursting into the arena. I panicked for a moment, then grabbed one sword from my locker and followed him.

We got to the gate and he knocked Jeremy off his feet, then swung at Angel with one hand. It took a great deal of strength to be able to lift the axe at all, let alone with one hand; his adrenalin was pumping and he was angry. He fiddled with the camera to turn it on; then he held it up, setting it so it would broadcast his message live.

"Burned my evidence ... destroyed my equipment. The Beauty works for the doctor! The Beauty is against all of us! Gemini..." he paused and kicked Angel while she was down, sweat dripping from his nose. "Gemini will burn!"

I was frozen in place as he spoke and again kicked my former roommate.

"Gemini ... caused the problem... Gemini work for the doctor... Take this as a message, *boys*! Take this as a warning that if you continue to hurt and bleed and *scar*, you ... will ... *burn*..."

He tossed the camera on the ground and crushed it under his boot. I knew I had to move quickly but I only started to walk. Stress tugged at my stomach as I watched him heave his axe out in front of him, then onto his shoulder. I gradually picked up speed as he raised it above his head. As I reached them, I flung my sword out over Angel, calling out and falling to one knee as I narrowly stopped the axe.

Crow stepped back and stared at me, both angry and surprised.

I silently watched him as he shook his head, raising his axe again and trying to go after Angel once more. She screamed and tried to crawl away. I jabbed at him, but he dodged to the left and wrapped the handle of his weapon over my neck as he stepped behind me. I was forced to drop my sword as I grabbed at his arms, using one hand to pry his weapon away from my throat.

"Soul, don't do this!" I shouted as I gasped for air.

"Need to send a message... Need to show them we're stronger!"

"Soul, we're the good guys! We..." I suddenly got light headed and slipped back, resting against his chest.

"K9 ... is wrong ... become a bigger monster than the one you're fighting... R-right?"

I shook my head slowly, then let my head roll to the side. "No, we need to show them. We're not going to kill an innocent woman."

I felt his hair brush against my cheek as he put his head down and shook it.

"Not innocent. Not going to leave unpunished..." He rubbed his nose on my cheek, and I continued to push the axe away from my neck. "*Sorry* ... my K9."

He quickly dropped me to the ground, then bolted back towards Angel. Yes, she was a traitor, but she wasn't as bad as Jekyll and Hyde. She didn't deserve to die. I pushed myself to my feet and tackled Soul to the ground. I straddled his middle and leaned over him, digging my nails into his wrist and hoping to make him let go of his axe.

"Listen to reason! We don't need the evidence. We can't just kill her!"

He gritted his teeth and let go of his weapon. I wheezed slightly as I consciously slowed my breathing. My arms still felt weak.

"No!"

Soul started to struggle and easily reversed our positions as he shouted at me. I turned my head to the side as he rambled, "K-K9 might... No, not possible. Maybe ... dog ... needs to pay, needs to pay. *Hell*! Hell to pay, no angels. Not here!"

I chanced a look back up at him, worry plain on my face.

"C-can't... They all think the bird is a monster anyway. Just want justice..." His lip quivered and his raspy voice cracked. "J-just want to be good enough! Teach them a lesson!"

"Then embrace it! If they all think we're dangerous, we're going to be! We're going to fight as hard as we can — as hard as we *have to* — in order to win! Once people have made up their minds, we can't change what they think. Let's prove to them that they *should* be afraid of us. But if they're already afraid, then we don't have to make it worse. We'll wear their masks if they make us, if that's what it takes, but there is still a line."

"No... There's no angels, only monsters and demons... Some not as bad as others?"

I shook my head and softly smiled. "Exactly, and monsters like *us*, the not-so-bad ones, don't leave collateral damage."

He wiped his nose against his shoulder, then looked back down at me. My arms were still pinned above my head, and I was still partially out of breath. Slowly, he removed his grip and sat back, allowing me to sit up.

"You are good enough."

"A-angry…," he muttered to the ground, a look of frustration playing on his thin face. "And … *scared…*"

I gave a small sigh and draped my arm over his shoulders. "Yeah, me too."

He looked startled as he twisted his neck to look at me.

I inhaled deeply and shook my head. "I don't know what we're going to do. I'm kind of scared too."

He nodded slowly and leaned against me.

"For now, we should focus on the tournament. That was our goal from the beginning, right?"

Soul nodded and helped me to my feet. I walked over to where I had dropped my sword and picked it up as Angel glared. A grim chuckle left my lips as I started to scowl back. I pointed at her. "Don't think this means you're off the hook."

Twenty-Two

I was starting to stress about how we were going to prove Soul's innocence.

Some of the locals didn't seem too happy that the man who had been attacking their favourite warriors was now one of them, and the warriors were still pretty cranky themselves. Obviously, *we* knew what happened, but how could we prove it? We knew that Jekyll and Hyde were the ones enforcing Dr. Frankenstein's requests. We also knew that anyone who potentially worked for him — No… There was no way.

I was sitting beside Soul and across from Chrissy at our usual table in the cafeteria as my face drained of colour.

"That … that can't be right."

"K9?"

I turned to Soul, disappointment written on my face "W-were they all involved?"

My hands shook but I had to laugh, mainly out of disbelief. "Randy, Ronin, Jeremy, Robert — that new reporter — and Jekyll and Hyde all have code names based off of old monsters from either books or movies, right? They're also all favourites of the boss."

Both of my co-workers shared a look, then shot their focus back at me.

"If anyone caused a problem, Ronin would be pitted against them as punishment. Randy has been caught sabotaging Jeff's kits, but he was never punished for it. Jeremy is a complete suck-up, though I don't think that worked in his favour. Robert has been put in charge of any media coverage involving this city, and Louis used to be put in charge of making sure all the favourite warriors got proper medical treatment," I explained.

"Think about it." I bit my lip as my hands continued to shake. "Who were the only four people to have taken part in every qualifying battle three years in a row?"

Chrissy silently nodded, and Soul clenched his fist.

"Beast, vampire, and the gemini… He really is Dr. Frankenstein…" he growled.

"Ben, are you sure? If you accuse him and you're wrong, you could lose your job. You two are in hot water as it is," Chrissy warned, her perfectly arched eyebrows creasing slightly.

"I'm hoping I'm wrong. I want to be wrong but it's the only… Everyone who was taken out — maybe that's the connection!" I jumped up and ran out into the hall.

I slid on the tiles of the white floor and made my way to my room with Soul quickly following. I reached my door moments later and unlocked it, only to see the room was trashed. Dan hadn't been exaggerating.

I stared at the mess on the floor for a moment, then shrugged my shoulders and scowled. I couldn't worry about that now. Soul followed me in and closed the door, stumbling over a small pile of clothes. Those weren't part of the search; I had left them there in the morning.

"Do you remember who you took out?"

He begrudgingly nodded and gave me a confused look. "I'm going to need their names."

He wrote down everyone he could remember and I got to work. He sat down on the bed behind me and picked up the picture of my brother off the table beside him.

"Good man."

I smiled to myself. "Yeah. He is."

"K9's sad? Wh-when she thinks about him?"

I stopped typing and swivelled my chair around to see my

dishevelled Crow watching me intently. With a slight nod I started to speak, "He was a warrior too, but after my run-in with Jekyll and Hyde, he was left nearly unable to walk. It's only been recently that he's started to walk without a crutch. It was really bad. I worry about him."

"Sorry," he muttered quietly.

I stood and stepped over to him. "Don't be. It was a long time ago." I fell onto the bed beside him. "And we're making up for it now."

Humming softly, Soul slipped his hand over mine, keeping his eyes fixed on the floor.

"Little girl, little girl
The one I love the most
Falling down, falling down
And I am just a ghost
Can't help, can't help
But still my girl will boast

Little dog, little dog
I will do all that I
Your crow, your crow
Will say 'you should have ran'

But never, but never
'Because we'll fight together.'"

He leaned against my shoulder and turned his head enough to let his nose touch my cheek lightly. I grinned and he nuzzled me slightly, making me smile wider.

"I have a question," I said softly. "Why me? Why didn't you just … shove me around and tell me to get lost like the others?"

His breath hit my face as he chuckled. "S-saw you fight… You were like the bird. You were strong but … *scarred*. Unafraid but aware. You got better. You … y-you were lonely and the bird … wanted to fix it." He placed his hand on my cheek and forced me to look at him.

"Wanted to tell you, didn't want to hurt the dog. Thought ... thought that maybe she could help the bird. After all, we are the same. D-didn't think it would go like this... Never expected..."

He shyly looked away from me. I leaned forward, gently kissing his cheek. His face instantly changed to one of shock as his cheeks burned. Leaning back, I looked at him. His eyes were wide and he had a goofy grin, like he was trying as hard as he could not to show how baffled he was. Shaking my head, I stood up and hopped back over trinkets and clothes to my desk chair. I started to research all the people on Soul's little list and what they had been doing before they were taken out.

I went through as many people as I could, looking up history and stats. The common factor between all of them was that they were rising in ranks. They were all major contenders for the tournament. They had booted out all of the monster-clique boys, and that must be why Frankenstein sent Soul after them. I just don't know why that would be important to him; none of them have ever won anyway.

I must have been sitting there for a while. My back was sore and when I turned around to ask Soul if there was anything else he could remember, he was fast asleep, lying across my bed, his arms spread out to the side like a bird's wings. I couldn't blame him. It *was* 1 a.m.

I sighed and closed my search pages, then pulled my boots off, carefully stepping over a sweater on the floor and turning off the light. I could hear Soul grunt and sit up as I tripped over myself, trying to find my bed. Bumping my shin on the edge of it, I fell forward.

"Oh no…"

My face hit the comforter and I sighed. I am the single most uncoordinated person I know. Soul chuckled softly and wrapped his arms around my shoulders, pulling me close and burying his nose in the front of my hair.

I welcomed his warmth and fell asleep in a matter of seconds, letting my mind wander far, far away.

My neck cracked as I rolled onto my back.

"Benji, get up we have to — *oh my god!*"

I gritted my teeth as I opened my eyes. Matt and Chrissy were standing in the doorway with Dan and a camera. One of the three (guess who) was blatantly disgruntled and the other two were just shocked.

"There is no way…! You two didn't…!" Dan stammered, face red.

"Calm down, Danny-boy. We're big kids now." I sat up and rubbed my neck. I looked to my left and saw Soul lying face down with one arm draped across my stomach and the other tucked under his chest, very much like a cat. I shook his shoulder and he bolted up, looking around and then looking down at himself, disoriented.

"Oh my god…" Chrissy mumbled again, pressing her hands to her cheeks. "Oh. My god."

I scowled at her and Soul licked his lips as he ran a hand over his hair. "M-morning?"

I nodded and he stood up, stretching his arms above his head and grunting. Chrissy just shook her head, while Dan was in the process of mangling a water bottle.

Soul turned his back as he smirked at them.

"Did you all want something, or…?" I waved my hand around as I stood and went in search of my sweater.

Matt nodded as he stuttered, "Yeah, Johnny just released a statement explaining what happened to Soul and why you're helping him. He refused to release any evidence but people still bought it. Now that someone's said something, most of the Valiants are backing you now too!"

I smiled from my closet door. "My brother's always been good at setting people straight." I pulled out a black jacket and held it up — not what I was looking for but it would do.

"Remember, you guys leave tomorrow night, so gather your things today," Matt instructed.

I scowled and nodded curtly. "What time is it?"

"Eleven, why?" Chrissy asked.

I smirked and left the room, following a few white halls to Frankie's room. When I pushed the door open, he was standing in the centre of the room in his boxers with a hairbrush in his hand. Some kind of pop song was playing from his radio. His room always smelled like musky aftershave. It tickled my nose. We simply stared at each other for a moment before I shook it off and walked over to his desk, opening a drawer and pulling out the small metal piece that was previously fixed to the end of the electric prod.

"Thanks for looking after this." I sauntered back out and tossed the piece to Matt. "Keep an eye on that. If it goes missing it's your head on a platter."

The thirty-six hours went quickly. We were told that a few of our friends would be going to Rhys-Mordred a few days after us. We were also told that any family we had would be invited as well, so I called Soul's mother and Tina. The little girl was so excited that she started to pack right away.

"Careful out there. Louis is going to be there as a representative and as your main medic, so talk to him if you need anything," Matt instructed as I handed a gym bag with my armour and weapons to a man in a suit. He nodded nervously and bowed to me.

The wind sweeping his grungy hair to one side, Matt shook my hand and grinned. "You're going to do great!"

"I'm going to do my best. Look after the place while we're gone."

The next thing I knew, I was being held tightly around the neck and had a face full of dirty old sweater.

"Relax, Matt, it'll be fine."

He nodded quickly, then let me go, turning to Soul who was in the process of saying goodbye to his sister — and it was a *long* process.

"I'm so excited, I told all my friends. I said, 'That's my brother!

That's him and he's going to the Tournament of Survivors. We have to root for him because we want him to win!'" She stood in front of him and danced around with stars in her eyes.

I started to make my way over to them as Tina tripped and fell onto her stomach. Embarrassment took over her delicate features. Soul tucked his hands under her arms and lifted her up, holding her against his chest.

"I can't wait to see you there!" his mother told him. She was standing proudly behind them. When she saw me, she reached out and shook my hand. "Please keep him out of trouble. We'll be there in one day."

I looked at her children and shrugged. "One day... I think I can avoid trouble for one day."

Soul squinted as his sister pressed her hands against his cheeks.

"Th-thank you … going to win for you," he told her. She grinned so hard her cheeks must have hurt.

"See you tomorrow," she said as he placed her on the ground and straightened his shirt again. Soul lifted his bag onto his shoulder and waved to her as we walked back to the nervous young man in the suit.

"Calm down, kid. This isn't a place that's used to private jets; we barely even know how to handle a guy taking care of our bags." I told him.

He seemed to calm down a bit. "It's my first day... I don't want to make a mistake."

Nodding, I patted Soul's arm as I followed him up the steps and slid into a seat. I sat across from him and looked out the window. I'd never flown before, but something told me I wouldn't particularly like it.

"Nervous?" Soul asked suddenly. I turned my head back to him and shook my head.

"I don't get nervous, bird."

He crossed his arms and shook his head, the corners of his mouth turning up slightly.

The flight itself was only two, maybe three hours but the tightness in my stomach lasted far longer. I constantly had to grip the seat to keep myself from getting physically sick, and I tried to keep my cursing to a minimum. Tripping and stumbling down the steps, I grabbed my bag from the young man, who sheepishly led us into an old brick building. It looked more like a mansion than a base. The air was a lot warmer here, but that could change very quickly.

"Here are your keys. Your rooms are across the hall. If you need anything, your friend Louis will be down the hall. The kitchen is always open. What else…" He thought for a moment. "Oh yeah! Feel free to roam about the town. Other warriors are already here, and more will arrive soon. Someone will come and talk to you about the details. Good luck!"

I unlocked the door and tossed my bag down. The room looked very old, much like the rest of the building. There were two windows on either side of a canopy bed, and the walls were a dark navy blue. There wasn't much light. I kind of liked it.

I pushed my hand onto the bed and fell face down onto it.

"A featherbed. I think I'm going to stay here forever." I pushed myself up and looked around a bit more. There was a small chair in the corner and wooden beams in the ceiling.

Rhys-Mordred Isle is a resort town, mainly for skiing and snowboarding in the colder seasons, but it was also one of the only places used for the Tournament of Survivors, as it was the only town that *didn't* have a proper arena or even an organization. No one has an advantage here; it's a fairer game this way. The large landscape ranged from forest to field to beach to lake. It gave the competition a little bit of variety. Someone from Lilithia Heights might do better in an open area with few places to hide because that's how we train. Someone from, say … Grizelda would do better in a mountain environment.

I hadn't realized that I was standing and staring into a mirror until Soul stepped behind me, making me jump. He leaned over slightly, resting his head just above my shoulder and smiled at our reflection. Grinning, I brought my hand up and played with his hair. He grimaced at his bird's nest and pulled my hand away.

"You realize that I'm going to have to fix that at some point, right?" He shook his head and stuck his lip out like a child. I turned my head enough to see his gentle face, which was calm and slightly tired at the moment.

"E-explore?"

"I'll follow you wherever you want to go," I told him as I grabbed my green army jacket. I pulled the sleeves up, feeling the fur on my hood tickle my neck as I followed Soul into the hall. I looked around the hallway … creepy wallpaper and old paintings, the kind with eyes that follow you. This place was unnerving.

Soul pushed open the door at the end of the hall and stopped in his tracks. I reacted defensively, an alpha wolf protecting its pack, and pulled a knife from my belt. I slipped around him and through the door.

"Whoa!" A man held up his hands and jumped backwards. "R-relax, would you?"

"Sorry about that." I carefully placed my knife back into the woven fabric on my belt. I nodded in Soul's direction. "I get a little wary when I see that look."

The man dropped his defences and ran his hand through his chocolate-brown hair, nodding. "I recognize you two. Lilithia, right?"

I shook his hand with a nod. "K9 and Crow. Call me Benji."

"So I'm guessing he's Crow?" He pointed his thumb at Soul, who nodded silently. "I'm Greg. I'm here with Fred Burnham — he's kind of an ass, though. We steer clear of each other."

"You're not forming an alliance?"

"Hey, if he wins, good for him. If we both end up the last two standing, good for us, but if I'm lucky, someone else will take him out and I won't have to deal with him."

I was sensing some bitterness there.

"I know the feeling. Where are you from?"

"Dwyer. I'm on my way out to the tavern. You two want to come?" I looked at Soul. He shrugged, then nodded.

"This place is kind of creepy. Lots of bad energy here," Greg muttered as he looked around.

"D-don't understand," Soul replied as he leaned forward to get a better look at Greg, who was nearly a full two feet shorter.

"Well, you know how this place is always used for the tournament, right? You have to think about how all that energy — that anger and pain — would have to leave some kind of imprint, right?" He waved his thin arms around.

Shaking off the sudden chill that ran down my spine, I followed the two men to the door as the shorter of the two droned on about the history of the building. Soul absentmindedly rubbed his shoulder against mine as we walked, so I slipped my hand into his and he blushed. As he always does.

Greg glanced out of the corner of his eye and smirked. "You two are going to have to be careful. Couples get targeted."

I scowled and squeezed Soul's hand a little bit tighter. "I'm not new to this."

I pulled my shoulders in closer and looked up at the buildings around us. Most were made of brick and looked relatively old, maybe a little imposing. Soon, I caught sight of a big red sign swinging in the breeze. It read "Mayfield's Pub."

I sighed out of relief and let my hands fall back to my sides as I stepped in front of Greg and Soul, pushing the door open and looking around. The taller and grimmer of the two joined me at my side and cast a look around. I noticed a few people stop and stare when I walked in, but the second they noticed Soul, the place went dead silent. He nervously hunched his back and wrung his hands as he looked at me.

"K-K9?"

"It's okay. We're fine," I stated quietly as I marched myself over to a table near the bar counter, hidden behind a low bookcase.

People slowly started to turn back to their conversations, and Greg looked around curiously.

"People look at me funny sometimes, but I've never gotten *that* reaction before…"

"Eliminating half our city's recruits will usually do that for you," I muttered as a waiter walked over.

"What can I get for you?" he asked shyly.

I shrugged. "Something strong."

"I've got just the thing." He winked.

I grimaced as he turned to Soul, who suddenly seemed calm, far calmer than I'd ever seen him before anyway.

"Local brew," he said.

"I'll have the same," Greg stated. The waiter left with a nod and let us go back to talking.

"You said people give you funny looks. How so?" I asked.

"My eyes. People think it's weird that I have different-coloured eyes." He blinked and brushed his hair to the side of his face as I leaned forward to look. He really did have one bright blue eye and one dark brown eye. "Wow," I muttered quietly. "That's actually really cool. I've never seen it before."

"They say it's really uncommon. I used to get made fun of, but I think it makes me stand out a bit — it's called complete heterochromia." He wrung his hands as the waiter placed our drinks on the table. "How high in rank are you guys back in Lilithia?"

I bit my lip and thought. Lilithia didn't really have a proper ranking system; it's still mainly an online polling system more than anything.

"Soul's only been there for a few weeks, but I'd say he's at about … ten out of forty. I'm a little closer to the top, maybe six or seven? We haven't set up our system yet so we only have a basic idea."

"Dwyer just set it up. Our qualification tournament is an obstacle course. I'm not sure how *you* did it."

He looked expectant, so I quickly swallowed my drink, which caused me to cough. "Boy, that is potent. We have a smaller version of the big thing. Less people, smaller space, but same deal."

Greg nodded as he looked around again. "So far, only ten out of fifteen city reps are here, so that's…" He started to count on his fingers.

Soul cleared his throat. "Twenty."

"Yeah, twenty warriors," Greg said as he leaned forward again. "You two ever fight together — like as a team? Or are you just dating?"

I don't really know if you can even say we're "dating." We hadn't really gone out other than to train.

I looked up amidst my thoughts to see a small monitor in the corner of the room, just above the fireplace, showing clips from all of the current warriors' qualifications. Sadly, the clip they decided to show of Soul and I was our little bout against Jekyll and Hyde in the market, which changed to him going after Angel. The footage was shaky since Soul had the camera in one hand and a forty- to fifty-pound axe in the other. What the hell were they thinking when they chose that?

"See for yourself." I crossed my arms and nodded towards the TV. It showed Robert, Johnny, and another man talking about our styles of fighting and how Lilithia — as pretentious a name as it was — bred warriors like no others. We were a gruff and tough place that, compared to some other cities, seemed pretty barbaric. We weren't the worst this world had to offer, though.

They showed our fight at the warehouse against the two brutes in the background as the third man tossed his questions about.

"Now, Robert, is there any significance to these men that they're currently fighting?"

"Yes, there is, in fact. If you've noticed Crow's face, he has a long scar running down to his neck (along with various other scars). That was caused by these two men. They've been known to use a pipe and razor wire, or whatever they could find, in previous fights to tease and torture their opponents, going back long before their time with us. They say that those two had done so much damage to Mr. Ravin that he no longer has a proper grasp on reality. He was apparently looking to get some revenge against them..."

"Actually, Robert, that's not true," Johnny interrupted.

Anger was building in my stomach, but my brother's voice washed that away and I sighed gratefully.

"They did do a lot of damage, yes, but he has a perfect grasp of reality. He just has a hard time forming proper sentences, though he has started to readjust and speak much more clearly."

I watched the recording of our fight. Soul choked out Jekyll with the wire and I finally noticed the look on my face. It was humorous, somewhere between pants-wetting terror and complete adoration.

"And what about K9? I believe it was revealed a few weeks ago that she too has a history with these two."

The screen flashed and showed an older video of me in the black vest and loose-fitting cargo pants, both of which had covered most of my scars.

"Indeed, and if you could see her arms here" — Robert pointed to the rings around my upper arms — "you can see circular scars, likely from razor wire."

I gritted my teeth as they showed Soul and I going after each other in our training.

"She wears a much more revealing outfit now. Now I'm not one to tell a lady what she should wear, but why do you think that is?" He paused, then answered his own question. "Most likely to show off these scars. She was shot quite recently and I can tell you, she is still very bitter about it. She most likely wears this now because she wants to remind these two men of what they did and to elicit sympathy from the crowd."

Johnny piped up again and shifted in his seat. "These scars are her war paint. She takes great pride in showing off what she's accomplished. She wears this to remind herself and to warn others." He stressed the last part of that sentence, looking into the camera to emphasize it even further. My brother really was good at this media stuff. They hadn't asked all the questions I'm sure Johnny had braced himself for, but years ago, he had some tech-savvy friends scrub the video from most streaming services. I'm sure it's still out there but after Viktor hired me, we tried to cover it up as best we could.

Greg stared with wide eyes and I scowled.

"What's your problem?" I said. I didn't like so many people knowing so much about me.

"What else can you tell me about Crow?"

Robert looked down at his hands with a frown. Johnny spoke up again.

"He fights like a true warrior, and he is very dangerous to anyone *who poses a threat. He won't hesitate to take down anyone in his way, but he is a very kind-hearted man generally. He would never hurt anyone he didn't absolutely have to."*

I silently praised my older brother as Soul glanced gratefully at me. They showed the rest of our training battle, right to the very end, including the point where Soul had lifted me off the ground and I sheepishly held out my hand. I smiled at the memory; it was a nice one that I wouldn't mind keeping at the front of my mind for a little while.

Greg turned back to us, his blue and brown eyes looking from me to Soul, then back.

"I heard about this. Some people are crying conspiracy, you know? I-I believe that; I think there's something bigger going on."

"You'd be right. We know exactly what's going on, but we can't explain it yet, so you better watch out for our big reveal," I told him with a smile as I finished off my ... whatever it was the waiter had brought me.

"How long has this been going on?" he asked as he leaned forward. Soul bit his lip and mouthed something to himself, so I spoke up.

"You know what was happening to our fighters, right?" I asked him.

Greg nodded and his eyes widened. "Y-you... That was him, right?" he said, pointing at Soul.

I nodded and Soul grabbed my hand, which I had placed on his arm. "It had been happening for quite a while, two or three months. We were down to about twenty warriors. As luck would have it, he came after me, only he didn't leave me hurt or tell me to go — "

"What did he do?"

Greg was leaning far over the table, listening to us like it was the most interesting story he'd ever heard.

"I'm still a little fuzzy on the details. He knocked me out, and when I was functioning again, I was sitting in his office, in the dark. Once I realized that he was doing everything against his will, I promised to help him find the people who put him up to it."

The look that passed over Greg's face rivalled my brother's own disapproving scowl. "I'm sorry, all I heard was that you were suffering from Stockholm Syndrome…"

I groaned as I leaned forward and rubbed my temples. "N-no, it's not… He didn't — I'm not… No, it's not Stockholm Syndrome. I-I don't have to defend myself to you!" I slammed my fist on the table.

Soul's face was bright red but he seemed to chuckle, along with Greg, who let out a hoot of laughter.

"You two have an interesting story, I'll give ya that. People like that."

"That's all well and good, but this is the real deal. No popularity contest here," I shot back.

"You're just full of snappy comebacks, aren't you," he said as he pointed at me and then took a drink of his beer. "I *like* that."

The bar was starting to get packed, and we ordered another round. We sat there for a while, laughing and joking with Greg and sharing a bit of gossip about our fellow competitors. Soul mocked Greg's laugh, and Greg teased Soul about his rat's-nest hair. It was a great time, that is, until Soul jerked his head up, spotting someone at the door. He leapt to his feet. Once I turned, I saw them too.

Them.

"Why are *they* here?" I mumbled as the grip on my glass tightened.

The brutish Irishmen pointed at Soul and I, then made their way over. Hyde had thick bandages over his refined features, mostly on the left side of his face, which still appeared to be bruised. Jekyll had bloody gauze around his neck and a small butterfly bandage over his right eyebrow.

At the time, I didn't think that Jekyll and Hyde would honestly be dumb enough to attack us here and now. I discovered I was quite wrong when one slammed my head onto the table and pinned me down.

I struggled and grunted as blood fell from my nose. I could see Soul stand up out of the corner of my eye and swing a punch, only to have Jekyll grab his arm and twist it behind his back. My Crow was too stubborn to let them see him sweat. He grunted as Jekyll grabbed a handful of his black hair and made him look at Hyde, who seemed to lean on his hand, still pressing my head into the table. I pulled out every weapon in my arsenal of derogatory names, statements, and curses — and trust me when I say I was well armed — and strung them together, aiming them at the *absolute jerk-face* standing behind me. I admit, if given the time, I would have thought of something better than "*jerk-face.*"

Soul struggled even more and tried to throw his body back, but failed. Jekyll was still much taller and much wider than him, and that made it easier for him to taunt and poke and shove my Crow around.

"Oh, little Vixen. You keep running and we keep finding you. Maybe someday you'll be rid of us," Hyde said in his smooth and unnerving voice. "But that day is not today."

"I swear to god, we're going to kill you both, you sick freaks. Damn the league, we should have just done it." I settled for a second, letting Hyde relax his muscles before I tried to heave myself off the table again. I kicked the chair back as Hyde leaned over me with even more pressure. "Damn you! You bastards!"

My eyes burned and started to water.

"You hear that, Jekyll? We aren't just monsters, we're *nightmares* too. We've gotten inside your head," he taunted, almost singing with that grizzly voice.

I cried out as he leaned over one last time, then let me up and hauled me to my feet by my jacket collar. I was facing a seething Soul. If Jekyll were to put any more strain on Soul's arm, he could easily break it. Still, he struggled and snarled at Hyde. I grunted softly as Hyde shook my shoulder and forced me to step closer to my partner.

"Get a good look at each other..." Hyde said breathily as he leaned toward me. "Take a good long look at your man, Vixen. You're both going home in a hearse."

"We're going to run Lilithia," Jekyll said, smiling cruelly.

"Over my dead body!" I shouted, not giving Jekyll a chance to finish talking. Soul gasped and shouted in pain as Jekyll continued to punish him.

"That can be arranged!"

I let the blood pool in my mouth as it dripped from my cheek and nose for just this moment. I spat at Jekyll, spraying blood across his face. All it seemed to do was make him cringe and curse at me very loudly. Both men let us go for a few short seconds, letting my pain fester into agony, then into anger. Soul attempted to grab my hand and pull me away before I could rush forward and take someone's head off, only he was too late and Hyde did the same, spinning me around and attempting to jab a concealed knife into my side. I barely managed to sidestep the blow, knocking the knife away with my elbow. A hand — belonging to Greg, I assumed — shot out from under the table and snatched the knife away.

"God damn, no good — " My temper flared.

"Shut it! Before my brother does it for you..." Jekyll hissed, pulling his own knife. Soul clenched his fists, and his face burned red as he glanced from me back to the twins.

"N-not now ... please..."

They shared a look, then broke out in raucous laughter. All emotion other than blind rage fell away a second later as Jekyll shoved Soul back against the wall and pressed a knife into his cheek, directly over the already existing scar.

"I swear to god I'll kill you both!" I said, my voice dripping with venom. I swung my elbow back, narrowly missing. I felt Hyde readjust his grip on my arm as he chuckled softly.

He pressed his nose into my hair and sighed. "I bet you will."

I grunted and struggled more, only to be stopped and frozen in place by the sound of Soul's small whimper. I dropped my arms to my sides and looked over at my friend. He wasn't bleeding and he looked more frustrated than nervous, but he definitely wanted me to stop fighting. I must commend him for his composure, that's for sure.

Jekyll slowly sunk down to his height, taunting him. "She wants to kill us for what we did to her boyfriend. You want to kill us for what we did to you ... but have you thought about why *we* want to kill *you*?"

He trailed the knife down Soul's cheek again, barely earning a flinch.

Soul looked confused, even curious.

"Okay fine, I'll tell you. Your little pet K9 tricked us. She made us look like fools so we destroyed her mind and body — "

"And now we're going to destroy her Soul, too!" Hyde let out a hoot of laughter as his brother and I (and probably anyone else watching) rolled our eyes, exasperated. How long has he been holding that one in…?

Nevertheless, he was right. They went after Henry and I because we made them look stupid. They were our first opponents in a real fight, but they weren't the same people back then. We pulled a dumb trick on them, and we won at the cost of the twins' dignity. They never forgave us. People laughed for weeks.

We pretended it was a three-team battle, that even though the other team was running late, we had to just go ahead and start. They fell for it, and when they got me on the ground, Henry started shouting that the other team had arrived. When the twins turned to look, we jumped them and choked them out. They disappeared from the circuit for a few years and when they came back — absolutely ripped — we were their first targets.

"We thought we got our revenge, you know. We killed that boy and broke her brother. I thought that was enough, but here she is, still mocking us and running around like *she's* the top dog!" Jekyll started to wave his knife towards me, then angrily turned back at Soul. "I thought we could work together. I never had anything against you. You were just in the wrong place at the wrong time … with the wrong person."

"Do you have a point? Some of us kind of have better things to be doing." I scowled, attempting once more to pull my arm from Hyde's grip.

"The point is" — Jekyll growled, pointing his knife at me — "that we're coming for you and you will die. Either in the competition or not. It's up to you. But you will die slowly and painfully. Which one do you think would hurt more from watching the other die, Hyde?"

I'd been around death, I could handle it. Almost every warrior from Lilithia Heights has killed someone, but I can't lose someone to Jekyll and Hyde, not again. I couldn't even feel Hyde's cold, calloused hands anymore. I was practically shaking with anger, frozen in place. Soul's composure had started to crumble too. He glanced between me and the twins, a hint of fear shining in his eyes. He reached up for Jekyll's wrist, pulling the knife away slightly.

"Don't touch my K9."

"Aw, is the doggy afraid to play war?" Jekyll sneered.

Soul wasn't taking any of this from him and leaned closer, fear replaced with contempt. "Are the gemini afraid to let her?"

Hyde shoved his brother out of the way and tried to intimidate my Crow. He puffed his chest out to look bigger, but Soul only shook his head.

"Listen, bird —"

"Hyde. Crows are just dirty, careless birds. Not worth our time."

I had to bite my tongue and clench my fist, otherwise there would have been bigger trouble.

Soul, on the other hand, startled me with one last comment and a merciless growl. "Murderers too. Don't forget that." The look on his face was demonic, carrying more anger and hatred than I had ever seen before.

They were taken aback by this, but just for a second. Collecting themselves again, they went back to taunting us.

"Hey, Jekyll? Want to play with the puppy?"

"Why not, Hyde?" I was thrown off guard momentarily, as they simultaneously turned to me and jumped forward.

"Don't."

They paused at Soul's instruction and shared a humour-filled grin.

"What's going to happen if we do?" Hyde asked, tauntingly holding up his knife.

"The bird's going to peck our eyes out?" Jekyll added.

I watched the raven-haired man contemplate the words, rolling his eyes back and shaking his head.

"Possible."

I hid a dark smirk as they started to chuckle more and that wicked grin took over Soul's face.

"You'll die, but what to do with your eyes…?"

I watched the jokers suddenly start to look a bit uneasy as Soul's chest rumbled with chuckles. Pride tugged at me. They stopped laughing at this point and shared a nervous look as Soul stepped away from the wall and tilted his head, keeping his shoulders hunched and cracking his knuckles. There was barely a trace of my gentle Crow in this man; he just looked unstable and … scary.

I liked it a little bit too much. It wasn't him, and that worried me.

"The gemini will burn. Whether it be by K9, Crow, or neither. The gemini will die, leaving ash and ember where they once stood tall. They. Will. *Burn.*"

Soul gave Jekyll a small shove. Jekyll stumbled back but stepped back up to Soul, taking his button-up in his grasp.

"Jekyll, don't," Hyde muttered as he tossed me back against the table. His eyes were focused on something just over my shoulder. "Now's not the time. We're done here."

Soul stepped forward as Jekyll released him. He rushed forward and got one good shot to Hyde's nose. There was a solid *crack* as Hyde fell back against his brother.

"Don't … touch her!" Soul growled after them.

Jekyll hauled his brother up and quickly pulled him toward the door, passing two familiar figures on their way out. Louis and the boss had just walked in. They were coming toward us, fast. That explained brothers' sudden departure.

You see, if contestants attack each other outside of training before the tournament begins, they get disqualified. *If* they get caught. Now I no longer trusted Mr. Viktor for obvious reasons, so his concern was pretty … concerning.

"What on earth happened here?" Viktor said hotly.

Ignoring him, I gritted my teeth and pulled out some cash for our drinks; then I stood and tossed it on the table. I made my exit by keeping my eyes fixed on the door and flipping off the twins.

"Benjamina, what on earth…?" Viktor asked.

I pushed past our boss and the medic and into the cool night air. Soul was, luckily, right behind me and caught me as I started to stumble.

"I-I should have ordered another drink…" I muttered with a grin.

Soul wrapped his arm around my back and helped me make sure I wouldn't end up in a ditch. It's not exactly the ideal place to be when you wake up after a night out, trust me. My world was spinning, the blood still flowing from the cut on my forehead as I leaned into my friend. "Carrying me home from a bar… That's usually Chrissy's job."

Soul wasn't going to have any of my jokes tonight. I kept forgetting I didn't need to fake my way with him. I couldn't even if I tried; he wouldn't tolerate it.

With a sigh, I touched his arm. "Are you okay?"

"Dead … die, the demons will die. Burn, little monsters, burn in hell for what you've done. If hell is too far then Apollo shall come to you, crow-black feathers left in his wake…"

I sighed again and continued to walk. I felt the same as I always did whenever I drank too much, only this time coffee wouldn't fix the pounding in my brain. The walkway of the temporary base came into view, and Soul sighed out of relief.

"Sorry to be a burden."

He ignored my sarcasm and rolled his eyes as he kicked the door open with his right boot.

I was getting a little lightheaded, and I started to find playing with his hair very amusing. I giggled like a child as he picked me up off the ground and carried me bridal-style into the lounge-kitchen. I started to braid a piece of his bangs, and he grunted at me as he continuously pulled his head away.

"Come onnnn. I have to make it look pretty at some point anyway!"

"Not now."

I giggled again as he set me onto the arm of a leather loveseat. Slowly, I fell onto my back on the seat, kicking my legs back and forth as I listened to his boots stomp on the old wooden floorboards. I absentmindedly looked around the room, blood still staining my nose and lips. I put my arms above my head and puffed my cheeks out like a chipmunk.

There were about five people in the room, three of which left nervously once they saw me and my cohort. That was a funny word — "cohort." I didn't really know what it meant, but I laughed a little anyway.

"What in heaven's name happened to *you*?" a man who was reading a book asked. He looked utterly appalled. "Appalled" … that was another one I wasn't really familiar with. It made me sound smart though.

I snapped back to my senses and sat up quickly, getting dizzy again from moving too fast. The tap was running in the kitchen as I carefully touched my right eyebrow, feeling a slight sting.

"It's a long story." I shook my head a little bit and received a flick to the arm from Soul.

"Hold still…" he instructed, with a tad bit more sympathy than before.

I pouted as I reached up and tugged his beard, bringing him down to my height. "Do not treat me like a child."

Scowling, he dragged a wet rag over my cheek. He cleaned up a little bit of blood and then examined my face, stopping at my lips. "Don't act like one … and … d-don't get *hurt*."

I smiled up at my handsome Crow. "For my Crow?"

A gigantic grin took over his face. "Who else?"

His green eyes looked from my hazel ones to my cheeks to my lips, then back to my eyes. He seemed to falter for a second; then he grinned wider and planted a soft kiss on my nose. I hopped back and smiled despite the small throb of pain it caused.

"Watch it, would you?" I giggled and gave him a half-hearted shove. He put a hand on the left side of my face — the non-bruised, non-bloody side of my face — and continued to wash off the blood.

"Jekyll didn't hurt your arm too badly, did he?" I asked.

Soul shook his head and stretched his arm out as he silently worked. The man with the book was still staring, and the girl that was with him grinned.

"Oh my *god*! You're them! You're Crow and K9!"

"Good guess, captain obvious," the man responded.

The man sighed as he surrendered his book and turned towards us. "Again, I ask, what happened to you two?"

I was about to answer him when I heard a door slam open and several voices talking over each other.

"We'll slaughter them! Those two have no right to be taking our spot in the tournament *and* have the gall to think they can win too!"

"We can't kill them here, Hyde! Too many eyes on us. We'll wait until the tournament begins. Then I'll slit the dumb girl's throat like we should have when we met."

I bit my lip angrily and slid my knife out of my belt. Then I leapt, half stumbling, over the back of the seat and toward them. The men walked into the room, and I shoved Jekyll into the wall as hard as I could, pressing my blade into his neck.

"This dumb girl just might slit yours first," I spat at him. "Because of you two, I'm pretty good with sharp objects."

"Ms. Keanin!" Another voice from behind. Mr. Viktor.

Arms wrapped around my middle and pulled me away from my prey. Soul was still pretty angry, but at this point, he had more self-control than I did. I fought him a little bit, but he grabbed my wrist and pinned my arm back, then took the knife and let me go.

"*Someone* isn't happy," a man muttered as he crossed his arms and rolled his eyes. He looked like Viktor's PA, but I'd never seen him in person before. He looked bored under his frizzy black hair.

"What on earth just happened?" Mr. Viktor asked cautiously.

"They tried to kill us! Again!" I shot back.

Viktor chuckled and shook his head.

"You must be mistaken; they are aware that they can't attack anyone unless they agree to train in the arena."

I was shocked and hurt that he really didn't care if we were killed by these two.

I turned my back, mouthed a few choice words, and then turned again and looked at Hyde. "How's your nose feeling? I've taken a few blows to the face myself. Stings doesn't it?"

Hyde lurched forward, and I cringed as I hopped away.

"You two best stay away from here," Mr. Viktor instructed the two brutes as he led them out, along with the other man I wasn't familiar with.

As they left, I started cursing up a storm and waving my fist in the air. Soul had crossed his arms and walked out of the room, leaving me to trip over the side of the couch and hit the floor.

"You know what? This is good. Just leave me here, I'm good."

Eventually, I grabbed the arm of the couch and hauled myself up.

"You two are going to get hurt if you keep instigating." Louis smirked. He was leaning against the wall, arms crossed. He must have slipped in behind Viktor during the shouting.

"They are going to kill us anyway! Why not let them do it sooner rather than later?" I clutched my head and scowled at the floor. He calmly walked over, pulled his penlight from his pocket, and shone it into my eyes, roughly grabbing my chin to hold me still.

He chuckled darkly and shook his head.

"You have a concussion — "

"Thanks, Mr. Doctor! I could have told you that!" I shoved him away from me and stood again, starting to pace back and forth in front of a large stone fireplace. I thought about how we could defeat them until I realized that they weren't even supposed to be here. They lost our qualifying tournament; they should be at home sulking.

"It's a set-up! Who … who authorized this, and why were they talking like they're part of the tournament?"

I had to sit back down. The room had started to spin again.

"Forget about them; just focus on your training," Louis instructed. "We actually have decent warriors this year. We have a chance. Don't blow it."

"'*We have a chance, don't blow it*,'" I mocked, gripping the side of the couch to stay upright. "Louis, you ain't seen nothin' yet."

Twenty-Three

I caught Soul rolling his eyes as we talked to Ignatius, the man with the book, and Agatha, the girl who sat beside him. They were cousins from Grizelda village, but they acted more like siblings. They seemed nice enough. Almost everyone else who would pass through the room would avoid eye contact and move quickly. Despite witnessing the incident at the bar, Greg didn't seem to be afraid to be seen with us. He contently plopped himself onto the couch beside Ignatius, who seemed more than a little bit disgruntled.

"Don't mind Iggy. He's always a little bit cranky," Agatha — or Aggy, which she preferred — told him. She was leaning over a pillow and making conversation with Greg, who seemed very pleased that she was taking an interest in him.

Iggy scowled and held his book to his chest, not at all happy to have his reading time interrupted by us. He had dark, almost black, hair and bright blue eyes. His cousin had red hair and freckles underneath her round glasses. She was shifting her gaze between the members of the small group, finally resting it on Soul, who, for the most part, had been ignoring the conversation as he toyed with a puzzle box.

"What's his deal?" she asked me quietly.

Soul looked up at that moment, causing Aggy to look away and try to be inconspicuous.

"What do you mean?" I replied with a small laugh.

She shrugged. "The entire time you've been here, he hasn't said anything. He doesn't look too happy either."

"I'm not." Soul muttered as he went back to his puzzle.

"You never are, oh bird of mine." I turned back to Aggy and rolled my eyes.

Out of my peripheral vision, I could see him silently mocking me as he pressed buttons and slid panels.

Aggy giggled and then grabbed the remote. "Let's see what those reporters are saying about the others."

All of the other warriors that had arrived had already made alliances by now, and they were all staying very far away from Soul and me.

"Don't worry, we're going to help. I'm sure they're all misunderstanding the scenario anyway," Ignatius stated with an unimpressed look, which I doubted ever left his face.

I thanked them, making sure they all understood how much we appreciated it, then rubbed my head and turned to Soul.

"It's late."

He shrugged and followed me back out of the kitchen, into the purple halls. We passed two jet-lagged warriors that just had arrived. I offered a small nod, but they simply grimaced at me and kept walking.

My face was throbbing and no amount of feathery pillows could help that. Apparently, breakfast wasn't going to help either. I just stared at my toast as I stood at the island in the kitchen. Soul was still sleeping, as were most of the other warriors, but my nerves couldn't be calmed that easily.

I shook my hair out and went searching through cupboards and drawers, hoping for coffee. There was a kettle but I only found tea. That's not enough caffeine. I stood up and rubbed my head again. Maybe there was a little shop around here I could walk to, but was it wise to leave on my own? What if I ran into Jekyll and Hyde? Oh, I didn't want to think about them...

"Coffee's above the fridge." The voice came from behind, making me jump.

I spun around and prepared to defend myself. My heart was pounding as I gritted my teeth and looked at the man sitting across on a bar stool.

Sighing, I leaned against the counter. "Ignatius, don't do that."

"Yeah, kind of dangerous to sneak up on a girl who put someone out of work her first week as a pro because they belittled a boy no one knew." He bit into an apple and smirked. "Dog-girl."

One of the reasons no one would team with me was because of what I did the first week I was employed. That guy never should have said that about Henry, so I lost control. People don't *need* all their limbs, right? I pulled my knife from my belt and jammed it into the island. "There's a story there, and if you call me that again no one will find your body."

Ignatius was frozen with ... either fear or plain old shock. I'm not really sure. I pulled the apple from his hand and walked away.

Goddammit, I forgot the coffee.

Stalking through the maze that was our building, I grumbled to myself. Finally, after getting lost for a few minutes, I knocked on Soul's door.

"O-open!" he shouted back.

I opened the door and he was sitting on the end of his bed, still looking half-asleep.

"Coffee?"

He was squinting like a hamster in daylight but nodded and stretched, his beater top lifting up and his unbuttoned pants falling down. I stood against the doorway staring as he scratched his hair and dug around for his clothes.

"That looks fine, you know."

Slowly, he stood and turned back to me curiously. Looking down, he shook his head like he wasn't sure why he was already dressed. I laughed at him as he ran a hand over his face, then grabbed his long black coat and followed me out.

As we walked, he seemed thoughtful about something. He had brought his hands to his chest and started to fiddle with a button. "F-feeling ... better?"

"Hmm? Yeah, I'm fine," I assured him.

He nodded, then looked back up. He was standing on my right side, so he had a perfect view of the fresh bruises and cuts.

"Don't lie, not to the bird ... please."

I stopped walking and faced him with a grumble. "Okay, my head is pounding, my face is throbbing, and I'm pretty sure my self-confidence was taken out with the trash this morning. This is pretty much the new normal for me, so I'm doing pretty darn good, considering!"

My hands were shaking, and I had snapped at Soul pretty badly. I dropped my head out of guilt. Soul had stepped away and hunched his back, looking like a dog being scolded.

"P-please don't ... don't be m-mad at the ... bird." His voice cracked and I felt pins and needles in my chest. He squeezed his eyes shut and tugged at the collar of his shirt, biting his lip to keep himself calm.

"No, Soul, I'm not mad at you. I'm mad at the world! What did we do to deserve this? You — you're such a good man and I'm... Well, I'm not the best person but I don't think I'm all that bad. Maybe it's just the universe getting me back for what happened to Henry — "

Soul pressed his hand over my mouth and stared at me, probably waiting for a reaction. Giving a snort, I stayed still nonetheless. After a second, he pulled his hand back quickly, the way someone might if they had gotten burned.

"Y-you are *my* K9..." he told me with determination. "Hmm ... w-we will..." He fought to speak calmly but ended up pulling at his hair and taking deep breaths.

"The good guy always wins," I told him. "But I don't feel like the good guy, Soul."

"No! Th-this time ... wolf ... K9, r-right? K9 ... survival of the fittest..." he whined and pulled his hair a little harder, clearly frustrated with himself. I gently pulled his wrists away, and he took one long breath before looking back up at the sky. He started humming, first inaudibly, then harder.

> *"Wolves breed wolves*
> *And crows commit murder*
> *So stand up and run*
> *Before we take it further."*

I nodded and thought about it. I'm not hopeless. I'm not a loser and I never have been. I'm not going out so easily. Hell, I'll go mad before I get dead.

"I *am* a wolf," I stated. "And I'm sorry."

Soul started to look like he had settled, so I smiled and nudged him to start walking again. He grunted as I wrapped my hands around his strong forearms, looking away shyly.

"I'm going to stop freaking out. I'm going to try harder for you," I told him as I went back to searching for any signs of coffee.

"My K9," he muttered happily. He was barely audible.

We eventually found a small coffee shop. I threw money at the woman as she handed me my dark roast coffee.

"You two are here for the tournament, right? Is it true that you already got into it with some other contestants?"

I had started to walk away but froze and swung myself back around. "'Got into it' is a little … vague, lady. Anyway, they weren't supposed to be taking part in the tournament."

"Oh, be careful. No one really follows that rule." She waved to us as we started to walk again. "And … um … you don't seem to know this, but Bell Hearst's warriors dropped out, so Mr. Vince Viktor volunteered those two guys."

My stomach dropped about three hundred feet and I shook my head. "Oh, no, we didn't. Uh, thanks for letting us know."

She nodded and went back to work. I stewed in my discontentment and opened the door.

When walking through town, I was used to cobblestone roads, not perfectly smooth dirt streets. I tripped a few times but managed to save the coffee. My mind kept drifting to Soul as I let my drink cool. I needed to get my mind off of Jekyll and Hyde, so I asked him a question. "You like poems, but what about riddles?"

He thought a moment, then nodded and waited for me to remember most of it.

> *"Patiently, I'll sit and watch*
> *Though my attention cannot be bought*
> *Tell me why, dear prince of mine*
> *Why must I stand aside his kind*
> *To the left of which, I see*
> *Tell me why this has to be."*

I waited excitedly for his answer. I was quite proud of my riddle. His eyebrows creased for a moment before his eyes widened and he whipped his head around to look at me proudly, his loud laugh ringing out like a crow's call. "A knight. The prince was a knight, r-right?"

I nodded and grinned. "It started in medieval times. The sword was drawn from the left. How did you know that?"

Soul straightened his jacket and stuck his chin out. "Gentlemen know."

My shoulders shook as I laughed. He *was* a gentleman though, even if he was joking. As if to demonstrate his manners, he opened the door of the mansion and bowed as I walked inside. We quickly exchanged more poems and riddles as we finished our coffee — or in his case, tea — then made our way to the training room.

In order to get there, we had to walk through a few tunnels in the basement. It was kind of creepy. The main training room was full of warriors, but the practice arena was empty, so I made a call to Johnny so he could give a shout-out to any locals who wanted to see a free show.

Within half an hour, the place was full and we had hauled our equipment to the lockers. These rooms were separate, unlike the ones at home — one for women, one for men, and another separate change room entirely. I tightened my shoulder pads and walked past Ignatius and Greg into the pristine, white arena. They nodded and then headed back into the change room to suit up for their own battle. The officials had put barriers up but there was no dirt, only slippery white tiles. I looked up into the stands, noticing that there were also wires and poles to hang from.

I threw my arms into the air and people shouted, whether they knew my name or not. Soul, on the other hand, was already waiting for me, flicking at a long tear in his shirt.

"We're going to have to fix that before we're sent back out into the cold," I said as I casually started to walk towards him. He hadn't realized I was there, and he looked a little bit startled. He smiled sarcastically and walked towards me, holding out his hand, the same as he did last time.

I eyed it. His tape was already bunched up from clenching his fist, but I shook his hand roughly. We both took a few steps back and he held his axe ready. I waited until he started to rush forward again before I tossed a smoke pellet onto the ground and jumped up to one of the beams. When the smoke cleared, he stood straight and scratched his head. I balanced on one foot as I watched him check behind the barriers. I only blew my cover by laughing obnoxiously at his confusion.

I twirled in place, then jumped around, showing off a little bit as Soul reattached his axe to his back, then leapt to the beam, struggling to pull his weight up. He grumbled and dropped back to the ground. I paced on the thin bar as he left the weapon on the ground and went for a second attempt. He grunted in frustration and I twirled again to face him.

"Would you like it more if I got down?"

He grunted once again and nodded. "P-please?"

Like I said, I'm a show-off. So what? I dropped down and grabbed the bar before I hit the ground. I kicked myself over the top, perching like a bird. Soul got the idea and did the same. He did pretty good despite the fact he nearly fell backwards. I was small enough that I could balance fairly well as I slid my swords from their sheaths, but Soul continued to hold his arms out as he wobbled back and forth.

Once he'd steadied himself and glared at me for making him do this, I swung my swords at him. One, two, one, two. He knocked them out of the way and reached for my collar, so I leaned back, nearly falling off, having to drop one sword in order to grab the beam and swing myself around again. The second I was back up, my partner decided to use his knife to knock my other sword away.

I gulped and then grinned. "This isn't how I planned it…"

I faked a jab at Soul's nose and he bent his knees, pulling himself a little bit lower — low enough for me to leap over him and start running. He groaned and carefully jumped back onto the white-tiled floor, chasing after me. Once I looked back at him; he was standing below me with his axe. My first instinct was to drop onto his shoulders, but that could get me hurt. I was in mid-air, leaping over him to the next beam, when he pulled me to the ground.

His hand was still on my boot as I landed on the floor and grabbed my cheek, throbbing once again.

"The crow better fly away…" I grumbled.

I pressed my hands onto the floor and shoved myself up, pulling my boot free and throwing punches, jabs, and then kicks. My partner grinned as he dodged left and right. He continued to dodge as he started to walk towards me, backing me against a barrier. I tried to hide my glee as I dropped to the ground and the axe followed. I pushed myself forward and rolled across the ground to my swords. The thin handles slid perfectly into my hands, just in time for me to be kicked in the side, which rolled me onto my back and forced me to hold both in a defensive position above my chest.

I deflected swing after swing until a voice — a voice with a strong Irish accent — made us stop dead.

"Well, isn't this cute? Little lovebird and his puppy, play fighting. I wonder how they'd fare if someone they loved was on the line." This was Hyde. I could tell by the hair-raising manner in which he spoke.

Soul, who was still leaning over me, slowly started to turn his head, with rage and fear in his eyes.

Once he had straightened his back out, he let out a whimper and tensed his muscles. His axe was raised, and he started to mouth some poem to himself. I understood his terror once I turned my head to Hyde as well.

His usually well-groomed face was a mess of unshaven *scruff* and ugly bruises — not to mention that his nose was completely crooked now. The most horrifying aspect of this entire scenario wasn't his looks, though; it was that he was a holding a tiny girl with long black hair and porcelain skin. Tina Ravin.

"Let me go! You ... you big bully!"

Tina kicked her legs and struggled as hard as she could. I had to give her credit for not looking remotely scared. She mostly seemed annoyed.

Kicking my legs up, I jumped back to my feet and aimed one sword at the man. "This is too far and you know it, Hyde. Set her down and walk away."

Hyde smirked and tossed Tina into the air, catching her in his other hand, then producing a knife. Soul was grinding his teeth and clenching his fists. "Put down the girl and fight like a man; best fight hard because the bird is not a fan…"

He started to stalk closer, hauling the axe along the ground and producing sparks.

Tina was kicking and screaming for her brother and me, anger strong in her little eyes. I sneered at the hulking brute of a man as he pressed the knife into Tina's cheek, cutting her ever so slightly. She bravely bit back tears, keeping silent.

"You probably want to stay where you are. You don't want me to do to her what I did to the doggy, do you?"

Soul stopped walking and dropped his axe, raising his arms as fast as he could. All the rage drained from him in an instant.

And then Hyde turned to me. "You too, Vixen."

I tossed my swords down as hard as I could and scowled. "You know you can't do this. You know this is too far; no innocents, no *children*! This is low, even for you!" My throat was burning as I screamed at him. Soul's rage returned as tears fell from his eyes.

The ghoul simply sighed overdramatically and dropped the knife to his side. "You make such a big deal out of nothing. I can promise you that, if you were on your own here, you'd be far too *busy* to worry about it."

The way he suggested this made it seem like *busy* had some undertones I wasn't quite comfortable with. And by that, I meant thinking about it almost made me wretch.

"S-stop!" Soul grabbed his hair with both hands and hollered angrily. "Not yours, never going to be. Let the little girl go ... s-so I-I can kill you."

Hyde's hollow laugh rang through the silent arena.

Just as Hyde was about to retort, he growled in pain and fell to the floor, crimson dripping from his right leg. The gate had splintered open, and Greg jammed his heel into Hyde's spine as Ignatius carefully pulled Tina out of his grip. He held her tightly to his chest as he ran towards us, scowl still planted firmly on his face. Really, I think that was just his face.

I bolted for my swords and ran to Greg's aid. Hyde had turned the tables and was in the process of strangling him. The floors were unluckily slippery, especially since my boots were made for dirt and rugged surfaces. It was difficult to get any traction. Still, I threw my body into Hyde's and we both tumbled off of Greg, who grabbed his throat and coughed violently.

Hyde had the same plan for me; however, sadly for him I had a plan too. His knife was lying on the ground next to me, so I reached for it as his thick hands gripped my neck and squeezed. My fingers started to go numb, but I still managed to get a decent grip on the little box cutter, as my vision started to fade. I jammed it into his arm, but that only caused him to grunt and lean down harder. Kicking my legs against the floor, I gasped and dragged the small blade over his wrist. His dirty demon-blood dripped onto my neck and partially into my mouth.

"Oh Hyde, we need to keep her alive, remember ... until the tournament. You don't want to be kicked out, do you?" His brother's rough voice sounded from my left. I let my head roll to the side as I tried to swear at him. My voice only came out as a breathy whisper.

"You ought not talk like that, Vixen. It's unbecoming of a lady, and it makes me *think* things..." the man leaning over me said, in a tone that only he could consider seductive.

I was nearly completely unconscious, but I could feel the pressure in my face from the bruises and the blood. I had to keep my eyes closed to keep them from rolling back, but I managed to knee him where it counts.

"Go to hell!"

Hyde's face changed from one of amusement to one very true to his name, something deformed and sinister, and he doubled over in pain and let me go.

I heard a few footsteps as I resisted a cough as much as I could, then I heard worried mutterings and a call from my Crow.

"K-K9!"

"She's dead!" Jekyll mused. "Sorry, bird, you're going to have to fight alone. Alone again, just like you've always been! No one cares for you. They're all afraid of monsters and that's exactly what you are. All alone again ... so sad. I thought crows travelled in flocks."

Oh. He was just asking for it with that one. I smirked and launched myself to my feet. I quickly grabbed my sword then ran up behind him and kicked his knees out. Gripping both the blade and the hilt, I held my sword across his neck from behind, letting it cut into my hand.

"Didn't you know?" I taunted in his ear. "A group of crows is actually called a 'murder'" — I leaned down and sneered — "which is exactly what I'm going to do to you."

Ignatius sighed and shook his head, evidently unimpressed with my wordplay. He took over watching Jekyll for me while Greg held Hyde in place. After nodding a thanks to them, I keeled over and coughed like I was dying, which I guess I nearly was.

I shook my head as Soul ran over and placed both hands on my shoulders, disapproval and relief playing on his face all at once. I inhaled one last time and stretched out my neck, cracking it to the side. I threw my hand up and gripped the underside of my hair tightly as I grimaced. My partner sighed and I sheepishly grinned at him. His face fell into an expression of disgust, and then he smacked my arm.

"Don't do that!" he cried in aggravation. Grinning, I coughed and wiped my lip.

"That's my girl! Go, K9!"

"Yeah!"

I looked into the crowd to see an ecstatic Chrissy and a proud Dan. I hadn't realized they would come out for the tournament. I guess not much went on around Lilithia while it was on. Soul let out an unhappy grunt when he saw Dan. He looked at me again and bit his lip as he frowned, but his expression quickly changed from frustration to a much softer look, probably caused by his younger sibling clinging to his leg.

My tall, dark, and handsome companion dropped to the ground, and Tina threw her arms around his neck; she really did admire him to no end. Her little crow was tightly wrapped in her shaking fingers as Soul pulled her away and put both hands over her cheeks, carefully wiping away a little bit of blood. The bright red was a startling contrast to her ghostly skin.

"O-okay now?" Soul asked quietly. She nodded, shock still filling out her already wide eyes.

"She's a strong girl, just like her brother. She'll be just fine," I said.

I strode back over to Jekyll and Hyde, pacing in front of each before quickly bringing my boot up to Hyde's chin. Then I jumped to the right, grabbed Jekyll's hair, and brought his face down onto my knee. My voice was raspy because of what they did, but I didn't mind; it made my next words seem that much more ominous.

"I don't care if I get kicked out of the tournament or the league or the goddamn country. If you ever, *ever* go after family again, I won't be this kind."

I turned my back and gently took Tina's hand as Soul picked up his axe and pretended to swing it at Hyde's throat, eliciting a small shriek of terror.

He stopped short and sneered, "Like the final line of a nursery rhyme; the ghost in the wreckage of my mind … no longer a spectre, just a trash collector. Oh…" he chuckled grimly, sending a shiver up my spine, "how the mighty fall."

He stood again and lurched towards Jekyll, who fell onto his back. Soul's maddening cackle rang out as he walked out of the arena, still echoing as he walked into the locker room. Jekyll and his demonic twin shared a concerned look.

"Good job, boys, I guess Soul was right. '*Pity the man who has none, and fear the man who has but one.*'" I smirked.

I contently looked up to the ceiling, feeling all hope return from the cold, black hole it had previously taken up residence in. Tina giggled as she swung my hand back and forth, glancing over her shoulder and waving her fingers at Jekyll and Hyde. I cast one last glare at them as I ushered her into the locker room.

Tina was raving about the entire thing, no longer afraid of them after seeing how badly we'd beaten them, though it was four on two. After changing and waiting outside the training room for Soul, I tried to be mature and shake it off. We finally took a step forward, but I didn't know what was coming.

I high-fived Tina as Soul walked over. His lip was split again, but he didn't notice the blood trickling down his chin.

"Soul, you're hurt!"

He lightly touched his face then shrugged. "Fine…"

I was thrown off balance and shrieked as a mop of blond curls fell into my face and arms wrapped around my neck.

"Oh my god, that was amazing!"

"H-hey Chrissy… How's it going?" She allowed me to breathe again and stepped away.

"That was pretty grim, man." Dan smirked as he patted Soul's arm. Soul recoiled at Dan's touch, scowling at him.

"Dragon!" Tina hugged the tall, sandy-haired man.

"Hey, kid. How you been? I don't even remember the last time I saw you." Dan ruffled her hair, and Soul made a sound similar to what I imagine geese make when protecting their young.

I crossed my arms at him. "Down, boy. I already told you, you can slug him as hard as you want *after* we get things sorted out. Got it?"

"Promise?" he pouted angrily.

"Wait, what?" Dan turned to me, clearly offended.

Chrissy violently shook my arm and grinned. "Now that that's over, we need to go shopping!"

I scowled. "Why is that?"

"The big show tomorrow! They introduce everyone and tell a little bit about their fighting styles, history, and everything. You have to wear something nice, both of you!" She poked Soul in the chest and started dragging me away against my will, my partner giving a half-hearted wave as Ignatius and Greg joined him.

I forgot about this part of the tournament.

"I don't want to do this, Chrissy."

"Oh, come on! I'm sure you look great!"

I did, but that was beside the point.

"Just come out!"

I scowled as I left the change room, glaring daggers at my so-called best friend. She shook her head and handed me a different dress. We weren't finding anything that we agreed on; everything she liked had flowers and everything *I* liked was lace.

"Just let me try that one, please! It's so pretty!" I pointed to a floor-length dress that was black and electric blue. There was a blue band similar to my gear across the top, but the rest was fairly see-through — enough you could probably still see the X across my front.

Chrissy finally groaned in aggravation. "Fine, go amuse yourself while I look for something!"

Smiling victoriously as I pulled it from the rack, I bounded back to the change room.

Now, by no means am I a girl who likes painting myself in makeup and wearing fancy dresses; *however*, I had to bite my lip and grin as I looked in the mirror. Yes, it was a tad revealing, but I could show off my scars enough, and the blue part of the skirt wasn't too vibrant. I bounced up and down and giggled. Then I threw open the door, standing proudly as Chrissy's jaw dropped.

"Is this nice enough for you?" I asked smugly.

She scowled back. "Yeah, that will work."

Once I got back to my room, I found Tina wearing one of my belts, passed out on the couch in my room, and Soul was lying face down on my bed.

But that's okay, I could share.

I rubbed his arm, and he moved enough to let me fall down beside him, then sleepily wrap his arm around my shoulders. Smiling softly, I reached over to the bedside table, turning off the light.

Twenty-Four

The day went quickly but everything felt ominous, probably a side effect of giving Dr. Frankenstein and his men a good scare. It's hard not to expect retaliation. Agatha was sitting in my room with me while we got dressed, chatting and talking about how she was so excited to fight people other than the warriors from her hometown.

"I hope you realize that the only reason everything is moving so quickly this year is because of you and Soul," Agatha stated in her usual, bubbly tone.

I grimaced as I painted the white stripes on my cheek with fresh ink. "What do you mean?"

"Well … they all know that people die in this competition, and they also know you're at war with those two goons, so they figure that the faster they get the competition started, the faster you'll kill each other and everyone can stop dealing with property damage."

Her round spectacles slid down her nose as she readjusted her little pink dress and stumbled around on high heels. Her hair was up in pigtails; as juvenile as it all appeared to me, it really suited her personality.

"Oh, good to know just how unwanted we are." I grabbed my combat boots and tried to slide them on under my dress — the thing was quickly getting on my nerves.

"Don't you dare."

My head shot up to see Chrissy standing in the doorway with a pair of heels in her hand. I rolled my eyes and she tossed the shoes at me. They were pretty tall, and I didn't have much experience with heels taller than two inches.

"Are you kidding me?"

In response, she kicked my boots aside and shoved me, barefoot, towards the door.

Agatha, Chrissy, and I ended up in a small room full of other fighters, all in fancy suits and dresses.

"Why do we have to get all pretty like this anyway? We're just going to end up beating each other to a pulp in two days anyway," I said, concentrating on balancing on Chrissy's ridiculous stilettos.

Aggy cringed. "I don't have a clue but I feel pretty!"

Her forced smile told me she was nervous. After allying herself with us, she should be.

"There's Iggy and Greg." She dragged me towards them. Greg excitedly took her hand and kissed it. Aggy lost her cool and giggled while Ignatius's face went completely red, a vein in his forehead throbbing as he pinched the bridge of his nose.

"Agatha, please…," Ignatius whispered. "You don't need to get mixed up with him."

I scoffed at the irony and looked around for Soul. I hadn't seen him yet, which was unnerving, considering how many times we'd been jumped since getting to the island..

Thankfully, a few minutes later, the door swung open and he peeked his head in. My eyes widened slightly as I watched him skulk towards us. His usually untamed black mess of hair was pulled back neatly into an elastic. The shaggy front remained down, falling in his eyes. As he took his place by my side, I hid a smile as I reached up and tugged on a braid. There were two of them right below his left eye and a piece with a few blue and green beads hanging down. He pushed my hand away and looked around, grunting then ripping off his tie and shoving it into his pocket. He was grumbling a poem to himself as he undid a few buttons. Same as he always did.

"It won't kill you to smile, Soul," I whispered playfully.

He quickly turned his head and exhaled, slowly meeting my eyes. "F-for K9?"

Smirking, I grabbed his hand. "Who else?"

Looking away, he sheepishly grinned and kicked his boot against the tile floor. "My K9…"

"You couldn't be bothered to wear real shoes?" Greg asked.

Soul was still wearing his combat boots. It must be a Lilithia thing. As I was looking up at him, I couldn't help but feel annoyed. Even though I was wearing four-inch heels, I was still nowhere near being close to his height.

I watched Ignatius get increasingly annoyed with Greg, and Soul playing with the thin black string tied around my wrist for a few minutes more. Then they finally called us all out in front of the audience.

Jekyll and Hyde were standing *very* far away from us but still managed to glare daggers at us. Soul hadn't let go of my hand, and with the knots in my stomach, I really didn't want him to. I wasn't used to having so many people watching me for something that wasn't a brutal fight. It was pretty unnerving.

Luckily, time moved quickly and they were already halfway through the group. I spotted Johnny sitting in the crowd beside Chrissy, Louis, Matt and Josh. Louis was falling asleep already, but I noticed Matt holding Josh's hand. He seemed to notice me watching him and shifted uncomfortably. I smiled and gave him a small thumbs-up, at which Josh smiled broadly and Matt blushed. It was about time those two got together; we'd all been trying to set them up for years.

Soul's grip tightened on my hand, and I saw Robert walking over to us, bringing a very bright spotlight with him. Strategically, he wrapped his arm over my shoulders and smiled at the audience. Though the look on my face was probably a little less than pleased, I made an attempt at smiling.

"Lilithia Heights' very own K9 and Crow." Robert pinched my arm slightly, making me flinch. "Who I see is still true to the name, keeping her dog collar around her neck at all times, even while in formal wear."

Chrissy's head snapped up from where she was sitting. She motioned that she was going to punch me when this was over. I had replaced the necklace she'd lent me on the way over when she wasn't looking.

Robert turned to the screen and held his microphone up once more. "You're known as one of the most brutal and bloodthirsty fighters known to the Central Main land mass, but it seems you have quite the surprising soft spot for your friend."

The end of the qualifying tournament was playing on a big screen in the middle of the room, and Soul had to look away in order to hide his smile.

"Uh, well, yeah ... I mean, we've been through the ringer, so to speak. That kind of thing creates bonds, you know?" I stammered.

"Yes, but what's truly amazing is how you came to meet — some would even go so far to say *unhealthy*."

After hearing him say this, I burst into laughter and had to grab my leg to support myself. I was stopped dead and spun on my heel when I heard a video start playing again.

"*Matt, get the lights on!*" Viktor's voice echoed through the room.

"*I'm trying!*"

I calmed down as the video flickered, showing Soul toss Dan to the side, then quickly sock me in the nose and grab the front of my shirt to keep me from hitting the ground. My first instinct was to scowl at him, but his face was already red and he turned away, scratching his head and looking guilty.

"Oh, ladies and gentlemen, it gets better..."

We shared a curious look and leaned forward to get a good look at the screen. His old office.

All the monitors were still set up, and the screens flashed with faces of warriors Soul had attacked.

I aggressively smacked Soul's arm but kept my eyes fixed on the screen. "I thought there weren't cameras in there!"

"N-not supposed … to be…"

"Nameless and faceless
A monster at the core
Useless and careless
Here forevermore."

Soul's voice sounded so raspy in the video. I hadn't remembered how rough it was when we first met. His posture had changed too; I hardly recognized the slouching man in the video. Beside me, Soul let out a short grunt of aggravation, and I let go of his hand.

"How did you get this? There were no cameras in there." I sneered at our host.

"Well, obviously there was."

I snatched Robert's tie and pulled his face closer to mine. "How did you get it?"

"Th-there was an email… They told me to play it!" he stuttered as he shook his head.

"It was from Frankenstein, wasn't it?!"

He dropped the microphone to his side and pushed me back by placing his hand around my collarbone, pressing into the hand-shaped bruise with his thumb.

"You're perceptive, aren't you?"

I gripped his wrist and gritted my teeth, hurting myself in the process because of how crooked they were. Soul stepped in and swatted his hand away, staring him down menacingly. Robert blatantly regretted making a move. As he started breathing faster, I ran to the edge of the stage and waved Matt over. The second he reached me, I pulled him closer and whispered in his ear. "Don't trust the boss. He's Frankenstein. He was the one picking us off one by one!"

He stepped back and looked at me in shock. He nervously nodded nonetheless, and bolted out of the room.

I stumbled back to Robert, who turned to the screen again, "Well, now that we know what they've been up to recently, how about we find out how this started?"

All mercy had clearly left him. Playing over the big screen was the video of a much-younger Soul facing off against the two monsters all those years ago. My partner looked away and inhaled sharply. He did his best to look calm, but his eyes betrayed him. It hurt him to see that video again. Dan held his head down as the video played. I cursed them all in my head as Robert held out his microphone.

"Thoughts?"

"Sheer brutality for the sake of it. The only way they're leaving this competition is in a body bag, and the guys they work for are going to be next." I shot a glare at Mr. Viktor, his greying hair swinging in a ponytail. He sneered discreetly.

"And what about you? How do you feel about what they did to you?" Robert smugly pointed upwards. I watched the video switch. My young face was on the screen, awash in a nightmare of blood.

I had never been able to bring myself to watch the video. I knew what happened; I didn't need to see it again.

And yet there it was.

I already felt dizzy when the part I was dreading the most hit the screen.

"*Get out of here!*" A pudgy, purple-haired boy ran forward, carrying a baseball bat above his head. The camera flashed to an unimpressed Jekyll, holding a gun out in front of him.

I put my head down and bit my lip so hard it bled, the only way to keep from having a fit. With one last glance, I saw Henry's determined expression change to one of confusion, and then his body dropped to the ground, blood pouring out of his chest. I grabbed Soul's hand as my eyes burned with tears. I wouldn't have let them see me cry if I could have controlled it, but I simply couldn't. I felt a sheen of sweat and tears coat my cheeks. I clenched my fists and apologized to Henry and Johnny over and over in my mind.

"Enough."

"I'm sorry, Crow, what was that?" our host smugly asked.

"Enough! Tormenting... They — they beat and bloodied ... killing too many and..." He paused and ran his hands over his hair. "*Enough*! N-not going to happen anymore!"

He stepped forward and menacingly snatched the Invisible Man's tie. "Dr. Frankenstein ... Jekyll and Hyde ... the Invisible Man ... Dracula ... the Mummy ... all of you! T-tried to turn the bird into a demon!"

I watched him back Robert up to the edge of the stage and give him one good shove. "Set fire to my office ... took *years* to get that equipment, and Crow — *Death! Plague!* Going to do the same, no matter the cost! It's over. You're beat! Surrender or *burn*!"

"He's raving mad!" Vince Viktor stood up and shouted, pointing at Soul. My friend was in a rage, but he had zero intent of looking like a fool. He pulled a knife from his belt and prepared to throw it straight at our boss, glancing to the left just in time to see Hyde barrelling towards him. He ducked just as the larger man leapt and sailed over him, hitting the ground with a thud.

I debated getting involved as other warriors stood in shock and terror. I hadn't let Chrissy know, but I had shorts on under the dress. She'd have killed me. As my war tape was already in place, I just undid the zipper and stepped forward.

"Oh my god, *seriously*!" I heard Chrissy call from the crowd.

Ignoring her, I slid my own knife from a holster on my thigh and lunged at Hyde as Soul was forced to defend himself against Jekyll. After a few missed punches, I sent a kick to Hyde's stomach, the heel catching his rib. He fell from the edge of the stage, which gave me enough time to reach the microphone before anyone's senses returned.

"D-don't think we're crazy. It's Vince Viktor! He forced Soul to go after those warriors. He was going after everyone that was threatening his job, and if Soul refused, he would let Jekyll and Hyde hurt him!"

Soul punched Jekyll in the jaw, and then Josh directed the camera man to the burn. The skull was still very prominent on his skin.

"Tell them, *Doctor*!"

The enraged and aging man stood tall. Glaring, he shouted, "She's delusional! That lunatic told her lies. I bet he even burned himself!"

Robert waved his hand and a few men in uniforms very much like Josh's grabbed Soul and I, dragging us off the stage. They pulled us past the row of Lilithia guests, and Viktor glared daggers at us. "We will speak once this is over, Ms. Keanin."

Twenty-Five

The training room on Rhys-Mordred was nothing like ours. More often than not, we had blood smeared across the tiles and props that were half-broken. It was a small room, but it was more than enough for me. In a strange way, being there made me happy. It was like a second, maybe third, home for me.

This place, on the other hand, was dark like a warehouse with concrete walls. Everything was clean, and the equipment was spread out rather nicely, with target practice in one area and strength training in another. The weights, treadmills, and rowing machines were all in one corner.

When I got there, I looked around for anyone that I knew. Of course, Soul was struggling to climb the rock wall. Fight-or-flight training, and flight wasn't his strong suit. I made my way over and dropped my weapons on the ground.

"Hey, Benji!" an unfamiliar voice called.

Nerves reacting before my common sense, I half jumped, half turned around, prepared to defend myself, my arms instinctively brought to my chest. The voice belonged to a short, bald man who was standing very close to me. He kind of looked like one of those hairless cats with the pointed noses.

"Relax, little lady. My name's Fred Burnham," he said, holding out his hand. "I believe you've met my partner, Greg?" I stood there staring at him, refusing to shake his hand.

"Just wanted to let you know that those two guys said they'd be here today," he continued, dropping his hand. "But something tells me you don't really care…" His face started to fall.

Boots hit the ground beside me. I knew Soul was waiting for me, so I decided to send the man on his way.

"Thanks, Fred, but I don't think they'll be a problem."

I turned my back and smiled at Soul, who was watching me with curiosity in his eyes.

"Y-you … you don't want my help?" he asked.

"Why would we need it?" I retorted over my shoulder.

"You're going to regret it. Those guys have it out for you! You *need* me!" He ran off like a child.

I turned to look at Soul. He shook his head. Right away, I could sense that something was wrong. He wouldn't look at me and I couldn't get him to speak. At least his hair was down again, sticking out the way it does. He looked more like himself. Fresh ink was also splattered across his cheek and arm. It collected in the scars down his right arm and into his ear.

I was worried, so I decided to speak up. "Did something happen?"

He quickly shook his head and dumped his axe onto the floor beside my swords. I followed him back to the rock wall, and he attempted to avoid me by pulling himself up as fast as he could. Sadly for him, he only managed to get about a metre off the ground before he grunted and kicked his long legs around.

With a laugh, I leapt off the ground and grabbed at a small handhold. "Will you tell me what's bothering you if I beat you in a race?"

He grunted and dropped back onto the ground. "U-unfair… K9's better — smaller!"

I let myself fall back to the floor, crossing my arms as I stared him down. "What if I teach you and then we race?"

He hunched his back and wrung his hands, debating it before finally biting his lip and meeting my eyes. "O-okay. The dog won't … get mad that the bird can't fly?"

"It's going to take you a while to understand that I won't be mad at anything you do, isn't it?" I stated it more than asked. He looked at the floor and sighed, then hesitantly reached for my hand, keeping a tight grip on his tank top with the other.

"D-don't ... f-forget. Please ... don't forget."

I tilted my head, confused by what he meant. "Forget what?"

"The dog is too careless... The bird is fighting too — Crow is fighting too. K9 isn't ... isn't a-alone," he stuttered out in a whisper, stepping closer.

I squeezed his hand and softly smiled. "I know."

"No ... too careless! Going to get hurt and then ... and then the bird will be alone again! C-can't let it happen, don't want you to get hurt!"

He cringed and started to tug at his shirt collar.

"Don't forget... Can't lose you, can't let you get hurt." He whimpered and looked at the floor. "S-still love my K9... Don't want to lose her..."

I had to take a deep breath and collect myself. I was a little bit hurt that he thought I'd be so reckless as to get myself killed. My fingers brushed his cheek and he started to calm his ragged breathing. Again he told me he loved me, and again I didn't know what to do. There's a reason I didn't tell anyone I loved them, at least not in a very long time.

"There's no way that's going to happen — ever. The K9 and the Crow are a team; we'd be useless without each other."

"S-still my K9?"

"Who else's?"

He was still looking down, but he smiled and stepped forward again, wrapping his arm around my back and pressing his face into my shoulder. "My K9."

I let him stay there for a moment as I looked over his shoulder, mentally kicking myself. This was the second time I hadn't told him that I loved him too. If I'm not careful, my stupid fear of commitment would come back and bite me in the ass, and it'll be too late. What if something happens to him? What if he leaves? I don't want to do that to myself...

His hand was still in mine as I hugged his neck and gripped the back of his hair with the other, squeezing my eyes shut, promising myself that I would tell him next time. I put on a strong face before I finally let him go. He walked over to the rock wall and started to climb. He was struggling less than before and successfully dug his boot into a crack in the rock. He was almost halfway to the top when he stopped and called down to me. "Race!"

"Wait, no! That's cheating!" I leapt up and started to pull myself to the top, using mainly my upper-body strength. I threw my hand to the top of the ledge at the same time as Soul, and we shared a look before kicking and clambering to get up before the other. After a second, I hauled myself up onto my stomach as my crow's foot slipped and he dropped about a foot. I threw my arms up as I swung my legs over the edge, watching him claw at the smooth edge before he used his knee to push his large body up.

He sat beside me and rested his hand over mine as we looked out over the other warriors. We were unique if nothing else.

He kicked his legs back and forth. "T-talked to worm..." I turned my head to look at him. He absentmindedly rocked his head side to side. "Said the K9 would leave ... said you always did."

"Not this time. I ... I would leave because I was looking for something better. But this time I found someone who knows how to fight for himself. I've never met *anyone* better. Ignore Dan. I'm not going anywhere, not without you, Soul," I said, smiling softly at him. "Still going to beat him though."

Soul chuckled as he looked up at the large projection screen, smirking. Johnny had earned enough of a following that he was now regularly covering the tournament on the Rhys-Mordred city news channel. He was damn good at it.

I pursed my lips as I watched the live interviews. Ignatius seemed rather displeased to have to do them but answered my brother's questions and kindly shook his hand before leaving.

Johnny had his crutch again. His limp looked worse lately. I chalked it up to stress and watched as they introduced our city's first interviewee, Dan. The tall blond man stayed perched on the stool and gave a half-hearted wave to the camera.

"Now, Dan 'Dragon' Stanton — "

"Dragon isn't much of a nickname... Kind of feel like I have to earn it back from people. I didn't treat them the best." He grimaced, but shook it off and smiled painfully back at Johnny.

My brother chuckled and agreed. "*That sounds like a good idea. Do you have anything you would like to say about Lilithia's warriors in this competition, maybe anything you would like them to know?*"

Dan thought for a moment, then nodded and looked back at the camera. "Yeah. *Benji Keanin is one of the most intense and intimidating warriors I've ever seen. Jekyll and Hyde have made a huge mistake by getting on her bad side. Hell is going to be brought down on them. They won't know what hit them.*"

I smiled to myself. I liked that people were a little bit afraid of me.

"*When I knew Soul ... I was a really worthless guy. I was a jerk to everyone and left him when I shouldn't have. We all know that. But this guy is a good guy, and he would fight to the death to keep this from happening to anyone else. When those guys got to his sister, he snapped, no mercy. He's going to leave them bloody and broken, if not dead.*" Dan laughed to himself and shook his head. "'*Fear the man that has only one*' ... or something like that.

"He likes poems," Dan continued. "*He was always showing off with his stories and riddles. I never gave him enough credit. I — Soul, man, if you're listening, I know I already told you this, but I'm so sorry for what I did. You're lucky. Keep Ben out of trouble and protect that sister of yours. I'm going to do everything I can to make it up to you.*" He paused again and uncrossed his arms, pulling out a piece of paper then looking up again. "*I'm not great at writing poems but, uh ... I got one I think you might like...*"

Dan cleared his throat and looked up again.

> *"He is so hopelessly in love with her*
> *Black and white are the colours of his dog's fur*
> *Nothing can stop an angry man*
> *Who only wants revenge*
> *There's nothing stopping him*
> *And anyone willing would be too dim*
> *To see he at least deserves a chance*
> *To try his hand with a lance*
> *Everyone thanked him, even the pastor*
> *And he will never be damned hereafter."*

His blue eyes flipped back to the floor as he smiled softly, quite proud of himself. His cheeks were bright red as Johnny smiled and patted his arm. *"Thank you, Mr. Stanton."*

I looked at Soul, who was sitting rather contently. "That was pretty cool of him, even if it was a pretty lame poem. That being said, I won't blame you for still wanting to slug him. I do."

Soul smirked and shook his head. "F-friendly fight... Scare him a bit."

I grinned and bumped his shoulder with my own.

"K9! Crow!" A man with a clipboard was looking around, shouting our names. "Interviews, then you can go."

I shrugged and stood to my full height, stretching out my back. Soul slid down the wall to the ground.

"Quickly, guys! We only have a few minutes!"

I scowled and mocked him as I looked down at Soul. He waved for me to follow him, so I backed myself against the wall and took a running leap into the air, flipping myself around so I wouldn't land on my face. My Crow grunted out of displeasure and disapprovingly bit his lip as I hit the ground. I was forced to somersault to keep from cracking a bone, which left me lying on my back giggling.

My partner pulled me to my feet and grabbed his jacket, still disgruntled. The man with the clipboard stood with wide eyes and stumbled as he led us out into the hall and then to an office outside an interview room where Johnny had the camera set up. Chrissy was sitting down there and gushing to him about something, and then she saw me through a big bay window and started to gush about us.

Johnny politely finished the interview, then scowled playfully and shooed her away. Johnny pulled Soul in and closed the door. He sat down and pouted sleepily, resting his hands in front of him in his lap.

"So," Chrissy started, "this is exciting!"

I shrugged. "You know, the whole 'public eye' isn't my thing."

"But you have to admit, you like people knowing your name —"

"I like people knowing what I'm capable of, yeah. I guess you're right."

She grinned, red lipstick framing her white teeth like they belonged in a museum. She did love proving me wrong.

We watched a small TV screen right outside of the dingy room for a moment; it was fixed to the ceiling and tucked behind a thick grate.

"*You've known K9 for a short while, and it seems like you two get along well. Is there anything you want to say about that?*"

Soul played with a button on the bottom of his shirt and slowly started to smile. He looked away from the camera and muttered. "*My K9. Strong, smart, ruthless and reckless ... but mine.*"

"*A 'good with the bad' kind of relationship, then?*" I frowned and promised to smack my older brother later. He seemed to be having a good laugh at my expense.

Soul smiled so wide his crooked lips stretched the scar on his cheek out of place. He was still buttoning and unbuttoning his jacket, his cheeks as pink as a cherry blossom. He cleared his throat and glanced at me quickly through the window, his face softening enough that the smile stayed but appeared more content than giddy. He was a beautiful, beautiful man.

He started over and rubbed his head lightly as he spoke, a little smile staying firmly in place as he stared at the floor.

"The dog said to the crow
He shouldn't furrow his brow

For someday he'll soon join the crowd
The crow said to the dog
He'll appear as a frog
And really he has nothing to tell
The crowd shunned the bird;
This time was the third
Because he never sang the right song
The dog did the talking
While the crow did the walking
And the act went on for long
They said to the crow
"What a great show!"
Though it was never his to explain
The dog and the bird
Made such a good herd
That the crowd no longer detained
The notion of price
Is set to despise
Those who need it the least,
For those who win
Will never have sin
Unlike those at the feast
The Crow and the K9
Were doing so fine
The party they did decline
As the monsters behind
Staggered (sublime!)
They could not hurt them this time."

Joy tugged at my lips as I grinned and wrung my hands together, getting slightly shy. Chrissy frowned and waved her hand in front of my face. "I-is there something I'm not getting?"

"Usually the poems he recites are old ones he's found in books …

but he wrote that one." I bit back a soft smile and shook my head. "It's sweet."

Chrissy gasped and fanned herself overdramatically, feigning holding back tears. "Isn't it just so adorable? My little K9's all grown up and falling in love!"

I backhanded her arm lightly as I continued to watch the interview.

"Keep my little sister safe out there or it's on your head. I may be out of the game but I remember how to play," Johnny warned.

"P-promise..." Soul sheepishly nodded as he slid from the stool and shook my brother's hand. He made Johnny look very small, both in height and muscle. That used to be a lot harder to do.

Before I got a chance to say anything to Soul as he left the interview room, Johnny dragged me inside and closed the door.

"K9! My very own sister, anything you would like to say?" He grinned crookedly at me and waited.

"Yeah. I want to thank the people who helped us," I said, looking at the camera. "You trusted me just enough."

"What about your partner, anything you want to say to him?" I quickly sent a scowl to my brother, then bowed my head.

"He ... he's amazing — and dangerous. Which brings me to our opponents: we're going to crush you. It's nothing personal, but we're here to win. We kind of have to. If we don't, we're pretty much dead meat..."

"And Jekyll and Hyde?" he interrupted.

I smirked. "Johnny, you and I both know what's going to happen to them. They're as good as dead... They've threatened the people I care about one too many times — Soul, Tina, you. They better be training right now; otherwise they better be scouting hiding places."

"Be careful out there," he said quietly. I hugged him and left the room.

Soul was waiting with Chrissy. She appeared to be teasing him about something. He sheepishly looked up at me, then bolted to my side.

"Wait, are you leaving me already?"

"Chris! We have to train, maybe you can help us with techniques tomorrow."

My friend scowled and crossed her arms, begrudgingly nodding after a few moments.

We spent the rest of the day training. By eight o'clock, we were exhausted and had to drag ourselves back to the main room. There were other warriors hanging out and watching other interviews from earlier in the day, unlike before.

"You two look tired." Greg smiled as he tossed a package of candy at me. "Your friend said you like to snack."

Nodding, I tore into the package and dumped most of it into my mouth, then handed the rest to Soul — or at least I tried to, but he was fast asleep. His mouth parted slightly as his chest rose and fell, and his head was wrenched back toward the ceiling. I watched him for a few moments before turning back to the TV, where Jekyll and Hyde had pushed their way into the interview room. They shoved Johnny against the wall and trashed the place as my brother angrily watched.

"*I'm trying to work here!*" he yelled.

"*And we've got a message for the other competitors!*" said Jekyll, grabbing the camera and aiming it at his face. "*Stay out of our way and you won't get hurt. Join us and you won't get hurt. But lay a hand on the bird or the puppy and you* will *get hurt. They're ours to do with what we will.*"

"*Thanks for your time, Johnny-boy.*" Hyde shoved my brother again, then followed his shadow out.

Johnny angrily stormed towards the camera and shut it off. The video was on a loop and started with the first pair of warriors again, completely shaking off the final event of the day.

Greg shook his head and looked at me disdainfully. "Did I make a mistake by saying I'd work with you?"

Twenty-Six

"Chrissy!" I shouted. "We've been over the other warriors already. I just need to know about Jekyll and Hyde!"

My airheaded friend dramatically shrieked at me, causing me to scowl and step back from the table. The dim light from the little lamp cast four dark shadows across the kitchen as Dan, Chrissy, and I argued. We'd been over the warriors' stats, weapons, and fighting style multiple times, but the brothers had changed the play. They weren't fighting with their regular weapons. No one actually knew what they were using, but what we did know was that they'd stocked up.

"You know their tricks. You need to figure out how you can beat everyone else!"

"But they are the targets. They're who we're after!" I growled back. "I don't care whether we win or not if we can get them out of the way for good!"

I pushed my white bangs out of my eyes and looked around the group, stopping at Soul, who had kept his eyes fixed on the table. This is the only opportunity Soul and I would ever have to kill them without our reputations getting seriously tarnished. I momentarily doubted every choice I'd ever made and worried that any form of consequence would be my fault. It wouldn't be the first time.

Soul lifted his eyes and stubbornly shook his head. "Revenge."

"He's right. This competition isn't important right now but closure — revenge — is. I want to *feel* like we won; I want to know they can't *ever* do this to anyone again!" I could feel my eyes starting to water, despite how much I fought it. "I need it to be over so it never happens again." The edges of my teeth rubbed together as I avoided looking at the rest of them.

Chrissy had no idea what it was like to live while being hunted, to have someone's blood on your hands. She didn't come from the background most of us had. She'd never seen an underground tournament, and she'd never made it far enough into our qualifiers to be forced to do anything that would scar her for life. She continued to argue with me, not understanding what I had been going through. Dan, however, stayed quiet the entire time.

"J-just … dog is right, cat is wrong. Don't know — don't know what it's like, constantly looking over your shoulder…" Soul's hoarse voice startled me. Somehow he managed to make his way around the table to my side and placed his hand over mine. I heard Dan exhale as he rubbed his neck.

"He's right," he said. "No one's going to sleep properly until these guys are gone, and you two know them best. Chrissy, just let them do what they want. It's not like we can stop them anyway."

"Thank you, Dan." I looked expectantly at my blond friend. She was staring at Dan with a kind of rage that I would usually be slightly scared of, though given the moment, it hardly affected me.

"They are going to get themselves killed!" she snapped.

"Then that's their choice! We can't stop them, and if we cared about them or anyone else, we wouldn't even try!"

"Kill them," Dan said quietly. He turned to Chrissy. "If letting them face their demons makes me a bad guy — if it means I'm going to hell — then so be it." He shook his head and looked between us. "Benji, I manipulated you from day one, and you knew it. Why you didn't call me out on it I have no idea. Soul … I messed up! I watched that video day after day, week after week. I never forgot what I did, so give me a break and let me help take them down before I snap! I can't help much now, but I can let you off your leash. Forget about the competition and the other warriors. Ignatius, Agatha, and Greg can take care of that. Find the twins and kill them."

He paused and met Soul's eyes. "You deserve it." The rings around Dan's eyes were dark, like he hadn't slept in days. He shoved the papers at me, then stormed off. Soul let out a short sigh and looked at the floor, dirty black hair covering the majority of his pale face. I shot a glance at Chrissy, who was still glaring down the hall at Dan.

I shot up and followed Dan down the hall, grabbing his shoulder once I reached him. His body tensed instantly, and he growled as he spun to face me.

"What do you want?"

"I want to know why you're such an ass," I said.

"What?"

"I said I want to know why you've been such a jerk, and why you suddenly want to redeem yourself."

He roughly pulled his shoulder out of my grasp. His eyes seemed darker, with all sense of his usual mischief gone. "He's like a ghost!" Dan pulled his hair back. "Ever since he came back, I can't sleep, I can't eat, I haven't been fighting like I usually do… I feel like I'm being haunted. I thought he was *gone*! I came to terms with the fact I was a coward years ago, but now he just shows up? How do you expect me to live with what I did? He's never going to forgive me. *You're* never going to forgive me. *Hell*! I don't think I can forgive myself!"

I watched him carefully as he leaned back against the wall, exhaling. He shook his head.

"I-it was easy…" he whispered bitterly, barely a hint of his thick Boston accent in his words. "It was easy to forget him when he was dead — kind of a *put him out of his misery* type of deal, you know? His father left for business when he was thirteen, barely coming home after that. When he was sixteen, his mother found out she was pregnant with Tina, and the guy was gone for good. He was a drunk. Moses was his name … total jerk. Soul started fighting to help his mother out — extra cash. She hated what he was doing. Thought he was going to get hurt, so she told him that if we continued, she wanted nothing to do with him. H-he was so miserable…"

I crossed my arms and let him continue.

"When … it happened, I kind of figured maybe … maybe it was his way out. I came to terms with the thought that it was over, that he wasn't so miserable anymore! It was over! But when he came back, he… It was like *a ghost*. He was suffering all this time and it was my fault! I wanted to save him but I just killed my *brother*… He was just a kid. He's not even the same person anymore!"

Leaning against the wall, Dan slid to the floor and cradled his head in his hands. I knew what it was like. That didn't mean I was okay with what he did.

"Blood on your hands," I muttered, though I wasn't completely sympathetic.

Dan met my tired eyes with his red ones, then angrily shook his head. "What do I do?"

"Don't ask me; I'm still trying to get a little redemption myself."

I turned my back on him and started to walk back to the kitchen. Soul was standing by the door with anger-filled curiosity. He stuck his face in mine, physically shaking as he sneered. "Th-thought he was *helping*?"

The hurt in his voice hit me hard. He looked like he was sick to his stomach, despite the rage. I closed my eyes and shook my head. After a moment, I stepped back and opened my eyes to look at him again. I could tell he was furious. Because of past experiences with him, I thought I knew how to comfort him slightly. But when I tried to reach up and rub his shoulder lightly, he frowned and pulled his body away from me, storming off down the hall. As I watched him disappear into the dark, I sighed. He'd find me if he needed me.

"Chrissy, what else do we know about how they fight?" I asked suddenly.

Her shoulders rose, then slumped in defeat. "They don't have any specific techniques. They just like to make people bleed." She gazed into the empty hall. "W-was this my fault? Ben, I am so sorry — "

"No, part of me has been waiting for them to break since the day they confronted each other."

I started to drag my feet back across the wood floor to a barstool. I was starting to get claustrophobic in the little windowless room. I kind of wanted to go home.

"What the hell? *Ow*! Knock it off!"

Sharing a look, Chrissy and I both booked it down the hall, only to see Dan lying on the floor, trying to protect himself from Soul's boot.

As he stomped the blond man, he muttered under his breath. "C-couldn't just stay... No, had to leave, had to flee, just so he wouldn't see!" Soul's voice ripped from his throat as he screamed, "Feel shame, guilt ... feel *fear*! When the bird is done with the gemini, he will come for the worm!"

Soul kicked Dan once more, then allowed me to yank him back by the arm. I kept my hands tight around his forearm as he wiped his mouth with the back of his other hand. Keeping his gaze fixed on the traitor, he ripped his arm away. I grunted as I stepped forward, keeping myself from landing on my face, and stepped in front of Soul.

"What do you think you're doing?!"

He breathed heavily as he briefly gave me a look of worry and then reverted back to rage.

"K9 ... sh-shouldn't get...," he paused and squeezed his eyes shut, clenching his fist and pursing his lips slightly. "Stay away from the bird!"

He stomped back down the hall towards the kitchen and into the main room. I watched him pause a moment to breathe as his hands started to shake. He let out a grunt, then stomped off towards his room.

"Put some ice on that..." I absentmindedly muttered to Dan as Chrissy helped him up. I rushed after Soul.

I followed the purple-wallpapered halls back to our rooms, ignoring the clunk of my boots on loose floorboards. His door was closed, but I could hear him rummaging around inside and talking to himself. He sounded stressed and hurt.

I didn't blame him.

"Soul?" I gently knocked on the door and heard a sudden crash. "Are you okay? Can I come in?"

"Go!"

A scowl took my face as his growly tone of voice rang through the door. I knocked harder and leaned against the door. "Soul, I need to talk to you. Open this door before I do!"

I heard the small creak of the wooden door and had to catch myself by grabbing the door frame. I gave a frustrated look up at Soul. He was breathing heavily and glaring at me, but he held his chin high, telling me this was more than just hurt. This was betrayal, something I honestly hoped he would never feel because of me — partly because he was big and could probably snap me like a twig. But mostly because I never wanted to hurt him.

His hair was drooping over his right eye as he waited for me to say my piece.

"I know what he did was wrong. I know his philosophy is wrong. Everything about the situation we are in is wrong, Soul, but it isn't over yet — "

"Stop that."

"Wh-what?"

"Stop saying that. Crow may get revenge, Crow may beat the gemini, but he is still just a crow. Absolom is gone ... not coming back. Still scarred, still ... *stupid*... We lost. K9 and Crow lost. It won't be better just because it ends."

He took a small step forward. "Doesn't it hurt? Doesn't it *burn*, K9? H-how — still ... still scarred, torn, and *broken*... Oh! Hmm — mm." His face changed and he looked bitter and sad. I stood as still as possible as he gripped his hair in one hand and traced the scar across my chest with the other, suddenly becoming incredibly solemn. My breathing started to get shallow. He pulled his hand back up to my shoulder and rested it there, calming himself down a little bit.

"I-is it really winning if we've lost all that we had in the process?"

My head fell as I took a deep breath... Was he right? I still felt empty, the kind of empty that feels like a broken heart, but not out of loss or anything ... just ... *inferiority*. But...

"Yes, losses are in abundance but think of what we've gained. We took out their entire team, we won the tournament. We met each other, right? Isn't that a win on its own?" I asked him desperately.

I had taken a few steps towards him without realizing it, though he still hadn't moved. He was still staring down at me with anger and confusion in his tired eyes, with no hint of a smile. I was starting to feel light headed and tired, not to mention the emptiness in my chest and ball of stress in my stomach. I just wished he would say something.

"Soul, come on! We can beat them. We are warriors. It's what we do! We can beat them and then we can start over. We'll be free of them for the first time in our lives."

"*The black crow flies free, and sings his very own song,*" he muttered. That was the poem he recited the day we met. I think it was called "Ravens' Revenge," an older tale. I thought about it for a moment. Maybe it's his favourite? Maybe ... it just fits.

"K9?"

"Yeah?"

"S-still ... love you..."

I looked back up at him as he played with his shirt and blushed. This time I think I blushed too. He had calmed down now and grabbed my hands as I leaned myself against his chest.

"Want to ... w-want to start over but only if ... only if my K9..." he stuttered. He drifted off as he kicked his toe on the ground. He tilted his head from side to side as he thought, probably debating what words he should use. I didn't bother letting him try to figure it out for himself. I didn't like it when he did that. I could see him struggling and I hated it.

"I want to start over too," I jumped in. "But only if you will come with me, my Crow."

He didn't look at me, but he grinned as his cheeks turned an even darker shade of pink. He nuzzled my nose and rested his forehead on mine.

"We should clean up, and then we can go see Tina. After that I need to try to get some sleep." I grabbed his hand once again and dragged him away from his room.

Johnny had left the pub early to go prepare himself for his commentary tomorrow, which left us to socialize with Soul's mother and sister. She was a nice woman, but she couldn't get used to seeing Soul as a grown man.

"He looked so different, smaller. He was always a relatively average size, but in his early high school days he was only tiny —well, maybe I'm exaggerating, but look at him now…"

She shook her head and I glanced over at Soul, who had smeared ice cream all over Tina's face. I smiled softly as he slowly looked back, a grin still playing with his features and a soft chuckle escaping his lips. The grin was replaced with a much more charming smile when our eyes met. His hair still fell over one eye but he looked content for once. I couldn't really describe it.

He slowly reached across the table and tapped my nose, ice cream dripping and falling down my face. I kept my eyes fixed on his while he tried to keep himself from laughing, a scowl meeting my lips — along with vanilla ice cream. I pretended to sigh and shake my head as he folded his hands in front of him and bit his lip. Tina was giggling beside him, so I shook my head at her too, making her laugh harder.

We all stood, pulled our jackets on, and walked out of the little café and into the cold street. It was snowing lightly while the four of us walked in silence down the narrow streets until we reached the hotel where Soul's family was staying. It was a fancy old building with ribbons taped to gold pillars and bright lights shining through glass doors. The air smelled like pine needles, and a thin layer of snow had accumulated on my shoulders.

"You were right," Soul suddenly told his mother. "The crow made a mess, can't fix it."

He wrung his hands. I hugged myself tightly as I shivered and watched what could be our final farewell. I just prayed it wasn't.

"Soul, we have argued a lot in our time together, but you've never made a mess you can't get yourself out of. You two are going to do great tomorrow," she reassured him. Her lip shook. He slowly let his eyes close as the older lady lightly touched his cheek. "You better win, boy. You better win for the three ladies who love you most. Don't get killed, Soul, just don't…"

He nodded and gave a small smile before suddenly embracing her, to her shock. He buried his face deep in her scarf and shook his head, "Made a mistake… C-can't — can't fix it. I-I'm sorry…"

"Now" — she patted his back — "don't tell me that. You don't need to do everything yourself. I've said that but it's never stopped you before, so now I have to put my foot down. You can't do this yourself and I don't want you to. K9 is not going to sit back and watch you fight, and she shouldn't have to, so listen to what she says and let her help."

He wiped his hand across his nose and stepped back, nodding and then getting down on his knees in the snow. Tina sniffled as she threw herself at her older brother and knocked him onto his behind.

"Don't die!" She softly cried into his hair, and he let her. His arms fit uncomfortably around her because of her small size. "Don't leave me again. I missed you so much! I can't let you leave me again!"

Soul shook his head, but she clung to him as hard as she could. "Won't — can't."

"But those guys could kill you!"

"They won't. The bird has the K9 now… Won't let anything happen to each other … r-right?" He looked up at me. I nodded back at him and shivered again. My mind was numb from sleep deprivation, and my toes were numb from the cold. But I was willing to let them spend as much time as needed together, even if it took a while.

Soul closed his eyes and stroked Tina's hair. Then he pried her off so he could stand up. She still cried and clung to his leg. His mother turned to me with determination and roughly grabbed my shoulders. "If he ever says he thinks he's going to lose, or he says that he can't do this, then I want you to hit him on the head to knock some sense into him. Take care of each other."

I nodded and hugged her tightly, her nails digging into my jacket. I sighed as I let her go and got down on my knees, motioning for Tina to come over. The tiny girl did and silently leaned against me. "My friend Louis will be around if you need him. He's a little bit scary but he's nice. He'll do whatever you need while we're at the tournament, okay?"

She sniffled but nodded. "You have to keep him safe though! You have to win and keep him safe!"

"I will, I promise."

Twenty-Seven

My stomach was in knots — so was my hair — and the ink on my cheek was smudged. My hands were shaking, I couldn't breathe properly, and my pants were too tight.

Soul, however, stood as still as a statue beside me as I desperately tried to readjust myself. Swords sitting awkwardly at my hips and a knife concealed in my boot ... all articles of clothing too tight. I nervously tugged at the tape around my chest, and the cloak hanging from my metal-plated shoulder pads brushed haphazardly against Soul's trench coat.

He barely flinched.

"I'm going to freeze out there," I muttered. I wasn't permitted to bring a jacket because they wanted us to wear our ordinary armour, so instead, Chrissy stitched a thick fur lining under the metal and stitched on thin sleeves made of fleece instead of spandex. Soul had reattached the sleeves to his jacket with some green string he found, making it look messy and probably not at all warm.

We were going to freeze out there.

It had warmed up overnight — enough that a sweater was warm enough for a walk — but we all knew that could change in an instant. Who knows? Maybe this place was part of Canada before the land shifted around again.

I had to stop letting myself get distracted! This was serious, we could die! And there was the stomach ache again…

"S-scared...," Soul stated suddenly.

We were moments away from being let into the battlegrounds, and the anxiety levels were on the rise. Every warrior was nervous, not just Soul and me, but I think we had the most to lose here. They were in the process of briefing us on the rules, which we already knew. The only ways to eliminate our opponents were to attack until their vitals dropped to threatening levels or to drive them out of bounds. It wasn't that hard to understand.

As they continued to give examples of past years' elimination tactics and a little bit of first aid training, I pulled Soul out of the tent.

Johnny was waiting just outside. He was leaning on both crutches and wearing a fancy suit, a pink daisy tucked into the pocket. I'd never seen him so dressed up.

"Benji, I should have told you this before I left; I don't have much time. I love you more than words can say, and I don't want you to do this — "

"Johnny, no. You can't do this to me again. I don't want to hear it!"

"Well tough!" He shouted, his eyes tearing up. "You're the only family I have! I'm supposed to keep you safe, and I can't do that out there!"

I stared at him. "You don't get to say this again! You knew what I was getting into when I joined the league. I'm doing this for you and you know it!"

"I don't want you to get revenge for me! Benji, I don't care about them. I don't want you to *die*! Our parents left you with me — they trusted me to take care of you. What will they think if I just let you walk into this?"

"You're an idiot!" I shrieked at him. We stared at each other for a second, and then he dropped his crutches and wrapped his arms around my neck. I hugged him back and supported most of his weight. His cologne was overpowering; it almost made me sick.

"I know," he sniffled, "I'm panicking for no reason. I wanted to remind you that you'll always have a way out, even though I know you won't take it. I won't be there this time. If it goes south I can't help you. Do your best out there for me. I don't want to see you bleed."

"You won't be there this time. I think that might help." I let go of my brother and kissed his cheek.

"I love you, Benji."

"I love you too. If things get bad, please don't watch. Promise me that."

He nodded and touched my hair, then took his crutches and started backing away. His finger crossed his chest and he choked as he gave a sad smile. "I can promise without a doubt."

I felt Soul wrap his arm over my shoulders as we watched Johnny hobble away. My eyes started to water and I rubbed my face. My stomach was hurting for a completely new reason. "Come on, let's go catch the last of the briefing."

As we pushed through the fabric, we ran smack into our biggest threats, Jekyll and Hyde. Without a word, Hyde produced a few photos from his ratty jacket and shoved them into Soul's hands. They looked like crime-scene photos, but I knew exactly what they were and took them from Soul before he registered what had just happened.

"We know how to get inside your head, K9. We know you," Hyde stated, snarling.

Jekyll's guttural bellow followed. "But there isn't much to know about that bird of yours. His head is empty, unpredictable. He doesn't think when he raises that axe. But his head isn't empty all the time, is it? What do you hear, boy? What do they tell you to do? Day in and day out, whose voices do you hear? Is it silent, or is there screaming — or maybe it's the blank and mindless filler of elevator music?"

"That's enough!" My cheek twitched as I demanded they stop. "We are only human! We don't deserve this abuse and your horrible tormenting. For the last time, our pasts are not your playthings. You can't make up our stories to make us weak! You can't use them against us anymore!"

"Oh, Vixen" — Hyde grasped his chest — "you've moved me."

"Oh, I'm going to move you in a second...," I growled. "Soul's health isn't yours to dictate. He is who he is. We are who we are. Pain is pain, and the world has done nothing to heal us, so thank you. Thank you both for teaching us how to take care of ourselves, how to lick our own wounds. Today I'm going to show you just how grateful I am."

I turned my back to them. Listening to their taunting wasn't going to help us, and it wasn't going to make us feel better. If I had to fake my strength in order for Soul to believe that I was not afraid to go head-to-head with those brutes, then that's what I would have to do. He had to believe we would do it. It was the only way we'd be able to.

Soul squeezed my hand and started to shake his head. His voice was stronger than I expected it to be, though he still stuttered, "C-can't — won't let them ... hmm-mm... They are wrong about the bird. They are wrong, K9." He leaned into me slightly while we walked out of the tent. It was comforting to have him this close. He was warm, alive.

"I wish ... I wish I could tell you that it's going to work out. I wish that I knew it's going to be okay, but I don't know! I can't lose you too!" I looked away from him and sighed. "We just... We can't let them scare us."

We started walking again, but the air was different. The rest of the warriors started to gather at the boundary of the battlegrounds, and we could hear them all chattering.

I swallowed my own fear and grabbed Soul's hand. He flinched but kept his eyes forward. The tournament's music sounded loudly and onlookers cheered, knowing very well that they were about to see people get slaughtered. I shivered slightly, and Soul squeezed my hand to reassure the both of us.

We could hear Agatha yelling from a few metres away, at her wit's end. "But what if we get separated? Or what if they make us go in separately? Then what? How do I find you?"

"Aggy, relax," Iggy said, looking annoyed.

"How can I relax? I'm marching to my death!"

"Ladies and gentlemen, this year's Tournament of Survivors will begin in a few moments." My brother's voice paused, with a hitch I knew all too well. "The warriors must decide between themselves who will enter the competition first."

Soul quickly flinched and turned his entire, large body to me. "K9 goes first!"

I slowly shook my head. "Nope." I bit my lip and looked up at him. "I went first last time, remember?"

Soul protested by grunting and whining, even shaking my arm. I laughed softly, but he roughly grabbed my shoulders and forced me to look at him again, determination pulling at his features.

"Have to!"

I shook my head again and grabbed him by the back of the neck, his straw-like hair getting caught in my fingers. "Once Jekyll and Hyde are finished and done with, I have nothing. All I have is Johnny, but it would be easier for him… Look, you still need to knock some sense into Dan! You have to take care of Tina. I've lived my dream and it wasn't too great! But you have so much that you never got to do. You need to get out of Dodge first! I can handle myself perfectly fine and you know that. If warriors decide to camp and wait to eliminate the second round, I can move faster than you. I'll run. I can get past them! You … might not be able to dodge them all."

His breathing increased. Violently shaking his head and swallowing hard, he shut his eyes. I yanked him closer again, his nose inches from mine. Those green eyes were filling me with guilt.

"Soul, just do it! You still have work to do, and it's important—"

"B-but, K9!"

"Crow … please."

He dropped his hands to his sides and sighed. I looked at the ground as he slowly started to nod, choking on his breaths.

"F-for my … K9?"

"Who else?" My voice caught and he bit his lip. My throat burned, but I stood ready as Soul stepped back beside me and tightly held my hand, fingerless gloves scratching my skin.

"My K9."

I nodded and placed my other hand on the hilt of my blade for reassurance. The other warriors were still buzzing and discussing, but we stood in silent fear. *God!* I really wanted Soul to be safe. Please be safe...

"Now I lay me down to sleep," I breathed, "I pray the lord my Soul to keep — "

"If I should die before I wake," Soul joined in. "I pray thy heart to never break..." He trailed off and grunted as he held in a frustrated shout. Every time he had to deal with something that was emotionally painful, he dealt with it like he was in physical pain ... which made it harder on both of us. That prayer... I didn't know what it was actually supposed to say, but he taught me his version the other day — or rather, he muttered it in his sleep.

"Alright, I hope everyone's ready because the forty-sixth annual Tournament of Survivors is about to begin!" Johnny yelled.

Soul exhaled, his face draining of colour even more if that was at all possible. I fought the urge to tell Johnny to get on with things. Luckily, a loud bell sounded and the first group was released. Soul started to step forward, but I wasn't quite ready to let him go yet and yanked him back by his arm.

The breath was momentarily knocked out of me as Soul quickly fell back and threw his arms around me. My nose pressed into his neck for a second, and then I shakily kissed his cheek, his hair tickling my ear. I squeezed my eyes shut and kissed his cheek again, harder this time. He started to turn his head, but before he had a chance to reach my lips, I stepped back and pushed him off. Why should I let him do that to us when I don't even know if there will *be* an us by the end of the day?

He took a few steps backwards but kept those tired eyes fixed on me. The shadows cast over him by the trees reminded me of the day we met, when his office was completely dark and I was at my wit's end. The tired and cautious look on my face must have resembled that of when we met as well, because my partner smirked and grabbed his axe before he disappeared. He shouted back to me as he started to run: "Mystery, mystery, what can I say?"

I shook my head and unsheathed my swords, biting my lip and getting antsy. A few minutes passed and the second group — including Greg, Ignatius, Hyde, and me — prepared ourselves.

The final bell rang out, and most of the warriors started running for the woods. Ignatius hung back and grabbed Greg's arm, whispering something to him, then walking towards me.

I still hadn't moved.

I had noticed that Hyde was stalking towards me at a relatively slow pace. I faced Ignatius. "Get out while you still can."

He shook his head and turned his back to Hyde. "There's a small cave a ways into the forest. If you need any of us, we'll be there."

I nodded curtly, then shoved him to the side, bringing both swords up to shield myself from Hyde's spiked mace. It was heavier than I was ready for, and I had to take a small step back in order to keep my balance.

"Why don't you run, little dog?"

"Because I'm not a puppy," I shot back. "I am a wolf, I am a hunter, and I am the best damn warrior you've *ever* made the mistake of pissing off!"

I shoved him back and roundhouse kicked him in his probably already broken nose. He hollered and swung at me again, blinded by tears and rage. I ducked under his arm, but his weapon caught my arm and threw me to the ground. I tried to hit him on the back of his neck but missed and slid my body through the mud to get away instead. A fistful of dirt in my hand, I leapt up again and threw it in his face. I brought my sword down on the back of his leg then shoved him down long enough to start running for shelter, holding my bleeding shoulder.

❦

The frost on the ground crunched under my boots, and my fingers were already starting to go numb, not ideal for the situation. My lungs burned and breathing quietly was becoming difficult, so I stopped and rested my back against a tree. I was starting to see my breath and could hear shouting extremely close by, so I pulled myself up onto a branch and waited.

Since it was damn cold and I didn't want to be there all day, I decided to pursue whoever was there, attempt to take them out. Little bit of practice, right? Balancing on thick branches and hopping between trees, I followed the sounds until I found a standoff between three men. They stood in a circle facing one another — a blond, a redhead, and a man with an eye patch. A fourth man was lying on the ground, eyes glazed over, clutching his chest. I couldn't tell if he was breathing or not, but I wouldn't be surprised if he were dead already.

"Well, boys, what do we have here?" I dropped from my perch and swung my sword around, the beads on the end wrapping themselves around my wrist.

"Look, lady. We're not going to hurt a girl, so just go find your boyfriend and — "

I cut him off by swinging my weapon directly down on his shoulder, tearing flesh and spewing blood across the forest floor. He fell to the ground and cried out for help, begging for the pain to end.

"I can make it stop, but I kind of want to maintain my status as a good guy, so I'll give you another option: quit. Leave the competition and someone will come get you. Otherwise you'll bleed out in a very short time," I offered as I rested the tip of my bloodied blade on the ground.

"Okay, I quit! Send in the damn medic."

I smiled and turned to his friends. They shared a look and one held his hands in the air.

"I quit too!"

"Are you kidding me? Fight like a man, will you! It's just a girl!"

I lost my temper again and kicked the sexist pig back, pinning him against a tree with my blade at his neck. "Are you sure you want to do this?"

I caught sight of a glass shard in his hand and felt a sudden stinging in my cheek; he made it clear that he was ready for a fight. I stepped back and punched him in the nose, cracking my knuckles and knocking him out. His friend thought he'd be smart and tried to hit me with his baseball bat. I leapt to the side and sighed as he went headfirst into a tree trunk.

"*Twenty-five of our thirty warriors are left!*"

I heard Johnny's voice faintly as I pictured the eliminated fighters' faces flashing across the bottom of every screen in the city, the same as they had every year I'd watched the tournament.

My brother. I'd put him through so much...

I shook off the feeling creeping up in my stomach and prayed that Soul wasn't the other person eliminated from the competition. I know the man on the ground was out, and so was the blond pig that quit. I wondered who the other three were. After dragging my sword across the ground to clean it, I looked into the trees and heard leaves rustle in the wind. I heard something else too. I recognized it but never would have known it was the sound of the strong, black wings of a crow if he hadn't perched himself in the exact spot I sat minutes ago.

There's no way it was Lock. Crows were smart, but that would be crazy, right?

"Hey, little guy." I held my arm up and he tilted his head. I gave a sigh and dropped my hand. "I must be crazy. I know, birdy, I should find *my* Crow." The bird squawked at me, then hopped to a different branch, his black feathers sticking off of him in the cold air.

"Look, I can't help you right now, but if I see you again, I'll try to find some food."

Hearing boots on the ground behind me, I quickly hauled myself back into the tree, hoping they hadn't heard me. I balanced carefully and waited. Maybe I could take out more warriors if I was lucky. I gave up hope of that when I saw the slick brown hair of Jekyll. The two men were stalking around and whistling, as though looking for a dog. This wasn't a fun game for me, but it clearly was for them. Following the little black bird that hopped along through the trees in front of me, I made my way deeper into the woods.

I'm not sure how long I was following the bird, but my knees were aching from all the jumping and crouching, and my hands were nearly torn to shreds by the frozen bark.

"I'm sorry, little crow, but I can't do this anymore. I need to get down." I shook my head and recklessly dropped onto the dirt, earning another caw of protest. My nose was frozen and I was tired. My skills ranged from long range to melee. They didn't include endurance and stamina. Clearly, I needed to work on that.

I scrunched my face to regain feeling and cracked my neck. Judging by the light in the sky, it was around the time that the warriors back home would be cleaning themselves up. But around here, families would be sitting down for dinner. Maybe if I hadn't tried to be like my brother, we'd be sitting at the table right now, waiting to see who would be the next warrior out, instead of him praying that his sister isn't next and me praying that the numbness in my body is just lack of blood flow and not hypothermia.

The crow's call pulled me back again. I shivered as I pulled my hood over my ears. He continued to complain and make noise as he jumped around.

"Thank you for your help, but as you can see, we are lost and you don't know where you are going."

I turned my back to him and muttered about how there's always some weirdo in the group; this year it must be me. Suddenly, the crow flew at me. I fell back and my behind hit the cold dirt as I avoided being pecked and clawed by the winged beast. He didn't seem happy, but he also wasn't about to leave anytime soon, so I stood and shushed him before starting to follow him again.

Yawning and shivering, I shook my head as I stepped around fallen trees and broken branches, dragging my feet more than walking at this point. There was a sudden three-part whistle from behind a wall of bushes beside me, and my body reacted by bringing my fists up and crouching down. The crow disappeared over the little white flowers on our right, which climbed over brush and wrapped around tree trunks. I could heart faint footsteps on the other side. After collecting myself, I pushed through the bushes. As soon as the treads of my boots hit the dirt, I shot forward and stuck out my arm to pin down the person standing behind the bush. My other hand was wrapped around my small dagger, ready to pull it out and use it if need be.

Muscles spasmed from the cold as I lifted my head to see under my hood.

"O-oh! Sorry." I stuck my weapon back into my boot and pulled my hood down so my beautiful Crow could see my face. He had blood running down the side of his head, and his lips were nearly blue. Still, he didn't seem to be shaking half as much as I was.

My bangs fell into my eyes as I stepped away from him, even though I really needed his warmth. He slowly sighed, took a step towards me, and reached up, lightly touching my hair and resting his ice cold lips against my forehead.

"S-stupid ... what my K9 did... C-could have gotten herself killed by the gemini! Don't want my K9 taken away..."

I closed my eyes as his lips moved against my skin. I nodded and mindlessly swung my body from side to side. The cold was making me sleepy and hazy. Not the best combination for this competition.

I shook my head and leaned away from him again, thinking about Dan, Angel, Johnny, and Henry. "I had a plan. I knew that if you left first, you would be fine but ... I'm sorry. The last few times I've depended on someone else's skills it hasn't ended well."

"We should start a fire. It's starting to feel like winter," I muttered. "I can't feel my ears."

We had been walking a while, deeper and deeper into the forest. I didn't like how far away we were from where the competition started. It would take a long time for someone to get here if one of us were to get hurt.

Soul silently nodded and then started to gather some small rocks and sticks. The crow watched for a while, then noticed how dark it was getting and left for his nest, wherever that may be. Soul gave a small and silent wave, then continued to gather supplies for me. I suppose it really was Lock after all. Soul wasn't entirely sure what he was supposed to do, but I took what he had gathered and dumped it on the ground beside my little, makeshift firepit. I put in only what I absolutely needed to so we didn't have to gather more. Rooting around in the dark might draw too much attention.

"M-match?" Soul questioned as he shivered.

"Don't have any." I tugged my knife out once again and hit it against a rock. "The old-fashioned way will have to do." I heard him give a small chuckle, almost more like a giggle, as his jacket dragged along the ground behind him. I sat back as the leaves started to burn. "I guess we should thank that bird of yours. It would have taken me a lot longer to find you otherwise."

He nodded, then slid off of the fallen tree trunk and onto the ground beside me, pulling his knees to his chest. "R-remember … when the dog met the bird, he said nary a word but the dog still wouldn't wander? He told her to go; she of course said 'no,' and the crow only grew fonder. Th-that day … said … and never got to — said and never finished…"

He scratched his head and tugged his coat closed. Grunting and shaking his head, he didn't bother to continue. He kept his eyes closed a moment, then looked back at me with a piercing gaze. He was very intense sometimes. I kind of liked that about him.

"C-can I…" he muttered, then held up his hand. I smiled, knowing exactly what he wanted. The scar on his cheek pulled his lips down as he contently sighed and rested his chin in the crook of his elbow. He searched my face like a curious bird searches for dropped food. Sometimes, he looked completely uninterested in everything around him, but now his eyes were wide and his pupils were dilated, something that happened whenever we were close, even since the day we met.

"My Crow…" I started as I felt my throat choke up. "You are very strange, and very kind to such an undeserving mutt."

He raised his head, shaking it vigorously. He hesitantly took hold of my hand, gently pulling it close to his face and warming my half-frozen fingers with his breath.

"N-no… K9, if anyone doesn't — if anyone shouldn't — the crow must not go, the crow is the one — "

"Soul, do you remember that video that they showed a few days ago?"

He nodded and I carefully lifted my fingertips to his pouting lip.

"And do you remember that Johnny has a little bit of a limp?" He nodded again and tilted his head. I scoffed at myself and shook my head. "It was my fault. I — we basically created those two demons… *You* were my fault too, and every time I look at you I remember that. Henry and I made idiots of them; we unleashed Jekyll and Hyde." I couldn't look at him.

"They never used to be like this. They were the stars of the underground. How can you be okay with this? How can you be okay with someone who has *your* blood on their hands?" I could feel the exhaustion through my entire body. I sighed. Soul rested his strong but gentle hand on my cheek. I still wouldn't look at him.

"My K9 … has *no idea* … the things the crow has done. F-fear and loneliness … can make a person do things they'll regret. But the gemini… They are not human, they do not feel regret. And they are not your fault." Soul hesitantly put his other hand on my other cheek, worriedly laughing and starting to smile. "Why sh-should *we* regret what we do to *them*?" He ran his tongue across his bottom lip and focused on playing with my tangled hair. "K9 and Crow … don't need to regret. Done with pity, done with sadness… The crow has *everything* he could ever want."

I didn't know what I was feeling. I'm not great with identifying emotions in general, but I'm pretty sure I was *glad* that he was happy. I know I was grateful for being the one fighting in this little war. I didn't think anyone else could do it and live with the things I had planned for the twins.

"You know what the worst part is?" I pulled his hands away and he scooted closer. "The *only* thing I feel bad about is not letting everyone else they hurt take a few shots at them first."

Soul's devious grin returned once again. His body swayed back and forth as he hummed a creepy little song and looked down at his hands, which were currently playing with the three silver rings on my right hand, distracting him from the conversation.

"Wolf…" he muttered as he tugged on one that looked like fangs. He continued to hum to himself absentmindedly as he rubbed my bloodied hand. I couldn't help but giggle softly about how concentrated he looked. Startled by my movement, he looked back up and blushed. His nose was touching mine, and he struggled to keep from glancing at my mouth as he opened and closed his own, trying to find something to say.

"Soul?"

I straightened my back and leaned forward, catching him off guard. He barely managed a squeak of a response as his eyes widened and he started to stutter. I shushed him quietly and reached under his jacket. He grunted again and nodded, eyes widening but staying fixed on mine. I smiled gently as I felt the hilt of a silver, engraved dagger. I wrapped my fingers around it and then pressed the palm of my hand against the matching shoulder armour in front of me. Soul sat with wide eyes and shallow breaths, still stuttering.

He seemed lost for a moment until he heard the same noise I had heard moments ago. Sometimes the easiest way to hit a target is to look distracted. I shoved Soul back, whipping the dagger out of his belt and throwing it towards the clicking I had heard in the bush. A moment later, there was an arrow from a crossbow embedded in the ground beside my leg.

Now, I'm not fond of pain but that doesn't mean I can't take it — but I'd really rather not be shot, as a rule.

I pulled Soul to his feet, and we ran out of the small clearing into the much darker forest. I didn't like the tree cover; I preferred open fields where I can see my enemy and take them down quickly. Soul, however, was able to navigate in the darkness far better than I was, so I simply followed him. The boots and voices behind us were getting louder and seemed to come from all directions, leaving few places for us to hide.

Soul looked back to make sure I was still right behind him, then kept running.

Cursing myself and then muttering an apology, I stopped and dodged to my left through the branches. The tags on my collar rattled as two men ran past me. One stopped but the other kept going. Carefully, I slid my sword free and raised it up. Then I kicked myself into the air and brought it down on the short man. It was Fred Burnham, Greg's fellow warrior from Dwyer. That made it far easier to bury my sword deep into his abdomen.

"I suggest you don't make a sound. It will be far less painful."

He gasped and wheezed, but nodded and then dropped to the ground the second I pulled my weapon, bloody once again, out of his seeping wound. He clutched at his stomach, and I set my boot against his shoulder, pushing him into the dirt and pinning him down.

"They'll pull you out of the competition soon — assuming you want to quit?"

"Y-yes, I quit!"

Burnham whimpered pathetically, but his expression shifted a second later and he sneered, "Th-they're coming for you, you bitch! Greg will kill you once he knows what you did to me, and Jekyll and Hyde are going to skin your boyfriend alive!"

I gritted my teeth and snatched him by the neck, choking the little rat. "Fear … will not work on me, don't you know that? *Fear* doesn't affect *me* anymore. You know, once you use something too much, the effects start to wear off. It's like a drug." I sneered and squeezed tighter.

His face went purple as he clawed at my hand, smearing blood down my arm. "I hope they find you... I hope they gut you like an animal! You're a traitor!"

Traitor.

"What the hell did you call me?" I gritted my teeth, bringing his face very close to mine. "You'll shut your mouth if you know what's good for you. I did what I had to do."

"You sided with the guy who attacked your comrades without a second thought... You're a goddamn traitor." He half coughed, half chuckled, spraying my face with blood. "And where is the greasy bird now? You took off on him, didn't you? To save your own skin. You're a real piece of work..."

He slowly slipped from my grasp and I stood straight. He smirked as he lay in his blood, which was now pouring out of his mouth too. I kicked him in the head. Then kicked him again and again. He grunted and groaned as his teeth got acquainted with my boot.

"Yeah," I murmured as I glanced at my crimson-coated hands, "I really am."

He met my eyes only for a second before I stomped on his abdominal wound, and he screamed for his life. He passed out quickly after that. I stepped back. I didn't clean my sword. I didn't shout for a medic. I just stared and wiped my forehead, grimacing as blood stained my white hair and pale skin.

I didn't leave until his chest stopped rising.

Twenty-Eight

I felt ... hollow.

My mind didn't wander. I wasn't curious about Soul, I wasn't worried about being found... I just wandered for a few minutes and thought about what Burnham said to me.

A traitor to what? A bunch of monsters who tried killing their own people to save themselves? A traitor to people who believed *I* was in the wrong? A traitor to Soul, who loves and admires me, for not believing his abilities? For running off on him and hoping for the best? For making him think everything's going to be okay!?

Gasping for air, I reached for the nearest tree in order to steady myself. I wasn't even sure where I was exactly. Sweat started to form at my hairline and I pushed my bangs back. I singlehandedly alienated anyone who even remotely liked me in order to help one man I wasn't even sure I could trust ... *on a hunch*. On a hunch that he was a victim in all this too. I had no proof at the time, and I just went along! I was so stupid! My empathy got the better of me — stupid emotions that were going to get me killed, my pride and empathy...

No sane person would have done what I did. No sane person would purposely bring *hell* down on themselves. People look at me differently now; people don't see the same warrior they did two or three months ago. They see someone who was manipulated, someone who did something reckless for the sake of making a statement. That's not how it was though. They didn't get it. Soul wasn't like that.

Even Chrissy looked at me differently…

Yeah, it was reckless and stupid of me to put so much faith in him, but they didn't know the full story, they couldn't see the *fear* in his eyes. That fear was practically tangible, and the pain hurt me too. It wasn't as bad now; now I was just angry. We were going to have to kill the source. Soul was not weak and I was not a traitor, not to anyone. They should've known that by now. They knew who we were and what we'd done. They just didn't know what we're *going* to do…

Fear and pain was their game, but rage and vengeance was ours.

We were going to burn. Them. *Down.*

I looked up with watery eyes and determination in my chest. This would be *their* kingdom come.

Twenty-Nine

The air was still freezing but I wasn't the least bit cold. It burned my throat and lungs but I was *excited*.

I looked up through the frozen branches and caught the faint light of the moon. Grinning, I bolted through the trees, hooting and howling in excitement. I made my way back to the embers of our fire and looked around. The arrow was still sticking out of the ground, but there was no one around.

"K9!"

Spinning to the north, I heard Soul's faint call. From the other direction, I heard running and panting. I started running towards my Crow, the reason I was in the mess in the first place, and the best mistake I'd ever made. Branches and twigs were cutting my arms and face, but I was still faster than the person following me.

I slid to a stop and stared forward, where Soul was waiting with a scowl. His coat was swaying behind him as he stood amidst falling snow. A smile slipped across my crooked face and I shook my head, then leapt forward and swung myself into a tree above him. He grunted as he reached for my hand and did the same.

"I told you that being able to pull your weight would be useful." I grinned and nudged his arm.

Rolling his eyes, he leaned against the trunk of the tree and scowled like he was angry with me. I started to worry about him; I could understand him being upset but he was also clutching his left shoulder.

"Are you okay?" I asked, a little more solemnly.

He shrugged, then bit his lip. "K-K9 left … again." He looked away from me and down at his hand, soaked in blood.

"Soul, I promise I won't leave again. I promise, now sit so I can look at your arm."

I didn't know why I kept trying to help with cleaning and covering wounds. I didn't know what I was doing when it came to that. Yes, that was most definitely a wound, and it was most definitely bleeding. My friend silently did as he was told and moved his hand, but he was upset and wouldn't meet my eyes.

"H-how … could the K9 do that? W-worried the bird sick…"

"I know, I'm sorry. I was just scared and I don't want to — I don't want to see something happen to you. If they got us, I wouldn't be able to handle watching you get hurt."

He pursed his lips and shrugged it off, then examined me. Blood was still caked onto our skin.

"Hurt?"

I shook my head. "It's not mine."

"What happened?" he asked softly as he huddled closer, resting his cold nose in the fur of my hood.

I exhaled and grimaced as I pulled the black leather away from his skin, once again soaking my hands. "I lost my temper."

He sat back and watched me move.

"Burnham said they're going to gut us like animals, and he called me a traitor. I thought about it but he's wrong."

"K9 is a survivor, not a traitor." He paused and wrung his hands. "B-but … Crow was never going to hurt the K9… D-didn't mean to force you to help…"

I chuckled softly and shook my head as I went back to his arm. I unwrapped the tape from my wrist and wrapped it around his sleeve, earning a grunt and a wince.

"You never forced me to do anything. You did give me a good scare, though."

He shrugged and hesitantly wrapped his good arm across my back.

"K9 got hurt *so* many times because of the crow ... s-so many times..." He whimpered and bit his lip. *"Have to run, have to hide, don't want to meet you on the other side..."*

I ran my hand through my hair as he looked at the stars. "Not yet, anyway."

After a few minutes of silence, he swung his leg over the branch and rested his back against the trunk. I could hear his jacket scratching the bark as he sighed, his blue-black hair shining in the moonlight. Did he even care that he was the strangest man I had ever met? Strange could be very elegant and beautiful in the right light. I wondered what was going through his head...

Slowly looking back at me, he offered a nervous smile. I pulled myself closer to him and grabbed his hand. "Tina said you used to tell her stories. What were they about?"

Soul tilted his head and shrugged his shoulders. "Warriors ... exaggerations of what would happen. C-can't ... tell her anymore... Too — too hard to put..." He squeezed his eyes shut and shook his head, repeating that he couldn't tell them anymore. "Mm ... no more stories..." He chuckled but I could see his eyes watering behind his dark hair.

"I'm sure she'd like some of your poems," I responded, letting him play with my hand again. "You tell stories through them, too."

He nodded and looked up again. He was tired, and his arm was probably in much more pain than he was letting on. He still looked hurt that I left him, but I didn't know what else to say. I'd apologized already but I still felt like he was conflicted or angry — and he had every right to be.

"Soul, I — "

"She loves me
She loves me not
Once I'm buried

Why bother be sought?
No one loves me
Except she who rots
But even then
She had to be bought
With flowers and a kind word
That was learned by the bird
Even though it was completely absurd…"

Soul's hand left mine, and he tugged me closer to him as he shivered from the cold. I could hear him sniffle slightly, but he continued his poem.

"It was a lie
Told by the boy
That had played me
Like I was his toy
She did not care about
Such petty joys
She only loved me
Because what I destroyed
Was the remains of a place
That hurt a pretty face
And thought she was a complete disgrace,"

I watched Soul wrestle with conflicting emotions. He started to shiver even more, keeping his eyes fixed on mine for a moment before his cheeks took on a pink hue and he stuttered. He looked down and licked his lips, which were starting to get chapped in the cold air. The poor man was starting to feel the result of his injuries, combined with the cold. He intertwined his fingers with mine and smiled to himself, looking innocent and content, and ignoring his pain.

"She was so beautiful
She'll never understand
All the sadness that I felt

> *When I couldn't hold her hand*
> *She told me that I shouldn't*
> *And it wouldn't be so grand*
> *I told her she was wrong*
> *And I'd take her to a safer land*
> *Where all we'd be is her and me*
> *And she'd never ever feel so free*
> *And all I wanted was us, and she…*
> *But the boy hated every second*
> *Of not having her alone*
> *So he wanted to kill us*
> *And threw a great big stone*
> *She laughed at his misfortune*
> *And we ran all the way home*
> *But he followed us there*
> *He didn't want to roam*
> *He lit the place on fire*
> *'Please tell me why?' I did inquire*
> *'Because it's she he did desire'*
> *And then he threw me in a tomb.*"

Soul clung to my hand and continued to stare into the darkness, refusing to look at me or let me go. My stomach was tense and my throat was starting to feel dry, but the best way for me to put this is that I felt a little bit … *struck*. I might have been delirious, but even in the middle of a battleground, he made me feel safe.

"Soul, was that like your stories?" I asked quietly.

He nodded and spun a ring around my finger. "J-just thought — because the worm… H-he wanted my K9. He said I'd never be lucky enough to have my K9! He said you would fall for *him* and the bird would be alone … because no one could love a … a *broken toy*."

Pins and needles in my heart. I sadly placed my hand against his cheek. "I always did like to pull the heads off of my dolls."

"S-still scared the dog will leave…" He leaned into my hand and closed his eyes. His lip shook as he sniffled again, despite his small chuckle.

"Soul, I'm afraid that losing people we love…" I paused as my voice caught and I had to take a breath. "Losing people we love is something that happens far too often. The ones worth loving don't leave — "

"No … they are taken."

"I'm not going to be taken, by anything. I swear I'm with you until the end." Satisfied with my quick comeback, I nodded and gave a soft smile, watching my breath swirl in the air in front of us. My attention was brought back to my partner as his body shook. Tightly holding my hand, he shook his hair out by shaking his head vigorously from side to side.

"C-confused by my feelings, certain about others… The crow knows he is yours but he doesn't know why. Certainly don't want to be alone again," he muttered as he held his shoulders close. He grimaced and grunted as he struggled to hold his arm in place, but denied my help.

"I know. I don't want to lose you either, but I'm very afraid I might."

He shook his head, gritting his teeth. "Never."

Thirty

I felt like my fingers were about to fall off.

I sat up and looked around with a groan. Frost covered the trees, and my hair was frozen stiff. Soul was lying against the tree trunk, shivering. I poked him and he snorted as he bolted up. He blinked repeatedly and looked around.

"Nice nap?"

Scowling, he looked away from me and started to rub his arm. After a few seconds, he made an effort to slide from the tree. He hit the ground and started to stretch his spine out with a grunt, so I followed him and checked my weapons. We started to walk through the forest, back to where Ignatius had told us to meet him and the rest of our friends yesterday. I held Soul's hand tightly, partially to reassure him but also to keep my hand warm. At least he had pockets in his jacket.

"*Eighteen warriors left!*"

My eyes shot to Soul, who was trying to hide a small grin. I shook my head and looked through the trees, hearing dogs howling and crows calling. Nature is dangerous around here, and I didn't know much about most of the wildlife ... but it was kind of nice. If, you know, we weren't being picked off one by one. Again.

We both spun at the sound of rustling bushes and footsteps. Soul's first instinct was to free his axe and step in front of me, blocking my view, which was *not* helpful for me.

"Whoa! Relax, big guy!"

I peeked around Soul's large body and saw Ignatius holding his arms up in defence as Aggy and Greg ran up behind him.

"You never showed so we got worried," he said.

"Sorry, we got a little caught up — "

"H-hey … pretty boys and their toys…" an unfamiliar voice sneered.

Cringing, we all whipped around as fast as possible. There was a very pale and sickly-looking man with hunched shoulders and red eyes. He looked like he had gone insane a very long time ago and was only seeing the world now. I really didn't feel like getting in his way, so I stepped to the side as he raised his machete to Soul, who dodged him fairly easily. Ignatius and Greg pulled their knives out, but the lunatic didn't seem to care about them. He went straight for Aggy, catching her across the chest. There was a long tear in her tunic, and her blood seeped through, soaking her clothes. I watched her gasp and fall to the ground as the man laughed and made a face at her cousin.

His sickly outline was prominent in the green-and-white forest. He was dressed in red and black armour. I recognized it from a couple towns over from Lilithia; they'd always seemed so tame in previous years. Things change, I guess. He continued to taunt us until I swung my left fist at his nose and he stumbled back. He started to shriek and curse, taking a swing of his own and reopening the tear in my cheek. The ground was cold when my shoulders hit it. Greg leapt up and deflected another swing of the machete away from me. The man turned on Greg and thumped him hard on the head. Greg collapsed in a pile, apparently unconscious.

After the man turned back, trying to take *another* shot at me, Ignatius grunted, then made one quick slash at the man's back and struck him down.

"Agatha…" I stumbled towards her blood-soaked figure. I tore her jacket up and wrapped it around her as best I could, but blood still soaked through.

Ignatius knelt at her side, giving a pained look.

"What do we do now?" I asked.

"Agatha, hang in there. I'll get you help." He turned to look at me, his normally bored expression given over to worry. "She's out of the game, and I can't leave her like this alone. Good luck, you two." And with that, Ignatius wrapped his right arm around his red-haired cousin while taking a firm hold of Greg's belt. He lifted them both, and they walked away.

Soul gave a small, uncertain wave as our ally started making his way back to the entrance. My brother's voice faintly rang out in the distance, letting us know there was only sixteen people left, us included. I sighed and shook my head. I was starting to feel sick again and I missed Johnny. I should have visited him more often.

"K-K9 ... okay?"

I absentmindedly nodded at my crow and let him grab my hand as he started humming.

> *"Burn to ash*
> *And crumble to ember*
> *You get what you give*
> *And don't deserve to live*
> *You wreak havoc*
> *So reap what you sow*
> *Your time will come*
> *And you're completely numb."*

I smiled slightly and swung our hands as I looked back up at him. His breathing was shallow, but he was content with just holding my hand and watching the sky. Looking back down at me, he took a quick breath, his bottom lip shaking slightly.

> *"A group of three*
> *That had hired thee*
> *Has gone down in flames*
> *But I'm still not happy*
> *Burn to ash*

And crumble to ember
I could learn to forgive
And just be positive —"

Soul stopped dead and slowly took his hand from mine, once again reaching for his weapon. I did the same and grimaced when twelve men and women stepped out of the woods, led by Jekyll and Hyde. They had waited until our friends had gone, apparently. I wonder if the lunatic was their idea too.

"But you wreak havoc
So reap what you sow
And what you've done
Will be your Kingdom Come…"

Soul raised his weapon but I stopped him; we needed a plan. He stuttered angrily for a few milliseconds before listening to me.

"Soul, we should split up — "

"No."

"I know I said I wouldn't leave you again, but we can both handle a seven-on-one situation, right? We're better than them. We're Lilithia warriors! If we let them all go at once, we have to worry about them and each other. They'd overpower us; we don't know how to work as a team. Just … just go."

After a second of glaring at the group and scowling at me, he reset his axe in its place. Then — without looking away from the group — he walked a few paces backwards and started to run, Jekyll shouting for Hyde and his team to follow. The rest stayed and stared at me as I drew my swords.

Jekyll ordered everyone else to make a move against me. They each took shots, one after the other, but I dodged enough that they kept hitting each other instead. Eventually, I had to retaliate by slashing and shoving, using more energy than I would have liked to. This would be a long fight.

I had taken three down when Jekyll jumped into the fight. I started to panic and jump away from him as much as possible, but I only succeeded in cutting my arms and torso on branches and other sharp weapons. My left arm defended my face while the other worked as offence, though still keeping a distance from the Irishman. The most impressive part of all this was that I managed not to step on or trip over my cloak even once.

Fifteen minutes later, I had taken out all but one of Jekyll's warriors. The last woman left standing, who was horribly scarred and burned, looked desperately between Jekyll and I, terrified.

"I can help you. I know he threatened you. Help me and you'll live..." I offered darkly — desperately.

She nervously shook her head, contemplating my words as I tried kicking at Jekyll. His grim, grey eyes followed like a hawk's. His mouth was twisted into an evil grin. It was a grin I wish I never saw, one that will be burned into my mind for the rest of my life.

"Don't listen to her! She's a killer and a traitor!"

I glared daggers at him and kicked his accomplice out of my way before sticking my sword deep into Jekyll's forearm. I stood up and looked at the woman as blood shot in every direction. She looked horrified, but Jekyll wasn't going to give her a chance to decide and ripped her throat wide open with a small dagger he plucked from another fallen warrior's hand. Blood and bone spilled onto the ground, something else I will never forget.

Her body fell and Jekyll chuckled. "You shouldn't have left your boyfriend, Vixen..."

This entire situation was paralyzing and depressing; the human body is still so weak for all we put it through. Instinctively, I started to run in the opposite direction, mumbling Soul's poem to keep myself in the right mind.

> *"You created me*
> *As long as you live you'll never be free*
> *But I'm a busy girl*
> *So dead you'll have to be."*

I grabbed a tree trunk and redirected my path, but Jekyll was still close behind me.

I stumbled over myself and hit the ground with a curse and a grunt. My armour bounced against my jaw and I started to bleed, frost forming around my mouth. I sat up as Jekyll ran over and pulled me off the ground. My mind was getting hazy from the previous concussion, which he and his brother had caused last week, as well as from the one I just took. I half-heartedly tried to kick myself out of his grip as the brush behind him began to rustle.

"Give up and I'll let you live — with a catch, of course," he snarled.

He looked over my armour and unhooked the buckle across my shoulders. I spat copper-tasting liquid at him, and I started to recite once more, this time meant to distract him.

> *"Burn to ash*
> *Crumble to ember*
> *Isn't it all so provocative*
> *By how short we may live?"*

He dropped me onto the ground, landing on top of my armour. He kicked my ribs as he aggressively wiped away blood from his face, growling and shouting as he kicked me again. I started to bleed even more as I whined. I made sure I had all my weapons, then slid across the ground and away from him, kicking up dust and frozen dirt as I did so. A moment later I heard heavy footsteps and grabbed a tree branch to pull my aching self up. I waited and watched for who it could be, praying that it was Soul.

Luckily for me, it was.

Unluckily for Jekyll. Soul looked angry. He didn't even give Jekyll a chance to move. He walked straight over and used the blunt end of his axe to knock him down.

"Run."

I stuttered and looked around as I grabbed my head, bitterly snapping back. "Wh-why? There's no one — "

"*Run!*"

Soul snatched my arm and pulled me out of the clearing as fast as he could. He didn't let go. I was forced to follow him through the forest, his hand the only thing holding me upright. A gunshot rang out and a nearby tree splintered. That was more than enough to motivate me. We both started to pick up the pace, tripping over each other and feeling the sting of twigs and the frost on our faces.

After a few moments, we could hear Johnny with the announcements. "*Four warriors left. This has to be the quickest a tournament has ended. The remaining warriors are Benji 'K9' Keanin and Soul 'Crow' Ravin, both from Lilithia Heights; James Utterson, otherwise known as Jekyll; and Howard Utterson, otherwise known as Hyde, competing for Bell Hearst.*"

"Oh god…"

Soul pulled me into a clearing and looked around. "N-need to … to hide…"

He rested his hands on his knees as he tried to catch his breath.

"Fighting them is going to be an effort, I don't know if we can — "

"Not leaving you!" he shouted, incredulously.

"Soul! Listen to me! We will fight for as long as we can, but if we *can't* — if we get too tired — I want you to run as fast as you possibly can and I will do the same, okay?" I grabbed his shoulders and he glared at me, hurt and confused.

"Not going to leave. Not again… You promised!" Soul shoved my hands away and stood to his full height.

He was much taller than me and still very intimidating. If I didn't know him, I wouldn't want to get on his bad side, even when he looked as miserable as he looked now.

"We have to!"

"No, we don't!"

Soul was going to stand his ground, and I felt like he'd take them both on himself if he had to. At that thought, my anger took over. I smacked his chest and shouted, "Why don't you listen?!"

He calmed down slightly and looked down, still very conflicted. The sudden bitterness in his voice hit me almost as much as what he said did: "You were a mistake…"

I froze on the spot. I wasn't going to cry, not for him — not about this. But I felt like I was, so I used my best defence and shoved him. He stood relatively still, not bothering to stop me.

"Say something rational, Soul! Anything other than that!" I could hear my voice crack, against my will. "Why won't you trust me? I know what I'm doing!"

He grunted and scowled, shaking his head. "Do *anything* for the K9… The bird would *die* for the dog but the dog doesn't care! The dog … K9 doesn't… K9 *never* loved me … can't even say so … n-not going to waste my time. O-owed you my *life*… Not going to waste my time anymore."

I watched him turn his back to me and wait for Jekyll and Hyde, weapon tight in his grasp.

"The crow flies west. And then…" — he choked up and looked down, whispering bitterly — "and then … K-K9 won't have to deal with the crow anymore. S-sweep me away so you're not responsible…"

I stopped breathing for a moment. Did he just … *dump me?* Did I just lose Soul? I could feel my throat close, and my vision blurred as tears spilled down my cheeks. Of all the ways I could possibly have lost him and it would end like *this*?

I stood, cold and heartbroken. I partially nodded and carelessly tugged at my swords. I was not ready to fight. I was too distracted —

but Jekyll and Hyde were still running towards us. When they were a just a couple of yards away, they looked at each other. Hyde finally broke the silence after a tense few seconds. "I'll take the bitch, you take the bird."

Soul tugged his jacket farther down his shoulders and cursed at the man who scarred him. Guilt was nagging at me and I was still light headed, but I couldn't let Soul go, especially if I might never see him again.

"Soul!"

"K9, go!"

"Soul, please…"

He clashed with Jekyll, sliding each weapon against the other, daring their opponent to make a mistake. Hyde lumbered over and raised his own weapon behind him. He brought it down against my swords, creating sparks and pinning me to the cold ground.

"Asshole…" I snarled at him.

He grinned menacingly and leaned over me, taking another swing. I barely had enough strength to push him away, letting out a small yelp. More of a cry for help really. I prayed Soul would turn around as quickly as possibly because Jekyll had produced a gun and tossed it to Hyde. I kicked at him as I continued to use all my strength to push the man off of me, not doing well since he was winning with only one hand.

"You know, this is a shiny little toy, but I like doing things the old-fashioned way," Hyde muttered, his lips curling back as he tucked the pistol away. "It's more fun."

"Soul!" My shout didn't seem to register, but he gave Jekyll a good shove and the man collided with his brother. I jumped up and alternated between kicking Hyde and stomping Jekyll, until Soul grabbed my arm to turn me around.

"Bleeding."

My arm stung where he was holding it but I kicked Hyde once more, then ripped my arm free from Soul. "Don't touch me."

It would seem we were too busy glaring bitterly at each other to notice that one of the men had gotten up. Hyde lunged at me and ripped my sword from my hand. We both smashed our fists into his head, making him drop the sword, then Soul jumped to the left and picked it up, begrudgingly tossing it back to me and then grunting as he cast one last glance and then ran off.

Things were fine yesterday … even this morning. Why does the world turn into hell whenever we need it the least? How can we fall so far, so fast? And once again, Why *us*?

Soul bolted through the trees, ignoring the remorse that was blatantly written across my face. I was ready to make amends. I didn't mean for this to happen…

I was so focused on Soul that I was forgetting the battle at hand. Jekyll scrambled and stirred up dust and leaves as he followed my Crow. At least Hyde had the common decency to let me wallow in self-loathing for a minute before he attacked. He was carrying his spiked mace and that razor wire, neither of which put me at ease. He lunged forward and I stumbled back, storming right through the treeline.

I knew we were close to the main entrance, but I wasn't sure I even wanted to find it.

After running and wheezing for a while, I tripped and twisted my ankle. Groaning and whining, I pulled myself up by a branch, resting quickly as blood trickled from my arms and face.

"So, Hyde," I started, thinking I could hear his footsteps, "how does it feel to have lost to a girl after being the biggest thing in Lilithia all those years ago?"

Silence. I couldn't hear anything anymore so I looked back, but no one was there. I stood on one leg in the cold, but as far as I could see, Hyde hadn't followed me.

"*Goddammit!*"

I let go and fell forward. After pulling myself up off my knees, I started to look for tracks, or anything. Panic was hitting me hard. If they both caught up to Soul, he'd be dead. I couldn't let that… I couldn't see that happen!

"N-no … no, no, no!" I stumbled and clawed my way forward, hoping for any sign of any of them.

Suddenly, the voice of my brother was coming from all around me, booming out through the speakers in the little drone cams. I had forgotten about them.

"*Jekyll and Hyde have made a request that we tell 'Vixen' this: 'You were close, but gambling with death means you're going to lose your Soul.' Ben, I'm so sorry…*"

I started to fall apart at Johnny's words. I bit my lip as hard as I could and pulled my hair back, smudging almost-dry blood across my forehead. My breathing quickened and I fell to my knees, covering my mouth. My voice ripped through my throat in a long, harsh cry that felt like it was shredding my vocal chords. I couldn't lose Soul — he didn't know! I never got to tell him … I-I wanted him back! I *needed* him back! I leapt up and ran back to the entrance. If they gave Johnny that message, then they should still be close.

It might be a trap but I'd give my life to save his. To stop this.

Thirty-One

"Come out, come out, wherever you are…"

By this point my entire body was numb and my leg was killing me, but I had found the gate. I rested my head back against a tree and, drawing my sword, limped forward. My face was numb, and my lips were so cold I couldn't even speak properly. I should have trusted him, should have told him how I felt. I should never, *ever* have left any room for doubt.

"You wanted me, you got me!" I shouted into the air futilely. "Come out and fight fair!"

There was nothing. Sighing, I continued walking to the west and towards the setting sun. It cast a golden glow through the frozen trees.

"Jekyll! Hyde!"

I called to them over and over again until I noticed that all of the spectators behind the barricade were gathered a little farther down, staring and yelling about something. And then I noticed the large screen they were watching. I ran to the gates. All I could see was Jekyll dragging Soul by his jacket. He was unconscious and slashed right down his chest, which worried me, considering the amount of blood staining the ground below him. I didn't know where they were; all those damn trees looked the same to me.

A few people turned to me, the heat from my face melting the frost while I glared at the screen.

"Benji!" I heard a familiar voice from inside the crowd. "Benji!"

Suddenly Louis Crane stepped forward, pushing spectators out of the way to get to the gate. "He's hurt badly. You have to try to bandage him up until I'm let in!"

"Louis," I muttered as I watched the screen, "which way did they go?"

He glanced around, knowing that he shouldn't get involved. I turned my body towards him and snatched his dirty green shirt from across the barricade. His buggy eyes went even wider.

"*Ichabod!*" I hollered in his face.

He shook his head and pursed his lips. "Y-you know it's against the rules!"

"The rules aren't in play anymore! I need to find him. You saw what happened! If I lose him, then he at least needs to go out knowing that he's loved. You, of all people, should know what loneliness does to your sanity."

I was holding him close by the collar of his jacket, looking him straight in the eyes and breathing hard. I would never be able to truly show them the real rage behind my eyes.

Louis started to stutter and nervously glance around until he finally broke. Though aggravated, he held his hand up and pointed. "They went north."

I nodded and patted his chest as I started to step away. He simply scowled and shook his head. Past him, I could see Johnny up on a stage of sorts, calling out various actions, grimacing and cringing every few seconds. He seemed to be taking the stress badly. Chrissy stepped up and grabbed his hand to comfort him, and he seemed to relax a bit. I nodded to myself again and caught Dan's eye. He slowly started to turn to me as I took a few steps back, only to stop.

"Benji, look out!" Dan called.

I was about to duck or turn around or something — but two hands on my arm prevented that from happening, slamming my shoulders back onto the cold ground instead. Even through all the choking and wheezing, I knew who it was.

"T-took you long enough to find me."

My words were met with the dark chuckle of a madman, a chuckle that could only belong to Hyde. I sat up, only to be kicked between the shoulder blades. My lip started to sting as I fell back down and lay still, spitting and drooling in all my bloody and dignified glory. Discreetly, I slid the knife from my boot and got ready to slash. Hyde rolled me onto my back and I sat still, looking up at him and waiting for the best moment, which happened to come as he prepared to snap my ribs with his boot. I grabbed his leg and tore into it with the knife, ripping open the flesh of his calf.

I admit, it didn't exactly save my life, but it did buy me time.

As the large man fell back, I reached across the ground for the sword I dropped when he first threw me down. The light frost was melting under my stomach. I felt for the hilt and wrapped it tightly in my hand, then brought it over one shoulder and across my back, blocking Hyde's weapon and bending the blade.

I lay face down and protected myself with the bit of strength I had left for a moment. Then he rolled me over and ripped the sword from my hand, grabbing it by the silver blade with his ungloved, bloody hand. He only made his existing wounds worse. I still, however, lost the weapon. He tossed the thing to the side like a toy, and it clattered against the bars of the barricade. I tensed my muscles as he relentlessly started to kick at me. I cried out and bit my lower lip as I felt a stabbing pain in my side.

"How does it feel to die alone and unloved?" Hyde hissed as he flicked his hand at me. I shook my head and started to choke, blood running from my nose to my throat. You know when you feel like you're about to throw up but you can't, so your mouth just starts to shake and water? That's what I was feeling. Hyde pulled me off the ground by my upper arm and chuckled as I gagged.

"You ... tell ... *me!*" I stuck my small dagger into his shoulder once again and he dropped me. I cried out — landing on a broken rib tends to do that, I guess. I pushed myself to my feet with a grunt and stumbled a few feet before landing on my knees. I got yanked back again by my hair.

"Before I rip your insides out through your mouth, I have something to show you."

I took another shot to the head, and blood blinded me as Hyde pulled me up again. He glanced over my face and sneered, mimicking my voice, "Say something, Soul, anything!"

He let out the most raucous and sinister laughter I had ever heard, and that included Louis's. I grunted and swung my fist at his nose, missing narrowly. He continued his laughter as he dragged me through the trees and into the dark forest.

I wasn't sure how long he made me follow him, but I was starting to lose consciousness — maybe from the cold, maybe from the blood loss. He started to get tired of dragging me behind him and chuckled. When I heard that devil's laugh, I knew something was up, and it probably wasn't going to be good for me.

And then he tossed me to the ground again. I landed in a deep pond that wasn't quite frozen over yet. I rubbed my face, washing the blood away from my eyes, but I scrambled to get out as fast as I could. I tried to climb out multiple times as my fingers lost feeling and my muscles seized up, but Hyde simply laughed and dunked me under again. Do you know what happens when you inhale ice cold water? The water itself burns your lungs.

I silently pleaded and begged Hyde to let me up, and he did, after a few agonizing moments. He hauled me out of the water, letting me rest in the dirt before pulling his wire from his belt and grinning like the savage he is. I scrambled to my feet, gasping for breath and slipping all over the place. I crossed my arms around my body and shivered. But Hyde continued to smirk.

"Please, just let me see Soul... You can do whatever you want to me after that." I stepped forward and clutched his jacket in my hands as I begged. I *begged*. Benji Keanin had *never* begged for anything in her life and yet here I was, practically on my hands and knees begging to see some wild-eyed, messy-haired … *guy*.

I started to feel angry and bitter. I betrayed his trust… If I hadn't let myself be ruled by cowardice… And for what? Everything had backfired so badly, and I didn't even know why anymore. I didn't even know what's going on. I should have had a plan.

"Please just let me see him…"

Another dark chuckle, and then he tilted his head with a grin. "Where do you think we're going, Vixen?"

My confusion must have been written on my face. Hyde shook his head, amused, and started to shove me along a worn path and into a clearing.

Thirty-Two

My heart sank. There was razor wire strung up in the trees of the clearing, but what caught my attention was Soul. One of his legs was wrapped tightly in the wire, and he was hanging about eight feet off the ground, upside down. His coat had been torn in many places, and his shirt was practically nonexistent. A long gash across his chest was dripping blood from his collarbone to his hair, and pooling on the ground below him.

He was out cold, but I had no idea how long he'd been like that. It could already be too late.

I had one sword left. I quickly ripped it out of its sheath and pointed at Hyde, his brother at his side now. I didn't get a single hit in. They circled me, and then one took the sword from my hand while the other shoved me down. Choking up, I sat on the ground between them and glared daggers.

"The last thing you two did was argue. How does it feel to watch him die, knowing that he no longer loves you?" Jekyll asked.

I wouldn't meet his eyes. I just sort of stared over my shoulder at my Crow.

"I'm going to hurt you," I whispered.

My eyes shifted back to Hyde, with my weapon in his hand. Looking at the ground, I gritted my teeth. I used the last of my strength to launch myself towards Hyde. I elbowed him in the nose and repeatedly kicked his stomach until his brother wrapped his large hands around my neck. I fell to the ground, where they both proceeded to swing fists and razor wire.

Each slash opened a new wound. My body started to go cold, colder than the ice, water, and weather had already made me — the kind of cold your hand would get after it fell asleep, numb. I blinked to clear my vision as I lay on my stomach, waiting for my death. My entire right arm was soaked in blood and throbbing like there was no tomorrow, which there probably wouldn't be...

I lay still and the twins backed off, Hyde stepping behind me and lifting my head by my hair for the second time today. Grinning, Jekyll took a small knife engraved with birds and golden inlays, then walked closer to Soul.

"Don't you d-dare touch him," I hissed. Blood filled my eyes for the most part, and I couldn't move my leg in the slightest. I was helpless and I hated it. My mouth wouldn't move properly — it was too cold and too numb — but I managed to scowl at him.

"Look at this realistically, K9!" Jekyll shouted at me. "You are *done*! Your boyfriend is *done*! You are both going to die here, and you can't stop it!"

Hyde tugged my hair again and chuckled giddily. I felt sick to my stomach.

"M-maybe that's true, but there's always going to be someone around who wants you gone. Even if we die here ... you won't make it back to Lilithia..."

I spat blood in his direction, and he slapped me hard across the face. I hit the ground again with a grunt.

Hyde's yellowed teeth showed under a curled lip. "Get it through your thick head. You're going to see him die, and then you are going out too. Your friends can't save you, and your *loving brother* is useless."

He started to walk backwards, past Soul. He fiddled with the wire that held my Crow up. Choking up, I grabbed my hair and slowly started to sob. Each breath burned my throat, and all feeling in my fingertips was gone. Tears mixed with blood — so much blood, and not just mine. I rested on my knees and let myself fall forward onto my elbows. My heart was beating so fast I thought it would burst out of my chest.

"Soul..." — I shook my head as I cried into the frozen blades of grass — "Soul, I'm sorry! You were right. I *was* a mistake."

I heard Hyde lightly chuckle as he rested up against the tree, playing with his knife.

"That doesn't mean I don't love you..." I dragged my fingers down my cheeks as I looked back up at his still silhouette. He was swaying back and forth slightly, his lips parted. I glanced at a smirking Jekyll, then at his brother, who was mindlessly grinning and twirling the knife behind me. Sighing sadly, I glanced back up at my ... *former* friend.

I silently pleaded for a way out of this, some sort of plan. Anything at this point would be nice, but I didn't have the energy or brain power to think of anything. I felt like I was going to pass out again...

I pushed my hair back with my left hand — the only part of my body that didn't feel like it was going to fall off — and continued to watch Soul. And then he moved. Groaning as I leaned forward, he slowly lifted his finger to his lips and grinned menacingly, eyes still closed.

I held in my surprise and shakily covered my mouth. My eyes watered even more. I could barely see.

"Aye, Vixen, what's got you so quiet all of a sudden? No more threats?"

I muttered no and watched Soul unclip the heavy axe from his back as the wire let go and he dropped to the ground, flipping his body right side up in the process. In turn, I scooted back and watched in horror. Brother number one shouted and cursed as he hobbled towards Soul, both of his legs still bloody. Hyde hardly managed to get a swing in before Soul drove his fist straight into Hyde's nose. He fell to the ground, where my Crow stomped his chest as hard as he could, earning the squeal of a pig about to be slaughtered, a beg for mercy.

"Oh, birdy," Jekyll started. "You've made a mistake..."

Soul still had his back to the larger man and he chuckled, then winked at me as the corners of his mouth started to turn upwards. He spoke very beautifully … poetically…

> *"You wreak havoc*
> *So reap what you sow*
> *Whether its few or some…*
> *We will be your Kingdom Come."*

I watched him use the blunt end of his weapon to knock Hyde out. Jekyll got closer.

"Soul, look out!"

He nodded, keeping his beautifully twisted smile. The scar tugging his skin looked jagged and irritated; it had light scratches as though he'd been rubbing it throughout the day. The world seemed to blur around him, all the dull colours fading into each other. I was unable to focus.

> *"You created me*
> *Drowned innocence in the sea*
> *This is your Kingdom Come*
> *So dead you will be!"*

Soul grabbed his axe as Jekyll, standing a few feet behind him, hollered bloody murder and ran towards him with his hammer raised.

Jekyll stopped dead. Soul had grabbed his weapon in one hand and had swung it behind him. He knew what he did… He knew he had hit his mark. He grinned as he turned around to look at the damage he had inflicted. His axe was embedded in Jekyll's flesh. The look on the man's face was one of shock; his pain had clearly not yet registered. Soul yanked the blade free from Jekyll's neck.

"Don't *ever* touch my K9."

Jekyll's blue eyes widened momentarily. Then blood spilled from his mouth and sprayed out of the wound on his neck. My breathing quickened as I watched him fall to the ground. Jekyll was out, dead. His brother was unconscious, bleeding profusely from a crack in his skull … and Soul was standing in front of me, smiling contently, with his shirt torn to shreds. He dropped the large axe and rubbed his hands across his chest, smearing the blood that oozed from criss-crossed wounds. I shivered and stuttered as he ripped the fabric away from his body and sniffled.

The ground felt like it was shaking. I wobbled, sliding back to the ground. I was too dizzy to focus properly, but all I wanted was to make sure Soul was okay. Shrugging his shoulders with a look of indifference, he glanced down as he pursed his lips. One of us let out a small sob — I'll let you guess who — and tears starting to stream down my cheeks as I stumbled closer to him. I fell against his body, legs finally giving out and my body going numb, but it was worth it. Oh god … it was so worth it. I wrapped my good arm around his neck and shivered as I kissed his cheek repeatedly. I tangled his hair around my hand and touched his chest. The fact that I was smearing blood across our bodies didn't even cross my mind.

"I love you!" I whimpered, quickly and desperately.

I continued to mumble to him and rub my face against his shoulder, but he stood perfectly still. Soul wouldn't move and he didn't speak. *I didn't care.* I was too wrapped up in soothing my own stress to notice his reaction.

"I-I never told you … and then I almost lost you! I'm s-so sorry," I stammered.

"K9?"

"Yeah?"

"You're hurt … and cold."

I leaned away from him and nodded, still miserable. Guilt still had a hold on me. Swallowing a lump in my throat, I attempted to keep my eyes open and trained on Soul instead of the shadows and spots in the corners of my vision.

Soul became slightly more sombre, dragging his soft fingers along my cheek and up into my hair, then pushing it off my face. "The bird … never should have said what he said. Didn't mean it… J-just … just thought … maybe K9 didn't care."

"I will always care for you." I shook my head, then continued with a wispy voice. "You terrified me!"

I shoved his chest lightly, throwing myself off balance and quickly grabbing onto him again.

"You — oh god…" I started to feel my throat burn again. "Never do that to me again! Please!"

"Never?" He chuckled.

"E-ever!"

He laughed softly and rested his arms around my torso, pinning me against his bare, bloody chest. I shook against him but held him closer as best I could with only one arm. Wallowing in his warmth, my breath started to synchronize with his.

"I should have told you sooner. I'm so sorry, Soul…"

He shushed me and shook his head; his hair tickled my face and got in my eyes. He started to let me go, but I stuttered and whined in protest, muscles and body aching. He kept me at arm's length and placed his thin, pale hands on my cheeks. My body was numb and it was getting worse. He had pride in his eyes, which shone intoxicatingly bright in the gloomy weather. Fighting to gain control over my voice, I managed to get my words out.

"I love you…"

His lips parted slightly as he looked at my drifting eyes, and softly smiled. Without either of us noticing, we had managed to tangle ourselves together again.

"I know … *my K9.*"

My body was still throbbing and my vision was blurred. I couldn't tell whether it was from the loss of blood or the concussion. Either way, it probably wasn't good, considering how laboured my breathing was getting. His soft touch below my left eye brought me back for a moment as my Crow ran his thumb back and forth.

As I smiled back up at him, my body decided to give out. He quickly wrapped one arm around my lower back to keep me close to him.

"I-I don't think I can stay up much longer…"

"Not losing my K9 again."

All shock had subsided, and throbbing pain turned into agony. I bit my lip and shook my head.

Soul looked focused, almost as if he was in his own world entirely. He kept his hand in place and once again rested his nose beside mine. Then he took a breath, and — as if my head wasn't already spinning — he slipped his warm lips over mine. His eyes closed the second our lips met, and he furrowed his brow. After a second of haziness, I did the same and tightened my grip on his jacket. It probably would have been nicer if I wasn't tasting coppery blood. Despite the joy of finally getting to feel his smooth, yet slightly cracked lips, this pain was worse than I had ever felt. Almost like when I met Jekyll and Hyde.

If not for Soul, I would have given up, lay down right there and then, and let myself freeze to death. I let him continue to tug and pull at me as he desperately pressed himself against my body, trying to stay as close as possible.

A sudden wave of dizziness washed over me, and I started to protest against him, pushing my arm against his chest and whining. Soul stopped kissing me. Once I opened my eyes, I noticed that he had kept his closed. I had also, apparently, been digging my nails into his collarbone, judging from the light red scratches on his skin.

"W-we need to … f-find Louis…"

I slipped again but Soul didn't let me fall. He wrapped his arms under my legs and made me holler in pain. My right side was completely limp in his grasp as he started walking, and I held in as many complaints as I could.

Blood that wasn't frozen to my body was dripping to the ground and mixing with Soul's. He was in bad shape too, but he was still able to walk. Once again, he was saving my life.

"I'm … sorry for everything I've said, Soul."

He gave me a confused look and shook his head.

"For everything… I got us into such a mess — I-I … uh…"

"My dog was scared, the crow was never mad. Love means fear, sometimes makes us sad."

His eyes stayed fixed on mine, even though I had let my neck go limp. He seemed content — honestly happy — but there was still that little bit of sadness… It was always there. His past broke him, and you can't pick up the pieces from something like that. He was always going to remember it but that wasn't why it hurt me. It hurt me because I knew I was dying. Because I was going to be contributing to his pain.

I'd easily lost about a pint and half of blood. Much more and I would be dead. Soul knew that. I could see it in his face, but he didn't say anything. I shivered harshly, and my brain was getting foggy.

"G-going to be … okay," he muttered to himself.

"S-Soul?"

He muttered a response, so I continued as he slipped and slid over patches of ice, making me dig my left hand into his jacket even further.

"My chest hurts. I can't … b-breathe properly… Are we almost there?"

His perfect green eyes widened and he nodded quickly. After a moment, he stopped walking and sighed miserably, shaking his head. "D-don't know — K9?"

I grunted and tilted my head to look at him.

"C-can't do this — don't want to… Please don't leave me…"

Blood was pooling into my mouth and running down my nose. It poured into my eyes. I couldn't promise him anything, as much as I wanted to. My throat started to swell and tears washed the blood from my cheeks. "Don't do this, Soul. P-please… I'm scared…"

Suddenly my chest burned. My lungs barely registered that I was taking breaths, and I started to shake harder. "Don't *let* me leave! I w-want to stay with you!"

Shame. That was definitely the word I would use to describe how I felt about begging like that, but a lack of warmth, oxygen, and blood makes you do crazy things.

Warm drops of water hit my chest. With dreary eyes I looked up at Soul, who was biting his lip hard enough to make it bleed. He shook his head and painfully looked down at me as he started to stumble forward again. He didn't have anything to say; we were both bumbling messes. He put on a strong face and I lightly touched his cheek, my own rubbing against his vest. He had started to shiver from the cold too...

I heard him sigh lightly as his warm breath grazed my wrist. I wanted to look at his beautiful face, but I had to keep my eyes closed; I couldn't keep them open anymore. He whimpered my name and sobbed slightly, so I used the last of the strength in my left arm to haul myself closer. I was grunting and moaning, having to force my head up. Soul had adjusted his grip so I could rest my face in the crook of his neck. His skin was just as warm and smooth as his face. And just as bloody...

I want to kiss him again... I just... The blood in my mouth kind of made that impossible. I tried to tilt my head away from him and spit, but it just slid down my neck, covering me with thick, red drool. I was gagging and sobbing as I cuddled back into him. Without my consent, my hand started to slip from his cheek. It fell and rested in my lap. That only made me more upset. Please, just let this be over soon...

Soul rested his forehead against mine and took a deep breath... It was the exact opposite of what I was doing, which was quick breaths and painful gasping. Soul...

"K-K9 ... *K9*, stay awake!"

"For my ... Crow?"

"Wh-who else?"

I closed my eyes but nodded and licked my lips, trying to breathe slower... Blood mixed with bile and I choked as air eluded me...

"Louis!"

I spat as much as I could, and coughed and retched... I cried out for Soul between breaths and ... writhed in his grip ... a-after that...

Black.

Thirty-Three

"K9! K9 — Benji! W-wake up, p-please … K9!"

I watched my sister die as the man — as her first and last … love violently fought to be by her side.

It was seconds ago that he ran out of the woods carrying her half-limp body. Her right side was covered in gashes. She'd soaked them both. She was shrieking bloody murder, you know, crying and yelling for Soul, choking in the blood and saliva that was dripping from her mouth.

I'd only seen her cry once before.

Right before Louis got through the barricade, she got silent. She stopped moving. Soul had fallen to his knees and pleaded with her to wake up. He told her over and over how much he loved her, recited numerous poems … but her elegant hazel eyes were glazed over. No … amount of words could tell you how much it broke me. I just started to pray, curse, and lament for her. My voice cracked and my throat bled, but I didn't stop. I deafened myself for a moment.

Louis had to force Soul to let her go as he repeatedly performed CPR. Soul was struggling to escape Dan, and a few other fighters. He was crying for her, clear tears dripping and slowly turning red, his nose running. His mouth was set in remorse.

He just kept telling her he loved her.

I leapt from the stage, cracking my leg and dropping both crutches. Benji's friend Chrissy called after me, but I stumbled and slid across the ground until I was right beside my little sister. Soul had fallen into sobs as he still rested in the arms of others. His shoulders rose and fell with every harsh inhale, and his sweat mixed with his own spit and blood.

I fell apart again, so I wrapped one arm around Soul and we cried together.

One medic held a pouch of blood up while another inserted a thin needle into her arm. A third man started wrapping her wounds, but Louis continued to try to resuscitate her ... I can't watch! My little sister — Benji!

"Benji, wake up! Don't do this to us, Ben!" I screeched and cried out for my little girl...

At this point, Soul was holding me back. With one hand on my arm and the other arm wrapped around my torso, he gripped the front of my jacket as he leaned against my back and wept.

"Clear!"

I shouted quickly as her body jolted with the shock... Her angular and sickly face was stuck in sadness and ... guilt, maybe regret.

"K-K9..."

It was almost like ... even in death she blamed herself — she always did, you know. No matter what, no matter how tough or rude she seemed, she blamed herself for everything and she had a hard time letting go of that guilt.

"Clear!"

I gasped for breath and bit my lip as her body jolted again. When I looked back up, her face looked far more severe, shocked and worried. I fell into the dirt crying when I caught the last tear fall from her eye — it was the last she'd ever shed. No more crying herself to sleep and thinking I never knew.

Soul saw it too, and his sobs became more vocal as he reached out his hand for her again.

"You've got to call it, Doc!" Dan hauled Soul back as he frantically clawed and kicked for Benji.

"One more time. Clear!" Louis yelled.

"Forget it, she's gone!" Dan shouted back angrily. He was upset too.

Her love let out a blood-curdling shout and pounded the ground with his fist, his head down and hair starting to stick to his face.

The only reason I stopped crying was because of how light headed I felt. Instead, I sat emotionless...

I just lost my sister ... forever...

My little girl ... my little girl just died.

Thirty-Four

I couldn't move.

"S-Soul…"

I didn't want to move. I didn't want to wake up without him … and if I woke up now, he wouldn't be there. Because *I* was not there.

I was dead. Or I should've been.

I opened my eyes nervously. My right side shouldn't be this numb if I was in heaven — wouldn't think it would be this numb if I was in hell, either. That's where monsters go, right? But I would think there'd be more pain. Maybe I was in purgatory.

I couldn't see anything. It was too bright but too dark at the same time. Testing my left hand, I tried squeezing it into a fist — only … something very soft was pressing against it. The slight tension on it … felt … *alive.*

I tilted my head from side to side as I grinned wildly. The smell of flowers mixed with disinfecting spray tickled my nose. It smelled like home. I still couldn't see or hear anything, but I knew I was just lying under a blanket, so I tugged my hand free and rubbed my forehead. There were thin bandages over my eye, so I carefully slid them back, yelping as my skin started to sting. Blood had dried to it and stuck in place until I ripped it free. But I could see.

Bright fluorescent lights hit my eyes and I blinked, raising my eyebrows and wiggling my nose. I turned my head again, and something tugged at the right side of my neck. probably stitching and bandages.

I opened my eyes again and heard talking. Shouting actually. Probably from some doctors...

I'm going to be honest here. I had no recollection of what happened. I didn't know why I was in Jeff's office. I did know what waking up with bandages on fresh wounds usually meant: I just got my ass kicked in the Pit.

My eyes finally adjusted and I looked around. My entire right side was done up in rags, some looked fresh while others were soaked red around the edges. That was why I couldn't move, I guessed. Using the strength of my left side, I pushed myself up and looked around the pristine white room. There wasn't much in here except for a few chairs, one of which held my boots and jacket. The quick head movement made me woozy, and I had to close my eyes for a second.

I took a breath as I settled myself, opened my eyes again, and looked to my left. I gave a light sigh and smiled to see a beautiful raven-haired man hanging over Louis's small frame. Soul was being held back by the scowling medic, resting his left side across Louis's shoulders and letting his mouth hang open.

"K-K9, how do you feel?" a small voice asked from my other side.

I jumped slightly and looked at a little girl, Tina. She must have been the one who had held my hand. I can't describe the comfort I took in seeing her worried but hopeful eyes.

"I feel ... kind of funny, actually... Did someone pull a taser out?"

The hospital gown I was wearing rubbed against my sore skin, which was more painful than I had an explanation for. She bit her lip and left me confused as Soul tripped over Louis and shoved him away in order to get to my side. I tried to hide my smile by biting my lip as he recklessly put one knee on the bed and tackled me onto the pillow. Instinctively, I leaned myself back and embraced him like my life depended on it. His breathing was shallow and he was shaking slightly. After he picked himself up again, I couldn't help but notice how red his lips were, like he had been repeatedly biting or running his tongue over them. His pout was still as present as ever though. I tilted my head and smiled.

I could feel him start to relax, resting on his stomach and propping himself up on his elbows. I happily touched his cheek and stroked his hair with my left hand — it felt like forever since I'd done that. His skin was very soft, and I couldn't help noticing the ink smeared across his thin jaw. A soft giggle escaped from my lips, and he silently shook his head, removing one shaking hand and using it to push faded yellow bangs away from my eyes. I was kind of confused. He'd never done that before, but I wasn't going to stop him — why should I?

The tournament. I must have lost the tournament. Oh god, what happened? How did it end? What the hell did I do? We could have died out there!

My voice was hoarse and strained, but I remembered that I never told him ... that he never knew...

"Soul, I never got to tell you, but I love you, so much more than words can say. No poem could tell you... I-I wish I'd told you sooner. I could have died and you wouldn't know..."

Snorting, he choked up and shook his head.

"I should have told you before the competition. Who ... who won that, by the way? What happened after...?" I thought a moment. What was the last thing I actually remembered? Soul still wouldn't speak but tears started to form in his eyes. "Soul?"

He continued to purse his lips until he gasped for breath and looked away from me, chuckling sadly. I tried to bring my other hand up to make him look at me, but I still couldn't move it. Instead, I remembered a trick from a few months ago and tugged his scruffy facial hair with my left hand. He let out a whine and looked at me. He started to breath normally again but took a shaky breath. I tried offering a worried smile, but he shook his head and leaned down, tilting his head and rubbing his nose against mine. He smiled sadly as he closed his miserable-looking eyes. Soul was acting very out of character... I was worried for him. Still, I grinned slightly as he did this, which made him smile wider.

A second later, he pushed my head back to the pillow, pressing his lips to mine with his eyes still closed.

That was *really* out of character, so much so that my reaction was a quiet squeak and wide eyes. I could feel him chuckle lightly but he didn't move. I didn't really want him to. I had grabbed a handful of his hair, which was greasier and more tangled than it was ordinarily — not that it mattered. After the shock wore off, I closed my eyes as well, and smiled against his lips.

After a few quick, soothing seconds of his warmth and letting him move as he wished, I furrowed my brow. Why was he…? Why did he do that? He had *never* been this lovey-dovey in all the time I'd know him.

How did I feel about this?

I must not mind because when he pulled away and grinned again, I felt disappointed.

"Th-that was … *bold*," I said between heavy breaths, keeping my wide eyes trained on him.

His expression changed from amusement to confusion. "D-don't … remember?"

"Remember what. What happened to us in the competition? Jekyll and Hyde! What happened to them?"

"Dead."

I shoved myself up with one hand and bumped Soul's nose against mine. It stung but I hardly noticed.

"Wh-what ha — "

"Jekyll is dead … only one left. K9 — K9 got hurt…"

And just like that, everything came back: the multiple beatings, seeing Soul strung up in the trees … *watching him embed his axe in Jekyll's neck*. And kissing him. And I remembered he had to carry me to medical, but after that … nothing.

Truthfully, I was a little bit anxious. Waking up in a bed covered with bandages will do that to a person, but remembering what happened made me happy. Remembering how he forgave me made me very happy.

"What happened after … you know…"

I shrugged and looked around. He sighed and bit his lip, and then Louis jumped in to the conversation.

"You died." He smirked from where he was leaning against the wall. Soul whipped his head around to glare. "We tried to bring you back three times. I was about to call it."

I looked back at Soul, who had teared up again. He wouldn't meet my eyes.

"Oh my *god* … Soul…"

He whimpered, just like he did when we first met. His lip was quivering, and I threw my arm around his neck, squeezing him with the little strength I had. We both fell back down when he threw his arms up as well.

"Th-thought I lost my K9 … Sh-she was — s-so much blood… *I could not have dreamt up such death, for that is all I am; Not a killer, just a dreamer, and I won't hold my breath…*" He buried his face in my neck as I stroked his back.

"D-died," he murmured into my shaggy hair.

I felt like I got hit by a ton of bricks when he told me I had died, but I couldn't even imagine how Soul had felt. I died *in his arms*!

"Love my K9. Never do it again…"

I nodded and sat back so I could look at him. "Never again."

I looked back at Louis, hoping for a diagnosis or at least for instruction to stay off my feet or something. He pushed himself to his feet with a grunt and sat in the chair to my left.

"You were pretty scraped up, got a bad wound to your neck. You were losing blood faster than you knew. Every cut down your right side was pretty deep. They destroyed a few nerves. You might not regain full feeling again, and range of motion will be limited temporarily. You'll still be able to go back to fighting if you want, though."

I nodded and took a deep breath. "The light-headedness will go away too, right?"

He nodded like that was obvious. He stood to leave, then hesitated. "Glad you're okay," he muttered, then made his way to the door.

"J-Johnny's here," Soul stated quietly.

He motioned towards the door that Louis was making his way out of. Suddenly, he was shoved aside with a yelp and Johnny — looking dishevelled — stood in his path. Louis shot him profanities as he held his head and walked past. My brother looked like he had been through hell. His eyes were red and he only had one crutch, but the look of sheer relief on his face was enough to tell me he was perfectly fine.

My brother shoved Soul, making him tumble off of the bed, and then fell on top of me. He inhaled deeply as he stroked my hair—just like he used to do when I was little. I had night terrors for a long time, and he would do this to calm me down. I was starting to think he did it to calm himself too.

"God, Benji ... y-you died! You were dead!"

I held him tightly and nodded. What am I even supposed to say in this situation?

"I'm so glad you're okay."

"Yeah, me too."

"You're a fighter."

"I wasn't finished with you guys — I mean, do you have any idea of the kind of problems you'd get yourself into without me around?"

He chuckled and kissed my forehead. "I wouldn't make it through the day." Smoothing out his red plaid shirt he grinned and stepped to the side. "I brought a friend, too."

A second later, a massive husky jumped onto the bed and laid down beside me.

"Skipper!"

The huge, fuzzy dog kissed my nose and wagged his tail. Soul carefully and curiously patted the dog's head and scratched his ears. Skipper panted and wagged his tail and then turned to Tina, almost like he was waiting for her. With a grin and wide eyes, she held out her hand and he smothered her in fur and drool, his fluffy paws patting the blanket. It was gross but Tina didn't seem to mind, much.

I started to use my left hand to push myself to the side of the bed. I needed to get dressed. I hated hospitals, and being here wasn't helping anyone.

Soul jumped at the chance to be the knight in shining armour (or in this case, the crow in a ratty jacket) and nudged the dog out of the way. Childish habits kicking in, I swung my legs back and forth before sliding to the ground. The tingling in my leg caused me to stumble a bit, but I still managed to snatch my clothes off the blue plastic chair beside my bed and make it to the washroom.

I looked different. There was a long scratch on the side of my cheek, criss-crossing the faded white stripes and running up past my eye. I lightly touched it and it stung like nobody's business... It changed my face completely. It pulled my eye to the side, making me look like Frankenstein's monster. This was the first time I had ever hated the way a scar had changed me. Hopefully, it would heal the same as a small cut. Hopefully.

I guess that was what we got for trying to be showy with our so-called armour, though I had a feeling the brothers would have ripped it all to shreds anyway. I walked out of the washroom and sat back down on the bed, leaning back as I started to get dizzy again.

"My K9," Soul whispered to himself as his cheeks turned pink.

I touched the side of his face, the way I always did, and ran my bruised knuckles over his cheekbone. He tilted his head down and put his hand over mine... He was so *happy*. For the first time since I'd met him, he looked genuinly happy, and it made me feel terrible. Soul never deserved any of this. He was just a kid when they hurt him — then again, so was I. It couldn't happen again, though. That was what mattered. I didn't care about myself, but from now on Soul was going to get everything he'd ever wanted. I was going to make sure of it.

He pulled me out of my thoughts with a small grunt. I watched him look at the floor, struggling to make himself speak. This always happened whenever he wanted to ask for something but was afraid of my reaction, despite the very obvious fact that I would always agree to give him what he wanted.

"C-can the bird ... wants to... Can he s-stay w-with you?"

I laughed lightly as his cheeks burned again. "Soul, you're always with me—"

"N-no ... meant tonight. Alone again for so long ... scared to let you go again..."

He wouldn't meet my eyes. He looked embarrassed for being worried but I simply nodded.

"Of course. There's no need for me to go anywhere, and I *promise* this time. I promise..." I wrapped my arm around his neck, and he clung to me like a child would. His hair tickled my cheek, so I started to grin as I pushed him away.

It was one of the rare times he made eye contact with me for an extended period of time. After what seemed like ten minutes, Soul sat back down and Johnny held out a cup of coffee. I was about to take it when he jerked his hand away and hopped back. The next thing I knew, I was pinned down under a mop of blond hair. It was suffocating me as big, wet lips continuously kissed my face, leaving sticky, pink lipstick across my cheeks.

"Pain. Chrissy, I am in pain."

"Oh, I'm so sorry!"

She sat up and looked at me. Tearing up, she threw her arms around me again.

"That was awful. We were so worried. Almost everything is settled now. Jekyll is dead and his brother has refused all contact with anyone, including the doctors. You two left him in bad shape."

I patted her back and she wiped her eyes. I noticed Dan had also joined us. I was ready to scowl, but he slowly walked over and shrugged. Soul was blatantly unhappy — borderline growling, actually — but he backed down after I shot him a warning look.

"I'm sorry for everything I did and said," he whispered as he held out his hand.

I was uncertain but I shook it, then tugged him close. "I take it you're going to be civil towards each other from now on?"

He curtly nodded, then stood silently by Chrissy. Both of them looked weirdly joyous, given everything that'd happened.

We used to fear stepping into the arena if we'd done something wrong, especially since we would be thrown up against Jekyll and Hyde. But now we didn't have to. No one did. Ever again.

The both of us had tossed and turned all night, kicking each other and maybe falling out of bed once or twice. Soul kept yelling, and though I don't know what he meant exactly, I could have guessed quite easily. But this is a new day and our city is starting over, just like us.

We will never forget what happened, but we will be free of it.

The dust was getting kicked up from my boots, and the sun was shining through the arena's panels. Soul was standing beside me and I had the biggest smile on my face; no one *blamed* him. Maybe the details were still fuzzy, but no one held him accountable and they finally understood what a gross misunderstanding it all was. Someone even told me that we were heroes for what we did. At this point, I was just happy to be alive. I didn't want to be a hero.

All the praise was nice for a while, but everyone knew what was about to happen. Locals had gathered in the stands and warriors lined the arena. I lightly squeezed Soul's hand, watching his hair fly about as he whipped around to look at me. He stayed quiet while Matt joined us and looked up at the stadium.

"Big deal, guys!" he said. "I hope you know what you're doing."

I gave a small nod and rolled my eyes.

Vince Viktor stepped up to us with his usual glory, but missing his suit jacket. His eyes drilled right through me. It just reminded me of the horrible things he's done. I couldn't believe he tricked us all so easily.

"K9, Crow. I understand the trauma you've both faced, yet the accusations you've made against the good people of Lilithia are unacceptable." He tucked his hands behind his back and looked down his nose at us. "I'm afraid this will be the end of your career here."

Soul dropped his gaze to the ground. His body was rigid and he was clearly uncomfortable. Just behind him, standing in the line of shocked warriors, Johnny waved around as though he was ready to stumble over and explain everything himself. Even Josh, who had placed himself on the opposite side of Soul, was ready to jump in.

"Sir, we won't be following that order."

"I-I'm sorry, Benjamina?" He had started walking away and when he faced us again, he practically stood over me.

"I said we aren't going to follow your orders. You were the one that hired Soul all those months ago. You were the one that rigged our system. You manipulated some good people into some dirty tricks. We have the proof."

"You don't need it, Vixen."

My gut wrenched at that voice. The five of us turned but all I saw was Matt hollering as he got tossed to the side. Before I could react, Soul was also off his feet and lying on the ground. On instinct, I grabbed my knife and turned, faced with a large, seething Irishman I hoped to never see again.

"H-Hyde?"

"Oh, Vixen! With all those people shouting and *crying* the other day, I hadn't noticed you actually pulled through! Unlike my brother, who had his throat *slit*…," he hissed at me.

He looked very … battered and bruised. Bludgeoned. The man took a good beating. He held a knife out at me, his hand shaking, rage and grief flashing in his eyes. While keeping an eye on him, I bent down to Soul and shook his shoulder. "S-Soul… Hey, are you okay?"

He offered a grunt but blood was slowly staining the ground. I could feel myself starting to panic.

"Little Vixen… Do you know what it was like for me? To, for a *second* time, be unconsious and unable to help my brother? To have him taken from me when I couldn't even say goodbye?!" His voice was shrill, cracking. There was madness in his eyes like I had never seen before.

"Sorry, big guy, but you were about to do the same to us. But maybe you missed that over all the *shouting and crying*," I spat back.

He shrugged his shoulders and flashed a crazy grin, full of chipped teeth. "You're a bitch, and he's an idiot. You deserve each other."

"Hyde! K9! That is enough! Please just clear out, the lot of you, and go home. I am sick and tired of this," Viktor interrupted, clicking the heels of his shoes.

"Oh shut up, you old goat!" Hyde roared. His voice rattled the arena. Warriors took steps back, and parents in the stands shielded their children's eyes, just in case. He hauled Matt up off the ground and then gritted his teeth, letting his grip loosen so my friend could scramble away.

"They're telling the truth. Yeah, Vinny hired us — he hired a bunch of us — but those other guys were too low on the totem pole to know what they were doing. They were punishment for anyone getting too close to information. He just chose them because he liked their names."

Josh was standing on my other side, glaring with a red face.

"When people started to look good to the public without his *professional expertise*, that meant that Mr. Viktor could lose his job to someone younger, someone more impressive. That's where bird-boy came in."

He clapped his hands together, then looked at the old man. "Sorry, boss, I'm done taking orders. You don't have anything for me anymore."

"The others never knew. They had nothing to do with any of whatever he was planning," I explained. I don't know why I defended them after what some of them tried to do to me. But they were just human.

Jeremy, Ronin, Randy, and Louis sat in disgust as they realized the connction between them, and all agreed that they had no clue that Dr. Frankenstein was our very own overlord. Instead, we all watched Josh wave in his security team, which quickly handcuffed Vince Viktor and Robert Harold, carting them away.

I tugged my hair back and growled. At least we won…

"K-K9?"

"Yeah, Soul?"

"I-is this … good?"

I let go of my hair and turned to him, anxiousness written across my face. "I think so. We can focus on training now. It's over," I said incredulously.

He pressed his forehead against mine, closed his eyes, and sighed. "Underwhelming."

Nodding, I leaned back on my heels, "Yeah, it kind of is."

"Of course, it is. I just took your last victory," Hyde muttered, his eyes going cold again. "And don't you forget, Viktor. Once I'm through with them, I'll be coming after you!"

Rage was welling up inside my chest. He ruined our chance to clear our names ourselves, so what more could he possibly have to say?

Hyde held out his arms and addressed the crowd, "You all think we were the bad guys — and maybe we are — but do you have any idea what it's like, what you feel like when you lose a *brother*?"

I rolled my eyes. Almost everyone here knew what it was like. No one knew better than Frankie, Soul, and I. Looking past Hyde, I saw that Soul was sitting up and rubbing his head with the arm he wasn't cluching to his chest. Seeing his frustration and his readiness to fight again wiped away my hesitation. He'd battled more than enough demons to fill his short lifetime. His job was done. Someone else needed to step up.

Hyde continued. "I want you to feel — "

"For your information, I *do* know what it's like to lose a brother," I said. "You should know that since you were the one that killed Henry!

He may not have been blood but he was sweet and kind and he deserved better. He was also far more merciful than me."

Hyde sputtered and gagged, grasping at my knife, which I had just stabbed deep into the tissue of his shoulder, in the crook of his neck. I twisted the blade and he cried out in pain, cursing and growling. He fell to his knee and I ripped my weapon free. I was standing directly behind him, so when I brought my knife down a second time, I prayed I didn't impale myself as well.

"Far, *far*, more merciful."

Hyde screamed and writhed as I plunged my weapon deep into his eye socket. I twisted it again and sawed at the bone. I closed my eyes and prayed my friends would forgive me — should I have any left after this. Then I shoved it in farther, soaking my sleeves and hands with red and scraping the bones of his face with the hilt.

He stopped shrieking. He stopped moving.

I let him fall to the ground. I flicked blood away from my body and dropped the small weapon, anger fading into worry.

"Soul, forgive me."

I turned to watch Louis wrap a bandage around my friend's arm. They were staring at me in awe and concern. Soul shoved Louis away while he continued to stare at me, his grin far more twisted than I had ever seen before. It scared me more than just a little bit.

But at least he wasn't angry.

He pushed himself to his feet in a bumbling haze, accidentally tripping over himself. I stood perfectly still as that grin stayed where it was. I started to take a step away from him as he stumbled forward and grabbed my arm.

"B-blood spills like wine when it comes to bad men and swine."

He was practically standing overtop of me. I struggled to pull my arm free, but he was digging his nails into my skin. I growled, "S-Soul, let me go!"

He chuckled and silently taunted me, creating much more tension. I could feel frustration, curiosity, and slight fear bubbling up inside me.

As I'd said before, this look... It wasn't Soul. I didn't know why, but sometimes he got this look. And at those times he turned into someone very scary. I didn't know why and I didn't know what to do. I stared at him silently as he started to grin wider, quietly chuckling as he stared me down. I shook my head nervously but didn't take my eyes off of his. Suddenly, Soul looked down at his hands, then at Hyde. He slowly gained control over himself, eventually returning to my ordinary, anxious Crow. He quickly released my arm before wiping his hands on his jeans.

"Good riddance. K9 — K9 d-did the right thing." He grasped my hand and looked even more shaken than I felt.

"You ... scared me for a second, Soul."

He swallowed harshly and nodded, signalling that he was ready to leave the dead Hyde — not only ready to leave him in the arena to rot, but also in the past. I hoped this would be the end of his nightmares.

"B-Benji, wait!" Matt called. He was biting his lip, holding back a small smile as Josh and Frankie threw their arms around him, urging him on.

"Now that Mr. Viktor is out of the picture, we don't have anyone to run the league. What are we going to do?"

I shrugged my aching shoulders and looked at all of them. "Why are you asking me? I don't know anything about that stuff. Shouldn't you take over, Matt?"

"Oh my god, Ben ... I can't do that! I mean, thank you, beyond words! But ... I-I don't know the first thing about running the whole show, and I'm happy doing what I do here. I'm sorry!" He smiled wider but his hands shook. He looked concerned, but Josh winked from behind him and nodded over his right shoulder to someone in the crowd.

"Okay then, if you won't do it then keep doing what you do here. We wouldn't be half as great as we are without our little nerd," I said, laughing. He shook my hand, tearing up. Soul started to chuckle. He patted Matt's shoulder and waited expectantly for me to continue.

"It's okay," I reassured our little blond friend. "Alright ... Johnny Keanin, if you are willing…"

I held my hand out in the direction of my older brother, who had been sitting between Jeff and Louis. He stood and did his best to make his way over quickly on his crutches. Then — for the second time this week — he embraced me like he didn't know his own strength. Which he probably didn't…

"Will you do it?" I asked.

"Without a doubt," Johnny said, breaking out into a grin. The crowd started to cheer for him, and the warriors that he had been friendly with applauded him and welcomed him into our ranks. It's where he's always belonged.

Casting one last glance upon the body, we wrapped our arms around each other's shoulders, and Soul grinned. Following me out of the arena, he kissed my cheek lightly, something he'd started doing whenever he got nervous — and something he knew I would never protest.

Thirty-Five

We'd decided that we would fight together from now on, for his sake and mine. I almost couldn't believe that after what I'd done — after what we'd both done — he still wanted to know me...

Hyde was right. We deserved each other's personal hells, if only to atone for our own sins. But what was hell to the demons that lived inside it? The hell-hound and her messenger, the crow.

Just as I was thinking about how badly I wanted to put it all behind me, the crow chose to speak up, just as we were walking out of the facility's gate and into the street, surrounded by locals and warriors cheering us on. Just as we were on our way to his long-abandoned apartment to gather his things. He had left all the books, clothing, papers and ink there because he'd never known a safer place.

"I'm scared of what you can do
Oh voices in my head
And why I'm always sober
Is why I'm not quite dead
With Apollo far behind me
And heaven far above
Every day I'm lying
When people see a dove."

It was the place he used to call home.

> *"Useless and faceless*
> *A monster at the core*
> *Careless and nameless*
> *Here forevermore*
> *Every night I burn*
> *My feathers turn to ash*
> *Like that of a young crow*
> *Rooting through the trash*
> *I do my best to please them*
> *And keep the voices down*
> *But sometimes when I hear him*
> *I feel I start to drown."*

We were no heroes, but just a couple of kids who got caught up in the worst side of life too soon. We were just angry warriors trying to fix whatever went wrong. We were in over our heads but somehow … somehow we did it. Somehow we fixed it. I owed so much to my brother. For all I screwed up for him … but we fixed it.

> *"I am no dove*
> *In a world full of gold;*
> *I am a crow*
> *And can't be bought or sold."*

A good warrior can get revenge. This is how that was possible. Our story is how that was possible; neither of us were meant to be heroes. We were only meant to survive as so many had to do before us, though none have been *like* us.

> *"It is not in my nature*
> *To do as they request*
> *For I must fly away*
> *As far from earth to rest*
> *He took away my beauty*
> *And burned my beautiful wings*

> *And now I'm left to hear him*
> *as others start to sing*
> *I am still a being of light*
> *Suffering in darkness*
> *One thousand degrees of anger*
> *Bring me such distress."*

The snow was heavy and hit his face, but he didn't notice. He just smiled and continued as a beautiful black bird flew overhead.

> *"Still they sing into my ear*
> *Telling me to flutter*
> *But the crow must not go*
> *And so they start to stutter."*

I clutched his hand and smiled while looking upwards.

> *"I keep my patience*
> *And trust my luck*
> *That someday I'll be pretty*
> *For now in ember stuck*
> *The flames that singed my torso*
> *Now burning back again*
> *Not for me this time*
> *But for a former friend*
> *I did all that he had asked*
> *And still it hurt me so*
> *Now he lies in agony*
> *While I'm pacing to and fro."*

I grinned wider and Soul started to laugh in glee, kicking at the snow and grabbing for my other hand. He started twirling me around in the cold, winter air as Lock soared high above us. But he was still so gentle with me…

> *"Finally he knows*
> *Just how it feels to burn*
> *Dream your last dream*
> *Because now it is my turn,*
> *The voices now have ceased*
> *And the monster now is gone*
> *A black crow flies free*
> *And sings his very own song."*

The man was remarkable.

> *"'Caw, caw,' says the crow*
> *'Down, down you will fall*
> *Deep, deep in the darkness*
> *Out of hell you will crawl.'"*

This town had seen some war — hell, this town had started some wars — and we were strong. We were smart, and we were fast. One thing we were not was scared. We would fight to the death for what we believed and who we loved.

Most of us had to; others wanted to. It's our story.

> *"Finally free*
> *These ashes that I'm from*
> *And now you will see*
> *Why they call me Kingdom Come."*

CPSIA information can be obtained
at www.ICGtesting.com
Printed in the USA
LVOW11s2037070518
576080LV00008B/6/P

9 781771 802109